STATION HELIX

Ash Greenslade

Text and cover illustration copyright © 2014
Ash Greenslade

Ash Greenslade has asserted his right under the Copyright, Design and Patents Act 1988 to be identified as the author of this work.

This novel is a work of fiction. Characters, institutions and organisations are either the product of the author's imagination or, if real, used fictitiously without any intent to describe actual conduct. Any resemblance to actual persons, living or dead, is entirely coincidental.

All rights reserved. No part of this publication may be reproduced, stored in or introduced into a retrieval system, or transmitted, in any form, or by any means (electronic, mechanical, photocopying, recording or otherwise) without prior written permission of the author. Any person who does any unauthorised act in relation to this publication may be liable to criminal prosecution and civil claims for damages.

This book is sold subject to the condition that it shall not, by way of trade or otherwise, be lent, resold, hired out, or otherwise circulated without the author's prior consent in any form of binding or cover other than that in which it is published.

ISBN: 978-1500582029

To Jenny

For the inspiration that turned an idea into a story; for the motivation that turned a story into a book.

ONE

1

Jonathan Cline staggered onto Tower Bridge, his bloodshot eyes squinting in the midday sunlight, his anxious breathing barely filling his lungs with enough oxygen to stay conscious. The taste of bile filled his mouth and throat. He collided with tourists as he grasped for the balustrade, trying to steady himself as his nervous system burned. People hurried to avoid him, alarmed and annoyed. Parents instinctively pulled their children closer as he stumbled towards them. Smartphones digitally preserved the schadenfreude. Insults were jeered about his drunkenness. But Cline wasn't drunk. He hadn't drunk anything since realising that alcohol was useless in combating the pain. It felt like the skin had been flayed from his body. A wave of nausea coursed through him each time he took a lurching step. He gripped the side of the bridge just to keep himself from collapsing on the crowded pavement.

He sprawled forward, his eyes straining to focus, his lungs feeling like every filthy molecule of traffic pollution had been sucked into his chest. His tailored suit was drenched in sweat. He grabbed furiously at his collar and ripped off two buttons in his panic to relieve the imagined constraint around his neck. His Magdalene College tie hung slack in a tight untidy knot. His expensive John Lobb leather shoes were heavily scuffed. Clawing his way along the pavement he dragged himself closer to the north tower.

More tourists stared at him with bewilderment and fear. He was in too much pain to care what anyone thought.

The irony of being a respected technology expert but unable to solve his own crisis was not lost on him. Cline's limitless capacity for innovation had failed him. His last best guess – oxygen therapy – had resulted in him screaming to be freed from the hyperbaric chamber. Now, three days later, he didn't have the energy to scream. His body felt like every fibre had been stimulated with an agonising electric current.

He neared the tower and glanced up at the grand Portland stone-clad building. He had walked this way many times before, always pausing to admire the Victorian architecture, but today he was oblivious to the details. The imposing arch gaped like the entrance to a dungeon. His muscles cramped and burned causing him to double over. He stumbled and fell against a fat man wearing shorts and a tasteless bright shirt, distracting the tourist from the photograph he was about to take.

"Hey, buddy, watch what you're doing!" the man shouted with an American accent, his voice seeming unnaturally loud in Cline's hypersensitive eardrums.

He pushed away from the tourist, groaning loudly with the effort, and continued his chaotic journey across the bridge. The American watched him, his expression changing from irritation to concern as he saw Cline's lurching momentum. "Are you okay?" he called out.

Cline ignored him, the man's words becoming lost in the cacophony of noise on the London landmark. He shoved his way past more pedestrians and regained his grip on the railing. He was a few feet from the tower. His legs gave way and he fell again.

No more. I can't stand this any longer.

He spotted a police officer hurrying towards him from the south side of the river. She was shouting into the radio clipped to her body armour.

You can't help me. No one can.

Summoning his last reserve of strength he forced himself to stand and clambered onto the balustrade. The police officer started to run, pushing her way through the throng of people. He heard her shout the words *urgent assistance*. He briefly made eye contact with her. She wouldn't reach him in time.

Cline threw himself off the bridge.

2

The evening ferry crossing from the Hook of Holland had taken longer than expected. A westerly weather front over the North Sea had been gusting for the last nine hours and still showed no sign of abating. The storm hadn't been strong enough to prevent the giant Stena Hollandica from sailing but it had slowed her journey. Most passengers stayed inside the vessel when the wind buffeted rain-laden clouds over the ocean, but Marek Gorski loved the coldness of the night air and had positioned himself resolutely on deck for most of the crossing, his oil- and grit-smothered fluorescent jacket protecting him from the wind chill and spray. The ferry was nearly at her destination. The darkhaired Pole glanced down at his watch. It was already eight-forty and the ship should have docked on the hour, but even with the delay he had several hours to spare. The longer trip had given him more time on deck.

Pulling the sleeve of his coat back over his watch, Gorski looked ahead at the lights of Harwich and Felixstowe on either side of the River Stour. He estimated the ship would moor up at Harwich within the next twenty minutes. He'd made this trip several times before, hauling exports from his home town of Poznań to their eventual destination in the Midlands at least fortnightly for the last four months. He'd established a routine, and, unlike many of his fellow hauliers, he preferred not to sleep on the ferry.

He was a light sleeper and found that the drone of the vessel's engine and the chatter of the passengers disturbed him too easily. He'd found a truck stop about half an hour's drive outside the port where he could sleep comfortably in the cab.

He took a deep lungful of cold sea air, tasted the salt on his lips, and turned towards the nearest door. As he stepped inside he heard the end of an announcement in English asking drivers to return to their vehicles. A moment later the instruction was repeated in Dutch. Passengers moved around him, making their way towards staircases. He unzipped his jacket and reached for an internal pocket, reassuring himself he still had his passport and transport paperwork. He grasped steel handrails to steady himself as he descended to the lower deck. He reached his articulated lorry and checked the tamper-proof locking handles on the rear of the trailer. He checked the underside of the vehicle as well, not wishing to be caught out by illegal immigrants. Satisfied, he climbed into the cab and waited for the instruction to disembark.

An hour later Gorski cleared Customs, acknowledged the official who waved him through, and drove out of Harwich International Port.

3

Bob's Transport Café was an unwelcoming truck stop just north of Ipswich. The single-storey, flat-roofed building was in need of maintenance, but it provided sufficient sparse comfort for the truckers who rested here. Food was always available, no matter what the hour, and there was a shower block behind the café. The facility had been designed with practicality rather than luxury in mind. The restaurant section was laid out in typical truck stop fashion with eight plastic tables bolted to the walls, a serving counter leading to the kitchen, and hard orange plastic chairs whose moulded texture attracted grime. Cardboard trays of eggs were stacked behind the counter and the smell of fried onions never seemed to dissipate. The yellowing paintwork on the walls was covered with rock'n'roll memorabilia, photographs of Elvis Presley and Buddy Holly, and half a dozen colourful American number-plates. A replica jukebox with sulky aged neon tubes stood in a corner near the door which led to the toilets. There were no neatly folded menu cards; just laminated sheets of A4 paper listing fried breakfast variations as the only available options. Food here was sourced from a cash-and-carry; not local purveyors of organic produce. Juice was always from concentrate; never fresh.

Marek Gorski pushed open the café door and walked inside, causing a bell above the entrance to ring. He'd slept briefly in the truck and now wanted to eat before setting out for the Midlands depot. With a clear run he'd arrive there in a few hours, deliver the load and then head back to Essex before the major routes became busy with rush hour traffic.

The café was empty except for two drivers who sat together at a table but read newspapers rather than conversed. One glanced up at Gorski momentarily before turning back to his paper. A woman in her middle fifties looked from behind the counter as the bell went silent. He recognised her – she had been working most times he'd stopped here – and smiled at her.

"Give me a moment, love, and I'll be right with you," she said as she wiped her hands on her apron.

"Thanks." He chose a table and sat down, pulled a menu from its place between two cheap plastic sauce bottles and glanced at it even though he already knew what he wanted. To his surprise he'd developed a taste for Bob's all day breakfast. He reckoned that a fried breakfast once every couple of weeks probably wouldn't kill him, and it did seem to fuel him up nicely for his drive. The waitress came over and he ordered his breakfast and a black coffee. She scribbled something on her pad and walked behind the counter. Gorski picked up a newspaper and started to read. His English was good but the language of tabloid propaganda wasn't something his school had taught him. He grinned as he read yet another inflammatory headline about Eastern European immigrants stealing English jobs.

He heard rain gusting against the window and looked up. The reflection of the fluorescent lights inside the café made it difficult to see through the pane, but it was obvious the weather was getting worse. The rain fell harder, the drops tapping relentlessly against the thin glass, drowning out the noise of a coffee machine near the egg trays.

"Never gets any better, does it?" the waitress muttered as she placed a plate on the table. He shook his head in acknowledgment and thanked her for the food. He wondered why the British habitually complained about the weather. He unrolled a knife and fork from a paper napkin and began to eat. The bacon and sausages were good but the fried eggs were burnt underneath. He told himself to ask for scrambled eggs next time. As he ate the two drivers walked past him and handed over some money to the waitress at the till. They pulled up the hoods of their jackets to protect themselves from the pelting rain before opening the café door. The bell rang again. Gorski couldn't see where they went but imagined them hurrying across the yard in an attempt to avoid getting completely soaked. He took a sip of coffee and turned his attention back to his all day breakfast.

4

Andrew Mason was a patient, methodical man. Bald, square-jawed and with a rugged rather than handsome face he fitted a military stereotype, but his grey eyes betrayed a sinister focus. Every mission he undertook was planned to the last detail. He'd learned the importance of preparation when serving in Iraq. Too many times he'd seen operations go horribly wrong because of an oversight or the absence of a robust contingency plan. Despite this, he'd become addicted to the daily tension that the Middle East guaranteed. Staying in Iraq after his last tour, he'd left the army and moved into the profitable private security sector. He'd earned a small fortune protecting European and American businessmen, as well as several Iraqi politicians and diplomats who were too wary to entrust their safety to their own people. Mason's team, comprised of trusted former army colleagues, quickly earned a reputation for reliability. When Iraq had settled into an uneasy stability, he'd realised that his men's talents could probably be put to better use elsewhere. Besides, not all of their work had been legitimate. To stay ahead in the private security game you didn't question what the client wanted if you expected to keep earning large sums of money. Finally it had made sense to sever ties with the country and return to England for a short respite before seeking new opportunities elsewhere in the world.

Things hadn't quite worked out that way. The team had been offered a security contract by the British Government to protect various top level installations. It wasn't difficult work – in fact they had found it dull – but they viewed it as a temporary measure before continuing with freelancing operations overseas. But Mason had got the entire team fired, and, thanks to interference by the Government, employment opportunities had dried up, the team's reputation demolished by unseen people with considerable influence. He'd had a long while to think about what to do next. Mason was a patient man.

His black Range Rover was parked at the edge of the compound – away from the café's few outside lights which tonight illuminated little more than the driving rain with a dim orange glow. Mason watched the Polish driver leave the café and step into the rain-lashed yard. For the last two months his crew had been observing hundreds of hauliers passing through the site, looking for patterns and routines. Often there was *no* pattern – schedules were usually unpredictable – but some companies had regular contracts and therefore followed well-established timetables. It had taken considerable effort to identify a suitable target. Timing had been crucial. Mason had to act tonight.

The wiper blades flicked the rain from the screen, the rubber squeaking quietly as it swept across the glass. The trucker paused about thirty feet from the lorry and fumbled for his keys. A moment later he found them and resumed his hurried walk.

Mason pressed the transmit button on a small radio. "Let's go," he said softly. He pulled a balaclava over his face. His two men in the rear of the car did the same. They got out and walked towards Marek Gorski's truck, staying in the shadows and using a nearby lorry as cover. Moments later they were in position, waiting in silence, ignoring the driving rain.

5

Gorski was about to unlock the lorry's door when a voice in the darkness startled him.

"Got a light, mate?"

Gorski hadn't noticed the man approach, but he hadn't been concentrating on much besides getting into his dry cab. He recognised the man as one of the drivers from inside the café. The man was cradling a cigarette in his hands, trying not to get it wet. Gorski understood the gesture more easily than the man's vernacular. "Yes, one moment," he replied. He put his left hand into his jacket's breast pocket and rummaged awkwardly for his lighter.

Seconds later an unseen man grabbed him from behind and slammed his head against the truck door, dazing and disorienting him. The attacker placed his gloved hand firmly over his mouth to stop him from calling out. Hands grabbed his right arm and painfully twisted the keys from his grasp. A sharp painful kick to the back of his left knee made him slump heavily onto the wet ground. Gorski looked up but his eyes filled with rain water. He could only just make out someone opening the cab door above his head. He was dragged from his knees and forced to stand. Someone in black clothing clambered into the cab and slid across the seat to the passenger side of the left hand drive tractor unit.

"Get inside!"

Obeying the instruction fearfully, he started to climb up. His attackers evidently thought he was moving too slowly and shoved him inside the truck as he tried to negotiate the step. The man in the cab held a handgun to his throat while Mason entered the cab behind him and slammed the door shut.

"Don't kill me," Gorski pleaded, his eyes darting between the masked assailants.

Mason pulled off his balaclava and grabbed Gorski's face, turning it towards his own, forcing eye contact. "Listen to me! If I wanted to kill you, you'd be dead already! Try anything stupid, though, and I might change my mind." He turned the key in the lorry's ignition and the powerful diesel engine started instantly. Flicking on the headlights and engaging the gears, Mason slowly manoeuvred the lorry and exited the truck yard. The black Range Rover followed.

Mason's companion lowered the gun and placed it into a holster beneath his black coat. From a small backpack the man removed a bottle of Russian vodka. He twisted off the cap and dropped it into the foot well. He shoved the bottle against Gorski's chest. "Drink this," he ordered. The spirit's vapour filled Gorski's nostrils.

He made the mistake of trying to refuse. "No! What do you want?"

Holding the bottle with his right hand, the man grabbed Gorski's hair with his left and tugged his head backwards. He tipped up the bottle and forced the neck into his mouth. The liquid drained down his throat, causing him to choke and swallow simultaneously. Gorski tried to struggle against the man's grip. From the driver's seat Mason leaned over and slammed a clenched fist into Gorski's stomach. The trucker coughed and choked as Mason's companion carried on forcing the bottle down his neck. Mason raised his right hand, indicating for his associate to give the Pole a temporary reprieve. Gorski coughed, expelling spittle and mucus, his throat burning and his eyes streaming painfully.

"It's simple," Mason said. "You have no choice. Do you understand?"

Gorski nodded, terrified.

"Good. I told you I wasn't going to kill you. That's true. But you *will* drink. Take the bottle and do as you are told. Or do you need my friend to help you again?"

Even in the near-darkness of the cab's interior, Gorski glimpsed the malevolence in Mason's steel-grey eyes. "No help," he replied.

6

From the driver's seat of his silver Audi A3, Bill Hannay glanced in the mirror at his twenty-two year old son Alex – the new British foil fencing champion. "You and Jim should have a good chance at getting into the Olympic squad now," he said. He looked back at the road, gripping the steering wheel a little tighter. The downpour was causing surface water to accumulate. Bill kept his speed at fifty miles an hour, despite the seventy limit.

"Maybe," replied Alex from the back seat. "We still have to earn the points though, Dad. We need some good international results first."

"You will. Hopefully you'll do well at Valenciennes next month."

"I'm looking forward to that. Are you sure you can get the time off work?"

"Already sorted. Your mother and I are looking forward to going with you."

"I appreciate you taking me to all these competitions."

Sarah Hannay turned round in her seat, nudged her glasses with a fingertip, and smiled at her son. "Hey, we're only going so we can enjoy the French culture," she joked. "I'm really proud of you. You did so well today."

Alex returned the smile. "Thanks. It's been a good weekend."

"Apart from this awful weather." Bill gestured at the

windscreen. "The rain hasn't let up since we passed Brentwood."

Alex shifted in his seat, trying to stretch his tired leg muscles. He closed his eyes and visualised the last few moments of the final against his friend and opponent James Peters. Jim had reached the final on similar form. Alex had beaten him by only two hits. Beside him on the back seat was the trophy he'd won: a large silver statuette with the words *National Men's Foil Champion* engraved on the front. Alex picked it up. "Jim's *so* going to want this next year," he said.

"He'll have to work hard to beat you," Sarah replied.

"Well he almost did today. I lost concentration for a while. I fell for that broken time attack he pulled on me."

Sarah looked around again and gave Alex a bemused smile. She was fifty-one but looked younger. "I have *no* idea what that means. I just cheer when your light comes on."

Alex grinned. "That's good enough for me. I'll just have to respond quicker next time he tries that."

"Well you're fast enough – *if* you concentrate," said Alex's father. Bill was right. Alex wasn't just a good foilist; he was excellent. He had speed and fluidity of movement. His timing and execution of technique were precise. Bill frequently called him 'the Jackie Stewart of fencing'. Tonight's victory in Weymouth was the culmination of years of relentless effort.

"I'm going to sleep for hours tomorrow," said Alex as he closed his eyes and tipped his head back against the headrest, listening to the drumming of the rain on the car's roof.

"You mean *today*," Sarah said, glancing at the digital display in the Audi's dashboard. The clock showed 02.30. "Why don't you have a sleep now? We probably won't be home for another hour."

"Are you sure?" Alex replied. "Sorry for not being good company."

"Don't be daft. Your dad and I will be fine. We can cope without you trying to confuse us with your weird terminology for a little while."

Alex laughed. "Okay, wake me up when we get back. And don't sell my medal on eBay when I'm not watching."

"Promise."

Alex shut his eyes again. With the events of the day replaying in his thoughts, he quickly drifted off to sleep.

7

Mason kept his foot down, driving the articulated lorry at speed, untroubled by the pelting rain. He'd had plenty of experience driving large vehicles in difficult conditions during his military service. A waterlogged main road was not much of a challenge. The spray from the lorry's wheels surged up as the eighteen-wheeler accelerated. Beside him in the cab the Polish lorry driver was borderline conscious. The litre of vodka he'd consumed had begun to take its effect, the intoxication numbing his senses. His fear had been replaced with confusion and failing co-ordination. Mason didn't care if the man fell asleep. It was enough that the trucker had shut up and obeyed his captors' commands.

A voice from the radio broke the silence. "You're two kilometres behind. The road is clear. Dual carriageway for another eight."

Mason's partner Curtis Wheeler pressed the transmit button on the unit. "Acknowledged. Making progress."

"Right where we want him," stated Mason, looking ahead through the cab's broad windscreen. He pressed his foot down, pushing the truck to seventy-five miles per hour. Had the truck been fitted with a speed limiter, Mason would have been able to remove it, but the Polish vehicle didn't have one. It was one of the reasons why he'd chosen this truck after his extensive surveillance at the café. The wiper blades flashed furiously across the screen, trying to clear the hammering rain from the glass. Mason couldn't have wished for better conditions.

The radio crackled once more, slightly distorting the speaker's voice. "Gap eight hundred metres. Road still clear. Flash your lights." Mason saw the red lights of a vehicle ahead. He flicked the truck's spotlights on and off. "Yeah, that's you behind me," the voice on the radio reported. "I'll pull back and let you pass."

"We're going dark," Wheeler said into the radio as Mason switched off all the truck's lights. Ploughing through the downpour Mason never slowed, using only the illumination of the highway's fluorescent lamps to show the way. He moved into the outside lane and seconds later went hurtling past the black Range Rover. Mason noticed another vehicle's rear lights in the distance. The road curved and he lost sight of the car briefly. And then it was there again, maintaining a steady, careful speed in the inside lane. Mason pulled into the same lane, getting closer.

Seconds later he recognised the vehicle. A silver Audi A3.

8

Alex Hannay was torn from his sleep as the back of the car was crushed.

In the fraction of a second after Mason rammed the Audi, the Hannays' car became a scene of chaos. The rear window shattered, showering Alex with fragments of glass. The airbags activated with explosive bangs as their detection systems registered the impact and triggered the detonators. Bill lost his grip on the steering wheel as he was flung forward into the airbag, his seatbelt locking rapidly and tugging him back into his seat. Sarah groaned with pain as her seatbelt constricted against her chest. The car lost traction with the wet surface of the road and started sliding, lurching ahead of the truck and spinning out of control. Alex wasn't sure if he'd woken or suddenly been hurled into a nightmare. The spinning car's headlights briefly revealed the horror of the lorry bearing down upon them once more.

The car was side on to the lorry when Mason rammed it again. The car had lost its forward momentum so the impact was greater this time, the doors buckling inwards, shoving Bill and Alex into the middle of the car. Sarah's head lurched sideways, cracking against the passenger window. Glass shattered and metal twisted. Alex felt a searing pain in his right leg and side. He wanted to escape but nothing happened when he tried to move his hands. He looked up and saw the front of the lorry inches from his face. He heard only the roar of the engine as the truck forced the ruined Audi sideways along the wet road. There was another jolt and the sound of scraping metal as the front of the car caught the crash barrier. It slid a quarter turn so that it was now being propelled down the carriageway backwards. Sparks flew as metal screeched against metal, the car utterly at the mercy of the lorry.

Mason backed off momentarily and then accelerated once more, turning the steering wheel sharply to the right. The corner of the truck smashed into Bill's door, impaling the wrecked Audi and causing the frame and chassis to buckle further. Mason tugged at the wheel, urging the truck to crush the Hannays' car harder into the barrier. The tractor unit started to judder as its front wheels lost grip on the road, their angle at odds with the truck's momentum. Mason kept the power going as long as he could, knowing that he'd lose control any second. With a grinding wrench the Audi stuck fast against the barrier. The tractor unit lurched up over the stricken car and came to an abrupt stop, its mass crunching down on the Audi's roof. The trailer swung out, jack-knifing and twisting before sliding to a halt and completely blocking the dual carriageway.

Mason tried to open the door of the truck, but it wouldn't budge. "Damn it." He turned to Wheeler. "Give me your gun."

With pistol in hand, Mason smashed the door glass. He clambered awkwardly through the gap and dropped onto the wet road below. Wheeler grabbed the back of Gorski's head and slammed it against the truck's dashboard. Gorski slumped, unconscious. His assailant climbed over him and exited via the broken window. Mason and Wheeler ran around the jack-knifed trailer and looked up the road in the direction they had come. The black Range Rover was waiting a hundred yards back, its powerful headlights glowing in the darkness, illuminating the torrential rain.

9

Alex coughed and tasted salty blood in his mouth. The rain was the only sound he could hear besides his rasping breathing. The seconds of chaos had given way to an eerie stillness. It was over but he still couldn't escape from his confinement in the wrecked car. The pain in his leg seemed to magnify.

Alex blacked out.

10

Lucas Ingwe put his copy of *Wuthering Heights* on the sitting room table as he heard his wife's key turn in the front door lock. Francesca stepped inside the narrow hallway of the small terraced house and hung up her green paramedic jacket on a hook by the door. She took off her boots and walked into the room where Lucas sat. She smiled when she saw him. "Hey, baby, you're up early. I thought you'd still be in bed." She put her arm around his neck and kissed him.

"I thought you might want some breakfast before you slept," Lucas replied.

She sat down on the sofa beside him. "Yeah, maybe."

He put his arm around her as she snuggled up to him. He touched her face gently and kissed her again. "What can I get you?"

"Nothing just yet." She closed her eyes and rested her head against her husband's shoulder. Lucas looked at her affectionately, idly stroking her blonde hair. He could tell she wanted to talk. A moment later she spoke, but it wasn't about work. "How's the book?"

"Great. I didn't realise that Heathcliff was so sinister. I think I'm becoming a fan of nineteenth century literature."

"I'm glad you're enjoying it."

"I have plenty of time on my hands at the moment." Lucas groaned silently to himself, regretting the comment as soon as he'd uttered it. He hadn't meant to bring up the subject of his absence from work when Francesca needed to talk.

Francesca made eye contact. "It'll work out, baby."

"Yeah, I'm not worried," Lucas lied. "It's just annoying not being able to do my job." He prompted Francesca to tell him what was on her mind. "How was the night shift?"

"Not great. Double fatal on the A12 near Martlesham."

"Oh."

"Yeah."

"You okay?"

"I will be, sweetie." Francesca cuddled closer and Lucas squeezed her in response. "Thanks for being there for me."

"Always. Do you want to tell me about it?"

Francesca closed her eyes again and sighed. "A lorry driver fell asleep at the wheel and hit a family car. It was really mangled. The mother was dead when we arrived. Her neck was broken. The father bled out and died as Tony was treating him. There was a young lad in the back who I worked on. I don't know if he'll make it. He had a piece of metal in his leg and internal injuries. It took Trumpton ages to cut him free."

Lucas didn't allow himself to react to the affectionate emergency services' nickname for the fire brigade. He knew it was a reference to a children's television programme from the 1960s, and it amused him that the name was still used. He wasn't familiar with the show – his family hadn't emigrated from Namibia until the eighties – but he'd learned why the name had become ingrained in emergency services jargon. He suppressed the distracting thought and turned his attention back to Francesca.

"Sounds like a rough night. How old was the boy?"

"Not sure. Twenties? I hope he makes it."

"I know you will have done your best for him."

"Sometimes that isn't good enough."

Lucas gave Francesca another gentle squeeze. "Let's hope he pulls through." They didn't speak for a while but just held each other on the sofa. Lucas looked through the sitting room window and saw that the morning sky was clearer than he'd expected. The torrential rain had finally blown through about 4am. The early sunlight was welcome, but Lucas hoped it wouldn't keep Francesca awake when she went to bed. He doubted she would be disturbed by it though. She was obviously exhausted.

Francesca wriggled. "So are you going to make me a bacon sarnie, or do I have to do it myself?" she teased.

"I'll start that right away." He moved his arm and kissed her again. He was about to get up when he noticed her frowning slightly. "What's wrong?"

"You know, it's funny..." Francesca paused.

"What is it?"

"Well, Tony and I drove past the crash site an hour later. We thought the police would have set up a diversion, but there was nothing there. They'd cleared it up already."

"Are you serious?"

"Yeah. Weird, huh?"

Lucas didn't reply.

TWO

1

Eric McVeigh seemed to spend most of his working life at his computer, writing reports and answering a never-ending barrage of e-mails. He'd joined the police with the rather romantic notion of making a difference, but during his twenty-five years' service bureaucracy and statistic-chasing had become ever-increasing burdens. Solving crime had become secondary to the public image of the police force. *No, police service*, McVeigh reminded himself cynically. Most of his career had been in the Criminal Investigation Department and he had passed his sergeant examination early. He hadn't bothered trying to get promoted beyond that rank, intending to remain a detective rather than become a manager. He consoled himself that he had only five years to go before he could retire. The phone on his desk rang again. It was the third call he'd received in ten minutes. He was tempted to let the answering system kick in but noticed that it was an external number this time. He picked up the handset. "D.S. McVeigh, Colchester C.I.D.," he said wearily.

"Eric, it's Lucas."

"Damn it, Lucas! You know I can't speak to you while you're on suspension!" McVeigh's Glaswegian accent amplified his irritation.

"Hear me out, Eric. This isn't about the Teller case. In fact, it's nothing to do with *any* of my cases. I need a favour."

McVeigh frowned. "Please tell me it's not about work."

"I need you to look into something for me. Just a discreet phone call or two."

McVeigh groaned.

Ingwe continued. "Is your mate Tom Eldridge still the chief inspector on Suffolk's road death team?"

"I think so. I haven't spoken to him for a few months." McVeigh and Eldridge had joined together back when police recruits from different forces went to national centres for their initial training. They had become friends and stayed in contact.

"Good. Fran went to a fatal on the A12 last night. Something feels wrong about it."

McVeigh paused. One of Lucas Ingwe's talents was his ability to spot things out of the ordinary. He had an instinct for seeing details that other detectives missed. Acting on instinct was unfortunately also one of his failings. His suspension was the result of bypassing formal procedures in a high profile investigation. But if Lucas thought something was wrong it was worth looking into.

McVeigh knew he should hang up right now. "Tell me more," he said.

Ingwe described what Francesca had told him about the crash. "Since when do we clear up fatals in under an hour?" he asked.

"Sounds unusual, I'll give you that."

"Unusual? Eric, that's barely enough time to take the measurements. Look, I may be wrong about this, but will you speak to Eldridge and find out what's going on?"

Hesitating, McVeigh rubbed his forehead, knowing he

would regret agreeing to participate. "I'll look into it, Lucas, but nothing more."

"I appreciate it."

"This might take a few days. I'll give you a call once I've spoken to Tom." McVeigh replaced the handset, closing his eyes momentarily and shaking his head. "Lucas Ingwe, you'll drive me to an early grave," he muttered to himself.

2

A soft beeping noise from a machine was the first thing Alex registered as he awoke. He was lying on his back but propped up slightly. He opened his eyes and immediately squinted at the room's brightness. He turned his head slightly and saw some of the room's detail. A bag of clear fluid was hanging from a metal pole beside his bed. A tube led from the bag to a needle in his arm. There was a cabinet against the wall upon which there stood a plastic jug and cups.

He felt disoriented. Memory fragments vied for attention in his brain, confusing him. He recollected being in a crash but the details were sparse. A woman had spoken to him, trying to reassure him, but he couldn't recall what she had said. Alex moved his head again and noticed a man asleep in an uncomfortable-looking chair, his glasses dislodged slightly by a hand pressed awkwardly against his head. He recognised his uncle, Graham Field. Alex tried to speak his uncle's name but the only sound he uttered was a dry croak.

Graham woke at the noise. He'd dozed off in the chair but the hospital's lights and cheap furniture prevented him from sleeping deeply. He looked at his nephew through weary eyes, surprised and relieved that he had stirred. "Alex? Are you awake?"

"Yes," Alex struggled to reply, his voice rasping.

"Let me get you some water." Graham stood and picked up the jug. He poured a small amount into a cup and held it carefully to Alex's mouth. "Just a sip. How are you feeling?"

"I don't know... tired."

"I'm glad you're okay." Graham's voice couldn't hide his anguish. The last four days had been the worst of his life. The fifty-five year old removed his glasses and rubbed the bridge of his nose with his finger and thumb. "I'll get a doctor. I promise I'll be right back."

3

Alex had fallen asleep again by the time Graham returned, but he stirred as the door opened. The man who entered with his uncle wore a pale blue shirt but no tie beneath an open white coat. His dark hair was slightly too long and dishevelled for his forty years. A plastic National Health Service identity badge was clipped to his coat pocket. "Glad to see you're up and about," the man said with a positive tone. Alex decided he liked the doctor. "I'm Dr Wood," the man said as he flashed a small torch into Alex's eyes, watching with satisfaction as Alex's pupils reacted to the light. "Can you tell me your full name?"

"Alex Hannay."

"Not Alexander then?"

"No, just Alex."

The doctor nodded, apparently pleased with the responses. "Do you know who this gentleman is?" Dr Wood motioned towards Graham briefly.

"My uncle Graham," replied Alex, his croaky voice becoming more comfortable with each reply.

"Excellent. You had us worried for a while, Alex, but you seem to be doing okay. You've been in surgery to fix some internal bleeding, and a piece of metal cut your right leg pretty badly. There is extensive muscle damage."

Alex hadn't felt any pain since waking and assumed he was on painkillers. "What does that mean?"

Wood's expression became less ebullient. "It's likely that you're going to need some physiotherapy to help you walk comfortably again. You may have to come back for more surgery, but we need more time before we make those decisions."

Graham leaned forward. "Do you remember what happened?"

Alex shook his head. "Not really. How long have I been asleep?"

"Four days," replied the doctor. "You stirred and mumbled a few times, but you haven't woken properly until now."

Alex couldn't register the lost days. He breathed heavily. "I was talking to Mum and Dad about the fencing competition, then I..." He became anxious, his face and neck feeling hot. "Are Mum and Dad okay?"

His uncle and the doctor exchanged glances. Dr Wood spoke softly. "I think I should give you a moment. I'll be right outside." He turned and walked to the door, closing it quietly as he left the room.

Graham placed his hand on Alex's arm. "Alex, there's no easy way to say this. They both died in the crash. I'm so sorry."

Alex didn't reply. He turned his gaze quickly towards the ceiling as his chest and throat tightened.

4

Eric McVeigh left the office to phone Lucas, partly because he didn't want to be overheard, but also to get out of the police station for a while. It was early afternoon when he walked into the grounds of Colchester Castle, the warm sunlight a welcome change from the miserable weather that had swept through the eastern counties during the last few days. McVeigh sat on a bench near the castle's entrance and studied the impressive Norman construction in front of him. He knew it stood upon older Roman foundations – he'd explored the underground sections during a visit some years ago – but his scant historical knowledge made it hard to imagine what the town must have looked like during the Roman occupation. He reminded himself – again – that he really should take up some hobbies and learn something. He, like many of his colleagues, had become institutionalised in the police. There was a cruel irony to life in the force: it gave an insight into society that few people ever saw but, after years in the job, officers were unqualified to do anything else. McVeigh was determined to make his retirement rewarding. *Only five years to go*, he reminded himself.

He watched passers-by in the castle grounds. It was always busy here – at least when the weather was fine – with many people from nearby businesses taking a quick lunch break, sitting on the lawns and eating sandwiches, or just having a stroll to pass the time before returning to work. The location also attracted some of the local drunks and junkies. McVeigh recognised an addict he had dealt with several times for burglary sucking on a two litre plastic bottle of cider, the man's pallor and gaunt pock-marked face making him look older than his twenty-five years. A skinny teenager with closely cropped hair, cheap-looking earrings and expensive trainers walked past him. The kid hadn't reached his twentieth birthday but had already spent nine months in prison for a serious assault. The thin red lines all over his forearms revealed he'd been self-harming again. McVeigh wondered if it was good for the public to have no clue who was around them. *Probably better to be oblivious to the reality of society than worry about it*, he decided. *That's for me to do.*

McVeigh pulled his phone from his trouser pocket. *Lucas, you're too smart for your own good.* He swiped through his contact list until he found Lucas Ingwe's mobile number.

Lucas answered quickly. "Eric?"

"I phoned Tom Eldridge," McVeigh said.

"Go on."

"It was a Polish lorry driver. The traffic guys found him in the cab and arrested him on scene. He was drunk and had fallen asleep at the wheel. He wiped out the only car that was on the road."

"What did he blow?" Lucas referred to the device that was used in police custody blocks for evaluating drunk drivers' breath samples.

"Ninety-eight," replied McVeigh.

"Jesus, that's high."

"Tell me about it. Anyway, he's been remanded. The plea and directions hearing was yesterday. The magistrates referred the case to the Crown Court of course."

"That poor family. Sounds straightforward though."

McVeigh paused. "Yeah..."

Ingwe noticed his colleague's hesitation. "What is it, Eric?"

"The thing is, Lucas, it's not straightforward at all. You were right about one thing. It *was* cleared up too quickly. Tom wasn't on duty when it happened, but he found out about it the next morning. The night shift sergeant sent him a text – he wanted to let him know so he could arrange staff welfare interviews. The next day Tom tried to look up the report on the computer, but the incident was inaccessible. It had been locked down."

"Okay, but that's not unusual in itself. The control room inspector will do that for sensitive incidents."

"Sure, but if anyone should've been able to view it, it'd be Tom. Anyway, he did some digging. He spoke to the night turn silver commander whom he knows well. She had a call from the chief constable – at three in the morning – telling her to get the incident shut down immediately. He told her that it was for 'national security' and the scene had to be cleared."

"That's different."

"No kidding. The vehicles got removed by the recovery service and the site got swept up by the MOD Police. Tom's been told to – and I quote – 'lose interest' in the job. He hasn't even been allowed to arrange a family liaison officer for the kid."

"Which firm took the vehicles?" asked Ingwe.

McVeigh hesitated. "Lucas, this isn't anything to do with us."

"I know, Eric. I appreciate you talking to me. Fran will want to know the lad's okay. After this call I won't mention it again."

"It looks like the boy's going to make it." McVeigh paused. "Stay clear of this, Lucas," he warned. "Sometimes you just have to let things go."

"The rota garage, Eric?"

"It was Lord's."

Lucas changed the subject. "The car index must have had a tag on it. Someone saw it flash up as soon as the attending officers ran it through PNC." Records of particular interest on the Police National Computer – a database of UK vehicles and criminals – could be labelled with a *ghost marker*. A police officer checking one of these records would have no indication that it was of special interest, but the person who had placed the marker would be alerted that the record had been accessed.

"That's what I thought," McVeigh agreed, "but that's not enough to wake the chief constable in the middle of the night and tell him to close down an investigation."

"I guess we can be thankful it's Suffolk's problem and not ours."

"Make sure you remember that. Your instinct was right – as usual – but now it's time to drop this. Let Francesca know she did a fantastic job then forget about this conversation."

"I appreciate you looking into this."

"Give me your word that you won't mention this to anyone, Lucas. This can't come back to me, and definitely not Tom Eldridge."

"I promise. I was right about this being unusual."

McVeigh chuckled but there was little humour in his tone. "I haven't told you the strangest part yet."

"There's more?"

"The Polish guy kept insisting it wasn't him driving."

"Come on, Eric, lots of drunk drivers say that."

"Yeah, but they don't all claim to have been abducted at gunpoint."

5

Lucas touched the red graphic on his smartphone's screen to end the call then placed the mobile on the kitchen counter. McVeigh's report intrigued him. He'd never encountered anything like this before, despite a career filled with far-fetched circumstances. Policing was never predictable but very little surprised him any more. He'd witnessed the worst in human nature from simple greed to cold-blooded animalistic violence. Yet this incident – which ostensibly was a simple road traffic collision – was revelatory. From the tone of his sergeant's voice, McVeigh hadn't experienced this sort of direct involvement from a chief officer either.

He made a decision and picked up his phone. He flicked through his contact list and found a number. He hesitated before dialling. *I have to do this*, he told himself. *If it gets messy I can walk away*. He made the call.

"Lucas!" an East London voice answered. "What you up to?"

"Hi, Stan, just this and that."

"I heard about your suspension, mate. Don't let the bastards get you down." Scenes of crime officer Stan Driscoll's default opinion was that management victimised workers at every opportunity and Ingwe had been unfairly persecuted. Lucas often wondered why Stan hadn't ended up as a trade unionist.

"I'll try not to."

"What can I do for you?" Driscoll asked.

Ingwe hesitated once more. "Stan, I'm after a favour."

"Anything for you, chief, you know that."

"I'm looking into something and I need to keep it under the radar. I shouldn't ask..."

"Bollocks, you ask away," Driscoll interrupted. "I owe you. If you hadn't helped me when I first got qualified, I'd be out of a job." Driscoll had struggled when he first started working as a crime scene investigator. Lucas had given him considerable but discreet guidance, preventing him from missing important evidence on more than one occasion. Driscoll considered himself to be indebted to the detective for life.

"Thanks, Stan," Lucas said. "There was a fatal on Suffolk's ground the other night, and something's bugging me about it. The vehicles were recovered by Lord's of Ipswich and I want to take a look at them. Any chance you can find me a spare kit box?"

"I can do better than that," Driscoll replied. "I'm off tomorrow. I'll pick you up and we'll have a look together."

Ingwe's stomach tightened. "I appreciate it – but that's probably not a good idea."

"How else are you going to get into the yard? They've taken your warrant card. Besides, I know the guys up at Lord's. It'll be a doddle."

"Cheers, Stan."

"No probs, mate. I'll pick you up at half-eight."

Lucas ended the call. *Curiosity will be my downfall.* Part of him knew he'd hoped Driscoll would be up for some snooping around. His friend would consider this to be a snub at the management, even though he had no intention of ever letting his bosses find out.

6

Days of confinement in the hospital room were beginning to take their toll on Alex. Physically he was feeling stronger but mentally he was exhausted. He imagined the walls closing in on him, crushing him, returning him to the wreckage of the car. At times he didn't believe his parents had died and he saw them walking into his hospital room, joking about taking him to France for the fencing competition in Valenciennes. Sometimes he could visualise nothing but the inside of the Audi, travelling through the rainy night, heading for home. He relived their last conversation over and over. Often the words changed and that angered him. He wanted to remember everything exactly the way it had been. Many times he fell asleep, gaining a temporary reprieve from his thoughts, only to be startled awake by the imagined sounds of collapsing metal and shattering glass. Life in the hospital was diluting his senses. His room, the ward and the bathroom had become the limits of his world. His sense of spatial awareness – which he had developed acutely through his fencing – was being eroded. He wanted to go home and return to some recognisable reality. He thought he would be trapped in the hospital forever.

It was therefore a shock when Dr Wood came in and told him his uncle would be picking him up that afternoon. "Really?" Alex questioned. "I can go home?"

"What did you expect, Alex?" the doctor replied. "The NHS can't afford to keep you here rent free indefinitely."

For a moment Alex didn't recognise the joke. "Oh. I..."

"Don't worry," Dr Wood interrupted. "You've been responding well to your treatment and we've kept you under observation for long enough. You'll have to come back for some follow-up consultations – we need to figure out exactly what to do about your leg – but it's time you went home. I'll make sure your uncle has all the information you need."

"I appreciate everything you've done for me."

The doctor smiled. "You're welcome. I know this has been a really tough time for you. It's important that you rest properly for the next few weeks. Your body has been through a lot. Just take things steadily for a while."

"I will."

"Alex?"

"Yes, doctor?"

"There's something else." Dr Wood held eye contact with him. "It's not just the physical trauma you have to think about. Your parents *died*. Stuck here in the hospital you haven't had a chance to grieve properly. You'll need to find a way of restoring your emotional balance. Talk to someone if things get difficult. It may be hard, but – trust me – it's better than bottling everything up."

Alex felt his stomach knot. He hadn't wanted another reminder about his parents' deaths. "I will. Thanks." He extended his hand.

The doctor's handshake was strong and expressed confidence. "I'll let you know when your uncle arrives." He turned to the door and left Alex alone in the room.

Sitting upright on his bed Alex considered what the doctor had said. It hadn't occurred to him that the life he knew before the crash no longer existed. He would have to make adjustments. His view of familiar people and places would seem different – perhaps almost imperceptibly so – but different nonetheless. People's perceptions of *him* would change too. They'd try too hard to behave as normal, but the façade would be obvious. Alex Hannay would no longer be the champion fencer and aspiring photographer; he'd be the unfortunate orphan whose doting parents had met their end in a terrible car crash. He could imagine the nonsensical conversations that his neighbours would have about the cruel hand of fate.

His home would be changed too. The lovely old building, with its timber beams and pastel painted walls – so typical of homes in many Suffolk villages – would seem empty without his parents' chatter and warmth. They had made it a wonderful home but now there would be a void he couldn't fill. The familiar would feel marginally detached, as if the impact of the crash had somehow caused his sense of reality to misalign. But no one else's world would have altered. People's lives would continue, just as they had before, the crash having no other effect upon them except prompting temporary expressions of sympathy. Would he feel angry at watching life proceed around him, indifferent to his loss, when his world had changed so drastically? Or would he slip back into life, his memories of his parents and the crash that killed them gradually fading from his thoughts?

No, I won't forget them!

Once again he imagined himself in the car, looking

between the front seats at the rain lashing against the window in the darkness. He wanted his parents to turn around, to look at him once more, but they kept staring ahead. Suddenly he snapped out of the daydream and felt tears begin to form in his eyes. For a moment he had forgotten what his parents looked like and the thought frightened him.

7

The compound's attendant recognised Driscoll as soon as he and Ingwe arrived. He was sixty, overweight and had thick untidy grey hair. Faded oil-stained coveralls and persistent dirt on his hands identified him as a mechanic. A radio somewhere in the yard blared noisily, a pop song giving way to a traffic report. The man greeted Stan cheerily, his Suffolk accent revealing he was a local.

"Keeping well, Joe?" asked Driscoll as he pulled up by the metal gate.

"Can't complain," the man called Joe replied, peering inside Stan's car as he leaned on the roof. "What can I do for you?"

"This is D.C. Ingwe. He's looking into the crash at Martlesham. Am I right in thinking the vehicles were brought here?"

"Yes... nasty business," the mechanic replied. "Only the tractor unit's still here though. Park up and I'll show you."

Driscoll found a clear space in the compound as Joe closed the gate. It was a large yard and currently held around twenty vehicles. An open-fronted building doubled-up as a repair facility and a covered space for vehicles awaiting police forensic examination. A tow truck with Lord's of Ipswich livery was parked next to an old shipping container that had been converted into an office. A much larger heavy recovery truck – robust enough for towing commercial vehicles – was parked on the far side of the yard. Stan took a metal case from the back seat of his car and waited for Joe to join them. He questioned the mechanic about the Audi's location.

The mechanic shrugged his shoulders. "We barely had it unloaded when someone showed up and towed it. Showed me some identification and said it was going to a special garage for examination."

Lucas frowned. The reason was plausible but seemed too convenient. Examinations of vehicles – even those involved in fatal crashes – were usually conducted in the secure compounds owned by the recovery services for no other reason than the practicality of space. It didn't make sense to move the car from one suitable compound to another. "I wanted to see that vehicle," he said to Driscoll.

Joe spoke again. "Well, I can't help you with that, but I kept a note of the vehicle details the copper gave me. I can let you have a copy. It's in the office."

Lucas felt relieved. "Cheers, Joe, I'd appreciate that."

"No problem. I'll photocopy it for you while you have a look at the truck. I'll bring it over in a minute."

Ingwe and Driscoll walked to the lorry. It had been kept under shelter since being brought to the yard. Lucas was surprised to see that it looked relatively undamaged but reminded himself that the tractor unit, weighing around seven times as much as the car, was more likely to inflict catastrophic damage than suffer it. "I'm not sure what I'm looking for, Stan," he said.

"There might not be much to find," his friend replied. "As far as I can see, it matches up with how Francesca described the scene." Driscoll pointed at the front of the truck. "There's some damage here suggesting a straightforward rear-end shunt. But Francesca said the right side of the truck had ridden up over the car and crushed it. That was why it took some time to get the bodies out. You can see the silver paint scrapings. This part of the truck definitely hit the car. The bodywork is twisted." He pointed. "This is the impact point."

"Would that have caused the doors to jam?"

Stan shrugged. "Quite possibly."

Lucas walked to the driver's side of the vehicle. "It's a left-hand drive, and Fran said the officers forced the door with a crowbar to get the driver out. But the window is smashed."

"That could have happened because of the energy transfer during the crash." Stan joined Lucas at the vehicle's near-side and looked closely at the driver's door. He motioned towards an aluminium step ladder. "Slide those steps over here."

Ingwe grabbed the ladder and watched as Driscoll set it up next to the driver's door. He went to his kit box and removed a pen light. He turned it on, placed it in his mouth and climbed up the steps. "Interesting," he murmured as he shone the torchlight onto the top of the door, still holding the torch between his lips.

"Found something?"

Driscoll removed the torch from his mouth. "Yup. Dried blood. Fetch me some distilled water and some swab tubes. I thought you said the driver wasn't injured?"

"He wasn't." Lucas handed Stan the items from the scenes of crime kit box.

"Well, we can be pretty certain that the officers

wouldn't have tried to pull him through the smashed window."

"They didn't. They prised the door open."

"And the victims were under the *other* side of the truck."

"Definitely."

"In that case we appear to have found someone else's blood." Driscoll continued to work for a short time, swabbing the dried blood carefully in order to collect a useable sample. When he was finished he climbed down and placed the collection tubes back in his kit box. "I'll get these tested for you. With luck this could belong to someone on the police database."

Joe walked up to them as they left the covered section of the compound. "Sorry, got held up with a phone call." He waved a sheet of white paper. "This is the information you wanted. The traffic officer gave me the owner's details. He was called William Hannay and lived in Clayfield."

Lucas took the piece of paper. "Thanks, Joe. You've been very helpful." He handed the mechanic a ten pound note.

Joe quickly stuffed the money into a pocket in his coveralls. "No problem at all."

8

Despite his apprehension at returning home, Alex felt relieved when his uncle drove him into the village. He'd told himself that he was going to approach things logically and strategically. That was the way he won his fencing bouts. Preparation, studying the opponent, developing tactics. But, since his conversation with Dr Wood, Alex had realised that an objective viewpoint required him to lock away his emotions. Adjusting to his parents' death wasn't the same as outwitting an opponent on the fencing piste. The sporting analogy wasn't much use to him anyway: after the serious injury to his leg it was unlikely that he would be able to fence competitively again. That was something else he would have to come to terms with, but before then there was a funeral to organise. He found the thoughts intimidating and conflicting. He was supposed to be dealing with his emotional reactions and yet the formalities had to be dealt with methodically. The irony wasn't lost on him. Fortunately his uncle had decided to stay in Clayfield for a few days to help. Alex knew he would be glad of the company. Graham had begun to make arrangements with the funeral directors while he had been in the hospital. The service would take place in four days' time.

Graham parked his Ford Focus in the space outside the Hannays' house and turned off the engine. "Stay there,

Alex, I'll get your crutches for you."

Alex opened his door, clutched the doorframe and moved his legs. Graham held the crutches for him. He placed his arms into the supports and held the grips, steadying himself and trying to keep his weight off his right foot.

Seeing Alex was managing, Graham unlocked the cottage's front door and pushed it open as wide as it would go. "I'll get your things," he said.

Alex hobbled inside, looking at the details he'd normally ignore. The familiarity of the hallway was welcoming. His mother's good eye for design had given the old cottage a modern look that was elegant but still retained the charm and history of the building. It was comfortable without being quaint and spacious without feeling empty. Alex had joked that the house was a 'mini barn conversion'. Sarah hadn't liked wallpaper and had removed it throughout the house, choosing to paint the walls with light pastels instead. Some of the carpets had been sacrificed for wooden flooring. The bathrooms and kitchen had been brightened with carefully chosen tiles. Rather than overwhelming the older features the modern decoration had complemented them, emphasising the beams and brickwork.

Alex took a few more clumsy steps, supporting himself awkwardly with the crutches, and turned into the sitting room. Here hung several of his photographs printed on canvas. He hadn't wanted to display them at first, thinking that they weren't of a satisfactory standard, but his parents had loved his work. He'd mostly taken landscapes which captured elements of the Suffolk countryside: reed beds by the River Alde, heather in bloom on Dunwich Heath and the woodland at Rendlesham Forest.

Graham walked into the room. "There isn't much food in the kitchen I'm afraid. I didn't have time to go shopping before picking you up. When you're settled I'll drive into Halesworth."

"No, don't worry, I'll get a few things from the village shop," said Alex. "You've helped so much already. Have a rest for a while."

"*You* really ought to rest that leg."

"I've been doing that for ages in the hospital. Honestly, I could do with getting out and having a stroll. After days of air conditioning I need some fresh air."

"Fair enough. Look, I don't want to get in the way, but if you're happy for me to carry on going through your parents' paperwork, I'll do that this evening."

"That's fine. Thanks." Alex was glad to have the help. His uncle was a solicitor and would understand what he was looking at. "Graham?"

"Yes?"

"I haven't asked how you are."

"You've had a lot to think about yourself."

"I know, but you've been sorting out everything. I..."

"I'll be fine, Alex." Graham's tone was reassuring. "We both will be. Particularly when the funeral's over. Of course I miss my sister and your dad, but they wouldn't want us to mourn. They would definitely want you to put all of your energies into your future."

Alex exhaled slowly. "I'm not sure what my future will be like."

"Career-wise? I'm sure your parents would want you to

continue with your photography. You're really good."

"I always wondered if they were disappointed with me for taking a photography course instead of something scientific. I'm sure they wanted me to follow in their footsteps."

"They did. They loved their work, but they also realised that you had to follow your own path. Believe me, they may have tried encouraging you to be a biologist at first, but they weren't disappointed when you excelled at something else. They were very proud of you."

"I'm glad. It's not that I don't like science – in fact it fascinates me – but I felt like I needed to be creative. Photography gives me that."

"I can tell that from your pictures," said Graham as he glanced at the canvas prints on the sitting room walls. "You have a gift for it."

Alex contradicted him. "Not according to my parents – not a *gift*. I evolved the right way and my brain learned the skill."

"Of course," Graham agreed. "None of that supernatural mumbo jumbo in the Hannay household!"

They both laughed. It was the first time either of them had felt a moment's levity in a long while.

9

Ipswich's expensive Neptune Quay was a place that Lucas enjoyed visiting. The waterfront, just a short stroll from the historic town centre, had undergone an extensive renovation and was now home to yachts and apartments which he knew he would never have any chance of being able to afford. *Not as long as I'm working in the public sector.* Lucas frowned. *Assuming I still have a job.*

His phone rang, distracting him. Stan Driscoll's name appeared on the screen. "Stan?" Ingwe said as he answered the call.

"Lucas." The voice didn't have Driscoll's usual energy. "Sorry, mate, but nothing came back from that blood sample. Whoever it belongs to isn't in the police database."

Lucas groaned.

"Yeah, I'd hoped we'd be on to something."

"Thanks for the favour, Stan. I owe you."

"Not for that you don't, but I looked into something else. It might be unrelated, but..." Driscoll didn't finish his sentence.

"Go on."

"Do you remember telling me that police officers often overlook a basic fact, namely suspects have to get to and from a crime scene?"

"Sure," replied Lucas. It was a point he tried to emphasise to new recruits who sometimes didn't see the wider picture. Establishing how suspects travelled and what their routes were often led to more information being unearthed about their crimes.

"I asked a buddy of mine in the Suffolk ANPR office for a list of vehicles on the A12 that night, and something came up." ANPR stood for automatic number plate recognition: a camera system which read vehicle registrations and compared the results to the national database, revealing any information markers. "One of the Orwell Bridge cameras caught a black Range Rover heading east four hours before the crash. Only it wasn't supposed to be a black Range Rover. The index came back to a red Nissan Micra belonging to a pensioner in Luton."

"That's a long while before the crash. We get ANPR hits on stolen plates every day."

"Yeah, but that index flagged up again four hours later on a camera near Suffolk Police HQ. That's fairly close to the crash site and we both know it doesn't take that long to get from Ipswich to Martlesham. That Range Rover dropped off the radar then reappeared in exactly the right place at exactly the right time. It went past the camera less than a minute before the truck."

A link. Ingwe liked links. Connections became hypotheses. Now one piece of information – the strange circumstances of the crash – no longer stood in isolation. *A black Range Rover on stolen plates...* "It sounds like too much of a coincidence, doesn't it?"

"Not much, chief!" Driscoll's East London accent emphasised the contradictory speech.

"Stan, would you do something else for me?"

"Sure."

"It's a long shot, but have the blood sample rechecked – this time against military personnel records."

10

Clayfield's village store was near to Alex's house and, despite his injury and the unwieldy crutches, it took him only three minutes to get there. The old wooden shop door stuck in its frame as usual and required a light shove before it allowed admittance. Once inside he looked around, glad to be in familiar surroundings. It was a typically charming village store with a tiny post office counter in one corner, a freezer in another and a seemingly random selection of stock squeezed into every inch of space. Bread, cakes, cheeses and jams from local suppliers were displayed on a table in the centre. He saw that he was alone apart from the assistant, Abigail Jones. She was a short, slim woman with sparkling blue-green eyes, short brown hair, and a beautifully bright complexion. She was thirty-eight but looked at least ten years younger.

"Hi, Alex!" she said, her surprise at seeing him clear in her voice. She had a Cardiff accent; only slightly softened by living in England for nearly twenty years.

"Hi, Abi, how are you?"

"Fine, thanks." She paused, her face revealing she wasn't sure how to express what she wanted to say next. "I heard about the accident. I'm really sorry."

"Thanks," Alex said, unsure if that was how he should reply to a message of condolence. Abi wasn't just saying the words. She was one of the most genuine people he'd met. They had known each other since she began working at the store ten years ago. She also worked during the evening in the village's public house – The Green Man – to supplement her income. He was surprised when she came over gave him a hug. For a moment he found himself caught between the sadness of recent events and the gratitude he felt at her expression of sympathy. He felt a lump in his throat. "Thanks," he said again. "I needed that."

"Don't... you'll start me off." She raised her hand to her face and brushed a tear from her cheek.

There was an awkward silence until Alex thought of something ordinary to say. "I came in to get something for dinner. My uncle's staying with me until the funeral and there isn't much in the house."

"Oh, okay," Abi said. "I'll let you have a look around. Look, I was wondering..." she hesitated.

"What is it?"

"I don't know if you're just keeping it to family, but if you don't mind I'd like to go to the service."

"I'd like that. I don't think there will be many people there. The only family left is me and my uncle. Graham said he thought a few of Mum and Dad's colleagues might want to come, but that's about it. You'll probably be the only person there I know besides Graham."

"I'll definitely be there then."

"Great." Alex smiled at her then went to the freezer and opened it, the cold rush of air cooling his hand. He removed a small box. "I think simplicity is called for. Chicken Kievs and chips will have to do tonight."

Abi laughed. Instinctively Alex grinned. There was an unintentional mischievous tone in her laughter that always made him smile. "It might not be the healthiest choice, but I bet it tastes better than hospital food."

"No kidding. I wasn't sure what I was eating most of the time and it all tasted equally bad. Do you mind bagging these up for me, Abi? I'm not used to these crutches yet."

"No problem." Abi took the items to the till, waited as Alex picked up some more goods, totalled them and placed them in a carrier for him. He handed over a note and waited for his change.

"I was just about to lock up," Abi said. "If you can hang on a moment, I'll walk you back home so you don't have to carry these."

"Are you sure?"

"It's not exactly far," she joked.

"Okay, thanks. Maybe it was a bit ambitious to carry a bag full of shopping while learning to walk again."

They continued to talk as they left the shop. Abi tugged the awkward front door shut and turned a key in the lock. "If you don't mind me asking, how badly hurt are you?"

"The muscles in my right leg got torn by some metal in the crash. The doctor reckons I might need another operation and some physio. I guess my fencing days are over."

"Sounds rough."

"Yeah. I have a few changes to get used to."

"Let's hope for a quick recovery."

"I hope so. I'm in danger of getting bored out my mind."

They soon reached Alex's house. Their conversation had been surprisingly helpful to him. It had been good to have an ordinary chat with a friend. He found his key, opened the door and took the bag of groceries from her.

"Enjoy your dinner," she said with a grin.

He smiled back. "Thanks. I'll do my best."

Abi's expression became more serious. She touched his arm. "Let me know about the funeral, won't you?"

Alex nodded. "Yes, of course." He raised the bag slightly. "Thanks for helping me with these."

"No worries. I'll speak to you soon." She smiled again and then walked away as Alex went inside.

He carried his groceries into the kitchen. *Things will be okay*, he told himself. He put the bag on the counter and removed the bread and milk. A thought flashed randomly into his mind. *I have to find some pictures of Mum and Dad.* There were already a few family pictures on display in the house, but he wanted more. They wouldn't fill the void in his life but the memories would be important.

He had several seven by five inch prints of his parents. He'd photographed them a lot and luckily neither had been shy in front of his camera. He found spare frames and spent the next half hour choosing his favourite shots and placing the prints carefully into the wooden mounts. He chose various places around the house for his new prized possessions and spent another half hour looking at the images, gladdened that the faces of his mother and father would never fade from his thoughts again.

THREE

1

Standing in the waiting room at the crematorium Alex found himself contemplating what it meant to die. It occurred to him that one of the disadvantages of being the dominant species on the planet was the tendency to try to find purpose in everything. It was ironic – having evolved intellect humankind should have known better. People were not the subject of some grand design or the fateful whims of an omniscient deity. His parents had encouraged him to have an open but sceptical mind. They had instilled in him the need to question everything, to apply the scientific method to problems and to never accept anything which could not be tested rigorously. Amid the dozen mourners who had arrived for his parents' funeral he could see why many people sought comfort in notions of the supernatural, but the foolishness of it annoyed him. *The only role which can be assigned to life is the continuation of the species*, he reminded himself. *Death is simply the cessation of life. Don't apply religious delusions to a scientific process.*

"Are you okay, Alex?" Abi touched his arm. "You seem to be in a world of your own." She was smartly dressed in a white blouse and dark grey trouser suit.

"I'm fine," he said. "Just thinking." He glanced at his watch. "The hearses should be here soon."

Abi didn't reply.

Alex knew very few of the people in attendance. His uncle was talking to a tall grey-haired man who had worked with his parents. He had introduced himself but Alex had forgotten his name at once. The man had said some kind words about his parents but he didn't remember the conversation. He wasn't in the mood to chat with strangers. He recognised a middle-aged couple from the village; close friends of his parents. He'd spoken to them for a while but he could tell that they didn't really know what to say. He was glad Abi had asked to come. They'd travelled to the cemetery with his uncle, choosing to go in Graham's car rather than being driven by the funeral directors. Doing so would have added to the sombreness of the occasion.

He looked outside. It was raining heavily. Puddles were forming in the slightly uneven patches of the road which led to the crematorium building. The downpour and the darkness of the sky made Alex's thoughts flash to the night of the accident. He felt the sensation of the car spinning on the water-logged carriageway and for a moment he felt dizzy. He heard glass shatter and the truck's engine roaring inches from his head. He placed his hand on the doorframe to steady himself. Abi looked concerned.

"I'm okay," he told her quietly. "For a moment I was back... *there*."

Abi hooked her arm around his. "Try not to think about it." She didn't let go.

The hearses arrived three minutes later, pulling in under a covered area beside the waiting room. Everyone fell silent which Alex found unnerving. Graham walked outside, shook hands with one of the undertakers and spoke briefly. They both came into the waiting room. In a polite clear voice the undertaker invited everyone to make their way into the chapel. For a moment nobody moved and Alex realised that they were waiting for him and Graham to go first.

Abi gave his arm a squeeze. "Come on," she said so that only he would hear.

They went to the pew at the front of the chapel. As they sat down others filled the benches behind them, but Alex didn't watch. He looked at the interior of the room in which he now found himself. It was a modern building which had been made to look old. It was in stark contrast to his family's home. The wooden pews – uncomfortable and slightly too close together – were replicas of those he would expect to see in a church. Pale pink curtains – *Mum would hate those* – were draped from the high ceiling, presumably to soften the mood of the room and mask its functionality. The illusion failed to work on him. After this funeral there would be another one, and perhaps another half an hour later. It made him think of aircraft waiting to be allocated take-off slots by air traffic control. He wondered what the incinerator looked like and how hot it had to be to reduce bodies to ashes.

The coffins were carried in by the pallbearers. He couldn't tell if their expressions were solemn or simply devoid of emotion. The caskets were placed beside each other on stands at the front of the chapel. They were adorned with small flower arrangements. Graham had insisted the florist avoided the extravagant and ostentatious displays usually seen at memorial services. The funeral director stood in front of the coffins and gave a short bow. Alex knew it was to demonstrate respect but couldn't see the point. *You didn't know my parents. Never mind, you're just doing your job.*

Alex didn't pay attention during most of the service. He found his thoughts wandering frequently – sometimes back to the accident, sometimes to events from his childhood. He remembered fragments of conversations with his parents which he hadn't recalled in years. He found himself back on the fencing piste in Weymouth, beating Jim Peters with the final hit and seeing the pride on his parents' faces as he turned towards them in the audience, his mask in one hand and his foil in the other as he punched the air in celebration.

He forced himself to focus on the funeral, looked up and realised the grey-haired man – his parents' colleague – had finished a speech. The man glanced at him as he walked from the lectern. Alex smiled in silent gratitude even though he had no idea what the man had said. Beside him he saw Graham removing some folded sheets of paper from his suit pocket. They exchanged glances and then his uncle stood and walked to the lectern. Alex felt Abi squeeze his arm once more. She'd kept her arm linked in his throughout the service.

Graham cleared his throat and paused. Alex found himself listening attentively for the first time. He knew this would be difficult for his uncle. Graham glanced down at the paper and then back at the audience. "I spent a while trying to work out what to say today, but I realised that my sister Sarah and her husband Bill wouldn't want me to talk about loss and sadness or any of the emotions that one normally feels at a time like this. So, while I miss them both – and will no doubt continue to do so for a long time – I'm going to talk about their enthusiasm for life, not my sorrow at their passing.

"Sarah and Bill had a fascination with life that was inspiring. My sister found wonder in the natural world from an early age, and that curiosity stayed with her throughout her adult life. Sarah received a microscope as a birthday present one year and spent hours with it, studying the structure of cells long before she actually knew what she was looking at. Becoming a biologist was the inevitable progression, and genetics swiftly became her area of expertise. In Bill she found not only a loving husband but also a fellow enthusiast. But, like all good scientists, she – and Bill – researched many other scientific fields.

"You will have noticed that there are no religious elements to this service today. They maintained that the greatness of life began long before humankind evolved the imagination to invent creation myths. Sarah often expressed – only half-jokingly – her hope that the 'fairy tales of long-dead Middle Eastern goat-herders' would eventually be seen as fiction in the same way we now view the gods of the classical world. Bill, on the other hand, was much more forthright. He saw religion as a destructive absurdity – the antithesis of science and rational thought.

"Sarah and Bill had a great life because they understood the building blocks of life. Being a brief part of the universe's existence was wondrous to them, and it was that sense of awe that gave them the desire to enjoy life and to learn everything they could about it. They saw life as precious, fragile and something to be celebrated. When Alex arrived everything they believed was reinforced and gave them even greater vigour.

"They were greatly inspired by the visionary writings of Charles Darwin. It is therefore fitting to conclude this celebration of the lives of Sarah and Bill Hannay with the last few lines from Darwin's remarkable work, *On the Origin of Species*. He wrote: 'There is grandeur in this view of life, with its several powers, having been originally breathed into a few forms or into one; and that, whilst this planet has gone cycling on according to the fixed law of gravity, from so simple a beginning endless forms most beautiful and most wonderful have been, and are being, evolved.'"

2

In the days after the funeral Alex discovered his parents had been meticulous in ensuring their affairs were in order. With his uncle's help he learned that the house was paid for, they had roughly seventy thousand pounds in savings, and that their wills left everything to him. They had several life insurance policies and he was the sole beneficiary of those too. He would have preferred to inherit money under wholly different circumstances, but he was grateful that his parents had considered his future and made sure that nothing had been left outstanding. Graham ensured that all the administrative details were concluded carefully. Alex found himself in the fortunate position of not having to worry about money.

It occurred to him that the amount of money they had accrued seemed rather high. He wasn't familiar with scientists' income levels but imagined most in the profession didn't earn a great deal. He realised he knew very little about their genetic research work with East Anglia University. As far as he was aware his parents hadn't supplemented their income with any other employment. He assumed that one or both of them had inherited money some time ago. He'd met his father's parents but couldn't remember them. Bill's parents were in their middle forties when their son was born and they had both died before Alex reached his fourth birthday. His maternal grandparents died within eight months of each other when Alex was fourteen.

Graham was a quiet house guest but, after his departure, Alex thought the cottage felt overwhelmingly silent. It had never been a noisy household but it had always had energy and life. His parents' absence affected him and at times he struggled to shift the melancholy which absorbed his thoughts, despite his efforts to stay positive. He spent many hours navigating the house with his crutches simply to look at family photographs. The pictures kept him company. When he looked at his mother's face he heard her laughter. His father's voice spoke to him in supportive tones about his fencing and photography.

He thought about them a lot when he went walking too. He was determined to keep as active as he could, so he made himself take short strolls around the village and nearby farmland. Negotiating footpaths wasn't easy but he found the effort satisfying.

A week after the funeral he found himself in conversation with Abi in the Green Man. His rather unsatisfactory attempts at cooking finally prompted him to take dinner in the pub. Abi – working her second job – brought his chicken and ham pie over to him and set it down on the table. The hot food smelled delicious.

He thought Abi looked tired. "Thanks," he said. "Are you okay?"

She smiled at him but her expression showed she was forcing it. "I'm fine." She tried to change the subject. "When's your check up at the hospital?"

"Not for a couple of weeks."

"Oh, I thought it would be sooner. Enjoy your pie." She

began to walk away.

"Abi?"

She turned round and looked at him without replying.

"What's wrong?"

She exhaled and looked away momentarily in an expression of mild annoyance. "Look, Alex, you have enough on your mind without having to worry about me. I'll be fine."

"I'm sure you will be. But listening to a friend – particularly one who's looked after *me* recently – is no chore at all."

She sighed. "I shouldn't burden you with my problems."

"Come on, sit down. A problem shared and all that."

Abi pulled the empty stool from under Alex's table, repositioned it, and sat down opposite him. She held his gaze for a moment. "Money's a bit tight. My bloody landlord has told me the rent on my flat is going up by a hundred and fifty quid. There's no way I can afford that. I don't know what I'm going to do."

"That's criminal."

"No kidding. The flat's not worth the rent I'm already paying."

"Maybe I can help."

Abi raised her hands. "Look, that's kind, but I won't let you pay for me."

"That's not what I meant. I'm rattling around in the cottage on my own getting bored. Why don't you move into the spare room? I'd get some company and you'd be much closer to work."

"Really? Do you mean it?"

"Of course."

Abi looked relieved. "Thank you! I think I might take you up on your offer."

"Great. There's just one thing though."

"What's that?"

Alex lifted up one of his crutches. "I won't be very good at helping you carry stuff."

She grinned. "Never mind that. Just make sure I have room for my shoes."

3

The south coast of Essex – shaped by the tidal might of the River Thames – was a curious and unlikely mix of industry and open space. The vast docks of Tilbury and the refineries of Canvey Island were isolated between salt marshes and wildlife reserves. Farther east Southend's ugly seafront – with its neon-tainted arcades and neglected Victorian architecture – marked the last large town on the north bank of the Thames estuary before the river spilled into the North Sea. It was a region of paradoxes where prosperity stood alongside decline and the natural landscape held fast against the encroachment of modernisation. From the high ground at the centuries old Hadleigh Castle – once sketched by John Constable – one could see flocks of wading birds in flight against a backdrop of refinery towers and cargo ships.

Sally Edwards had lived all of her seventy-three years in the area. She had worked at Ford's Dagenham plant and taken part in the sewing machinists' strike in 1968 which had led to equal pay legislation for men and women. In her retirement she enjoyed summer walks near Tilbury where Elizabeth I was said to have delivered her legendary *Speech to the Troops* in 1588, lamenting having 'the body of a weak, feeble woman' but proudly celebrating her 'heart and stomach of a king'. Sally didn't know much about history but she was proud to be from an area with famous associations.

Dawn on the river was beautiful during the summer and Sally always rose early for her walk. It gave her an hour or two of quiet before the commotion of the day began. Watching the birds feeding in the mudflats as the eastern sky filled with soft pink morning light, she almost forgot that she lived in the most crowded part of the county. The solitude of the marshes felt calming and invigorating. The river path, snaking around Coalhouse Fort, provided an easy stroll and a splendid view of the river. It followed the meander of the Thames, celebrating its form and protecting the fragile coastline.

The outgoing tide had exposed the flats, attracting flocks of waders. The river often washed up debris and Sally noticed a half-buried car tyre and a dented oil drum. Gulls were perched upon the fragmented hull of a small boat, long-abandoned and now nearly without a recognisable shape. She didn't mind seeing the man-made waste which the Thames rejected. It was only to be expected along a river with such a long industrial history. It was part of the landscape. But then something caught her eye which she didn't recognise. At first she wondered whether a dead seal or porpoise had been washed ashore. Several jackdaws and gulls were paying attention to the object, squabbling noisily over it. She continued her walk along the footpath, getting closer. She lifted her bird-spotting binoculars and moved the focussing ring with her finger.

She gasped with fright as the bloated grey face of a human corpse came into focus. The body was lying on its front twenty metres away in the mud, its head turned towards her. With her binoculars she could see that the eyes were missing. The corpse was clothed but the garments were in tatters, exposing parts of the decomposed body. It was too badly swollen and damaged to be recognisable as male or female. In places the skin looked like it had been slashed or had burst apart.

Sally began to feel queasy and thought she was about to vomit. Evidently her constitution was not as hardy as Elizabeth's. She lowered her binoculars and let them dangle around her neck by their strap. Fumbling in her coat pocket she grabbed her mobile, dialled 999 and held the phone to her ear. A beeping sound told her the call hadn't connected. She glanced at the screen and saw that she had no signal. She took one final glimpse at the corpse and then turned around. She hurried back towards Coalhouse Fort, holding the phone in front of her, staring at the screen for the first indication of a signal reception.

4

The police officers of the Thames Marine Unit had to improvise to recover the body from the mud. Getting the launch close enough meant having to wait for the tide to turn, but the delay required them to work quickly when the conditions were at their most favourable. It was too risky to simply hook the body and pull it up. It might disintegrate after its lengthy exposure in the water. The officers had to place boards on the slick mud – both for their own safety and for preparing the body for transport. They wrapped thick plastic sheets around the corpse and tied them in place. Only then did they attempt to lift the body into the boat. They looped ropes around the package and rolled it slowly up and over the side of the launch. When the task was complete and the officers were aboard they manoeuvred the craft back into the deeper water, heading upriver to a nearby jetty and the plain black undertaker's van that waited for them.

5

Jack Caldwell didn't bother looking up at the CCTV camera in Holborn Underground Station. Being seen was part of his daily ritual. As the section chief in one of the Central Intelligence Agency's London offices he had to expect MI5 to be interested in his whereabouts. *You watch us and we watch you.* It was part of the routine. Often he'd be tracked by a surveillance team for no other reason than practice. His field officers did the same thing. Following an operative from another agency was a good way to refine skills. Being followed was also useful. It meant less attention was being paid to the agents under his command. He was content to be a distraction, although occasionally he practised evasion techniques just for his own amusement. Part of the game was to keep everyone curious. *Make it look like you're up to something when you're not; follow a boring routine when you are.* The intelligence version of sleight of hand.

His London posting had represented a significant promotion and recognition of his talents, although it had also meant an end to working in the field. But, at forty-five years old, Caldwell had welcomed the change. He'd been a supremely competent operative – his Special Forces background adapting perfectly to intelligence work – but he also recognised that it was time to give younger men and women the chance to prove themselves. As a section chief he now had responsibility for many agents and also had to understand the strategic and political role the agency played in world affairs. It was a challenge he relished but he wasn't sure if it were the job or just his age that had caused his hair to turn grey. He was a handsome softly spoken man with a calm temperament and the respect of those who worked for him.

Caldwell used his Tube ticket – bought that morning with cash – to get through the barrier at Holborn. He made a decision to head directly towards his office building, crossed the street at the nearby traffic lights and headed southwest on Great Queen Street. He passed the grand Kingsway Hall hotel and the grey imposing architecture of Freemasons Hall. Here the street was a mix of cafés, pubs and office buildings. Had he wished to distract any observers he might have continued towards Covent Garden and wasted twenty minutes pretending to be interested in the shops and stalls there, but today he didn't have time to play with MI5.

He entered a modern office block on Long Acre, waved at the girl on the reception desk and started up the stairs. Most of the people who worked here had no idea that the building was owned by the CIA. The cover story of its acquisition – by a wealthy American entrepreneur – was easily sold to the numerous local businesses who rented office space. But the top floor – protected by sophisticated security systems – was very different from the rest of the building. Small teams of experts sat at computers watching CCTV feeds or studying intelligence data.

Caldwell reached the top floor, held an access card against the reader and heard a clunk as the lock opened. He nodded at colleagues as he entered the room, keeping the greeting brief to avoid distracting them from their work. He went to his office, removed his jacket and hung it on a hook near the door. The office was glass-fronted, allowing him to observe his staff at work, although he preferred to talk with his operatives directly. Later on he would spend some time chatting to them. It was useful to know small details but Caldwell didn't view it as an intelligence gathering exercise; he simply liked to make people feel supported. Many of his team were a long way from their families back in the States. It didn't hurt to show some empathy.

Logging in to his computer he saw that several new e-mails had arrived – a mix of reports he had requested and invitations to meetings at the American Embassy. He concluded that there was nothing he needed to read before his morning briefing with his department heads. A knock on the door made him look up. His next-in-command, Clare Quinn, was outside. Caldwell invited her in.

"Morning, Jack, I have something that may interest you." The beautiful Texan always came straight to the point. She was a couple of years younger than Caldwell but looked closer to thirty. Her long black hair was tied in a ponytail, the style emphasising her elegant face and dark eyes. She wore a knee-length plain blue skirt and a matching jacket. Her perfume was sophisticated but subtle.

"Hi, Clare. What do you have?"

She waved a handful of papers. "You're going to like this. Remember Suffolk – three and a half years ago?"

It took Caldwell barely a second to recall the information. "Station Helix?"

"That's the one. The genetics research lab which the UK

Government managed to keep hidden for decades. Do you remember how we got hold of the information?"

He nodded. "An ex-soldier working security on the site. He saw an opportunity to make some money by talking to us."

"That's right. We didn't get much for our twenty thousand pounds, but it was more than we knew before. Site plans, security protocols... that was about it."

"He didn't know anything about the research there, but considering we weren't aware the site existed, we thought it was a good deal. What was the guy's name?"

"Andrew Philip Mason. Former squaddie and self-made security specialist in Iraq after the war."

"I remember his profile. Highly self-oriented and a thrill seeker."

"We can add something else to that profile. It seems this guy holds a grudge."

Caldwell leaned forward, his curiosity awakened. "Go on."

"You know how we monitor the UK's police and military databases? Mason's name came up on a DNA check. It took us a while to figure out why but we got there. We think he killed two of the scientists who worked at Station Helix – William and Sarah Hannay."

Caldwell frowned. "Those names are familiar."

"They should be. William Hannay was the one who realised Mason had leaked information and reported him. The Government terminated Mason's contract immediately."

"So the son of a bitch spent all this time plotting his revenge."

"He did a good job too – *nearly*." Quinn placed the papers on Caldwell's desk. "It's all in there, but the synopsis is he stole a truck and drove it into the Hannays' car as they were coming home from their son's fencing competition. Made it look like an accident. Suffolk Police arrested someone on scene."

"How do we know Mason was involved?"

"Oh you're going to love *this*. A suspended Essex detective found blood on the truck and submitted it for analysis. That's how our boys worked out what had happened."

"Why was a suspended cop sniffing around the crash?"

"He's married to one of the paramedics who attended the scene. He must've figured something was wrong. The whole thing got shut down really fast – presumably because the MOD didn't want questions asked about two dead Station Helix scientists."

Caldwell's frown deepened as he considered Clare's information. "Mason wanted to make it look like an accident and fitted up someone to take the blame for the crash?"

"Yes – the Polish truck driver."

"Oh, this *is* good," Caldwell said. "The blood sample wasn't submitted as part of the investigation because a suspect was already in custody. You see what this means, Clare? In their hurry to keep things quiet the Brits haven't realised this *wasn't* an accident."

She nodded in agreement. "If Mason hadn't cut himself the detective wouldn't have found anything."

Caldwell leaned back in his chair. "What do we know about the detective?"

"Lucas Ingwe, born in Namibia, emigrated to the UK. He's a good investigator but he's not one for following procedure. That's why he's on suspension. There's a good chance he's going to lose his job."

"So right now he's not sure what to do with the information he's unearthed. He's probably stretched his resources getting this far. It's unlikely he knows the Hannays' background, so he doesn't understand the context of the DNA result. He can't take what he has to anyone because the investigation is closed, and he can't be seen to be breaching protocol."

Clare grinned. "He's an island."

"I want you to keep an eye on him, but he's not the priority."

"Mason?"

"Mason," Caldwell repeated. "Can we find him?"

"It shouldn't be too hard. He's using his bank cards. We think he's in London."

"I want him brought in. We might be able to use him again now that we have this."

"I'll see to it."

"Let me know when you have him. I'll interview him myself. At the moment he thinks he's invulnerable. I'll look forward to shattering that illusion."

6

The Scottish hunting lodge wasn't the only home Edward Rhodes owned but it was the grandest. It was an imposing gothic construction; its walls and towers built from grey stone designed to resist even the fiercest winter weather that this remote part of the country could experience. The manor house stood on high ground overlooking the largest of the three rivers which flowed through the estate of several thousand acres. Isolated fragments of the ancient Caledonian Forest survived here alongside relatively new pine plantations; home to bird species such as the capercaillie and the goldcrest. Red deer roamed the hills in vast numbers and were farmed for venison. Salmon were plentiful in the rivers. Lilac heather spread across the estate's moorland, its heady scent filling the summer air. It was the remoteness of the place which appealed to Rhodes' desire to minimise contact with his fellow human beings.

The great-grandnephew of Cecil Rhodes – the politician and founder of the De Beers diamond company – Edward Rhodes had inherited both considerable wealth and the aim to be politically influential from his ancestor. He resembled him too, from his round face and hefty waistline to his wavy and slightly unkempt hair. The security he kept at his residences was comparable to his ancestor's guardianship of his African diamond mines, but in this case it was more because of paranoia than actual risk. The owner of many international corporations, Rhodes was content to exert his influence indirectly, using his businesses to control global economies. He had no desire to be a public figure – he paid numerous chief executives to take on that responsibility – preferring to remain far from the limelight.

He poured himself another glass of vintage Scottish whisky from an expensive crystal decanter. He always drank too much, but the news his companions had brought him had increased his nervousness.

The other three men in the large study were different from him in personality and demeanour. They were all of similar age – middle to late seventies – having met as young students at Oxford over five decades ago. The others didn't have Rhodes' fortune but were still extremely wealthy men.

Archimedes Falkner was an intellectual with a passion for history. Recruited from university into British Intelligence he had risen swiftly through MI6's hierarchy and supervised operations throughout the Cold War. He'd rejected the opportunity to become director, knowing it was wiser to remain discreetly in the inner circle a rung or two below the top. The decision preserved his anonymity and kept him free from public scrutiny. He was slim with a bald crown and piercing eyes, an avowed tee-totaller and a dispassionate man with little empathy for others. Many people found his unshakeable self-confidence unnerving.

Benjamin Barnard was a kindlier man than Falkner with round glasses and pure white hair. He was softly spoken and courteous. He dressed impeccably – even for the most mundane of occasions – a habit which had developed when working as an adviser to several minor royals. Like the others Barnard was intensely patriotic and had considered it a duty to protect those under his care for the benefit of the nation. His role had given him a rare insight into both the private and public lives of his employers. He was a preserver of traditions and understood royal diplomacy intimately. His influence – which continued even in his retirement – was subtle and well-measured. Barnard had the ability to suggest an idea and then nurture it in others' minds because his opinion was respected. The aristocracy trusted him because he was a man who could not only deflect unpleasant scandals but also enhance their public standing.

The fourth member of the group was a businessman with interests in fossil fuels and shipping. Arnold Rossington was a short, round-shouldered man with a neatly trimmed beard and only slightly thinning hair. He'd survived lung cancer eight years ago but it had left him a weakened man. For all his dignified bearing the toll of the disease was visible in his hollow cheeks and tired eyes. As a young man he'd rowed for Oxford but he didn't dwell on past glories. He'd made good judgements when investing some of his family's money as a young entrepreneur; the returns far exceeding anything achieved by earlier generations of Rossingtons. He'd sought business opportunities which challenged him but it was the power rather than the money which provided his motivation. Global business shaped political policy, despite politicians' claims they could regulate markets and bring the private sector to heel. It was rhetoric that Rossington knew he could ignore.

Over five decades of manipulation and influence had

made the four friends some of the most powerful men in Great Britain. Investment in significant figures on both sides of the political arena meant they had allies regardless of which party was in power, but they didn't always rely on ministers to accede to their wishes. Convinced of their purpose to keep Britain at the forefront of world affairs they would do whatever they considered necessary to fulfil their ambitions. They knew that money really could buy anything and anyone.

Rhodes glanced anxiously at his companions. "Are you sure it was Cline's body?"

Rossington nodded.

Rhodes didn't look convinced. "But you said the body was mutilated and unrecognisable."

"The effects of being adrift in the river for three weeks," Falkner interjected. "Boat propellers and wildlife. The damage was post mortem. Cline was dead as soon as he hit the water."

"We don't need to concern ourselves with trivial details," said Rossington. "We have to decide what Cline's death tells us and what we're going to do about it."

Barnard rose from his leather chair and walked to the window. He concentrated on the view of the nearby river valley as he spoke. "It's a damn shame he chose such a public place for killing himself. There are at least eight videos on the Internet of him jumping. We've told the press he'd been suffering arthritic pain but, because of who he was, the conspiracy theorists aren't letting go yet."

"The suicide of a high profile Government scientist is always going to draw attention," Falkner said in his matter-of-fact tone. "It happened in 2003 with David Kelly after the weapons of mass destruction debacle. Plenty of people still think he was murdered. Even though Cline's death was public, people are questioning what drove him to it. They think we're covering something up."

"In this case we are," said Rhodes.

"I'm happy to let the world think Cline killed himself due to a crisis of conscience," said Barnard. "He was a designer of military equipment. We can invent evidence to say he was unable to live with himself for building weapons."

Rhodes nodded. "It sounds plausible."

"Let's keep that as a contingency for now," suggested Falkner. "The problem with cover stories is that people doubt them. I'd rather not give *anything* to the conspiracy theorists. Eventually they'll just give up if we tell them nothing."

"The matter we should prioritise is what Cline's death means for the EHB programme," said Rossington. "We might have to deal with the others."

"Can we definitely attribute his pain to the experiment?" questioned Rhodes.

Barnard turned back from the window and looked at his companions. "They need to do more tests, but preliminary results have found evidence of some genetic degradation."

"So the experiment was a failure – at least in Cline's case."

Rossington raised his hands in a gesture of uncertainty. "We can't confirm that. There could be other causes such as exposure to certain toxins or radiation. But we don't have any record of that happening to Cline." He paused for a moment before continuing. "That's why we conduct long-term experiments."

"A problem, but not an insurmountable one," stated Falkner firmly. "The early research at Station Helix was looking into an entirely new concept. The study goes on and techniques are refined. We now know there was a problem with the initial trial. Perhaps Cline's body will assist with future developments."

"Yes, but that still leaves us with some outstanding issues," stated Barnard. "Cline wasn't the only one."

Rhodes frowned, his expression grave. "Is there any evidence to suggest the others will be affected the same way?"

"That depends entirely on what you deduce from Cline's death," Rossington said. "The logical conclusion is that the first experiment was inherently flawed."

"But you don't *know* that, Arnold! What if Cline had a hereditary condition?"

"Impossible. His provenance was checked thoroughly."

Rhodes gulped his whisky and thumped the empty glass heavily on the table beside his chair. "We're on dangerous ground if we start making unscientific assumptions."

"Eddie, we're not assuming anything," said Falkner. His voice didn't sound reassuring. "We'll look closely at what the scientists tell us when they have more information. But the danger lies in other people finding out. The EHBs are in high profile positions. We *engineered* it thus. If what happened to Cline starts happening elsewhere, we may not be able to control the fallout."

"What are you saying, Archie?" asked Rhodes nervously.

Falkner took a sip from his glass before speaking.

"Gentlemen, we may have to consider terminating the experiment."

7

After Abi moved into Alex's cottage she found herself taking up a new pastime. She hadn't played draughts for years, but Alex had enjoyed the game with his father and wanted to play again. He thought his dad would be pleased. Father and son had spent hours concentrating over the board – usually set up on the kitchen table after dinner – and had been evenly matched. Alex saw a similarity between draughts and fencing – both used a small number of moves and required strategic thinking. Abi didn't look into the game that deeply. She usually lost to Alex but she didn't mind. She'd soon realised that her chances of victory were greater when she encouraged him to talk because it broke his concentration. The ploy rarely worked but it compensated a little for her lack of practice.

Studying the pieces she saw that he'd just left himself vulnerable with his last move. "Hannay messes up!" Gleefully she took two counters from the board.

Alex grinned. "Yeah, I think you've won this one. Best of three?"

"Sorry, I have to start work soon."

"That's convenient."

She laughed. "I'm sure you'll get your own back soon."

"I wasn't really concentrating that hard."

"Bad loser."

Alex smiled. "No, I'm being serious. Actually I was

thinking about my crutches."

"Whatever."

He grinned. "No, seriously! I don't need them any more." To prove the point he stood up and walked to the kitchen door. There was no sign of a limp or discomfort. Abi stared at him in disbelief. "See what I mean? I realised I've been using them through habit rather than necessity. My leg feels fine."

"That's amazing," said Abi. "You're not dosed up on painkillers are you?"

"No. I guess I'm just healing really well."

"And much faster than the doctors thought. You're not in some hypnotic state where you can't feel pain?"

Alex laughed. "No, there's no pain. I'm just glad to be back on my feet. I'm going to go for a walk around the village tomorrow to see how I feel."

Abi stacked the draughts counters in their box and folded the board. "You can update me on the number of times you fall over. I'm really pleased for you. Looks like you won't have to go through all that physiotherapy."

"You know what this means? I might not have to give up fencing."

Abi sighed and gave Alex a sympathetic half-smile. "I really hope so, but one thing at a time."

"I know. It's just a reason to be optimistic."

"True. Look, I…" Abi's sentence was interrupted by a knock at the front door. "I'll get it." She left the kitchen and walked along the hallway. Opening the door she saw a middle-aged black man.

"Oh… hi," Lucas Ingwe said. "I was hoping to speak to Mr Alex Hannay."

"I'm Alex's housemate," stated Abi. "May I ask what it's about?"

"Of course. I'd like to talk to him about the accident he was involved in."

Abi frowned, reluctant to talk further. "That's a private matter."

"I understand, but this is important. I'm a police officer and my wife was the paramedic who treated him at the scene. My name is Lucas Ingwe."

Alex joined her at the door. "It's okay." He looked at Ingwe. "I never got the chance to say thank you to her. Please come in."

Lucas nodded in gratitude and followed Alex into the sitting room. Abi held back, leaning against the door frame, frowning. "Alex, I really have to go to work. Are you sure you're okay?"

"I'm fine... stop worrying."

"Okay, I'll see you later."

"Will do. Have a good evening."

She picked up her keys from the small table in the hallway and left the cottage. The door banged shut.

In the sitting room Alex looked at his guest inquisitively. "I have to say I'm surprised to see a police officer. No one from the police ever spoke to me about the accident."

"I'm aware of that, Mr Hannay," Lucas replied. "And *that* is one of the reasons I wanted to talk to you. There's something I have to tell you though. I'm not here in an official capacity. I'll understand if you ask me to leave, but I implore you to hear me out. Strictly speaking I don't work for the police at the moment."

Alex looked uncomfortable. "You said you were a police officer."

"I am, but I've been suspended pending an investigation into one of my cases." He bent forward in his chair. "I know this sounds irregular, Mr Hannay, but I'm taking a huge gamble coming here to see you. I'll probably lose my job over this but it is imperative that I speak to you."

"What's so important?"

Lucas paused, inhaling deeply. "I'm not sure how to say this without distressing you, so I'll get to the point. I don't think the crash was an accident."

8

Alex stared. The policeman held eye contact, silently expressing his sincerity. His words disoriented Alex. During the short time since the crash he'd started to come to terms with what had happened. He'd allowed himself to adjust to his parents' deaths, acknowledging his grief but also finding the motivation and purpose to continue living his own life. He'd found a sense of equilibrium that was suddenly in danger of collapsing due to the unexpected message of a stranger. He didn't know how to react. He wondered if the man was a prankster trying to provoke a response with a tasteless joke. Eventually he spoke. "Are you a reporter?"

Lucas shook his head. "I assure you I'm not. I understand this must be disturbing for you." He paused for a moment, recollecting something Fran had told him. "Francesca – my wife – said there was a trophy in the car beside you. She asked you what it was for but you weren't able to remember."

Alex inhaled, relaxing a little. "I remember her voice. She did say something about my trophy but I couldn't understand her question. I was barely conscious. I don't remember much about the crash or what happened afterwards. I didn't wake up until several days later in the hospital." He paused. "I'd just won the national title at foil. I'm very grateful to Francesca for all she did. Please say thanks from me."

"I'm sure she'd appreciate that."

"Mr Ingwe, I'm confused by what you said. They told me in the hospital that a man had been arrested for driving while drunk. Are you telling me that didn't happen?"

"No, it did happen. The traffic police arrested the Polish lorry driver and he was intoxicated. I just don't believe he was driving. And please call me Lucas."

"Okay… and I prefer to be called Alex. I'm still not clear on what you're saying. Perhaps you'd better tell me what you know."

Lucas nodded. "I only knew about the crash because Fran wanted to talk about it. We tend not to discuss our work in detail but sometimes we encounter things that aren't particularly easy to come to terms with. We're pretty good at – for want of a better word – debriefing each other. Fran was understandably upset by the crash. She knew your parents had died and she wasn't sure you'd make it. She told me she'd passed by the crash site later on and it had already been cleared. That's what made me wonder what was going on. Fatals…" he paused, realising the emergency services jargon was somewhat cold. "Sorry. I meant…"

"It's okay," Alex said. "So are you saying it's unusual for that to happen?"

"Not even unusual – it *doesn't* happen. A road death examiner will always go to the scene. Photographs and measurements must be taken. Sometimes the police helicopter will do that from an aerial perspective to make things a little quicker, but the weather was too bad for it to go up that night. *None* of that happened in your case."

"Surely if they found a drunk driver at the scene that

was all the evidence they needed?"

"It would be fairly conclusive, but it wouldn't stop the processes from being followed." Lucas groaned silently to himself, remembering that his suspension was due to his lack of procedural integrity. "I decided to call in some favours. I found out that a senior officer gave the order for the incident to be closed. They weren't even allowed to speak to you as a witness or allocate you a family liaison officer."

"I did think it strange that no one from the police talked to me. The hospital staff told me an officer came to the hospital soon after the crash but he got called away suddenly. They knew from him that someone was under arrest. But *you* think they've got the wrong person."

"Alex, I'm speculating with much of this. I can't look into this as much as I would like. Even if I could, I'm an Essex officer and this is a Suffolk matter. But there are too many things that seem wrong. The lorry driver claimed he was abducted and I found someone else's blood on the lorry's door. I asked a crime scene investigator to check the sample. We got a match on an ex-soldier called Andrew Mason. I have no idea who he is, but I doubt he has anything to do with the Polish haulage company."

"Do you believe the Pole?"

"Honestly I don't know. I never had the chance to speak to him. He's been remanded in custody. As far as I know he's never been interviewed formally."

"What'll happen to him?"

"He'll have to go to court soon. I've asked a contact to try to find out when the trial is scheduled. I'll let you know as soon as I can."

"You said the police closed the investigation."

"Yes."

"How can they prosecute the lorry driver then?"

"Technically the police don't prosecute defendants. The Crown Prosecution Service does that. We just gather the evidence on their behalf. It doesn't have to be the CPS though. If my suspicions are correct, it'll be taken out of their hands."

"By whom?"

"The Government."

Alex frowned. "You realise this is starting to sound like a conspiracy theory?"

"Trust me, I've been trying to convince myself that I'm getting this all completely wrong," Lucas replied.

"What do *you* think happened that night?"

"You understand that I can't give you anything conclusive?"

Alex nodded. "I accept that. I don't think you're lying to me, Lucas. You've obviously come here for a reason. You told me you didn't think the crash was an accident. I want to know exactly what you mean by that."

"I think someone killed your parents deliberately."

Alex's jaw tightened. "The ex-soldier?"

"At the very least I'm sure he was involved. There was another car – on false plates – that was in all the wrong places. I think it was a co-ordinated attack."

Alex realised he was trembling. A sickly sensation tasted bitter in his throat. "Wouldn't the police have looked into Mason?"

"Why? They didn't know about him. I identified him from the blood sample *after* the investigation was locked down. As far as my colleagues are concerned there was nothing sinister about the crash. They arrested someone who seemed entirely responsible."

"The closure of the inquiry must be unusual."

"If a chief constable gets a phone call from the Home Office in the early hours he does what he's told. The Government only has to say the words 'national security' and people get nervous."

"How would this be a matter of national security? What's so special about Mason that the Government has to intervene in a police investigation?"

Lucas leaned forward. "Alex, I don't think the Government knew about him either. It wasn't Mason who prompted this response."

"So who did?" Alex realised he already knew the answer to his question.

Lucas held his gaze. "It must have been your parents."

9

The room fell silent again. Alex found himself questioning what was more shocking to him: Ingwe's theory that his parents had been murdered or the notion that they were involved in something so secret that they could never discuss it with him. If Lucas was right, how deep had the pretence gone? What did the words 'national security' actually mean? He tried not to guess but his thoughts became occupied with illogical unprovable theories. Had his parents been at risk or had they *posed* a risk? Alex realised that, by having this conversation with Lucas, he'd taken himself to a place from which he could never claw his way back. He could ask the detective to leave right now – ending this insane discussion before it progressed any farther – but the doubt was now firmly implanted. He felt like his parents had suddenly become strangers to him. It felt like they had died again. He needed to interrogate them, to demand to be told what they had kept hidden. For the first time in his life he felt hostility towards them, and then he became angry with himself for making a judgement without any facts. His emotion shifted to embarrassment. His parents had told him to be objective and now he was dishonouring their memory by rushing to conclusions without evidence. The turmoil in his thoughts took him back to the chaos of the crash.

"Alex?"

"Sorry – I was miles away. This is…" the sentence trailed away but the sentiment was clear.

"I know," Lucas replied. "That's why I have to emphasise that I don't know any more than I've told you. We can't make suppositions yet."

"I accept that but, even if just a fragment of what you've told me is true, what I thought I knew has been turned upside down."

Lucas spoke quietly. "Tell me about your parents."

"What do you want to know? Were they *terrorists*? I don't even know what to think any more."

Lucas gave a half-smile. "I doubt they were terrorists. MI5 would have spoken to you by now if that was true. Let's stay focussed on the facts. What work did they do?"

Alex forced himself to be calm. "They were scientists. They specialised in genetics."

"Genetics? That's still a controversial field. Were they ever threatened?"

"They never told me if they were. Sure, they encountered a few dogmatic religious types who didn't approve of scientists 'playing God', but most people are generally much more objective. Cancer, multiple sclerosis, infertility and thousands more conditions can potentially benefit from gene research. People are broadly supportive of medical advances. My parents were fascinated by the fact that we can study the building blocks of life."

"They were obviously dedicated to their work. Where were they based?"

"At East Anglia University. I think they worked in Ipswich mostly."

"You never went to their workplace?"

"I did a few years ago when I was deciding which subjects to study. My parents wanted me to become a scientist so they took me to a few laboratories. It was good but I was more interested in photography."

"Did they ever discuss any projects they were working on?"

"Not really. We discussed science in general terms but I don't know about any specific research they did." Alex paused. He understood what Ingwe was trying to figure out. "Do you think they were doing some sort of specialised work?"

Lucas shrugged. "Without evidence…"

"But it makes sense though, doesn't it? A lot of scientific work has to be kept secret. Could my parents have been working on a Government project?"

"I suppose it's feasible," agreed Lucas. "The Government oversees work in many fields of science and technology."

"So let's assume – for a moment – that my parents were doing some research for the Government. How does that link to the accident?"

"I don't think we have enough information to join those dots yet."

"You must be used to making hypotheses as a detective."

Lucas grinned. "It's in the investigators' manual."

"So what's your theory?"

"I don't have one."

"Best guess then."

Ingwe hesitated. It was understandable that Alex wanted an explanation. It was a basic element of human nature, and he'd seen it many times in victims of crime. Sometimes, he had to explain, there was no motive. In the Hannays' case, however, he was deeply suspicious. "I'm not sure what I can do next. Remember, I'm on suspension. I'll try to find out when Gorski – the lorry driver – is due in court, but I'm running out of favours I can call in. I'd really like to know more about your parents' work, but I've a feeling I'll be warned off if I start asking questions."

"I'll do it," Alex said quickly. "No one will question why I want to find out more. They'll interpret it as me trying to find closure."

"You realise that's exactly what you *would* be looking for?"

Alex nodded. "I have to."

"Where are you going to start?"

"There was a man at the funeral. He spoke to me briefly but I can't remember his name. My uncle will know who he is. He worked with my parents. Maybe he can tell me something."

"Alex?"

"Yes?"

"Allow me to give you a friendly warning based on my years as a detective."

"Please do."

"Don't expect to find all the answers. People guard their secrets."

10

It was late when Abi returned from the pub and she was surprised to see Alex still up. "Hi," she called out as she put her keys on the hallway table.

"Hi, how was work?"

"Fairly quiet, thanks. What did that policeman want?" Abi joined Alex in the front room. She bounced onto the sofa, swung her legs over the end and laid down.

"He has a theory about the accident," Alex replied. "It's... far-fetched."

"What did he say?"

"He thinks Mum and Dad may have been killed deliberately."

Abi pushed herself up from the sofa and stared intently. "Jesus, Alex! Where the hell did that come from? You're not kidding about it being far-fetched."

"I know, but he told me some things..."

"Are you sure this guy is a real police officer?" Abi interrupted.

"He is but he's been suspended."

Abi's consternation was immediately apparent. She swore again. "I hope you're not taking this seriously."

"What else am I supposed to do? He said he found a blood sample on the lorry that didn't make any sense. It belonged to a former soldier called Andrew Mason. The guy who was arrested claimed he'd been kidnapped. Lucas

– the detective – also said the crash site should never have been cleared as quickly as it was because there wasn't enough time to investigate it properly."

Abi hesitated. "Look, I'm sorry for snapping at you. This just sounds really vague. I thought you said the lorry driver was drunk and was arrested at the scene."

"He was, but there are several things that seem wrong. I should have been allocated a family liaison officer by the police but that never happened. I was never asked about the crash. No one from the police even told me the lorry driver was arrested. The police were actually ordered to close the investigation."

Abi held eye contact with him. "Do you really believe your parents were murdered?"

He hesitated. "I don't know. Lucas can't say for certain either, but he's discovered enough details to make me wonder if something's been covered up."

"Why would anyone want to hurt your parents?"

"They might have been working for the Government. We don't know how that links to the crash though."

Abi bent forwards. "*If* there is any truth in this, what could you do about it?"

"Abi, I understand that my parents may have died in a tragic accident. That may be the truth. But if it isn't, I want to know."

"So what else did the policeman say?"

"He's going to find out when the driver is going to court. Details of the case haven't been published but Lucas thinks he might be able to find out from one of his contacts. We need to speak to that driver."

"So he can tell you he wasn't drunk?"

"No, so we can hear what he has to say about being abducted."

"It sounds ludicrous."

"I know."

Abi frowned, concerned. "But you're not going to let it go, are you?"

Alex shook his head. "I can't."

She stood up and walked over to him. She put her arms around him and gave him a hug. "Just be careful, okay? I don't want you to become a conspiracy theorist."

"I promise. Hey, do you remember that grey-haired man at the funeral? The one who gave a speech?"

"Yes. He worked with your parents."

"I can't remember his name. I want to speak to him."

"Michael something… Michael Hearn, I think."

"You have a good memory."

Abi shrugged. "I remember your uncle talking about him. What do you want to speak to him about?"

"I'd like to know more about my parents' research and whether they were working for the Government."

"That kind of stuff is usually highly confidential."

"I have to start somewhere."

FOUR

1

Standing on the steps of London's Saatchi Gallery, Andrew Mason silently congratulated himself. The meeting with the representative of a wealthy Pakistani businessman had, as far as he could tell, been successful. It wasn't unusual for an assistant to conduct negotiations on his employer's behalf. He'd encountered this arrangement many times before and knew he wouldn't meet his future paymaster until the assistant had evaluated him thoroughly. They had spent half an hour inside the gallery, pretending to study the modern art exhibits as the Pakistani quizzed him about his background. It was certain that the man already knew the answer to every question. They had also spoken about money and Mason hadn't been shy in asking for a considerable sum. In the field of close protection trying to undercut the opposition usually created the impression of being an amateur. The man had told him to expect a call that evening. For now he'd just have to wait.

He headed for Sloane Square, intending to catch the Tube to Blackfriars. He'd checked in at the Crowne Plaza Hotel yesterday and was staying there for one more night. What he chose to do after that depended on the outcome of this morning's meeting. As he turned right onto King's Road he noticed an attractive blonde woman hurrying past him. From the numerous branded shopping bags she had looped over both arms Mason assumed she's been spending a fortune on designer clothes in the famous street's boutiques. Mason followed her, admiring her long legs and short summer dress. He guessed that she was in her early twenties, probably one of the Chelsea rich and that she'd never done a day's work in her life. *With a body like that, you'll never have to*, Mason thought.

Suddenly the woman tripped in her heels and shrieked with pain. She fell and sprawled clumsily on the pavement. Still attached to the now crushed shopping bags she tried to push herself into a sitting position as Mason hurried up to her. "Are you okay?" he asked. "That looked nasty." Now close to her he couldn't help glancing at her cleavage. The woman didn't seem to notice.

"I think I broke my ankle," she wailed, her face red.

Mason helped her sit up. "You've probably just twisted it. Do you want me to have a look? I've had some medical training."

"Okay," she agreed. "Just be careful."

"I will. Just sit still for a moment." Mason shifted himself towards her legs. "You seemed to be in a hurry."

"I was. I'd lost track of time. I'm late for coffee with my friend Samantha. Too distracted by nice dresses, I'm afraid."

He looked at the woman's left ankle. He couldn't see any indication of swelling. "I think you've been lucky. It doesn't look damaged. You probably just caught a nerve when your foot twisted."

"It still hurts," the woman complained. "Would you help me up?"

"Sure. Put your arm around my shoulders. Don't put any weight on your left leg; just use your right to push up." He put his arm around her slender waist, trying and failing to ignore how attractive he found her. She clung to him with her left arm almost as eagerly as she held onto her shopping bags. Mason stood up slowly and lifted her.

Suddenly her hand moved and he felt a sting as she plunged a hypodermic needle into his neck. "Don't fight it," she said with cold authority.

Mason's vision began to blur almost instantaneously. He became unsteady on his feet, about to pass out. The shape of a silver van pulled up alongside him. Two men got out and grabbed him just before his legs gave way. The woman pulled a handle to open a sliding side door. The men shoved him inside.

Rapidly losing consciousness, Mason uttered a single word. "Bitch."

2

He woke to find himself handcuffed to a steel chair in a twelve feet by twenty feet room. The chair was bolted to the floor in the centre of the otherwise empty space. Grey concrete walls surrounded him; featureless except for a dark glass panel opposite him and a steel door to his right. Mason deduced the glass was a one-way mirror. The illumination was poor from several strip lights high above his head. He could hear their faint electrical buzz. One flickered intermittently making him blink.

His neck hurt but not from the serum the woman had injected. His head had been slumped forward for an ungaugeable length of time, his chin against his chest. He was still clothed apart from his shoes and socks. His trousers were damp. He guessed the drug had caused him to urinate. The coldness of the concrete floor chilled the soles of his bare feet. He turned his head, studying his surroundings. It was clear the room had been designed solely for interrogation. Its sparseness was the secret of its sophistication; the absence of features causing his brain to imagine details where there were none. The placement of the chair in the centre of the room exaggerated his vulnerability and isolation.

Mason closed his eyes. They would make him wait – two hours, maybe three. Trapped in here the passage of time was impossible to judge, but in the army he'd received training to cope with captivity and interrogation. He turned his thoughts to identifying his captors. He was certain the woman had been English, but that didn't necessarily apply to her employer. Perhaps the Pakistani businessman had decided upon a more intense recruitment process. He was confident he could stand his ground and show his mettle. The contract would easily compensate for a little discomfort. He inhaled deeply.

And waited.

3

Jack Caldwell closed the steel door quietly as he entered the interrogation room. The dramatic effect of slamming it shut wasn't needed yet. He intended to build up the pressure gradually. As he'd predicted, Mason ignored him. The ex-soldier kept his eyes closed and his head upright. The posture represented defiance. He disregarded it. Mason had no idea what he was up against. Not yet. "It wasn't hard to find you, Andy," said Caldwell. He positioned himself near to the wall and directly in front of Mason.

Mason made a decision to reply. "I wasn't hiding."

"That's fortunate for both of us."

Mason made a decision not to reply.

Caldwell walked to the door and exited as it was opened for him.

Mason kept his eyes closed. *Shit. They're going to keep me here until I break.*

4

Caldwell re-entered the room precisely ten minutes after Mason fell asleep. "Come on, Andy," he said. "We can't have you drifting off like that, can we? You need to be alert."

Mason couldn't stifle a groan but he didn't speak.

Caldwell spoke again. "You had a meeting at the Saatchi Gallery. What was the purpose of that meeting?"

Mason stared at the wall. "I don't know what you're talking about."

"I think you're lying."

Mason noticed a crack in the concrete and used it as his point of focus. "I don't care what you think," he replied, his tone measured.

"You're still lying. You know what I think matters significantly."

"You want me to stroke that ego of yours?"

"I want you to consider your situation very carefully."

Mason held Caldwell's gaze. "Perhaps you should tell me what my situation is."

Caldwell shrugged. "Very well. I want information that you have. You can give it to me with good grace and I'll let you go."

"You expect me to believe that?"

"I don't want you to feel paranoid about me lying to you." Caldwell took a few steps and turned his back to

Mason. "What was the purpose of your meeting?" he asked again.

Mason didn't reply. Caldwell counted sixty seconds. He didn't expect the basic interview technique of providing a silence for the detainee to fill would work on Mason, but *knowing* it wouldn't work helped him build a profile of the man. "You met Yasin Gandapur three days ago. What was the purpose of your meeting?"

Three days? Have I really been here that long or is this guy fucking with my head? Mason felt his body tense. He knew his stress reaction would be observed by the people hidden behind the glass. It didn't matter that his questioner wasn't watching him. Soon they would debrief this stage of the interrogation and devise a strategy for the next part. "I don't know who Yasin Gandapur is."

"That didn't stop you from having a lengthy conversation with him in the Saatchi Gallery. Tell me what you spoke about."

"I have nothing to say."

"Then I'll talk for a while." Caldwell turned around and slowly walked a circuit of the room, stopping behind Mason. He bent forward but not far enough to be injured if Mason decided to throw his head back. "Yasin Gandapur is the cousin of Daoud Gandapur, a very wealthy man from Islamabad. Do you know who I'm talking about?"

"No."

"That's a pity."

"You'll get over it."

"I'm not sure I will. You see, I'm particularly interested in Daoud's business network," Caldwell lied.

5

"I don't know anything about a Pakistani businessman's network," Mason conceded. The statement was true; Daoud Gandapur's enterprises were of no interest or concern to him. Security work was about keeping the client protected, not being intimate with his affairs. He decided that his best tactic was to give only non-committal answers which were essentially true. That way, he surmised, he could co-operate a little but without revealing anything to jeopardise his professional connections.

"You must be hungry by now," Caldwell said, deliberately drawing attention to Mason's discomfort. It was a simple trick. Mason would have blocked any thoughts about food. The former soldier tried unsuccessfully to ignore the remark. "Probably rather dehydrated too," Caldwell added. "I can arrange for you to get fed and cleaned up. There's no need for you to remain so uncomfortable."

"I'll cope," responded Mason. He swore to himself again. *The bastard's just provoked me into challenging him. Whoever this guy is, he's causing me to make mistakes. He hasn't even raised his voice yet. Think before you open your mouth again. Focus before he exploits a weakness. You've been trained for this.*

Caldwell decided to push a little harder. He changed the tone of his voice to a steely chill. "I don't want to prolong this."

The sentence was so evidently without genuine sentiment that Mason couldn't stop himself from mentally adding *but I will if I have to*.

Caldwell left the room.

The strip lights blinked out and the room plunged into total darkness.

6

It was the closure of the cell door as Caldwell returned that woke Mason. The lights were already switched on but their weak illumination hadn't been enough to drag him from his sleep. He couldn't tell how long he'd been allowed to rest, but the headache – worsened by the lack of food and water – told him he'd probably slept for no more than an hour or two. His captor now wore a different suit and shirt to confuse his attempts at calculating the passage of time. In the corner of the room to his left there now stood a low table. On it was a small pile of neatly folded clothes and a half-litre bottle of water.

"Your reluctance to talk is intriguing," said Caldwell. He took three steps towards the table. He took hold of the bottle, pretended to look at the label and set it back down. "Perhaps you think you're protecting your business opportunities. The work you had lined up with the Gandapurs won't be happening now. You missed your phone call. We answered it on your behalf and said you were indisposed." Caldwell walked slowly around the room. Standing behind Mason he spoke again. "Loyalty isn't a quality we associate with you, Mason."

Mason recognised the change of strategy and it unsettled him. The topic had shifted from the Pakistanis to *him*. The interrogator had also used the pronoun *we* for the first time. It stressed the imbalance of power. He remained silent but flinched as the man gripped his shoulder. He cursed silently. Allowing himself to be startled revealed his discomfort. The man's grip was strong but he held back from causing pain. It was enough to indicate that he *could* inflict pain if he decided to. Mason realised that the suit disguised a dangerous man. He glanced at the clothes on the table.

Caldwell noticed the movement and let go. "They might not fit you very well but they'll do temporarily. You can be out of here very soon."

"What is it you *really* want? You know I don't have anything to tell you."

"You spoke to us willingly three years ago."

Mason tensed. "You're the fucking CIA."

"Of course."

Mason clenched his jaw.

Caldwell spoke again. "What's going on at Station Helix?"

"I told you everything."

"Really? Or did you just give us what you thought we deserved for the money?"

"I told you everything," Mason repeated.

"It's not enough."

"I don't know anything else."

"I think you're lying."

"*I'm...*" Mason stopped and considered what to say next. "You *know* I told you everything. Your people from Grosvenor Square questioned me thoroughly."

"I'd expect nothing less."

"So what am I doing here?"

"You're going to tell me everything I want to know

about Station Helix."

"But you said…" Mason shut himself up.

"Station Helix," Caldwell repeated. "You were there. You had access to the facility."

"I have nothing to say to you."

"Do you want more money?"

Mason didn't reply. There was no point in responding to the provocation. He'd accepted payment from the CIA before. He'd told them everything he knew three and a half years ago. This situation wasn't going to be concluded with a business transaction. "Go to hell."

Caldwell removed a handcuff key from his trouser pocket and unlocked the restraints which secured Mason to the steel chair. "Get dressed," he ordered as he headed for the exit.

7

It was a concession to accept something from a captor but it was also foolish to reject anything that would improve comfort. He took off his clothes and replaced them with the garments from the table: boxer shorts, socks, plain trousers and a long-sleeved base layer shirt. He cracked the plastic seal on the water bottle and gulped down the liquid in one go. He knew he wouldn't be spoken to again until he returned to the chair, so he sat down and waited. Momentarily he considered attacking the interrogator when he returned, but he dismissed that idea as quickly as it formed. The American was more than capable of defending himself and, even if he could overpower the man, he wouldn't get far.

Mason understood the peril of his situation. He wasn't able to reveal anything more about Station Helix; he really had told the American embassy staff everything when he'd contacted them. His security access to the facility hadn't given him any insight into the scientific work that went on there. He'd never even had access to the laboratories.

Deciphering his interrogator's plan was impossible. The questioning was a pretence. Mason had been completely wrong-footed by the questions about his Pakistani connections. His decision to contact the Americans three and a half years ago had come back to haunt him. He inhaled deeply, stretched out on the chair, and waited for the CIA spook to return.

8

"Feeling more comfortable?" the American asked cheerily as he entered the room.

"Yes."

"Good." Caldwell stood directly in front of Mason. "You're one sick son of a bitch, aren't you?" Mason caught Caldwell's gaze briefly before looking down. The comment and change in tone threw him. It was yet another tactic and the first time the American had insulted him. He didn't respond. Caldwell raised his voice. "What's the matter? Decided to clam up again?"

"I don't know what you're talking about."

"Lying bastard."

"Look, I..."

"DNA," Caldwell interrupted. "What do you know about DNA?"

"What?"

"You heard me."

"I don't know what you mean."

"Of course you do."

Mason didn't like the way the exchange was going. "They must have been researching DNA at the lab."

"Not *there*, Mason. I'm not talking about Station Helix. I'm talking about *your* DNA."

"My DNA?"

"Yes, *your*s. In the blood you left all over the truck you

used to kill the scientists."

Mason froze.

"You're a vindictive vengeful maniac, Mason. And we've found you out."

Mason didn't reply. He tasted bile in his throat. He recalled the tiny scratch on his hand that he'd discovered after the crash. He hadn't even noticed cutting himself on the truck's broken window as he'd clambered out of the cab.

Caldwell paused before speaking again. This time his voice was quiet. "Your silence speaks volumes. Let me explain exactly what happens next. We *own* you. Everything we want you to do for us, you will do. Not only do we own you, but we own your crew as well. Is that clear?"

Mason reacted to the provocation. "Leave my men out of this!"

Caldwell slammed his hand under Mason's jaw and pulled him clear of the chair. Mason hit the floor where it met the wall, landing painfully on his back with Caldwell's hand still crushing his throat. "Perhaps you misunderstood," remarked Caldwell coldly, tightening his grip. "We have evidence linking your entire team to the murder. That evidence is not currently in the possession of the police. If you fail to comply the police will learn everything." He dragged Mason back to the chair and shoved him onto it. "You know the quaint English law called *joint enterprise*? Every one of your men will go down for murder."

Mason slumped in the chair. "You manipulative bastard."

"It seems you're finally getting the message." Caldwell smoothed the sleeves of his jacket.

"What do you want?" Mason asked, defeated.

"For now, nothing." Caldwell paused. "No, that's not strictly true. You'll be thinking of ways to get even. That's what you do because you're psychotic. Dismiss those thoughts. We are cleverer than you. We are stronger than you. We have more resources than you. And…" Caldwell paused deliberately to provoke a response.

"And what?"

"We're considerably more ruthless than you."

9

As Caldwell left the cell for the last time, two men stepped inside. They wore suits but looked like they'd be more comfortable wearing the uniform of an American football team. For a moment he feared they were about to deliver a final message to encourage his co-operation, but instead they just ushered him from the room without speaking. His shoes were returned to him. He was hurried along a narrow corridor and down a flight of concrete steps into an underground car park. A silver van was parked close to the stairwell, its engine running. One of the minders pulled a black cloth bag over his head then shoved him unceremoniously into the vehicle. He was pushed onto a seat as the van moved off.

Mason estimated the journey as no longer than ten minutes. The trip seemed to be at low speeds and involved numerous stops and turns, so he guessed he was still in London. The vehicle stopped, the bag over his head was removed and the van's side door was slid open. Mason found himself staring at the entrance of the Crowne Plaza Hotel. The sky was dark and many of the hotel's windows were illuminated. His wallet and mobile phone were shoved into his hands and he was told to get out. He touched the phone's screen and noticed the date. It was still the *same day*. They'd screwed with his sense of time. The whole ordeal had lasted only hours, not days. Behind him the silver van pulled away. He didn't bother looking. He entered the hotel and walked to the desk.

The pretty receptionist smiled. "Good evening, sir, may I help you?"

"Andrew Mason, room 427. Are there any messages for me?"

"427… no, Mr Mason, you don't have any messages. Is there anything else I can help you with?"

"No. Thank you."

"You're welcome, sir. Have a good evening."

10

After showering and changing into casual clothes, Mason ordered a bar snack from room service. He laid down on the bed, uncertain what to do next. He'd encountered a lot of dangerous people during his professional life and he'd dealt with some tough situations, but now he was out of his depth and vulnerable. *What do I say to my men? Don't say anything, you idiot. They don't need to know. One false step and the CIA will throw you to the wolves.*

His mobile started ringing. Glancing at the display he saw a name: *Yasin Gandapur*. Mason hesitated. It occurred to him that the CIA interrogator hadn't actually given him any instructions. He didn't know whom he could speak to or what he could do. He swiped the phone's display to answer the call.

"Mr Mason?" the Pakistani asked.

"Yes, Mr Gandapur. How are you?"

"Very well, thank you. How was your afternoon?"

Mason half-smiled. "It was interesting. There are all sorts of things to do in London."

"My sentiments exactly. A fascinating city."

"Have you had time to discuss our business arrangement?"

"What business arrangement is that?"

"I was wondering whether you had spoken to your cousin about my contract."

"My cousin?"

"Yes – Daoud Gandapur."

"I am afraid you are misinformed."

Mason frowned. "What do you mean?"

"I do not have a cousin named Daoud."

"My apologies, I thought he was a family member."

"No, Daoud Gandapur does not exist."

Mason hesitated. "Then what was our meeting about this morning?"

"You must have misunderstood my purpose."

"Then why are you calling me?" Mason's voice revealed his irritation.

"To deliver a message from our mutual American friends."

Jesus. Mason didn't reply. His palms began to sweat.

Gandapur – Mason realised that the name was a fabrication – continued. "They hope you fully understand your situation. They *own* you. Tell me you understand, Mr Mason."

Mason clenched his fist around his phone so tightly that the screen cracked.

FIVE

1

The number for the Faculty of Science and Technology at the university was listed on the department's website, but, as Alex had expected, individual numbers for staff members were not shown. He resolved not to ask his uncle for Hearn's number unless his inquiry with the university was unsuccessful. It was premature to involve Graham at this stage and he didn't want to have to lie about the reason for contacting his parents' colleague.

Alex picked up his mobile and dialled the number displayed on his computer's monitor.

"Science and Technology Faculty," a female voice answered.

"Hi, would you put me through to Mr Hearn's office please?"

"Is that Professor Hearn you want?"

"I think so. I'm afraid I only know him as a colleague of my late parents and I don't know his title."

"Oh, I'm sorry. May I take your name?"

"It's Alex Hannay."

"Please hold, Mr Hannay."

"Thank you." Alex heard a tone as the receptionist redirected the call.

Twenty seconds later a man's voice spoke. "Alex? How are you? Forgive me for not calling since the funeral. I wasn't sure whether to phone."

"That's fine, Professor. I didn't expect you to."

"As long as you're okay. Please call me Michael. You're not one of my students."

"Thank you, I will. Michael, I'm calling about my parents. I realised that I didn't discuss their work with them as much as I should have and I'm curious to learn more. I'm trying to fill in some gaps and I was hoping you might be able to help me."

"I'll try if I can. I thought you were familiar with their field of expertise though."

"I knew they were geneticists but I never knew what sort of projects they worked on."

"Oh, I see." Hearn's voice seemed less assured. He paused for a few seconds. When he spoke again his tone seemed to resume its earlier confidence. "It's mostly culture dishes and computer analysis, of course. Alex, I have a meeting with the bursar in five minutes. I was on my way out when I answered your call – you were lucky to catch me. I'm sorry to have to cut this short. Would you like to come to the faculty on Friday? I can give you an hour or so from ten o'clock."

"That would be great," Alex replied, surprised at the sudden invitation.

"Good. You know where the facility is in Ipswich?"

"Yes, not far from Portman Road."

"Famous for football and murdered prostitutes I'm afraid. See you on Friday."

"Thanks. See you then." Alex ended the call and put down his phone. *That was progress*, he said to himself. *Hang on, you haven't learned anything yet. Go to the meeting and see what Michael has to say.*

He stood and walked to the window, unsure how he should feel. If the professor knew anything – assuming there actually was something to know – it was unlikely that he would give him a satisfactory explanation. And what if Ingwe's assessment of the meagre evidence was pure fiction? Perhaps the wisest voice had been Abi's when she told him not to take the word of a disgraced policeman seriously. The quandary troubled him.

His phone beeped, distracting him from his thoughts. He picked it up and saw that a text message had arrived from Lucas Ingwe.

Chelmsford Crown Court next Tuesday. Closed session. Trying to find out more. I'll call you soon. Lucas.

2

Jack Caldwell and Clare Quinn stopped walking once they reached the middle of Hyde Park's Serpentine Bridge. By force of professional habit both had been looking for followers but neither had spotted any. The field of view was broad from here, the sightlines clear. They could watch every movement on the entire length of the bridge and observe pedestrians on the footpaths around the lake. Passing traffic created ambient noise.

Leaning against the balustrade Clare glanced to her left and right once again before speaking. "Mason's unpredictable."

Caldwell nodded. "That's why I've put him on a leash."

"Continuing with the animal analogy, it might be simpler just to throw him to the wolves." She leaned back and enjoyed the warmth of the sunlight on her face.

Caldwell shrugged. "He could be useful."

"There's a problem."

"Go on."

"Owning Mason means protecting him." Quinn's distaste for the notion was clear.

Caldwell looked ahead. "I'd considered that."

"I know we both abandoned our moral compasses a long time ago, Jack, but is he worth the steps we'd have to take?"

"Like I said, he might prove useful."

"I'm not asking you to justify your decision, but he can't

give us anything else regarding Helix."

"Don't apologise for being my conscience, Clare. I respect your judgement. And you're right – Mason can't go anywhere near Helix. But *we* have to. If our information is correct the Brits are way ahead of us in genetic experimentation. We have to acquire their research."

"How does Mason fit in to this?"

"He's our scapegoat."

Clare glanced round. "If our operation goes wrong we tell the Brits that Mason tried to sell us information?"

"Exactly. And the Special Relationship remains intact."

"Jack?"

He looked at her, silently inviting the question he knew she'd ask.

"What do you mean by 'if our information is correct'?"

Caldwell smiled. Clare Quinn was as astute as she was beautiful. "I have someone inside Station Helix."

She stared. "Since when?"

"Eight months ago. I was told to start a project after Mason went to Grosvenor Square. It took a long time to set up. The operative has been working alone and reporting directly to me. I wasn't able to discuss it with you before now."

"Never mind that – I know how the system works – but how did you pull that off?"

"We had an asset with appropriate training and a suitably robust cover story. The Brits don't exactly advertise in the job centre for Helix, but they do keep their eyes open for suitable talent."

"And Mason turning up again?"

"Entirely coincidental. But…"

"Useful," Clare interrupted.

Jack nodded. "It's time to step this up. That's why I'm bringing you in. My asset has spent eight months blending in and earning their trust. Information has been sparse so far – deliberately so. But that's about to change."

"I see why you want to use Mason."

"If it comes to it we can sacrifice him and his entire crew. We must protect our operation. This is industrial espionage against our closest ally."

"You want me to make arrangements to tie up the loose end?"

Caldwell didn't reply.

3

Nick Seymour piled the plastic shopping bags into the boot of his car, not caring for neatness. The effort reminded him how bitter he'd become since his wife's accident. A fall down the stairs at home had damaged her spine and limited her mobility. Seymour resented how he'd had to take on tasks like shopping for groceries and cleaning the house. He had better things to do on his rest days. His already strained relationship had worsened when he'd become his wife's reluctant carer. He knew she exaggerated the injury and wasn't nearly as incapacitated as she made out, but the disability benefit softened the blow. If Theresa were spotted pushing a shopping trolley around the supermarket their case would be reviewed and they'd probably lose the additional money. With a grunt Seymour shoved the last bag – containing cans of beer – into the car. He slammed the boot shut and wheeled the trolley to a nearby bay.

Now just past fifty Seymour had left the best years of his life in the distant past. He'd become a disgruntled irritable man, overweight with a flabby beer belly and the ruddy complexion of a habitual drinker. His receding hair was cropped short, his stubble flecked with grey. This afternoon he would open a few cans in front of the television and spend a distracting ninety minutes shouting insults at football players. For a while it would lift him above the monotony of his boring life. He walked back to his car, sat down in the driver's seat and put the key in the ignition. Suddenly the passenger door opened and an attractive woman got inside, startling him. She closed the door quickly. She wore jogging clothes and her long dark hair was tied into a ponytail underneath a pink baseball cap.

"Hey, Nick, how've you been?" she said with an American accent.

"What the fuck do you want?" Seymour replied nervously. He'd hoped never to see her again.

"That's no way to greet an old friend," Quinn replied.

"You're not my friend, Amanda." Seymour had always doubted it was the woman's real name.

"You know you're probably right. But I *have* come to talk about old times."

"Our business was done a long time ago." Seymour realised he was sweating.

"You don't really believe that do you?"

"What d'you mean?"

"Come on, Nick. You don't think that little favour you did for me made us even?"

"I gave you what you wanted." The onset of a stress reaction made Seymour feel out of breath.

"A few names in exchange for paying off your gambling and credit card debts? I hate to disappoint you, but you definitely haven't earned your thirty-five thousand pounds yet."

"I took a risk…"

"Shut up," Quinn snapped. "You're going to do something for me."

"You can't make me do anything." Seymour's nervous tone betrayed the disbelief in his own words.

She sneered at him. "Don't be a fucking idiot. I can make you do anything I want. My bosses have decided it's time for you to show your gratitude for their generosity."

"I was already grateful."

"My bosses disagree."

Seymour fell silent. He'd been willing to take the money, naively hoping that there wouldn't be consequences. At the time he'd realised how close his chosen lifestyle had come to losing him his job and house. He hadn't asked questions when the benefactor had made him an offer that was impossible to refuse. In return for the money Seymour had handed over personnel records of staff and contractors working in all of the UK's detention facilities. He'd provided rotas and protocols for prisoner transportation and details of prison procedures.

He decided to stand his ground. "Why don't you tell your bosses I'm not interested? I gave them what they asked for. Now get out of my car and leave me alone."

Quinn's scornful glare revealed what she thought of Seymour's attempt at bravery. "Let me make something very clear. This is not negotiable. Or perhaps you'd like us to tell your disabled wife that you're screwing her best friend? Or that you've substituted the casinos for online gambling and you're back in debt? You couldn't afford the divorce and you know we'd tell the Prison Service what you did. You'd get put away."

Seymour's face flushed red. "You wouldn't…"

"Don't even cling to the hope of me not being serious."

Seymour abandoned his defiance. "What do you want?"

"That's more like it, Nick. I knew you'd come around. The good news is that my employers will consider all debts paid once you do this little errand for us. How does that sound?"

"Like bullshit."

"I'm serious. We won't ever contact you again."

Seymour gritted his teeth. "Like I said, what do you want?"

"You're still working at HMP Cunliffe, right?"

"Yes."

"There's a man in the facility that we're interested in."

"Staff or prisoner?"

"Prisoner. His name's Marek Gorski. He's a Polish national."

Seymour nodded. "I know him."

"Good. Gorski is due to attend Chelmsford Crown Court next Tuesday."

"So what?"

Quinn held eye contact for a moment before replying. "It is imperative that he never gets to court."

"Jesus!"

"Do you understand?"

"Are you saying…?"

"You will ensure that Gorski does not get to the hearing. Is that clear?"

Seymour felt his stomach churning and his throat tightening. He couldn't speak. The blood drained from his face as he stared at the American woman. In that moment he wondered if he'd ever seen a woman appear so cold-blooded and malevolent. "You're insane," he mumbled.

Quinn ignored the remark. "As I said, this will conclude our business. Do this and we'll never speak to you again. You have my word."

"And if I refuse?"

"Don't ask stupid questions." Quinn opened the car door and climbed out. "Have a nice day." She slammed the door shut.

Seymour emptied his stomach over the steering wheel.

4

Alex was surprised at Abi's offer to attend the meeting with Professor Hearn but grateful for the company. It also made sense to have an independent friend present. However much he tried to evaluate Lucas's information rationally he knew his objectivity was not absolute.

They reached the modern glass-fronted faculty building and went up the steps towards the reception area. "You didn't have to come," he said as they went inside.

"I know but I wanted to," Abi replied.

They reached the desk. A smartly dressed receptionist looked up. "Good morning. May I help you?" she asked with a soft Irish accent.

"I have a meeting with Professor Hearn at ten," Alex replied. "My name is Alex Hannay."

"I'll phone his office for you."

"Thank you."

The receptionist made the call.

As they waited they studied the interior of the building. It was sparsely decorated in a minimalist modern style, elegant but not endearing. The waiting area had several chairs with plain pastel upholstery, chosen for style rather than comfort.

The receptionist put down the phone's handset. "Professor Hearn is on his way down." Alex thanked her again.

Hearn arrived moments later, appearing as the lift doors opened. He looked surprised when he saw that Alex was not alone. He extended his hand in greeting. "Alex," he said as they shook hands.

"Hello, Michael, thank you for seeing me. I hope you don't mind me bringing my housemate along. This is Abi."

"No problem at all." Smiling, he shook hands with her. "Yes, the young lady who was with you at the funeral. Shall we go to my office? I thought we could start there and then have a tour of the facility."

"Sure," Alex replied. They entered the lift. Hearn pressed the button for the third floor.

"I'm sorry I wasn't able to talk for longer when you called," Hearn said as the lift rose. "You caught me a little off guard. I wasn't sure how I could summarise your parents' work in a phone call. That's why I suggested a meeting."

"I'm grateful to you for finding the time."

"Here we are," said Hearn as the lift stopped and the door opened. He led them to his office. It was less tidy than the reception area with numerous stacks of documents in piles on the desk and bookshelves. A computer was on the desk and a discontinued model of inkjet printer sat on a drawer unit in the corner. A chair was already positioned for Alex in front of Hearn's desk. He moved a second from against the wall for Abi. "Please sit down," he said, closing the door. He walked around the desk and sat down. "It was a tragedy to lose your parents, Alex – a very great loss. They were lovely people and fine scientists."

"Thank you. My uncle and I appreciated you speaking at the funeral."

"It was the least I could do."

"I know my inquiry must have seemed odd." Alex was anxious to get on topic. "The thing is I didn't really know much about my parents' work. I'd like to learn about their research."

"It's hard to know where to start. They were researchers here and also conducted lectures for students. They were very popular."

"What was the nature of their work?"

"Genetics is rather a broad discipline of science. Your parents worked on numerous projects over the years. Our genes are like instruction codes; each with a specific function in the body. We inherit these instructions from our parents. Sometimes these hereditary genes are useful, sometimes they are damaging. Genetic research endeavours to identify their functions. Faults can be passed on from generation to generation. By studying what each piece of code does we're better able to repair the broken ones. I'm obviously simplifying things rather crudely, but that is essentially the science your parents studied."

"So they were working on medical genetics?"

Hearn nodded. "There are many diseases which have a genetic cause. The trick is trying to identify where the problem lies within the genetic code. For example, some people are more likely to develop cancer because of an inherited susceptibility to the disease. The goal is to correct that trait and strengthen their resilience."

"Would their research have put my parents at risk?"

"I'm not sure what you mean."

"Genetics is still controversial, isn't it?"

"Oh, I see. I wasn't aware that your parents had

encountered any serious opposition to their work. Although this field of science is advancing all the time, you must remember that the recognition of inherited traits goes back centuries. Everyone's familiar with the idea of breeding the perfect rose or racehorse."

"But surely that's not the same as deliberately altering the structure of DNA?"

"Isn't it? I don't think a distinction can be drawn that clearly. The end goal is the same – a better organism. I won't pretend there isn't some resistance to this field. Some people with religious beliefs find it deeply uncomfortable knowing we can build a life form in the laboratory. In 2010 the J. Craig Venter Institute created a synthetic bacterium. Who needs a creator god when you can do that? Even non-religious people are wary about having their food altered, even if the purpose is to make it resistant to disease and increase crop yield. But progress has to be made if we value life."

"Rest assured I understand the value of the science," said Alex. "I don't think my parents were ever intimidated by anyone." He paused, considering how to phrase his next question. He wanted to push this conversation a little harder without being obvious. "Presumably there was a lot of secrecy around my parents' research?"

Hearn nodded. "Of course. The nature of research requires confidentiality. There is considerable commercial competition."

It wasn't the direct answer that Alex had hoped for. "I didn't think my parents worked for the private sector."

"That's partly true. A lot of our funding comes from other organisations. It's a commonplace arrangement. A facility like this couldn't operate without sponsorship."

"I see. Can you tell me who sponsored my parents' research?"

"The money comes into the faculty as a whole, not to individuals."

"Do you receive public sector funding?"

"Some, although not a great deal. The Government spends around nine billion pounds of taxpayers' money on science annually. Only a proportion of that goes into higher education. It might sound a lot but in reality it doesn't stretch very far. Science is a long-term investment. Politicians aren't keen to invest in anything that doesn't bring results they can quote during election campaigns."

"I see."

"Forgive my cynicism. It's just that getting funding is a constant battle." Hearn raised his hands by way of apology and changed the subject. "Your parents did publish a handful of articles. Would you be interested in seeing them? They're probably a little hard to follow without knowing the jargon, but I can give you copies if you wish."

"Thanks, I'd like that."

Hearn leaned back in his chair. "No problem. Would you like to have a tour of the lab?"

"If that's okay. I did visit some years ago, but I'd like another look."

"Very well." Hearn stood and gestured towards the door. "Let's go and find you some lab coats to put on."

5

Forty-five minutes later Abi and Alex walked out of the faculty building. Under his arm Alex carried some cardboard sleeves containing copies of his parents' research papers. The tour of the research facility had been interesting from an academic point of view, but had provided him with even fewer answers about his parents than the discussion in the professor's office. He'd actually considered asking Hearn directly if his parents had conducted any research for the Government, but he'd refrained. Such a question would sound absurd if there was no truth in his theory, but, if the Hannays *had* been working in secrecy, it would have revealed he was in possession of information he shouldn't have. He didn't want to inquire too forcefully when he was only basing his assumptions on the theories of one suspended detective.

"How d'you feel that went?" asked Abi as they walked down the steps and turned onto the pavement.

Alex frowned. "About as well as I expected, I suppose."

"You don't sound like you mean that in a good way."

"I don't. Michael was very informative about the science in broad terms, but I still don't know about my parents' work."

"At least he gave you some of their papers to look at. Plus he said they worked on medical research."

"I knew that already. He didn't tell me anything new.

I'm beginning to wonder why he bothered arranging the meeting."

"He thought it was better to give you some time face to face rather than talking over the phone. I'm sure he just thought you'd appreciate the courtesy."

"I *am* grateful for that, but I'm frustrated that I didn't actually learn anything."

She stopped walking and turned to face him. "Alex, there may be nothing to learn."

He held her gaze. "I know. I might be misinterpreting everything Lucas told me, but there are too many unexplained parts to this. Why wasn't the crash investigated by the police? What about the DNA Lucas found on the truck? I'm not satisfied that there's a simple explanation for all of this."

Abi nodded. She turned her head away and didn't speak for a moment. She looked at him again. "I know this is difficult. I just want you to be careful, okay?"

He smiled at her. "Thanks."

She looked at him thoughtfully. "What do you want to do next?"

"I'll speak to Lucas."

"You're putting a lot of trust in that man."

"I don't have a choice. I'll tell him I drew a blank with Hearn. Perhaps we can find out something next week."

"The court case?"

Alex nodded. "Courts are public buildings so I'll be able to get inside easily enough."

"True, but if the case is being heard in a closed courtroom you won't be able to watch."

"We might be able to find someone to talk to. I'm sure

Lucas knows most of the barristers and ushers at Chelmsford."

"I suppose so," she agreed reluctantly. "Come on, let's go home. There's nothing else we can do here."

Alex adjusted the bundle of folders under his arm. They resumed their walk, leaving the gleaming glass façade of the university faculty behind them.

6

HMP Cunliffe was a category C facility for offenders unlikely to present an escape risk, but its imposing Victorian architecture was no less sinister than that of more secure facilities. Located in the heart of the Suffolk countryside the prison housed nearly seven hundred men. But today Nick Seymour was concerned with only one. As a prison officer with twenty-two years' service he was knowledgeable in every aspect of prison life. He knew he could isolate Gorski without much difficulty. Simple practicalities weren't the problem. Since receiving the shocking instruction from the American woman he'd agonised over the implications. He'd allowed strangers to manipulate him, never suspecting that their arrangement would ultimately lead to such terrifying consequences. He realised now that providing confidential data for money had sent him down a path from which he couldn't return. He hadn't just traded information; he'd sold his soul.

He'd spent hours trying to analyse what the woman had said. He told himself that her directive had not been specific, that she hadn't said she wanted Gorski dead. He failed to convince himself, knowing she wouldn't have spoken the words directly. The message was clear without explicit instruction. Gorski had to be eliminated and he was the person who would do it. It made him sick. He tried to rely upon his resilience of years in the Prison Service, telling himself that the people in his custody were the scum of society, that they'd sacrificed their rights by committing their crimes. His attempts to justify the action he had to take by thinking of his target as less than human failed to ease his thoughts. It would still be murder.

The word had jolted him into a sense of self-preservation. If he killed Gorski, how would he protect himself? He'd turned his thoughts to the practicalities of killing an inmate. He'd encountered several prison murders during his service and knew that the majority were never solved. For all their stupidity in committing crime and getting caught, many prisoners were highly resourceful. In prison they had time to think. Furthermore the environment was a library of criminal ingenuity. Some inmates left prison with vocational qualifications; *all* left with greater criminal knowledge. But some of that creativity rubbed off on the prison staff too. Seymour had learned plenty of tricks over the years by necessity. To stand half a chance against the prison population you had to be able to think like them.

He headed for the showers. His disgust turned into icy determination. Doing this was the only hope he had that his life would not be utterly ruined. He prayed that the American bitch would keep her word. Steam billowed as he entered the wash block. Gorski would be alone. He'd double-checked and triple-checked the rota. The Pole was standing under a forceful jet of water, oblivious to his presence. Momentarily Seymour wondered what was going on in the man's head. The Pole had been in a permanent state of disorientation and bewilderment since arriving at the facility.

He closed in, grabbing the back of Gorski's neck, ignoring the sudden drenching from the loud cascade of hot water. Without hesitation he slammed the truck driver's forehead against the white tiles with all the force he could muster. The impact stunned the Pole but Seymour didn't stop. He drove Gorski's head against the wall again and again. The man's body went limp but Seymour didn't quit. Blood poured from his face, staining the white tiles red. Seymour kept up the relentless assault, crunching his victim's head against the pipework, continuing until fatigue overcame him. He let Gorski's body drop to the floor.

For the first time he realised the damage he'd inflicted. The man's face was hideously injured. Seymour crouched down and checked for signs of life. There were none. He left the shower running, knowing it would wash away any remaining trace evidence which could link him to the crime. Satisfied his deed was done he rushed from the wash block and activated an emergency alarm. "Prisoner down!" he screamed. "Someone call the medic!"

7

Reading his parents' papers gave Alex a headache. Hearn had hinted that they might be difficult reading, but the professor's words understated the documents' complexity. He'd spent most of the afternoon and evening trying to decipher the technical jargon about proteins, chromosomes and DNA fragments. With dismay he realised that only a fellow geneticist would understand the essays. His parents had evidently been strict adherents of the scientific method, studying and testing their work with almost paranoid scrutiny. Knowing how concerned they were with assessing every minute detail of their experiments reinforced his admiration for them, even though he couldn't understand what their results actually meant. Frustrated, he reached the end of the fifth document and slipped it back inside its folder. He still had another two essays to read and it was getting late. He expected Abi to return from her shift at the pub any minute.

He linked his fingers together and put his hands behind his head. He shut his eyes and leaned back against the sofa's cushions. The chances of finishing the other documents tonight were extremely slim. He needed to rest and would have to take another look in the morning. He'd learned nothing. The experiments his parents had written about were, as he'd expected, predominantly concerned with medical research. He was glad he only had seven essays to study. Any more and his patience would probably run completely dry.

He bent forward, placing his elbows on his knees and his head in his hands. He rubbed his forehead and then glanced at the stack of papers beside him. He stared at the paperwork for a moment before grabbing the first folder he'd looked at. He started having a conversation with himself in his head. *Idiot, you didn't read the references. No one ever reads them. Just look at the bloody references.* He turned to the last page and glanced at the list of citations. The bibliography provided the books and other scientific papers the author – in this case his mother – had referred to in her essay. Flicking the pages over he saw that her text was dotted with several numbers in a superscript font. He turned to the last page and studied the list of source documents in close detail. Nothing stood out as being worthy of interest. He tossed the paper to one side and picked up the second. Once again the list was uninteresting, although he noticed a single entry where his mother had quoted one of her own studies.

By the time he started on the fourth set of citations he was beginning to wonder why he'd bothered looking. But now, two-thirds of the way down the list, something caught his eye. Entry 34 read *MOD Report WH-1994-003*. The reference looked out of place among the book and journal titles. He looked through the essay for the paragraph containing the number 34. The paragraph referred to a gene's susceptibility to decay when exposed to radiation. His father's technical jargon prevented him from understanding the details.

He was distracted by Abi opening the front door. She

peered into the sitting room. "You're up late."

"Yeah, I've been trying to read these papers."

"Have you learned anything?"

"My decision to become a photographer instead of a scientist was probably wise," he replied with a grin.

Abi chuckled. "So they're pretty heavy-going then?"

"No kidding. I don't understand a word Mum and Dad wrote. But I may have found something interesting."

Abi flopped down on the sofa beside him. "Tell me."

"I will, but before I do, don't you think it's odd that Michael only gave me seven essays?"

"What do you mean?"

"My parents worked at the university for years. I'm sure they must've published much more work than this."

"Maybe he thought these were enough to be getting on with. Going on how tired you look, he was right."

"That's probably true, but what if he just selected a few papers that didn't contain anything significant?"

Abi frowned. "You've become very suspicious."

"I know. The thing is, I reckon he overlooked something when he was choosing which papers to give me."

"How d'you figure that?"

"No one reads the citations."

"Excuse me?"

"The references to other works. I made the same mistake myself. But then I went back and found this." He handed the citation page from his father's work to Abi and pointed at the thirty-fourth entry.

"What does this mean?" she asked.

"MOD? WH? I think my father wrote papers for the Ministry of Defence. Something about resistance to radiation. And Lucas said it was the MOD Police who shut down the crash site."

"That's an interesting theory," Abi replied, raising her eyebrows.

"You don't look convinced."

"I'm not. MOD could stand for something else."

"Like what?"

"Oh I don't know, Alex! It might be an abbreviation for a gene or a protein or something."

He looked subdued. "You could be right. I'll see what Lucas says when I phone him."

"You haven't spoken to him yet?"

"No, I wanted to look through these papers first. I'll call him tomorrow."

"Okay. Look, I'm knackered. I'm going to get some sleep." She stood up and walked to the doorway. "You should too."

"I will. Sleep well."

"Thanks. See you in the morning." Abi turned into the hallway and walked up the stairs.

Wondering whether he'd found something significant or if he was losing the plot, Alex stacked the cardboard folders into a neat pile. He stood, walked to the door and turned off the sitting room light.

8

Acknowledging the call from her radio dispatcher, Francesca Ingwe pressed the switch which activated the paramedic response car's blue strobe lights and changed down a gear. Driving skilfully along the deserted Ipswich roads she mentally plotted her route. She was familiar with her destination – a narrow pedestrian thoroughfare known as The Walk which connected the town's two main shopping streets. She was only two minutes away. A man had collapsed and was vomiting blood. Most people had gone home by four o'clock in the morning – even the late night clubbers – so she guessed the victim was a vagrant.

Francesca pulled in at the west end of Buttermarket, grabbed her kit bag and hurried the short distance to the thoroughfare. Halfway along she saw a figure lying on the paving stones. She noticed some movement and heard groaning. The figure was a man with dirty dishevelled hair. A filthy blanket was wrapped around him. "Hello, can you tell me your name?" Francesca said loudly. "I'm a paramedic."

She crouched down and placed her bag on the ground. As she reached for her torch the man launched himself at her, grabbing her throat. Standing upright, the man shoved her against the nearest shop's security shutter. The metal rattled loudly. Pinning her tightly against the grill the man produced a knife and placed the point under her right eye.

He pressed just hard enough to draw blood. Francesca wanted to scream but his hand compressed her throat. "Drugs?" Francesca asked hoarsely, suspecting she'd been trapped by an addict. Offering him the contents of her kit bag might be the only chance of escape.

"No, not drugs," the man replied. "Just a message." He loosened his grip slightly.

Francesca stared, her eyes wide open with fear.

"Tell Lucas to forget the Hannay case. Do you understand?"

Francesca nodded, her heart pounding.

"Good. Make sure he gets the message. Now get out of here." He released his grip.

Francesca ran.

9

Lucas was already awake when Francesca came home. It didn't take him long to realise that something was wrong. Her face was expressionless when she saw him in the hallway. Without a word she hung up her jacket and walked straight past him into the front room. She slumped onto the sofa and stared at the television screen, not caring that it was switched off. Lucas followed her into the room and sat on the sofa's armrest. "Rough night?" he asked delicately.

Francesca scowled at him and looked back at the blank screen. "You could say that."

"Do you want to talk about it?"

Francesca ignored him.

"Are you okay, baby?"

She turned to look at him again, her expression severe. "Don't 'baby' me, Lucas. I don't want to talk to you."

"What have I done?"

"What have you done? I have no bloody idea! I wish I knew."

Lucas frowned. "I don't know what you mean."

"What exactly have you been up to during all this spare time?"

"What are you saying, Fran? You're not making any sense."

"Being attacked tonight didn't make any sense, Lucas! And it was because of you!"

He suddenly felt cold. "I don't understand. You were attacked? Are you okay?"

"Do I look like I'm okay? Of course I'm not bloody okay. Some bastard pretending to be a wino held me up at knifepoint. He had a message. A message for *you*."

Lucas swallowed hard. For a moment he couldn't speak. "Tell me what happened," he said quietly.

Francesca breathed deeply. She was a little calmer now – the outburst had helped to reduce her stress – but her face was pale and withdrawn. "Like I said, a man held a knife to my face – he *cut* me here – and told me to pass on a message to you. He said you were to back off the Hannay case. That's the name of the people who died in the car crash, isn't it?"

He nodded. "I don't know what to say. I'm so sorry you got dragged into this."

"Into what? It's not even your investigation."

"I know, but there were things that worried me about it. I spoke to some contacts and tried to find some answers. But I never thought it would come to this."

"Well it has. You *know* you shouldn't be snooping around when you're suspended. Now you'll definitely get sacked."

"No, this is different," he stated firmly. "Someone knows I've been asking questions but it's not the police. I'd have been visited by Professional Standards if they knew."

Fran glared. "So who is it then? Who stuck a knife in my face?"

"I honestly don't know."

"So what are you going to do?"

He knelt down in front of Francesca and took her hands

in his. "Fran, I'm sorry this happened. I promise I won't do anything that puts you at risk again."

"So you're going to heed the warning and let this go?"

"Yes. Nothing's worth you getting hurt. I love you."

"I hope so." Francesca pulled her hands away. "I need to get some sleep." She stood and walked quickly from the room.

10

Nick Seymour was surprised at how calm he'd felt since killing Gorski. The trepidation he'd suffered beforehand had vanished. He'd gone through the motions of writing a statement and talking to the police and prison investigators. The process had been straightforward. He stuck to his story that he'd found the Pole already dead in the wash block – which was an entirely plausible account – and hadn't encountered the merest hint of suspicion. The death was being treated as just another prison murder. The apathy at solving the crime and identifying the person responsible was clear from the outset. No one expected a result when the evidence had literally washed down the drain. Several prisoners could have had contact with Gorski on the morning he died and it was certain that not one would have anything to say.

His rota meant it was his weekend off and he decided to go to the pub for a drink. His wife shouted at him from the kitchen, telling him he'd better dare not come back drunk. He ignored her insult and removed his set of keys from the hand-painted *Home Sweet Home* key holder in the hallway. They'd bought the ghastly thing from a seaside gift shop many years ago. Seymour had no idea he'd be dead within ten seconds. Shoving the keys into his jeans pocket he opened the latch, walked out the house and slammed the door shut behind him. Theresa hated it when he did that, although the noisy cow made more noise than him. He tugged the belt loops of his jeans, trying to adjust the ill-fitting garment under his obese stomach, and walked down the concrete path towards the road outside his house.

A sniper's bullet tore into his forehead, shredded his brain and caused the back of his skull to explode.

11

"I'm sorry I snapped at you when I came home," Francesca said to her husband. Several hours' sleep had settled her thoughts, and she'd suggested to Lucas that a late afternoon stroll in the park would give them a chance to clear the air. Her arm was hooked around his. She squeezed his arm briefly and he responded.

"You had every right to. I had no idea how complicated this had become."

"What do you think this is about?"

"I don't know for certain. Someone's covering up the truth about the Hannay crash. Everything you told me about that night seemed wrong."

"Like how it was cleared up so fast?"

He nodded. "I tracked down the lorry and found a blood sample on it that didn't match anyone at the scene. Fran, I don't think it was an accident. This should be a murder inquiry."

She stopped walking. "Are you serious?"

He held her gaze and didn't reply.

"But didn't they arrest someone for drunk-driving?"

"I think he was set up."

"What if you're wrong?"

"What happened to you last night tells me I'm not."

She shuddered as she recollected the attack. For a while they didn't speak. They resumed their walk, passing tennis courts on their left and open grassland on their right. The warmth of the afternoon sunshine did little to soothe Fran's unease. "D'you think we're in danger?" she finally asked.

"I don't believe so," Lucas replied. "The message was clear. I'm sure we'll be fine if I stop asking questions."

"I know you, Lucas. You don't want to let this go, do you?"

He sighed. "Truthfully, I really want to know what happened."

"So what are you going to do?"

"Nothing. I made you a promise."

"I was angry. If the truth's being hidden about two people's deaths…" Francesca didn't finish the sentence.

"Not two. Three."

"Not the son?" she asked wide-eyed.

"No, not Alex. He's fine. It was the Polish guy arrested at the scene. He was found dead in prison."

"How d'you know?"

"From my contact who schedules court hearings. I had a text this morning."

"Is it connected?"

"Possibly. The case was already suspicious – it was going to be heard in a closed court. Now it seems that even a closed session was too much exposure for someone's liking. The driver told the officer who arrested him that he'd been abducted at gunpoint. He was never formally interviewed about that or anything else – just remanded in prison. They probably didn't even give him access to a lawyer."

"That's unusual?"

"It doesn't happen. I *know* the police were told to shut

down the investigation. That directive can only come from the very top."

"The Government? Why would they do that?"

"To control the information about the death of two scientists."

"The Hannays were working for the Government?"

"I have no idea. It's just a loose hypothesis."

"But if it's true – no wonder you've been told to back off."

He touched her arm. "That's what I'm going to do. I'm out of my depth and I don't want you getting hurt."

"I don't want *you* getting hurt either. You can't solve everything, detective. This is the right thing to do for *us*."

Lucas pulled her closer and they kissed. "I love you, Fran."

"I love you too."

Lucas's phone started ringing. "Always at the wrong moment," he muttered.

Francesca grinned. "Go on, answer it."

He looked at the phone's screen. He glanced back at her. "It's Alex Hannay."

"It's okay. You should talk to him."

Lucas answered the call.

12

"Hi, Alex."

"Hi, Lucas. Can you talk?"

"Sure."

"I may have found something. It's not much but I'd like your thoughts on it."

"Okay." Ingwe felt awkward. He didn't want to commit to a response.

"I went to the university to see Michael Hearn – the man who worked with my parents. He didn't say very much. I wasn't sure if he was being elusive or just didn't know anything, but he gave me some papers my parents had written. On one of them I found a reference to another document. It said *MOD Report* and had my father's initials on it. Do you think it means the Ministry of Defence?"

Lucas took a moment to evaluate the new information. He'd speculated that the Hannays had a Government connection, but this wasn't enough to substantiate his theory. "I don't know," he replied. "I'll admit it's an intriguing discovery, but it might refer to something else."

"I realise that, but it stands out from all the other citations. The others refer to documents by title and author. This one is almost anonymous."

"You could be right," Lucas conceded.

"So what do I do next?"

Lucas looked at Francesca before replying. She was

listening intently to the conversation. "Alex, I'm afraid I can't help you any more."

"Why not?"

"Something's happened. I've been warned to keep away from you."

"Are you serious?"

"Yes. I have to stop. And so should you."

"But doesn't this show that there *is* something going on? And what about the lorry driver? We have to talk to him."

"Gorski's dead. He was killed in prison."

Alex inhaled sharply. "To stop us from learning the truth?"

"I don't know. He may have just been the unfortunate victim in some petty dispute between inmates. Whatever happened there's nothing we can do about it. He was the only lead we had."

"But now we have this document," Alex insisted. "Surely we can look into that?"

"It's not worth the risk."

Alex hesitated. "It's all I have to go on. If my parents were murdered I want to know the truth."

"I understand, I really do. But this has got out of control. It's become dangerous."

"What do you mean?"

Lucas hesitated. "Francesca was attacked last night. She's okay but she was told to give me a message. I have to let this go. I can't risk Fran getting hurt."

"I'm sorry. I didn't realise."

"It's not your fault. I feel bad about telling you everything and then having to back away, but I don't have a choice."

"I understand."

Francesca put her hand on her husband's arm. "Let me talk to him, Lucas."

He nodded. "Alex, Fran's here. She'd like to talk to you if that's okay."

"Of course."

She took the mobile. "Alex?"

"Hi, Francesca. I never got to thank you for looking after me. You saved my life. I'm so grateful for everything you did."

"Thank you. I'm so sorry about your parents. These last few weeks must have been difficult."

"And confusing. But I'm okay. I don't know what to say about last night. I never imagined anyone would get hurt. I'm sorry."

"I'm not hurt – just a bit shaken up. I'll be fine. Lucas told me what he found out. I really hope he's wrong."

"I wish that were true, but I think he's right."

"He usually is. And that's the problem."

"You believe him, don't you?"

Francesca sighed. "Even if it's only half true, it's more than we can deal with."

Alex understood exactly what she was trying to tell him. "I understand. I don't expect Lucas to take any more risks for me."

"Thank you," she said. "It's good to talk to you, Alex. I hope your recovery continues to go smoothly."

"Well that's another surprise," he replied. "My leg is almost completely healed. The doctor thought I'd need physiotherapy to walk again, but I'm almost one hundred percent."

"That's fantastic. Maybe next year you'll be defending that fencing title you won."

"I'd like that."

"I'm glad you're doing okay. Thank you for being so understanding."

"That's okay, Francesca. Take care."

"You too." She touched the phone's screen to end the call and offered the device back to Lucas. He took the phone and returned it to his pocket. "That's odd," she commented.

"How so?" Lucas asked.

"He said he has nearly full mobility. It's impossible to recover so quickly from that level of injury."

"Maybe it wasn't as bad as you first thought. Or maybe he's just lucky."

"I hope so. That lad deserves some luck after what he went through."

"Well we can't worry about him any more."

Francesca looked glum. "Yeah, we have to look after ourselves."

Lucas noticed her expression. "What's the matter?"

"I feel bad about what I've asked you to do."

"It's the right thing. We both know that."

"But what about Alex?"

"He'll be okay."

"I feel we've abandoned him. He's on his own."

Lucas put his arm around her waist. "There's nothing more I could do for him. He understands that. Come on, let's go home."

"I suppose you're right," she agreed reluctantly. They resumed their journey along the footpath.

13

A dozen people were sitting at tables inside the pub when Alex arrived, but the stools at the bar were empty so he sat on one and waited for Abi to finish writing down a meal order for a customer. "Give me a minute," Abi told him as she disappeared into the kitchen. A moment later she returned. "How's your day been?" she asked.

"Nothing special."

"Oh." She leaned forward on the bar. "Did you make your phone call?"

"Yes. I don't think Lucas can help."

"So he didn't agree with you about the MOD?"

Alex moved closer and kept his voice low. "It's not that he didn't believe me – I think he does – but he's not in a position to look into it."

"Maybe he's not as sure as he made out."

"His wife was threatened."

Abi looked shocked. "*What?*"

"She was attacked at work and told to make Lucas stop."

"That's horrible."

"Yes, but don't you see? It tells me Lucas was right about everything."

She shook her head. "You can't draw that conclusion."

Alex gave her an intense look. "There's *something* going on."

"Alex…"

"And the lorry driver was killed in prison," he interrupted.

Abi stared at him. "You're sure?"

"According to Lucas's source, yes."

"That might not…"

Alex interrupted again. "Yes, I know. It could just be coincidence. But don't you think these coincidences are stacking up? I've got to find out what's going on."

"But you said Lucas won't help you."

"I'll do it on my own."

"Do *what* exactly?"

"I'll go to the MOD."

Abi glowered at him. "Don't be ridiculous!" she exclaimed, trying to keep her voice down to avoid being overheard. "What are you going to do? Wander down to Whitehall and demand to be seen?"

"If that's what it takes," he replied obstinately, knowing that her point was logical.

"Do you really think you can turn up at a Government building and expect them to answer all your questions? You'd just get yourself *arrested*."

"I can't forget all this," he insisted. "That crash killed my parents and could have killed me. If it was deliberate I have to find out why."

Abi noticed three customers standing at the bar waiting to be served. "Look, I have to get back to work. Promise me something."

"What?"

"I'm not working tomorrow. Promise me we'll talk this through properly before you do anything rash." Her voice was direct, her Welsh accent emphasising her insistence.

"Okay." Alex stood up and shoved the stool against the bar.

"Good. I'll see you later."

Alex walked out.

SIX

1

Alex and Abi's conversation in her aging Volkswagen was sporadic and superficial. He didn't ask where they were going although he saw that they were heading east to the Suffolk coast. Embarrassed at the bloody-mindedness he'd displayed in the pub last night he resolved to approach the matter in a more objective and adult way. But, right now, Abi didn't want to talk. Alex wasn't sure whether it was because of his behaviour or her indecision about how to discuss the subject. She'd risen first that morning but looked as though she'd had little sleep.

Alex noticed a road sign. "We're going to Orford?"

"Yes. Should be there soon. There's something I want to show you."

"The Cold War site? I've heard about it but I've never seen it."

Abi kept looking ahead, concentrating on the winding road. "Well now's your chance."

"Sounds good."

She didn't reply.

Ten minutes later they drove through the narrow streets of the picturesque coastal village. Abi pulled into a large gravelled car park and stopped the car. A number of people were already there, some with tripods and spotting scopes. Orford Ness – the long shingle spit located a short boat ride from the village's dock – was a popular location for birdwatchers and photographers on the infrequent occasions it was opened to the public.

"Come on," she said. "We have to buy tickets for the ferry from the National Trust office. We're a bit early. It might not be open yet."

They left the car and headed for the quayside, reaching the shop in a couple of minutes. The door was open. An elderly lady with grey hair and a National Trust volunteer's badge was arranging a display of leaflets and souvenirs. "Good morning," she said. "Are you here for the Ness?"

"Yes," replied Abi. "May I pay for two? We're not members."

"Of course, dear. What's your surname please?"

"Jones."

The volunteer wrote on a yellow card. Abi handed her some money. "Would you like a guidebook?" the lady asked, giving Abi the card.

"Yes please. My friend hasn't been here before. I'm sure he'd like to know more about the site's history."

"And a fascinating history it is too," the lady remarked, turning her attention to Alex. "It's hard to imagine that hundreds of people were stationed here during the First and Second World Wars. Then the Atomic Weapons Research Establishment tested detonators for nuclear bombs here during the Cold War."

Alex responded appropriately to the woman's eagerness to be informative. "It sounds really interesting."

"I'm sure you'll have a good day. The weather should hold out too. The first ferry leaves at ten and the last one back is at five. You can catch one every twenty minutes or so but they do stop at lunch time."

Abi thanked her. They left the office and walked to the quayside where half a dozen people were already waiting. Alex noticed a green painted boat moored at the dock. It was a small craft – large enough to carry about ten people only – with the controls mounted in the stern.

"This place seems great," he said.

Abi handed him the guidebook. "There's a map in there. It'll give you an idea how vast this place actually is. It only takes a couple of minutes to cross over – you can see the dock over there – but you don't get a sense of scale until you land."

Alex opened the booklet. The illustration revealed that the site was almost an island. A narrow pebble bank connected Orford Ness to the mainland at its northernmost point near the village of Aldeburgh. The vast shingle spit – formed by longshore drift over hundreds of years – extended for ten miles southwards, separated from the Suffolk coastline by the narrow River Alde. While the shingle was the dominant feature, mud flats and lagoons also occupied the two thousand acre site. Numerous military buildings – now abandoned and in an unhalted state of disrepair – had been constructed on the site during the twentieth century. He read that there were no plans to renovate the buildings. The priority was nature conservation; the area now a protected reserve.

The visitors were invited to embark by the ferry's skipper. With everyone aboard he untied the ropes which held the boat to its mooring then skilfully manoeuvred the vessel away from the quay. Minutes later they neared a pontoon. Alex noticed an old rusting military landing craft nearby as the skipper drew up alongside the floating dock.

The ferry was tied fast and the skipper indicated that everyone could disembark. He told them that a volunteer would meet them at the top of the steps and take their yellow cards from them. "You can collect them when you come back for the ferry," he said. "That way – hopefully – we don't leave anyone behind." His tone was light-hearted.

The man who collected the ferry tickets asked everyone to wait for a short briefing. Handing out maps, he summarised some of the key features of the Ness. "To the north lies the Cobra Mist site," he said. "It was built by the Americans to test a new radar system in the late 1960s. Unfortunately it didn't work very well and the experiment was shut down. After that the BBC World Service was transmitted from there until 2011. To the south the First World War airfields are now flooded and protected for wading birds.

"You'll be able to see AWRE pagodas in the distance, but they're closed for safety. They used to try to make detonators blow up by subjecting them to vibration tests. They wanted to make sure the bombs wouldn't explode inside the aircraft that carried them.

"If you follow the red route you'll reach some buildings used in the two World Wars, one of which is our information building. Inside you'll find a nuclear bomb." He paused for dramatic effect. "Rest assured, it's just the casing. Farther along this route is the Bomb Ballistics Building. This contained the instruments used to measure the bomb tests that were carried out here. And that brings me to the most important point. Please keep to the paths. The site has never been completely cleared of ordnance, so we don't know how much explosive is out there. And that's the curious thing about this place. It was so secretive that we'll never understand exactly what went on here. Enjoy your day and make sure you're back here in good time for the last ferry."

The walkers began to disperse. Abi and Alex walked slowly, allowing the other visitors to get ahead. Following the path marked with occasional red arrows – painted on the roadways or on lumps of concrete – they walked for thirty minutes before they reached the first set of buildings on the island. Alex had become absorbed by the site, enjoying the juxtaposition of the destructive military history and the thriving natural spectacle of the wildlife reserve. Eventually they found themselves among some single-storey brick buildings. Scattered nearby were piles of debris; steel and masonry. The guidebook described the place as the remains of a First World War hangar, but it was almost impossible to imagine what the building must have looked like. A rusty fuel pump stood on a stretch of cracked and overgrown concrete.

"This place is extraordinary," he said. "I'll have to bring my camera next time."

"You haven't asked why I brought you here," said Abi. There was tension in her voice.

"You said we should have a day out."

"Because we need to talk."

"To clear the air."

"Yes."

"I'm sorry for upsetting you, Abi."

Abi shook her head. "Don't apologise. I'm the one who's sorry."

"You don't have anything to be sorry for."

She reached forward, taking hold of his hands. "I do. I really do."

He held her stare for a moment. "What do you mean?"

"I've been keeping something from you."

"I don't understand."

"I brought you here for a reason. Not everything about this place is in the guidebook." Abi hesitated. "When I realised how serious you were about finding out what happened to your parents, I knew I couldn't hide the truth from you any more."

"What truth?" Alex pulled his arms away. "Do *you* know what happened to them?"

"No – well, not exactly. I genuinely don't know whether the crash was an accident or not. But I do know why the police were told not to investigate."

"Are you serious?" he demanded. "When were you going to tell me? What's going on?"

She continued, uneasy. "The policeman was right. The Government *did* cover up the crash because of your parents' work. The work they did *here*."

"Here? No one's worked here since the Cold War."

"That's not true. This is still an active MOD site."

Alex stared at her wide-eyed.

"Your parents were based here. They were conducting highly advanced genetic experimentation for the Government."

Alex shook his head. "This is crazy."

"It's true. Beneath these buildings is an underground laboratory. It was established in 1963 – ten years after Watson and Crick described the structure of DNA. The Government of the day wanted to be at the forefront of genetic engineering. The site is still being used. Its name is Station Helix."

2

Alex wondered whether Abi was trying to play a practical joke. What she'd said seemed so absurd that he almost reprimanded her for fooling him, but the absence of humour in her expression made him reconsider. She wasn't the sort to employ tasteless pranks on her friends. But, if what she'd said were true, it meant Alex didn't know her at all.

"Station Helix?" Alex repeated, not knowing what to say.

"After Watson and Crick's discovery," she replied. "And a sentimental nod to Bletchley Park."

Alex knew she referred to the top secret code-breaking facility in Buckinghamshire – known as Station X – where the Nazi Enigma and Lorenz machines were deciphered during the Second World War. "I'm supposed to believe there's an underground facility here?"

"Look around you. This is the perfect place for secrecy."

"But it's open to the public."

"Only on a handful of days each year."

"But surely people would know?"

She shook her head. "No one knew what was going on here for decades – even when hundreds of military personnel were based here. They still don't. It's convenient for the Government to let people think this is just a nature reserve and a crumbling monument to bygone eras, but it's strictly controlled. The National Trust is required to adhere to MOD rules, and that includes employing staff approved by Whitehall. All of the wardens are MOD personnel."

"And the volunteers?"

"Don't get carried away. They're local people who enjoy sharing their knowledge with visitors. But their knowledge is incomplete."

"So how do you know about this?"

Abi hesitated before replying. "I'm MOD."

"You work in the village pub and shop."

"It's – *it was* – suitable cover for my assignment."

"What assignment?"

"Let's go and sit down somewhere."

"I'm fine right here."

"I'm not." Abi's throat was dry. "By telling you this I'm breaching national security and will probably get prosecuted for treason. But I couldn't hide it from you any longer. You deserve to know the truth."

"The truth about your assignment? What was that *exactly*?"

"To observe."

"My parents?"

"No." Abi paused again. She felt like she was about to open Pandora's Box. She looked intently at Alex, fixing her gaze upon him with forlorn eyes. "I had to observe *you*."

3

Alex stared. He'd known Abigail Jones for nearly half his life but the woman in front of him was a stranger. The turmoil her words inflicted wrenched him back to the night of the crash. He felt disoriented once again – confused and angry in equal measure. He looked blankly at her, unable to process the information in a meaningful way. He couldn't speak.

Abi touched his arm and broke the silence. "Let's walk," she suggested gently. "I'll tell you what I know." She paused as they continued along the roadway. "I won't be able to explain everything. I'm not a scientist."

"But you have a good idea what was – *is* – going on here?"

"Alex, I'm going to tell you something that'll be hard for you to hear."

"About why you were sent to watch me?"

"Yes, but let me put everything in context first. I'll try to explain this as best I can."

"You have a lot of explaining to do."

Abi ignored the remark and indicated along the roadway. "Let's head to the Bomb Ballistics Building. You can see more of the site from there."

Alex nodded but didn't reply.

They continued walking and remained silent. The road took them to a modern steel bridge which crossed a creek and led them onto the shingle bank. Here the road became a track and the pebbles made walking more strenuous. Painted arrows on concrete blocks marked the route. An ominous sign warned them to keep to the trail to avoid unexploded ordnance. They continued their trek without speaking until they reached the next building. It was brick-built and had an external steel staircase which on any other building would have been a fire escape. Abi glanced inside the open doorway halfway up the steps to satisfy herself they were alone. She led Alex to the roof. They found themselves on a platform with a good view of the shingle bank. A lighthouse stood on the shoreline about a quarter of a mile to the southeast. The Cobra Mist building was a mile to the north.

Alex felt that the wide expanse of shingle, scarred by countless bomb tests, was an appropriate setting for his mood. He leaned against the railing and stared at the Cold War pagodas in the distance. "Tell me," he said.

Abi stood next to him, her hands gripping the railing. "Station Helix," she murmured. "Genetic experimentation. The project was set up to see whether humans' genetic structure could be altered in some way that might have a military application."

"What does that mean?"

"You already understand the principle of medical genetics, don't you?"

"Loosely – it's about replacing faulty genes with synthetic alternatives, or finding ways to switch them off."

"Yes. Well that principle is similar here. Only it's not about repairing faulty people in the medical sense. It's about enhancing healthy people by implanting desirable genetic traits."

"A kind of selective breeding?"

"Sort of. But it's not just about making someone more intelligent or less susceptible to disease. They're way beyond that here. Imagine being able to make someone's body more resistant to cellular decay from radiation, or able to store and process oxygen more efficiently. Think of how that could benefit soldiers in war zones. And that's just the tip of the iceberg."

"My father's MOD report… *that* referred to radiation sensitivity."

"I assume that was one of the projects he worked on. I don't know."

"How is this possible?"

"If you think about it, it isn't such a wild idea. They've been mapping the genetic code for years, and gene therapy isn't new science any more. Publicly the focus has been on medicine. Privately the same technology has been developed for strategic reasons. The Helix scientists take characteristics from the natural world and figure out how to apply them to humans."

"Such as resistance to cell decay."

Abi nodded. "Everything in nature is essentially made from the same building blocks, but variation exists because of how those blocks are arranged. Every living thing – whether plant, animal or bacterium – shares a common ancestor. We can measure how closely related we are by studying the DNA patterns. If you know what each piece of genetic code does, you can build your own model."

"So – theoretically – you can take a genetic trait from one animal and give it to another?"

"Yes, but it's not a theory. It's real. In the States you've been able to buy genetically engineered fluorescent fish for over a decade. The developers took genetic traits from jellyfish and corals and added them to ordinary fish. But here we're way beyond pretty pets."

"Are you saying they've actually modified humans?"

Abi nodded.

"And this is what my parents worked on?"

"Yes," she replied.

"How long has this been going on?"

"The laboratory was established in the sixties to work on the theory, but the first EHBs weren't designed for many years after that."

"EHBs?"

"Enhanced Human Beings."

Alex drew breath. "This is crazy."

"They said that in the sixteenth century when Copernicus claimed the Earth wasn't the centre of the universe."

"I understand the need for secrecy about my parents' work. Was that the reason the crash investigation was blocked?"

"Partly. But it wasn't just about your parents."

"You mean it was about me? Because I'm the son of Government scientists?"

"Not exactly."

"Then why?"

"Did you ever consider why your leg repaired itself so quickly?"

Alex stared at her. He suddenly felt sick. "What are you saying?"

"I told you this wouldn't be easy to come to terms with, Alex. You're not just the son of Government geneticists. You're one of their experiments."

4

The chill Alex experienced at that moment reminded him of stories about cold spots in haunted rooms. In an instant he became detached from the warmth and brightness of the day. The vast shingle bank of Orford Ness seemed vaster still, increasing and emphasising his isolation from the life he'd known. He moved away from Abi and stared at the lighthouse in silence, gripping the handrail tightly. Neither of them said a word for several minutes. Abi waited patiently, watching Alex watching the sea and sky. Eventually she joined him. She decided against placing her hand on his arm as a gesture of comfort.

"My life has been a fabrication, hasn't it?" he asked softly, the words barely audible.

She responded quickly. "Your life has been everything you've made it."

"No it hasn't. It's been engineered for someone else's purpose."

"So what?" Abi snapped. "What do you want me to say? Do you want me to agree with you? To encourage you to wallow in self-pity? Well I won't. You're an individual and you're part of something special. Don't go all 'woe is me' on me. You're better than that."

Alex was taken aback by her directness. "Are you saying I should be *grateful*?"

"So you'd prefer to have someone else's life now? Born

to a drug addict mother on a shithole council estate maybe?"

"That's not what I meant."

"Then what did you mean?"

"I..." Alex hesitated. "This is just so much to take in. Has my life been influenced because of the choices I've made or by what I am?"

When Abi spoke again her tone was softer. "That's the question everyone asks themselves. Life isn't equal for everyone. Background, education, health... they affect everybody. You have to take what you're given and make the best of it."

"How do I make the best of what you've just told me?"

She looked intently at him. "By accepting it."

"You think it's that simple?"

"It has to be."

He looked away. "So what did they do to me?"

"I have no idea."

"But you were sent to watch me."

"I told you I'm not a scientist. My role was to monitor you and report anything important back to the Government."

"Such as?"

"I didn't have much to report."

"Well what were you looking for?"

"Illnesses or failure to integrate socially mostly."

He shook his head. "I see. So am I considered to be a successful experiment?" His tone held a note of sarcasm.

"Not entirely. They wanted you to become a scientist so you could contribute to future research. But the MOD can only manipulate things so far without it becoming obvious."

"That's why my parents pushed me towards biology."

"Yes."

"The Government must be very disappointed in me."

Abi shrugged. "Your career choice is not a priority for them. The fact you've grown up to be a healthy sportsman with a keen intellect is what counts." She paused briefly. "I doubt they anticipated you'd be so bloody-minded though."

Alex allowed himself a half-smile. "There must still be some pieces of the genetic code yet to be deciphered."

"Looks that way," Abi replied.

Alex turned around and leaned back against the rail. "Is Michael Hearn part of this?"

"He's a supervisor here."

"Does he know who you are?"

"We never met before the funeral."

"Why did he agree to speak to me?"

"To reinforce the cover story. Your parents *did* work at the Ipswich faculty on occasion. The documents he selected were supposed to distract you, but you spotted something."

"The MOD reference?"

"Yes. Like you said, no one reads the citations. Hearn didn't think to check the papers that carefully. Other than that single reference to your father's MOD paper the documents didn't contain anything of use to you."

"But I found the reference." Alex paused. "I suppose that's gone in your latest update."

"I haven't said anything yet. Somehow I don't think there'll be any more reports." She sighed deeply. "I don't know what's going to happen, Alex, but I had to tell you the truth. We've been…" She hesitated.

Alex knew what she'd intended to say. "Friends?"

"I reckon you don't agree with that any longer, do you?"

He looked at her for a while before replying. "I'm not sure what to think. Did you move into the cottage so you could monitor me more closely?"

She nodded then looked away, ashamed. "I manipulated you. I invented the story about my landlord upping the rent. I'm so sorry. But being friends with you wasn't an invention. I always really liked you and your parents. It was awful when they died and you were hurt."

"I don't know if I can believe you."

"I understand, but if you didn't mean something to me we wouldn't be having this conversation. After that policeman told you about the crash, I realised I'd be faced with a dilemma."

"To stay loyal to your employers or to tell me the truth?"

"Yes. The more I thought about it the more I knew that being honest with you was my only choice."

"I'm glad you told me."

"I'll start packing my things when we get home."

"Why?"

Abi looked startled. "I don't suppose you'll ever want to speak to me again."

"I guess there's one thing about me that you didn't observe," Alex said. "When I become a friend, I'm a friend for life. I know we have to rebuild our trust, Abi, but you were there for me after my parents died. You kept me going during a very difficult time. Now you have another choice to make. Hold on to this friendship or walk away from it."

Abi found it difficult to speak. "I don't know what to

say."

Alex smiled. "Remember what you said earlier? You have to take what you're given and make the best of it. We'll be okay."

5

They left the Bomb Ballistics Building and followed the trail across the broad expanse of shingle towards the lighthouse. Pieces of concrete and metal were strewn across the landscape. They spotted a heavily-rusted shell casing just yards from the path. Its metal was torn and twisted where it had exploded decades ago. They saw the foundations of unidentifiable buildings which had been demolished, their purposes forgotten. The site was a peculiar wilderness, touched by the inventions and ingenuity of mankind but gradually being reclaimed by nature. The harsh cry of a gull passing overhead emphasised the Ness's remoteness.

Alex found himself experiencing emotions which seemed incompatible with one another. His thoughts took him back to the hospital room and the moment his uncle told him his parents were dead. Grief, bewilderment and anger vied for his attention and he didn't know which reaction deserved primacy. He thought about how he'd reacted when Abi had told him of his connection to Station Helix. The sickening feeling had been instinctive, completely beyond his control. He understood it was a natural stress reaction – he'd learned how to use stress positively when competing – but allowing its negative aspect to affect him caused him some embarrassment. He found himself wondering why the scientists hadn't found a way of removing that evolutionary defect from his body. His inner voice reminded him that it wasn't a defect but a survival mechanism. In a moment of clarity he realised that the principle response he was experiencing wasn't distress or infuriation but curiosity.

He pressed Abi for more information but there was very little she could tell him. She hadn't seen inside the Station Helix laboratory. Understanding what went on there wasn't her role. She described the little she knew. The staff didn't access the site from Orford because – unsurprisingly – such activity would have been obvious to the locals. Using the map they'd been given by the National Trust volunteer she showed him that an offshoot of the River Alde passed behind the buildings. The staff were brought by boat directly to the site of the laboratory, their route almost unnoticeable due to the cover from nearby Havergate Island.

They spent another two hours walking around the site. From the lighthouse they went onto the beach and headed southwest for a quarter of a mile. They reached a timber lookout tower – to which warning notices about climbing the structure were attached – and re-joined the footpath. Farther along they encountered an octagonal building called Black Beacon. Its shape and black wooden panelling made it stand out from the other buildings on the site, even though the entire collection was seemingly random and unmatched. From there they continued north, finally re-joining the path which traversed the steel bridge they'd crossed earlier.

As they headed back they spoke about matters unconnected with the site, but Alex's curiosity returned when they reached the buildings standing above Station Helix. He searched for clues of current activity but found none. It was with disappointment and reluctance that he accepted Abi's direction to return to the jetty and end their tour of the site. Orford Ness had captured his imagination – even without the revelation about the secret laboratory – and they'd only visited the central part of the accessible site.

After a short wait the ferry returned to collect them and half a dozen other visitors. They boarded the craft and were soon on their way back to Orford's quayside. They didn't speak during the short crossing. The return to the mainland seemed more profound than simply the end of a tour. Alex didn't know what to do next. He couldn't step off the boat and return to the life he knew. The River Alde might as well have been the Rubicon.

The skipper tied the boat to its mooring and thanked everyone for visiting. The group disembarked cautiously and climbed the concrete steps up to the quayside. Alex and Abi were the last to leave the boat. They noticed a large silver Lexus parked nearby. Two burly men stood beside it. They wore grey suits and Ray-Bans.

They stepped forward to intercept. "Miss Jones, Mr Hannay," said one. He didn't extend his hand when greeting them and his voice was emotionless. "We're with the Ministry of Defence. Please get into the car."

6

The glance that Abi and Alex shared at that moment confirmed they both understood they had to obey the instruction. Her expression told him she'd resigned herself to accepting the consequences of her actions. For a second Alex wondered if they could outrun the MOD men, but he dismissed the idea almost instantaneously. There was probably another team where Abi's Volkswagen was parked. Alex had wanted to speak to someone in the Ministry; he just hadn't anticipated it would be so soon and under these circumstances. They had no option. He resolved to protect Abi as best as he could, but he had no idea what they would face and how he could look after her.

"Where are you taking us?" she asked. Her voice was quiet.

"To London, Miss Jones," the man replied. He opened the rear door and indicated for her to enter. She did so and Alex climbed in after her. The man closed the door and got into the driver's seat. His companion waited a moment and then also entered the car.

"Where in London?" said Abi.

"To the office of your employer," the driver replied, pressing a switch. The door locks clunked. He drove slowly from the dock towards the village.

Alex needed to show solidarity with his friend. "Why are we going there?" he asked, realising the question was weak.

"I can't answer that, Mr Hannay," the man replied. "My colleague and I were sent to collect you. The reason why is no concern of ours."

"But you must know something." Alex knew he was talking for the sake of it.

"Even if I did, Mr Hannay, I wouldn't discuss anything with you."

"So you're just following orders?"

The man ignored the remark and continued driving. Abi placed her hand on Alex's arm to attract his attention. She didn't speak but the slight shake of her head told him that trying to provoke their captors was unwise and utterly pointless. He nodded slightly to acknowledge her. They hadn't been threatened and, despite the lack of conviction in the man's words, he'd spoken to them politely. Alex leaned back in the seat and tried to anticipate what would happen to them in London.

7

The drive to London passed without incident or conversation. Neither Abi nor Alex felt inclined to discuss anything. Talking about their current predicament seemed wrong in the company of their escorts, and talking about ordinary matters would have felt similarly awkward. With begrudging respect Alex recognised the skill of the driver whose flawless control suggested he'd received advanced police training. But he was in no mood to compliment the man and kept his thoughts to himself.

After passing through the Suffolk villages they took the A12 trunk road through Essex and followed it all the way into London. Less than two hours since being intercepted on the quayside at Orford they found themselves passing the neoclassical architecture of various Government buildings built upon the site of the Palace of Whitehall. The car passed under the elegant Admiralty Arch and pulled in immediately into a small drop-off area.

The driver's colleague turned to face them and spoke for the first time. "We're here," he stated. "Please follow me." He exited the car and held the rear door open as Abi and Alex obeyed.

They faced a grand four-storeyed building of grey and red stone. A bronze statue of the eighteenth century naval captain and explorer James Cook stood nearby. The MOD escort motioned them towards a doorway where a slim man with cropped grey hair waited. His straight back and aquiline features gave him an air of authority. He looked intently at them with sharp eyes, his gaze flicking between them. He nodded at Abi in recognition. Alex took an instant dislike to him. The man's mien revealed distrust and suspicion. Suddenly his expression relaxed a little. He handed over plastic-covered identity badges.

"Please put these on," he said. "My name is Stephen Jennings. Welcome to the Ministry of Defence. Please come this way."

8

Jennings strode purposefully along the Ministry building's corridors. Abi, with her shorter stature, found herself hurrying after him at an awkward pace. Jennings glanced back occasionally to check they were keeping up but he didn't slow down. Alex glanced at the high ceilings and wooden panelling that characterised the building's interior and wondered what happened within the dozens of offices they passed. He already knew that the estate extended southwards to the famous Horse Guards Parade, but he couldn't estimate its scale.

They were taken to a doorway which looked no different from those they had hurried past. Jennings knocked and waited. A female voice invited them to enter. Jennings opened the door and held it open for them. It was a courtesy but he made it look like he found it distasteful. He followed them into the room. Sunlight coming through the two tall windows was diffused by net curtains, softening the light inside. A hardwood desk stood in front of the windows. An old-fashioned brass reading lamp with a green shade stood at one end of the desk in contrast to the LED computer monitor which occupied the middle. Three chairs with luxurious red leather upholstery were positioned around the desk. But it was the woman who stood in the centre of the room who grabbed their attention most forcefully.

Her attire was tailored and impeccably smart. Over a white blouse she wore an elegant dark blue trouser suit. She was about five foot eight but looked taller because of the raised heels on her shoes. Her dark red hair was tied into a loose ponytail, the style revealing her face completely. She was beautiful and looked younger than her forty-five years, her demeanour professional. Abi had met her once before but hadn't spoken to her at length.

The woman smiled at Alex as she shook his hand. "I'm Charlotte Black," she said. "I reckon we have a lot to talk about."

9

"Forgive the arrangements I had to put in place to bring you here," Black began. "I'm afraid, Abigail, that you rather forced my hand." Abi ignored the comment. "When you were recognised on the security cameras at Orford Ness…"

"You mean Station Helix?" interrupted Alex. "Who exactly are you?"

Black held Alex's stare for a moment before replying. "I'm the person who decides how much to tell Government ministers about the research there. You, Mr Hannay, know more about Helix than some members of the Cabinet."

"And what do you think I know?"

"Well that's a good question," she replied. "I have to consider my response according to whether I think you know too much or not enough."

"What are you talking about?"

"I have to make a decision on what to do with you. Do I send you home and ask you nicely to keep quiet, or do I indulge that curiosity of yours and disclose national secrets?"

Alex frowned. She'd presented two unexpected choices and her tone told him that no alternatives would be considered. The decision she made would be heavily conditional. He realised that she'd prepared for this conversation, probably from the moment Abi had reported Lucas Ingwe's interest in the crash. He was being manipulated and found the lack of control unnerving. It was the same sense of irritation he experienced during fencing lessons when he wasn't on form. He'd mistime parries, his footwork felt heavy and his point placement was inaccurate. But poor training sessions could be remedied by taking a break and focussing on something else. Now he didn't have the ability to take charge of the situation. Charlotte Black had absolute control.

He decided to change the subject. "What are you going to do with Abi?"

Black sat down on the corner of her desk. Her smile revealed she'd anticipated this question too. "I'm intrigued by your loyalty towards the person who deceived you for so many years."

"She didn't deceive me – she had a job to do. Our friendship is intact."

"So what happens to Abigail remains of concern to you?"

"Yes."

"You understand she's broken with protocol?"

"She told me the truth."

Black smiled, her blue eyes sparkling. To Alex's chagrin she was enjoying the conversation. She spoke again. "Presumably you don't want me to prosecute her for treason?"

"Of course not."

"So are you asking me to disregard her indiscretion?"

"Yes."

"What are you prepared to give me in return?"

"What do you want?" Alex felt himself being cornered. "I want you to understand this isn't a barter in a

Moroccan souk. You aren't negotiating with me, you're merely hoping my decisions are favourable to you."

"Then why did you ask the question?"

"So I could gain a clearer perspective on your personality and your sense of loyalty."

"What does your perspective tell you now?"

Charlotte smiled. "I like you." The remark threw Alex and he didn't know how to respond. He looked at her for a moment but she turned to Abi. "What do you think I should do, Abigail?"

"I think you've already decided," Abi replied sullenly.

Charlotte glanced down at her fingernails momentarily before re-establishing eye contact. "On some matters, yes. I can see there's no point in trying to deconstruct the alliance you two have. You've decided to trust each other in spite of – or perhaps because of – the past. I admire that depth of loyalty, but I still have the breach of security to consider. You have to build that level of trust with *me*. And, because you're in this together, that means both of you." She stood and smoothed down her suit. "Is that acceptable to you?"

"You can't involve Alex in this," Abi blurted out. "He's not to blame for what I did."

"Oh he's involved already," Charlotte replied. "As for blame, that's hardly relevant now, is it? You're not in a position to make demands. You knew what would happen when you took Alex to Orford Ness. I'm giving you a second chance here, Abigail. Don't blow it."

Abi fell silent.

Black continued to speak, her words directed at them both. "I expect your co-operation."

Alex spoke again, defiant. "It wouldn't take much to leak the information. I don't see why we have to co-operate with you at all."

"Don't be naive. What would you do? Speak to a reporter? Post something online? We'd relocate Helix to the beta site and ridicule you as a conspiracy theorist." She leaned back on her desk. When she spoke again her tone was lighter. "You're mistaking me for your enemy. I'm not pretending we can end this conversation, walk away and forget everything. But we *can* work together. I can even keep Abigail's employment with the MOD intact and ensure her record remains unblemished. Your life has already changed, Alex. You *wanted* to know the truth. You just have to decide what to do with it. Are you going to fight me or be my ally?"

"Before I agree I want your promise that Abi will be okay," he replied.

"That's a good step."

"What do you mean?"

"By seeking my assurance you reveal that you're prepared to trust me. You know I could lie to you, but you believe I won't."

"That's an interesting analysis. Let me put it more plainly. Can I trust you?"

"That's for you to judge. You already know that loyalty is highly important to me."

"Well there's one way you can help me make a judgement."

Charlotte looked at him closely. "What's that?"

"Tell me everything you know about my parents' death."

10

"I agree with Detective Ingwe's assessment." Charlotte walked to one of the net-curtained windows, pulled the fabric to one side and turned her attention to whatever she could see outside the building. A moment later she let go of the curtain and turned back to face Alex. "His theory about Mason seems entirely plausible."

"Are you saying you don't *know* whether Mason killed my parents?"

"That's exactly what I'm saying. We didn't suspect foul play when we heard about the crash. There was nothing to suggest they hadn't been killed by a drunk driver."

"But you told the police not to investigate?"

"Correct. We were alerted when the car's registration number was checked at the scene. Vehicles owned by high level MOD staff are all tagged, so we get alerted if anything untoward happens. That's why the chief constable received a call in the middle of the night to be told we were taking over the investigation with immediate effect."

"But it wasn't an investigation, was it?" Alex retorted. "It was a whitewash."

Charlotte shrugged. "The point is we had the obvious suspect in custody. It was only when we discovered that your suspended police officer was digging around that we realised there was more to it."

"Is that why you threatened Francesca?"

"She was never going to get hurt."

"She was terrified."

"That was the idea," Charlotte responded coldly.

"You can't do that to decent people."

She looked at Alex intently. "I'm not asking for you to approve my methodology and I'm not going to justify my actions to you. The MOD has more important things to worry about than someone's hurt feelings."

"Are you going to leave them alone now?"

"Yes."

"What about Mason?"

"He presents a problem."

"What sort of problem?"

For the first time Charlotte seemed less self-assured. "We don't know where he is."

"Have you tried looking for him?"

"From the moment Abigail gave us his name. He's disappeared."

"What do you mean, *disappeared*?"

"He was using his bank cards here in London until very recently, but that activity stopped and the account was shut down. Normally we'd be able to find where the money went, but somehow he's covered his tracks. He doesn't own any property and the only family he has is a step-sister he hasn't spoken to in years. He usually rents accommodation or stays in hotels. His passport hasn't been used either. He's gone off-grid."

"How does that happen?"

"Put it this way – it's not something that a man of his limited resources could achieve on his own. He's had help from somewhere."

Abi looked up, her expression alert and questioning. "Is this connected to the prisoner's death?"

Black nodded. "I think so. There's been a development that you may not be aware of. The prison officer who found Gorski's body was shot by a sniper."

Abi looked incredulous. "*What?*"

"I checked his background. Someone gave him a substantial amount of money to pay off his gambling debts. *I* think the prison guard murdered Gorski and was then killed to tie up loose ends. These events were arranged to protect Mason."

"Was Mason told to kill Alex's parents?"

"I don't know that."

"But you do know something."

Charlotte nodded. "There was a connection between him and the Hannays."

Alex shifted in his chair, startled at the new information. "They *knew* each other?"

"Mason worked as a Government security contractor at Station Helix for a short time. Your father found out he'd leaked confidential information and reported him. We suspect the crash was simply a well-planned and merciless act of revenge."

Abi cursed. "The evil bastard."

Charlotte nodded in agreement. "That's why we've been trying to find him. Ironically we have Lucas Ingwe to thank for the information. If it hadn't been for him we'd never have made the connection." She paused. "Unfortunately we're at a disadvantage and trying to make up lost ground."

"How?" asked Abi.

"By keeping an eye on the people Mason sold the information to."

"Who are they?" questioned Alex.

"The Central Intelligence Agency."

11

Although the secrecy of recent events irritated Alex enormously because he was personally affected by it, in that moment he began to appreciate why Black had taken the measures to silence the police about the crash. Mentally he compared the pieces of information to the rusty shell fragments he'd seen strewn upon the pebbled landscape of Orford Ness. But it wasn't just Alex who'd been searching for fragments. He wondered how many metaphorical shell cases the CIA had collected since Mason had sold them information about the site.

When Abi spoke it was clear she'd been thinking the same. "How much does the CIA know about Helix?" she asked.

"That's difficult to judge," replied Charlotte. "It's unlikely Mason told them a great deal because he didn't have access to the labs and the data."

"It bothers me that he's resurfaced now and the CIA's protecting him."

Charlotte nodded. "It's an unanswered question."

"Is it definitely the CIA?" asked Alex. "It sounds like there's no evidence of that connection yet."

"That's true but I can't ignore the *earlier* connection," Charlotte replied.

"Why are you telling us this?" Abi asked.

"Because you're deeply involved," she replied without

a moment's hesitation. "I want you to understand how complicated this has become."

"What happens next?"

"I'm going to arrange a visit to Station Helix for you. If Alex is joining my team, I think he should have a look at the facility, don't you?" Abi didn't reply. "There is something else prior to that, though," Black added. "I require you both to sign paperwork regarding the Official Secrets Acts." She turned her attention to Jennings who had stood silently by the door throughout their discussion. "Stephen, would you find the necessary documents? Thank you." Jennings nodded and left the room. "One more thing, Abigail," she said. "I suggest you read what you're signing *this* time."

12

The two MOD men who had conveyed them to London from Orford were Alex and Abi's escorts once again for the return journey. This time the friends didn't feel the need to maintain their guarded silence. While the meeting with Charlotte Black had been unsettling, they'd left her office in a completely different capacity from when they'd walked in. They had no doubt that Black had discussed only a fraction of what she knew, but she'd confided in them, and that had given them both a sense of security. Alex had wanted to ask more questions, but Charlotte had drawn the meeting to a close on her terms.

"I think I've just been recruited," he said as the Lexus pulled into London's evening traffic.

"Yes, but as what?"

"That's the point. I have no idea."

"I'm amazed I still have a job."

"What exactly is your job now? You're in the same position as me. You don't need to monitor me any longer and try to prevent me from learning Government secrets." Alex grinned at her. It intrigued him how, in the space of a few hours, his anger at Abi's secrecy had evolved into amusement. He hoped it was a sign of their friendship's strength.

Abi shrugged. "Charlotte Black is the sort of person who only tells you what she wants you to hear. She has a plan for us but she isn't ready to reveal it."

"It bothers me that she doesn't *need* to do any of this. She could have shut us out completely."

"Perhaps she does need us."

"To take on the CIA? I'm confident that neither of us could offer anything in that respect."

"Maybe we'll learn more when we visit Station Helix."

Alex nodded. "I'm looking forward to that. Charlotte didn't tell me anything about *me*. Perhaps I'll find out when we go there."

"About what they did to you?"

"Exactly. I know I can heal from injuries quickly. I want to know how they achieved that."

Abi shifted round in her seat to face him. "Anything else?"

"What d'you mean?"

"You haven't spoken about your parents since we were on the Ness."

Alex held her look for a moment before replying. "The events of the day took over."

"Don't avoid the issue. You have another adjustment to make. They kept a secret from you that has, quite literally, altered your life."

"I can always rely on you to get straight to the point, can't I, Abi? You're right – this is something I'm going to have to think hard about. But at least I'm beginning to learn what happened. I'm not guessing in the dark any more."

Abi leaned back in the seat and closed her eyes. "I'm glad you're being objective." Another thought occurred to her and she turned back to him. "But can you be objective about everything? Mason's still out there."

Alex felt a chill down his spine.

SEVEN

1

As he left the British Embassy via a discreet exit, David Stone was instantly struck by Cairo's midday heat. The temperature wasn't uncomfortable for him – he'd worked here for four years and become acclimatised – but he nonetheless preferred the days when a breeze blew in from the Nile. Today the air was breathless and filled with the endless cacophony of car horns, characterising the modern aspects of the ancient city. He wore a white shirt and striped tie under a dark blue suit. Junior diplomats always dressed smartly whether the occasion demanded it or not. Ties were obligatory regardless of the temperature. Stone accepted and enjoyed the Englishness of steadfastly wearing utterly pointless neckwear.

He spotted his driver Maget Mahfouz standing in the shade of the building. "Maget!" he called out. "Izzayak?"

"Kullu kwayyis, al hamdulillah. Wa inta, Mr Stone?"

"Good thanks." They slapped their hands together in a loose handshake. "Is the car ready? I need to check out the conference centre again before the Prime Minister's visit."

"Yes it is ready. You want to go now?"

Stone nodded. "Apparently there's a problem with the catering. It's probably nothing serious, but I want to make sure."

"Mafeesh moshkila." Mahfouz fished the car keys from his jacket pocket and the two men walked towards a black

Mercedes. "Tomorrow is my daughter's birthday," the Egyptian stated proudly. He aimed the key fob at the car and unlocked the doors.

"That's great. How old is Halima now?"

"Six years old." Mahfouz held open the rear door and waited as Stone entered the vehicle. He got into the driver's seat and started the engine. "Her English is very good, but I want her to have an English teacher."

"I'm happy to help, Maget."

"Shukran, Mr Stone."

"Afwan."

Stone's fascination with the city hadn't lessened in all the time he'd been here. Every journey through the energetic chaos of Cairo intrigued him more than the last. Their conversation continued as Maget navigated through the seemingly endless maze of roads that criss-crossed the ancient city. The Egyptian had lived his entire life here and knew Cairo in minute detail, but Stone wondered whether a single lifetime was long enough to acquire the local knowledge his driver possessed. Mahfouz negotiated the bustling streets and picked the best routes with his customary expertise. The aroma of spices blended with diesel fumes.

The two men had become good friends since Stone's arrival at the Embassy. Stone had been a guest at his friend's house on several occasions and knew Maget's family. He appreciated the man's extraordinary generosity and hospitality. It was a typical characteristic of the Egyptian host, but he was always overwhelmed by the man's grace. Being in his company was good for his linguistic skills too. The Englishman had a knack of learning new languages incredibly quickly from books and recordings, but picking up local dialects and figures of speech could only be done in the company of a native speaker. In return he'd helped the Egyptian improve his already very proficient English and given English books to his children. He'd only feigned ignorance about Halima's birthday. He'd already bought her present and was looking forward to surprising her with it.

Their route to the conference centre was approximately eight kilometres, but the relatively short distance seemed longer in Cairo's crowded streets. Progress was typically much slower than it would have been on the desert roads outside the city, despite the frenetic pace set by many Cairene drivers. Stone had concluded that coping with the traffic required both alertness (to keep track of the swirling chaos), and numbness (to avoid thinking about it too much).

Mahfouz glanced at the rear view mirror as a white Hyundai accelerated towards them. The car bore the black and white checked body stripes and yellow roof sign of a taxi. The Egyptian frowned. Stone noticed his colleague's expression in the mirror. "What is it, Maget?"

"The taxi behind us," Mahfouz replied. "Something's wrong."

Stone turned around and looked through the rear window. Nothing struck him as unusual. "What do you mean?"

"Driving too fast. Two men in the front. Passengers sit in the back, Mr Stone."

The taxi veered out and accelerated, pulling alongside the Mercedes. The passenger raised a Misr assault rifle and fired a volley of shots through the open window. Rounds tore noisily into the Mercedes, smashing the glass and puncturing the doors. A bullet sliced through Stone's neck, ruining his carotid artery. Blood soaked his shirt and jacket as more bullets pierced his body. Mahfouz was slain a second later. He slumped forward against the steering wheel causing the car to swerve so sharply that it overturned and slid noisily to a stop. The gunman emptied the magazine as his companion dropped to third gear with a boost change and accelerated rapidly past the ruined diplomatic car.

2

Archimedes Falkner was alone in the office of his Kensington apartment when the telephone on his desk rang. The ring volume was low. He despised unnecessary noise. He picked up the handset and didn't say anything. A voice spoke briefly. Falkner didn't reply. He replaced the handset. His encrypted e-mail account was open on his computer and he clicked the button for composing a new message. He populated the recipient field with three names from his contact list: Arnold Rossington, Benjamin Barnard and Edward Rhodes. He lifted the glass that stood beside his computer's keyboard, took a mouthful of fruit juice and then set down the glass. He typed the shortest message he'd ever written.

IT'S BEGUN.

3

The remnants of a dawn mist lingered as the launch made progress northwards along the River Alde. Alex and Abi had boarded the MOD craft with Charlotte Black and Stephen Jennings at a remote quayside south of Orford Ness. The jetty was on a private estate. Alex had always believed that the manor house and grounds – which hosted weddings and business events – was owned by a private family. It hadn't surprised him when Abi revealed that the site actually belonged to the Government. It provided a discreet boarding location for the Station Helix workers. From the jetty it took about half an hour to reach the research site when the weather was mild.

The craft passed the Suffolk coastline – characterised by shingle beaches rising barely a few feet above sea level in most places – and soon they saw the tip of the Ness on the starboard side of the boat. It was here the river finally reached the North Sea after being trapped by the miles-long shingle spit. The view changed as the curve of the river guided them northeast. Mudflats and marshland dominated the coastline. It was a place of stark and peaceful beauty where seabirds thrived and few people ventured. Trapped in the strange geography of the river was the rarely accessed wildlife reserve of Havergate Island. It stood between the narrowest reaches of Orford Ness and the coastline, shielding the MOD boat from view.

Approaching the Station Helix jetty from this direction gave Alex a new perspective of the site. This section of the Ness was out of view from the footpaths which Abi and he had followed during their recent visit. He felt the same sense of curiosity as before. Then he'd been intrigued by Orford Ness's extraordinary past; now he was finding out about its secret present. Despite the circumstances which had led him here he felt privileged at being given access to the MOD site.

He turned to Black. "Charlotte?"

"Yes, Alex?" She raised her voice to be heard over the engine noise.

"I want to know how I fit into all of this."

"That's why you're here." She turned her face back into the breeze.

The boat entered a narrow tributary and Alex noticed some single-storey buildings near the bank. They looked like the First and Second World War buildings he'd seen before but he couldn't be sure if they were the same ones. The pitch of the boat's engine dropped suddenly as the pilot reduced power and slowed the craft. The boat manoeuvred neatly alongside a floating jetty. A crewman stepped onto the pontoon and tied the craft to its mooring. A framework of metal steps with a handrail was attached to a sturdy wooden post providing continual access to the pontoon, regardless of the tide's height. Alex spotted Michael Hearn walking towards them as he ascended the steps.

"Welcome to Station Helix," Hearn said. The greeting was meant for all of them but his attention was focussed on Alex. He extended his hand and Alex shook it. "I regret not being able to tell you everything when we spoke at the faculty," he said apologetically. "The secrecy of this place requires careful protection."

"I understand," Alex replied.

"I gather you spotted something I missed," said Hearn with a wry smile.

"The MOD reference? I nearly missed it myself."

"At least you now have clearance. We'll be able to answer your questions more helpfully this time." Hearn gestured towards one of the brick buildings. "This way. This is one of the entrances to the facility."

The small building looked much like all the other dilapidated blocks on Orford Ness but it was apparent that the disrepair affected only the outside. Hearn pushed open a weathered wooden door and led them into a clean and functional reception room. A security guard stood up from behind a desk and handed out access cards on lanyards. A modern internal office door, with a vertical rectangle of glass near the handle, was positioned to the right of the desk. Hearn held his access card against a square scanner beside the doorframe. A solenoid clicked, releasing the lock. He pushed the door open.

Jennings didn't proceed with the group any farther, remaining in the reception area with the security guard. The others found themselves inside a narrow windowless passage with a concrete floor and breeze block walls. Small fluorescent lights, humming faintly inside translucent plastic casings, illuminated the space. A flight of twenty steps descended a few feet from the door. Tubular handrails were mounted on either side of the stairwell. Hearn led the way. At the bottom of the steps there was a floor space barely ten feet long. Another security door – which Hearn opened with his access card – stood at the end of the tiny corridor. "Here we are," he stated as he deactivated the door lock.

Alex was reminded of a hospital waiting area when he entered the next room. Behind white glass-panelled walls people wearing lab coats sat at computers or occupied themselves with technical equipment. Several doors, similar to the one at ground level, led to offices and laboratories. He noticed a plaque above the door which led to what looked like the largest laboratory in the facility. The sign read *Standard Wing*.

Hearn noticed Alex's puzzlement. "The name's a tribute to Alfred Russel Wallace," he explained. "Do you know about him?"

"He was Darwin's contemporary," Alex replied. "He developed the theory of evolution through natural selection independently of Darwin. But I don't understand the reference."

"The standardwing is bird of paradise which Wallace discovered during his expeditions in modern-day Indonesia. The birds' posturing behaviour contributed to his understanding of evolution. Station Helix doesn't have wings in the architectural sense, but those who established the facility decided to call this lab the Standard Wing in honour of Wallace."

Alex smiled, amused by the reference. "It's strange that Wallace doesn't have the same recognition as Darwin."

"I think that's beginning to change, but yes, you're right. The two men were from different social backgrounds. Darwin held a different status to Wallace but they had considerable mutual respect."

Charlotte Black interrupted the conversation. "Professor, shall we go to the meeting room? There are matters – other than history – to discuss."

"Yes, of course," he replied. He held open a door for them. Alex, Charlotte and Abi sat down. Hearn closed the door quietly and joined them. "Where would you like to start?"

Charlotte answered. "Tell him about his parents."

"Very well. Alex, I'm not sure what you've been told already, but there's something very important to clarify about your mum and dad."

Alex held the professor's gaze. "Michael, I've already deduced that they're not actually my real parents."

"No, Alex, that's my point," Hearn said hurriedly. "William and Sarah Hannay really *were* your biological parents."

For a moment Alex didn't know what to say. He glanced at Abi and could tell from her look that she was equally surprised. Charlotte's expression, by contrast, didn't give anything away. He turned back to Hearn. "Are you telling me the truth?"

"Absolutely. I can show you the DNA records. Your case is the first time Station Helix staff have been directly involved in raising one of the EHBs, but it seemed like an appropriate next step in the project."

"I'm not sure how I should feel right now."

"What do you mean?"

"I've found out that Mum and Dad really were my parents, but they allowed me to be part of the EHB programme. They were happy to experiment on me. I don't know what that tells me about them."

Hearn didn't reply, unsure how to deal with Alex's remark.

Charlotte touched his arm. "This is something you'll have to spend some time thinking about. Professor Hearn can only tell you the facts. The ethical question is arguably more complicated than the science."

Alex nodded. Her remarks – seemingly out of character – surprised him. It sounded as though she was being genuinely supportive. For a moment he wondered if she was putting on an act, but her expression didn't seem anything other than empathetic. Alex realised he'd just seen the human side of Charlotte Black.

"Alex would like to know exactly what the changes to his DNA amounted to," said Abi. "We know he's part of the EHB project, but how was he altered?"

Hearn seemed glad to be returned to a subject he was more comfortable with. "I won't try to blind you with science. The adjustments to the genetic code are, through necessity, relatively minor. It isn't possible to alter the code in drastic fashion."

"You mean to create a hybrid species?" asked Alex.

"That's right. We have to remember what evolution tells us. While all living things are comprised of the same building blocks, each one has made its own evolutionary pathway. Those blocks can't be rearranged at will to create something new or a cross between species. That's the whole point of natural selection. The vast majority of possible genetic sequences don't work or, at the very least, don't last. Evolution gets rid of the weak and unviable models. We couldn't – even if we wanted to – create something that is fifty percent human and fifty percent something else. Those ideas are the preserve of mythology."

"Doesn't that create a contradiction, though?" Alex asked. "If you can alter someone's DNA to a small degree, where's the limit? Why not alter it to a greater degree?"

"That's a good question. The limit isn't clear. Think of the problem as a computer. You can keep upgrading the hardware, the software and the operating system as new technology becomes available, but at some point incompatibility will cause a failure. Here at Helix we call this the Chimaera Conundrum. We know the model will break eventually but we can't predict exactly when. That's why this project has been going on for decades, taking only tiny incremental steps."

"Evolution again," said Alex.

"The comparison seems fair."

"So what adjustments were made to me?"

"You already know that you can heal fast. Your bone structure is also sturdier, so theoretically you're more resistant to physical trauma. It's possible you survived the crash because of that, but we can't be sure. You also have faster reflexes and more flexible muscles."

"Anything else?"

"Physically? No. But your intellect is partly due to genetic enhancement, although your parents were highly intelligent, so most of that probably rubbed off from them."

Alex was amused by Michael's non-scientific comment.

Charlotte looked at him. "Now you know."

"A little more than yesterday. But surely there has to be an end game with all of this?"

"Explain."

"Experiments require results, positive or negative."

"The results comes from observing you."

"That's it? Just watching how I progress through life?"

"Yes. As Professor Hearn said, the EHB programme is a long-term study. The scientists observe what works and what doesn't. The potential for this science is being evaluated all the time."

"But if the MOD's been involved from the start, the goal must be a military application."

"It is, but we don't need you to be a soldier to see that you can heal fast."

Alex decided it was time to change tack. "Charlotte, why did you bring me here? You could have kept all this from me. You said as much in London. What exactly do you want?"

Charlotte smiled. "I need your help."

"To do what?"

"To make contact with the others."

"The other EHBs?"

"Yes. There've been some developments and I've changed the parameters of the experiment. I want you to bring them in."

4

Charlotte leaned forward. "The first generation of EHBs was developed ten years before you were born. They were encouraged to pursue demanding careers where their genetic alterations would, theoretically, give them advantages. Until a few weeks ago the experiment was going well, but then a problem arose."

"What sort of problem?" asked Alex.

"One of them committed suicide."

"Because of the experiment?"

"Possibly. His body was recovered and tissue samples were taken. The scientists here found some evidence of DNA decay but they can't pinpoint an exact cause. It could be unrelated to the EHB programme."

Hearn interrupted. "We don't know if there was an error that took all this time to have an effect or if he got bitten by something nasty on holiday. There are a wide variety of toxins which cause DNA to break down."

"But you're leaning towards a problem caused by the Helix experiment?"

"At this time, yes, but we still have more samples to analyse."

Charlotte spoke again. "Alex, you're the only EHB who knows about Helix. That's why I want you to speak to the others. You'll be able to explain why they need to come in for tests. You can approach them and build up a dialogue.

If we get this wrong, details of the project could become public knowledge."

"What if they *do* have genetic defects? What if *I* have one?"

Hearn shifted awkwardly in his seat. "Alex, we have a high level of confidence about the Generation Twos. We'll take samples from you to be sure, but there was a ten year gap between the first subjects and yourself. There were considerable advances in that time."

"I'm sure the scientists who worked on the Generation Ones had the same level of confidence," Alex said. The sarcasm in his voice was apparent to everyone.

Hearn hesitated. "You're right, of course. In science it isn't possible to make perfect predictions all the time – that's why experiments are conducted. The problem with Jonathan Cline may be unique. Each subject was given different adjustments. We just want to be sure."

Alex made a decision. "I'll help you, Charlotte. These people deserve to know the truth. I'll need information about them before I start though."

"You'll have everything you need. Stephen will provide any resources you require." Charlotte turned to Abi. "Abigail, I want you to assist Alex. You'll have direct access to me and the MOD staff who've been watching the Generation Ones. Let's keep the interventions as low-key as possible. You know how this works."

Abi nodded.

Alex spoke again. "I'm still unclear on the specifics of the EHB programme. If I'm going to speak to the others, they'll have a lot of questions that I won't be able to answer."

Charlotte considered his words for a moment. "Michael, can you give Alex a crash course?"

"Yes… although I have a researcher here who's probably better at explaining things than me," Hearn replied. "I had intended asking her to show Alex the lab today anyway. Would that be in order?"

"Whom do you have in mind?"

"Zoe Sibon. She's a team leader."

"That's fine. She can give him a quick tour of the lab and tell him what he needs to know." Charlotte stood and walked towards the door. The others automatically followed her lead. They left the room and stood in the hallway.

Hearn pushed open the door to the Standard Wing laboratory. "Zoe?" he called out. An attractive woman in a white lab coat glanced up from a computer. She was about five four, middle thirties and had a mop of untidy dark brown hair. The interruption startled her, her child-like expression revealing her mistaken assumption she'd done something wrong. Hearn – familiar with Zoe's habit of being self-conscious – qualified his reason for calling her. "Nothing to worry about, Zoe. There's someone I want you to meet."

"Oh, no problem." Zoe relaxed, pressed some keys on her computer keyboard to log off and walked to the door.

Hearn introduced Alex. "Zoe, this is Alex Hannay."

She recognised the name and drew breath. They shook hands. "It's a pleasure to meet you. I knew your parents well. They were lovely. I was so upset when they…" She didn't finish the sentence, fearing her choice of words was insensitive.

"Thank you, Zoe."

"I'd like you to show Alex our lab," said Hearn. "You may answer all of his questions. He has MOD clearance."

"Right... okay," Zoe replied. "Let's get started." She pushed the laboratory door and held it open for him. He stepped inside, glancing at the equipment and researchers. For a moment he felt nervous. She noticed his hesitation. "Are you okay?"

He nodded. "I'm fine – it's just that I've been finding out so much so quickly. Now I'm finally here. My first visit to Station Helix."

"Well that's not quite true," she said. "You've been here before. You were just much too young to remember it."

5

It didn't take long for Alex to see why Michael had suggested Zoe as his guide. She had considerable enthusiasm for her work and was genuinely fascinated by science. She reminded him of his parents. She had the ability to summarise concepts in a way that made them seem less challenging. He could imagine her on television presenting science programmes. She had a warm and charming personality with a hint of endearing clumsiness. He couldn't help but like her.

She'd been explaining genetic code to him when they sat down at a workbench together. "Essentially all living things have the same component parts," she continued. "We just have them arranged differently. We have instructions contained within our cells. These dictate what hair colour we have, how we process food, how well we fight off viruses… you get the idea. Genetic engineering is about adding or removing some of those characteristics."

"But not just within humans though?" Alex inquired. "You're taking non-human traits from nature and adding them to human beings."

"It might be helpful to avoid 'human' and 'non-human' as labels."

"But isn't that exactly how it is? For example, I know my father was looking at resistance to radiation. That occurs in scorpions. If you're trying to add some scorpion to a human, you're creating a hybrid."

"Actually, radioresistance occurs widely in nature. Scorpions are more tolerant than humans for sure, but nowhere near as resistant as some bacteria. The point is, it can't be labelled as a scorpion characteristic. It's a genetic instruction that happens to work well in scorpions. If we can add that quality to a soldier, we're just tweaking his genetic make-up, not turning him into an arachnid."

"But the soldier is no longer fully human."

"Why not? You're assuming there are rigid parameters. It's not like that. Take two ordinary people. One is healthy and has 'good' genes, the other suffers cancer because of a hereditary genetic defect. Is the cancer victim less human than the other?"

"I see your point."

Zoe grinned. "I knew you would. Let's put it another way. Lowry paints an industrial scene and chooses a certain shade of brown. You see the same colour on a sparrow in your garden. Is it Lowry-brown or sparrow-brown?"

"I guess it's neither. It's just brown."

"Exactly. It's a combination of molecules that reflects a wavelength of light in a certain way. The context varies but the fundamental quality is the same. It's the same as a musical note played on different instruments."

Alex smiled. "Okay, I get the idea! You're saying genetic code is like a kid's set of building blocks. The same pieces can build a bridge or a tower."

"Yes. It just depends on how you arrange them. We have Darwin and Wallace to thank for making this knowledge accessible to us."

"They didn't know about genetics."

"No, but when they figured out how evolution worked, modern science was born. They didn't know about DNA, but they *still* got it right. They are what science is all about. They tested their theories for years – in Darwin's case for decades – before publishing their findings. They were remarkable."

"Not everyone believes in evolution though."

"It shouldn't require belief. It's simply a scientific fact. Some people choose to remain ignorant and pretend science isn't real. That's their problem. You can either take the time to learn about this planet or you can decide to ignore knowledge and believe in mythology."

"You sound like my parents."

"We had similar views."

"I can tell you got on well."

Zoe smiled. "Yes we did. I miss them."

Alex nodded. "Me too."

She placed her hand on his arm. "I'm sure it's hard to learn that you're part of this programme, but try to look at it as something revolutionary and exciting. We have an inherent desire to learn and better ourselves. It's why we stick our noses in books, point telescopes at the sky or try to eradicate malaria. You could say – as the dominant species on this planet – we have a responsibility to gain knowledge."

"You're doing a good job of convincing me, Zoe, but I can't ignore the fact that this is a military research facility."

"It doesn't mean that our work will be used exclusively in that context." She paused and looked into his eyes. "You think I'm being naive, don't you?"

"Perhaps a little."

"You might be right, but my intention is to use science in a positive way."

"Trust me, I don't doubt your motivation."

"I'm glad. Now, what else do you want to know?"

"Everything you can tell me about the Generation Ones."

6

"Who's first?" inquired Charlotte as she stepped from the pontoon into the boat.

"Are you sure I'm the best person for this?" Alex followed her into the craft and sat down beside Abi.

"We're past that. The decision has already been made. But, yes, I do think you're the best person."

"Do you want to qualify that observation?"

"I could give this task to anyone under my command, but for them it would just be another assignment."

"And for me?"

"It's personal." Charlotte paused. "You're uniquely placed to understand not only the nature of the programme but also what it means to be part of it. And there is one other consideration."

"What's that?"

"What would you say if I prevented you getting involved any further?"

Alex grinned. "I'd ask you to reconsider."

"You'd *pester* me until I backed down. Your curiosity brought you this far and it won't let you stop. You told Abigail as much when the policeman spoke to you. Your obstinacy featured in her reports."

Alex turned to Abi and gave her a mock frown. "Thanks!"

"Nothing I didn't tell you to your face," she replied with

a smile.

Charlotte raised her voice as the boat's diesel engine coughed into life. "Back to my original question. Who's first?"

"Lily Carter."

"Why?"

"She's in London. It makes sense to begin with the closest."

"Very well. I'll make sure you have her observer's details." Charlotte turned to Jennings. "Stephen, would you get one of the MOD apartments allocated to these two? I don't want a paper trail. Let's stay clear of hotels."

Jennings nodded, his icy gaze catching Alex's eye momentarily. Alex assumed the man must be supremely good at his job to compensate for his lack of people skills. Every stare was judgemental and untrusting. Alex turned back to Charlotte when she spoke again.

"Carter's a lot like you," she said.

"Really?"

"She's a rebel."

"You're saying *I'm* a rebel?"

"In terms of the EHB programme, yes, you are. You were supposed to pursue science and put that enhanced brain to good use."

"I see. What did you expect Carter to do?"

"Become a pilot in the RAF."

"But she didn't want to follow the career path the MOD tried to push her along? I can relate to that. What did she do instead?"

"She became a singer in a country-rock band."

"That's different."

Charlotte nodded. "Apparently she's rather good. Doesn't help Station Helix much though."

"You can't have everything."

"Try telling that to the British Government."

"You *are* the Government."

"Just a little corner of it. There are many people with considerably more power and influence than me."

"That doesn't seem to worry you."

Charlotte smiled. "The trick is understanding the rules of the game. That analogy should resonate with you."

Alex grinned as the launch motored away from Station Helix.

7

The flat was a functional rather than comfortable residence, sparsely furnished and with little character, despite being inside the neoclassical architecture of the MOD building where Abi and Alex had first met Charlotte Black. Some of the top floor had been designated as accommodation for when Ministry staff had to stay at work in order to deal with a crisis, or when a defecting diplomat needed a temporary safe house.

Abi put her mobile into her jeans pocket. "That was Lily's observer." Alex poured orange juice from a carton and handed the glass to her. "Thanks."

"What did he say?" He returned the carton to the refrigerator. The space in which they stood served as both kitchen and living area. They sat down on fabric-covered chairs which looked and felt like they had been there since the seventies.

"He has a difficult time keeping track of her," she replied. "She has a flat near the Elephant and Castle but she doesn't spend much time there. When she's in London she sometimes stays with friends, but quite often her gigs take her around the country."

"And he can't follow her."

"Exactly. They aren't friends like us, so there's no personal contact. The observation has to be extremely discreet. In fact a lot of the time he just looks at her website to see where she's performing."

"Does he know where she is now?"

"She's performing at a place called the Phoenix tonight. It's a pub near Oxford Circus."

Alex grabbed the laptop from the small round table beside his chair and lifted the screen. "I'll look it up." He hesitated before speaking again. "I still haven't figured out what I'm going to say to her."

"Well I suggest you don't start with, 'Hi, I'm with the Ministry of Defence and we've been watching you because you're genetically enhanced'."

Alex frowned, unamused by her joke. "Thanks. That's helpful."

"Oh lighten up! You'll be fine. Apply some of those fencing skills to this task. Adapt and improvise." Abi decided to tease him some more. "Or are you just scared of talking to a woman in a bar?"

He shook his head in exasperation. "This spying thing is new to me. I'm just worried what'll happen if I mess this up."

"Don't worry. Charlotte will have a contingency plan ready. It's just better if we can use a low-key approach and do this without attracting attention."

Alex glanced back at the laptop's screen. "Found it. The Phoenix. It says Lily's playing at eight o'clock tonight."

"Good. That gives us time to get ready." She swallowed the last of her orange juice and stood up. "I'll call Charlotte and let her know. Check out the Tube routes and street names near the pub. Neither of us knows London that well, so we need to be clear before we go."

"Okay, I'll look those up."

"Be ready to go in an hour."

8

Alex had missed almost all of Lily Carter's show when he entered the Phoenix at 9.45, but watching her perform hadn't been part of the plan. The venue was a short walk from Oxford Circus Underground Station, occupying a corner of Cavendish Square dominated by coffee shops and ugly concrete architecture. The exterior of the Phoenix didn't have the aesthetic appeal to entice custom – had he been looking for a lunch venue he probably would have passed it by – but once inside he found the interior much more to his taste. Wooden wall panels and subdued lighting gave the pub a cosy atmosphere. The bar was busy and the sound of a rock band echoed noisily from the basement level.

Alex headed for the staircase and made his way down, hearing the audience burst into applause as a song finished. The room was packed with people. He looked towards the stage and noticed the band's casual attire and long hair. They had the confident swagger of a country-rock band who knew they were good.

One of the guitarists stepped up to a microphone and thanked the crowd for their support. "We've had a good time and we hope you have too," he shouted. The crowd roared their approval. "How about a cheer for Lily Carter?" The audience cheered again.

A woman stepped up to the microphone, grinning and

waving at the crowd. She wore jeans and a sleeveless Willie Nelson shirt. Her hair was dyed blonde with streaks of colour and numerous braids.

She pulled the microphone stand closer, glanced round at the band briefly, then turned back to the crowd. "Okay, I think we can manage one more for you."

She punched the air and the band reacted instantly, launching into a song that Alex recognised right away – Lynyrd Skynyrd's *Call Me The Breeze*. Alex regretted that he hadn't seen the whole show. Lily and her band were superb. The customers had obviously been entertained and were now dancing and singing along, determined to enjoy the last song of the night. Alex moved through the crowd to get a little closer to the stage.

He snapped a few pictures of Lily with his mobile as she sang. He sent the images to Abi's phone number. Although they'd seen pictures of her on the Helix file, the singer had changed her appearance since the photographs had been taken. He put the phone away and allowed himself to enjoy the performance, watching as one of the musicians went into the song's guitar solo. The playing was perfect and the crowd cheered as he gave way to Lily's next verse. Not to be outdone, the pianist emulated Billy Powell's part with finesse before the last verse of the song.

Moments later it was all over. The audience applauded as the musicians left the stage. Hoping in vain for another encore, the crowd waited a short while before leaving the basement. Alex walked with them, listening to their excited conversations about the show.

He crossed the street and waited where he could see both sides of the Phoenix's exterior. He reckoned correctly that the band would wait a short while before leaving. With the performance over most of the customers dispersed quickly. He felt increasingly conspicuous as the minutes passed, and decidedly nervous by the time Lily left the premises twenty minutes later. She walked outside with two other women whom he recognised as the band's backing singers.

Alex followed them as they headed towards Regent Street. They stopped briefly and Lily's companions hugged her before walking south towards Oxford Circus. She resumed her walk in the opposite direction.

Seeing she was now alone, Alex increased his pace. "Lily Carter?" he said as he caught up with her.

Lily glared. "Who wants to know?"

"I'm sorry to bother you." Alex's words felt clumsy. "I saw you in the Phoenix."

"So did a lot of people. Goodnight." She walked away.

"Actually I only caught the end of it." He hurried after her. "But that's not why I want to speak to you."

"Yeah, well, it's been a long night and I'm not really in the mood for talking to a complete stranger on the streets of London, if it's all the same to you." She walked faster.

"But this is important."

"Sure, sweetheart. Why don't you leave me alone before I get really pissed off?"

"Honestly, I'm not trying to upset you. It's really important that we talk."

"You're sounding like a fucking stalker. I don't care who you are or what you want, but if you don't back off right now, I'll call the police."

Alex hesitated. "Miss Carter, my name is Alex Hannay.

I'm with the Government. Like I said, I need to talk to you."

Lily stopped suddenly and turned to face him. "I told you to leave me alone." She pulled a mobile phone from her jeans pocket and held it up. "This is your last chance. Fuck off back to your psych ward right now, or I dial 999."

Alex took a step back. "My apologies for the inconvenience, Miss Carter. I don't wish to upset you. I won't trouble you any further."

"Damn right you won't. Now you're going that way." She pointed back along Regent Street. Alex nodded and walked away.

He mentally counted thirty seconds before turning round. Lily Carter was nowhere to be seen. He took out his mobile, found Abi's number and called her.

"Hey, Alex."

"I didn't manage to get her to listen."

"I noticed. Still, we didn't expect that to be successful."

"Did the scanner work?"

"Yeah, like a charm. We'll be able to track her as long as she keeps her phone switched on."

"Good. Where are you now?"

"Portland Place, near the BBC's Broadcasting House. Lily's just gone into a flat nearby. Are you still on Regent Street?"

"Yes."

"Okay, stay there. I'll come to you."

"Don't you think we should visit Lily tonight?"

"No, especially if she's staying with someone. We'll bring her in tomorrow when she's alone. It'll be easier to follow her in daylight."

"Okay."

"Alex?"
"Yes?"
"Good job. Welcome to the MOD."

9

Alex stared out of the coffee shop window wondering how the day would play out. The flat Lily Carter had gone to last night was several streets away but it didn't matter that they weren't observing the location directly. Abi tapped the screen of a tablet computer, checking the location of Carter's phone. The sophisticated software linked into the mobile networks, triangulating signals to within tens of metres. It was now late morning and the phone still hadn't moved. This was their second coffee shop and they'd been here nearly an hour.

"We should find somewhere else," Abi said quietly.

Alex nodded. "There's only so much of this coffee that I can drink."

Abi noticed a graphic move on the tablet's screen. "Hang on, I think we have something. Yeah, she's moving. Come on, let's see where she goes." They slid off their stools and left the coffee shop. Once outside Abi spoke again but it wasn't to Alex. "Are you reading me, Joseph? She's on the move." A tiny microphone attached to the collar of her t-shirt picked up her voice.

Alex heard a man's voice reply through the miniature earpiece in his left ear. Lily's MOD observer confirmed he'd heard Abi's transmission. "Which way is she heading?"

Abi glanced at the tablet again. "South towards Oxford

Circus."

"I'm at Regent's Park Tube. She's probably about five hundred metres ahead of me."

"That's fine. Follow, but keep your distance. She's closer to us than you." Abi glanced at Alex. "We need to make visual contact in case she catches the Tube. We'll lose the triangulation underground."

Alex spoke into his microphone. "Is Oxford Circus Station covered?"

"Foxtrot Two; I'm just by the entrance," a man's voice replied.

"Okay, Foxtrot Two, she should be in view any moment."

"Standby… I see her. No, she's turned left into Oxford Street."

Abi looked at the tablet. "We're close. Let's see where she goes."

When they joined Oxford Street from a side road the tracking software indicated that their quarry was about forty metres ahead of them, but they couldn't see her in the crowded street. Shoppers and tourists made progress slow but Carter was hindered to the same degree and didn't get any farther ahead. When she passed Tottenham Court Road Underground and continued eastwards towards the station at Holborn they began to wonder why she hadn't jumped on the Central Line, but their suspicion was alleviated when she changed direction before reaching the station. They finally caught sight of her once she'd left New Oxford Street. Abi put the tablet into her small backpack. Several minutes later they identified her destination as she approached the grand neoclassical façade of the British

Museum.

They followed her up the venue's steps, past its huge columns and into the entrance. Seconds later they found themselves in the museum's vast Great Court, but they didn't have time to admire the diamond patterned glass and steel ceiling high above their heads. They almost lost sight of her as she blended into the crowd. Hundreds of visitors filled the hall making progress slow. The centre of the Great Court was dominated by the circular Reading Room where special exhibitions were held, but Carter ignored that section and headed left. She passed a ticket vendor stand and continued towards the Egyptian sculpture wing.

"It seems Lily enjoys some ancient culture," said Abi.

"We EHBs need something to keep our superior minds occupied," retorted Alex, smiling. "A rock chick who appreciates history. I'm liking her more and more."

"Well now's your chance to speak to her again. Try not to upset her this time. I'll hang back and co-ordinate with the team."

Alex nodded and walked after Lily. He noticed she was waiting at the back of a small crowd to see the Rosetta Stone just inside the Egyptian section. As the people in front of her moved away she stepped closer to the glass-covered exhibit and spent the next two minutes looking at its famous inscriptions.

Alex stood beside her. "Good morning, Miss Carter."

Lily glanced at him, recognising him instantly. She glared. "Didn't you get the message last night?"

"I said I needed to speak to you about something important. I wasn't lying to you." He took her by the arm and led her into the exhibition hall.

She jerked her arm away, making him let go. "Something so important that you need to stalk me?"

"Surveillance would be a more accurate description."

"*What?*"

"I told you I work for the Government – specifically the Ministry of Defence." He held up an MOD identification card briefly. "We've been able to follow you because you gave me your phone number last night."

"I didn't give you my number!"

"Not intentionally."

"So how did you get it?"

Alex ignored the question. "I need you to listen to me."

"I don't care what you need."

"It's about your past."

For a moment Lily stared at him. "My past is none of your business."

"Actually, it's MOD business."

"Not any more."

"I'm afraid it is. I'm not talking about you growing up on RAF stations. There's something about your birth that we need to discuss. Walk with me." He took her by the arm again and guided her through the hall.

Lily stared at him, unsure how to interpret his apparently sincere expression. "It sounds like you know more than I do," she said. There was suspicion and anger in her voice but she made a surprising revelation. "I never knew my real parents."

"I know. You were adopted by Thomas and Sharon Carter when you were a baby. Thomas was a successful pilot and encouraged you to follow the same career that he had. As a teenager you rejected the idea and pursued your interest in music."

Lily frowned. "I got fed up following my parents around the country from one RAF base to the next. I told myself that if I had to go from place to place I'd do it for me, not anyone else. But what does my birth have to do with this?"

"The circumstances of your birth were... *unusual*."

"What does that mean?"

"It'll take a while to explain. I'd like you to come back to the MOD with me so I can discuss everything in detail with you."

"I'm not interested."

"I..." Alex stopped suddenly when he heard Abi speaking to him through his earpiece. "What is it, Abi?"

"I think you're being followed." Her voice was tense. "Get her back into the central area and mingle in the crowd. I'll keep watching."

"Okay." Alex looked back at Lily. "We might have a problem."

"What kind of problem?"

"My colleague thinks we're being watched. We need to move."

"I'm not going anywhere. I still don't know who you are."

"Lily, the reason I'm here is because *my* circumstances are very much like *yours*. I need you to trust me."

"*Right*. Give me one good reason."

"Your eyes."

"What about my eyes? And don't tell me they're the most beautiful you've ever seen or I'll make that call to the police right now."

Alex kept his voice low. "Your daylight vision is

supremely sharp and you can also see well in almost complete darkness."

She stared at him. "How the hell do you know that?"

"Please, Lily, let's get out of here. I'll explain everything later."

"Damn right you will."

10

Abi had kept a discreet distance from Alex and Lily, feigning interest in the ancient artefacts while following them through the Egyptian sculpture wing. Their conversation had given her time to co-ordinate the rest of the MOD team although she hadn't intended to use them now that Alex had made contact. But the sight of two men in grey suits watching Alex caused her concern. Like her, they weren't really looking at the exhibits. Their attire was conspicuous. Most visitors to the museum were tourists or students of history and they usually came much more casually-dressed. These men stood together but hardly spoke. She'd watched them watching Alex for a few minutes before alerting him to their presence. As she'd instructed, Alex began to look for a route back to the Great Court. Thankfully Lily followed his directions. He'd obviously said enough to cause her to pay attention.

The two men moved apart. One walked after Alex and Lily while the second crossed to the other side of the hallway, keeping track of his associate. He increased his pace, moving ahead of Alex. Abi hurried past a series of millennia-old statues, determined to get ahead of Alex's followers. She reached the end of the exhibition room and found a position where she could watch Alex and Lily strolling towards her. The second man stopped at the exit to the Great Court, keeping up his casual observation, ready to intercept.

Abi tried to keep her voice low as she spoke into her microphone but the tension in her words was clear. "Alex, there's a man in a grey suit blocking your exit. White shirt, no tie, mid-thirties. His associate is about thirty feet behind you. Give me about ten seconds and then start running." Alex didn't reply but took hold of Lily's arm and glanced towards the exit.

Abi took out her mobile phone and pretended to be distracted by it as she hurried towards the Great Court. She ran straight into the man in the doorway, causing him to lose his balance and step back. "Shit, I'm so sorry! Are you okay?" She stepped around him and his eyes followed automatically, breaking his concentration, distracting him from his task. "I should have been more careful. I'm really sorry." In her peripheral vision she saw Alex and Lily sprint past, followed instantly by the man who had been behind them in the hallway. The man she'd collided with tried to get past her but she placed her hand on his arm in an attempt to delay him.

The man removed her hand. "I'm fine, really," he said, his accent American. "It was a simple mistake. Don't worry." He put his hands on her shoulders and pushed her aside firmly but without aggression. "Excuse me." Abi stepped aside, hoping she'd hindered him long enough to improve Alex's chances.

11

Abi's distraction provided Alex with the opportunity to get Lily out of the Egyptian hallway, but he had no idea where to go next. Keeping hold of Lily's arm with one hand he ran with her into the Great Court, glad that she kept pace with him. But, despite its vast size, it wasn't easy to make progress through the museum's glass-covered centre. Hundreds of people walking in different directions meant their run slowed considerably. He resorted to pushing people aside just to get through the crowd. A glance over his shoulder told him that at least one of the pursuers was close behind.

Abi's voice shouted in his earpiece. "Alex! Back door, ground level! Keep running!" He didn't reply. He didn't know the layout of the building but Abi's instruction was enough. Shoving past tourists he led Lily out of the Great Court and into another section of the museum. The opposite end of the building to where they had entered was, he assumed and hoped, where they'd find the exit Abi meant. Her voice shouted again but this time the instructions weren't directed at him. "Rear exit! Alex needs an urgent pick up." A voice responded but Alex couldn't hear what was said.

He was dismayed when he saw that the route he'd taken didn't lead directly onto the street. They found themselves in another wing of the building, having to negotiate their way around exhibits and yet more sightseers. He glanced back. Their pursuer was almost upon them. Alex grabbed hold of an unsuspecting tourist and shoved him into the path of the suited man. The ensuing collision caused them both to fall, but Alex noticed the second pursuer running into the hallway. He grabbed Lily's hand and ran for the exit.

The double wooden doors were open and they barged their way out of the building. A black London taxi pulled to a sudden halt outside and Alex heard the driver yell his name. He grabbed the door handle and shoved Lily into the rear of the vehicle, following quickly. As soon as the door slammed shut the cabbie pressed a switch to activate the locks. One of the suited men ran from the building and pulled at the handle in vain as the taxi turned into the traffic.

"You okay, Alex?" the driver said, looking over his shoulder for a second.

"Lucas?" Alex was relieved and astonished to recognise Ingwe.

Lucas looked into the rear-view mirror. "I think we've lost them. Good to see you."

"Likewise. I wasn't expecting this. How did you get involved?"

"I met a woman named Charlotte Black."

"Not by accident, I'm sure."

"Oh, the meeting was engineered all right. You knew I was being investigated?"

"I remember."

"Well, I went to the police headquarters for my disciplinary hearing, expecting to get asked to resign."

"What happened?"

"I was asked to resign. There's a peculiar arrangement with the police. They rarely sack anyone; they just invite you to hand in your notice. So I did as I was asked because I knew I was screwed. As I walked out of the building, Charlotte approached me. She offered me a job with the MOD on the spot."

"And you accepted?"

"Not right away. So she told me you were part of her team and that I'd been right about the crash. Then I accepted."

"Does Francesca know?"

"Yes. We're both glad to be involved. We felt we let you down before."

"You didn't, but it's good to have you on board. So you know about the EHBs?"

"I do, but I can hardly believe a word of it."

"Well you now have two of us in the back of your cab. This is Lily Carter."

"Pleased to meet you, Lily. I'm Lucas Ingwe."

Lily didn't reply. She turned to Alex. "You told me you'd explain everything. Now what the hell are EHBs?"

Alex didn't answer, directing his next comment to Lucas instead. "Are we going back to the Ministry?"

"Yes."

Alex looked at Lily again. "I'll explain once we're safe." She scowled and turned away, gazing out of the taxi's window. He decided it wasn't worth trying to appease her.

As Lucas drove past Charing Cross, Alex's phone rang. Expecting the caller to be Abi he was surprised when Charlotte's number appeared.

She spoke as soon as he answered. "She's with you?"

"Yes."

"Good job. Where are you?"

"About a minute away from the MOD."

"Good," Charlotte repeated. "Get Lily inside and tell her what you know. I need to talk to you but I've been called to the Foreign Office for something urgent. I don't know what it is yet but hopefully I'll be out of there by this afternoon."

"Did you hear what happened?"

"Abi's just called me. That's why I need to talk to you. Meet me at Richoux on Piccadilly at 5. It's a little way down from the Ritz."

"I'll find it."

Charlotte ended the call.

12

"Am I going to get my explanation now?" Lily hadn't asked any more questions until Lucas and Alex had brought her to the MOD apartment, but now it was clear she wasn't going to accept any more deferments.

Alex realised that the woman who didn't hesitate to speak her mind would probably respond best to a direct answer. "Your genetic code was altered by Government scientists. That's why your vision is better than anyone else's."

Lily stared. "That's bullshit."

"You think the MOD would waste all these resources tracking you down just to play a practical joke?"

She hesitated, glancing at them both, searching for any indication that they were lying to her. She saw none. "You realise how insane this sounds?"

"Completely. I only found out that I was part of the same programme a short while ago."

"But you're younger than me."

"The programme's been running for a long time. You were part of the first group. I was part of the second about ten years later."

"How did you find out?"

Alex suddenly felt awkward. He hadn't thought about his parents for a while and he was annoyed with himself for neglecting to remember them. "My parents and I were in a car crash. They didn't make it."

"I'm sorry."

"Lucas's wife was the paramedic who saved me. When she told him, he looked into it."

Lily made eye contact with Lucas. "I heard you talking about the police in the taxi."

He nodded. "I looked into the crash because I suspected foul play. It turned out I was right."

Lily glanced at Alex but didn't speak.

"My parents were murdered," he said quietly.

"Oh my god."

"I found out they worked at a place called Station Helix on the Suffolk coast. It's where the EHB programme is based."

"EHB?"

"Enhanced Human Being. Station Helix is an MOD laboratory where genetic code is manipulated. In your case they've found ways to refine your vision. I can heal quickly. We're both apparently quite intelligent too. They're also looking at resistance to radiation, oxygen processing, auditory enhancement, and a whole load of other things. Ultimately they want to use the data from the experiment for a military application."

"This is crazy. Is this really possible?"

"Do I need to answer that?"

"So what are they going to do? Build super-soldiers?"

"I hadn't thought of it quite like that, but I guess that's one way of looking at it."

"What do they want with you and me?"

"Just to see if the genetic alterations were sustainable. We weren't supposed to ever find out. Arrangements were put in place to encourage us into professions where our skills could be tested. I was supposed to become a geneticist like my parents. You were supposed to become a pilot."

"Are you saying my adoptive parents knew about this?"

"Almost certainly."

Lily looked annoyed. "Well I'm glad I broke the mould. I guess you didn't do what your parents wanted either."

Alex shook his head. "They kept watching us though. They call them observers. Abi's mine. Yours is a guy called Joseph."

"I don't know anyone called Joseph."

"He keeps a discreet distance."

"Are there others like us?"

"Yes."

"Do you know them?"

"Not yet."

"But you're going to find them? Like you found me?"

"Actually, we know where most of them are. You tend to move around more than the rest."

Lily frowned. "Something's not right here. I can understand how you found out, but if I wasn't supposed to know, why did you track me down? There's no way I'd have discovered any of this."

"I'm not sure how to explain this. There may be a medical problem with the first group. There's a chance that the genetic alterations weren't as robust as the scientists had hoped."

"What does that mean?"

"They need to run some tests."

"I could be ill because of the experiment?"

"Possibly. You heard us talk about Charlotte Black? She's now in charge of the programme. She decided that the EHBs should be told and brought in for checks. That's why I came after you."

The door to the apartment opened and Abi entered. She held a plastic bag which she tossed onto the counter in the kitchen. "Are you guys okay?" she asked.

"Yeah, we're fine," replied Alex. "I've told Lily about the EHBs. Lily, this is Abi."

"Your observer? Yeah, I recognise you from the museum. We ran past you."

"Well spotted," Abi replied.

"Apparently I have good eyesight." Lily turned back to Alex. "There's something you're not telling me. How do you know there could be a problem?"

"One of your group committed suicide a few weeks ago. The autopsy found some evidence of DNA decay in his cells. His name was Jonathan Cline. He was a defence systems specialist."

"I heard about that. He jumped off Tower Bridge. Wasn't he supposed to be some kind of computer genius?"

"That's him."

"So why did he jump?"

"According to his observer he'd been receiving treatment for chronic pain. We think it got so bad he decided to end it."

She glanced away. "This could happen to me, couldn't it?"

"Honestly, we don't know. Cline's case may have been unique."

Lily didn't respond. She walked into the kitchen area,

pulled open the fridge door and took out a small bottle of Coke. "Any objection to me having one of these?"

"Help yourself."

She came back into the living room and slumped in one of the chairs. She twisted the lid off the bottle and took a swig. "Okay, I get it about the EHBs. I see why you want me to have tests. But there's one thing I don't understand."

"Go on."

"Who were those guys in the museum?"

Alex didn't reply. He wanted the answer to that question himself. Leaning against the kitchen doorway, Abi caught Lily's eye. "We're looking into that, Lily."

"What does that mean?"

"It means we don't know yet. It was unexpected. The obvious conclusion is that someone else knows about you or Alex."

"Well, you'd better figure it out soon. It didn't look like they were just after a friendly chat."

"We will." Abi turned to Alex. "Do you have a moment?"

Alex followed her into the kitchen. He kept his voice low. "You know something, don't you?"

"Maybe. They were American."

"CIA?"

Abi shrugged. "They found out about Helix three years ago. It's a logical conclusion."

"True, but they didn't know about me or Lily."

"That's what bothers me. Someone's got hold of more information."

"From Mason?"

"How would he know anything? He was dismissed once

the MOD found out he'd spoken to the Americans. He never knew the details of the programme. You're going to see Charlotte later, aren't you?"

"At Richoux on Piccadilly."

"It's close to here but I don't want you to go on foot. Get Lucas to drop you off in the taxi." She picked up the plastic bag she'd thrown on the counter and pulled a grey baseball cap from it. A New York logo was embroidered on the front. "I picked this up for you on the way back. It isn't much, but it'll make you less obvious. Change your clothes too."

Alex took the cap from her. "Thanks, Abi. I'll be fine."

"You'd better be. Find out what Charlotte wants us to do. I've a feeling this has just got a whole lot more complicated."

13

In the back of the taxi Alex tried his hardest to be alert for signs of trouble, but he realised that he didn't actually know what to do. He'd been thrown into something he'd never been trained for. His random glances at random passers-by were utterly pointless. Most of the people he saw walking along Piccadilly looked like tourists – a cover which, he assumed, would be ideal for an operative for that very reason. He had no idea how to distinguish between real tourists and fake ones. Or maybe an operative would choose a different appearance *because* an observer would be trying to spot someone pretending to be a tourist. He was letting himself become paranoid and decided he'd ask for a training course in surveillance. Charlotte would have the contacts.

Despite his inability to spot an enemy spy, he did catch sight of Stephen Jennings on the opposite side of the street at the entrance to the Burlington Arcade as Ingwe stopped outside the restaurant. Alex assumed he was there at Charlotte's request, but he still found himself deeply suspicious of the man. He turned his attention to Richoux's red-painted shop front, then glanced back at the clock on the taxi's dashboard. 16.59. The timing was ideal. He hadn't wanted to arrive any earlier for the meeting. "Thanks, Lucas. I'll see you later." Alex opened the door and stepped onto the pavement. He entered the café as the taxi's clock marked the hour.

Alex liked the layout of the restaurant as soon as he saw it. The dining room was long and narrow. Wooden panelling and wallpaper gave the place a cosy ambience. Framed prints of flowers adorned the walls, but the floral decoration was subtle rather than overbearing. The tables were set in shallow alcoves which permitted diners more privacy than they might usually expect in a London café. Alex wondered if this was how Edwardian railway dining cars might have been arranged. He saw Charlotte Black sitting alone at a table near the back of the room. She saw him arrive and gestured towards him while saying something to a waitress. The waitress walked up to him, greeted him politely and told him his friend was waiting. She led him to the table and took his drink order.

Charlotte handed him a menu. "I'll probably have the risotto but you might prefer the all day breakfast. I haven't tried it myself but I'm told the hash browns are perfect."

"I saw Jennings outside."

"Good, that's where he's supposed to be. Considering everything that's gone on today, I thought it might be prudent to ask him along."

"I don't trust him."

"Why not?"

"I'm not sure."

"Don't let his aloof character put you off. I've worked with him for a long time. He's a pro because he maintains that detachment."

"I still don't like him."

"He probably doesn't trust you either. You're an outsider to whom I've revealed eyes-only secrets. You haven't earned your stripes yet in Stephen's eyes."

"What about in yours?"

"Today went well. There's still a lot more work to be done."

"I'm not sure it was as successful as you think."

"Because of your encounter with the Americans? True, that was a close call, but that's how this game is played. Actually it turned out to be very useful."

"How's that?"

"We know more than we did this morning. It's certain that your pursuers were CIA."

"How do you know?"

"Stephen followed one of them back to a CIA office in Covent Garden."

"I didn't realise Stephen was part of the backup team."

"You didn't know Lucas was either. Focus on the matter at hand. We have to ask ourselves how the CIA found out about Carter."

"They already know about Helix."

"But not the EHBs."

"Therefore they have new information."

"How?"

Alex hesitated. "There must be a leak."

"Exactly. Stephen's going to check the Helix security protocols. Hopefully he'll come up with something."

Alex leaned forward. "They must have someone *inside*."

Charlotte nodded. "That's my conclusion too. Our starting point is to examine everyone who's been recruited to the project since Mason spoke to the Americans, but we may have to look earlier than that."

"Why would they come after us?"

"I can only theorise. I…" Charlotte hesitated.

"What is it?"

She frowned. "Tell me *exactly* what they tried to do today."

"Abi spotted them watching us. We ran out. They followed. Lucas got us away just in time before they grabbed us."

Charlotte closed her eyes and rubbed her forehead.

"What's the matter?" Alex asked.

She looked up. "The EHB data is valuable. The project has been running for decades and we're way ahead of every other nation with this science. The Americans may have stolen some of that data, but that doesn't beat getting their hands on one of you."

"You think they wanted to abduct us for *experimentation*?"

"Isn't that what you'd do in their position?"

"That means the others are at risk."

Charlotte frowned. "I thought so, but now I'm not so sure about my hypothesis."

Alex waited for her to explain.

"My meeting at the Foreign Office earlier. They told me a junior diplomat named David Stone was assassinated two days ago in Cairo. He was a Generation One EHB."

Alex leaned back in his chair. "Abi was right. She said this was about to get more complicated."

"That's an understatement."

"It can't be the Americans."

"Go on."

"Trying to kidnap one EHB and executing another? It

doesn't make sense. Someone else is involved. Maybe Stone's death is coincidental. There are plenty of people who dislike us in the Middle East."

"I don't believe in coincidences. If it had been another member of the diplomatic staff, I might accept the terrorist theory. But a junior officer who happens to be an EHB? You're right, Alex. It's not just the CIA. Someone else knows about Station Helix."

"Then we may have a second leak."

Charlotte shook her head. "*That* would be coincidental."

"And you don't believe in coincidences."

The conversation paused as the waitress brought Alex's drink. "Are you ready to order?" she asked.

"Can we have another couple of minutes?" said Charlotte.

"Sure." The waitress walked away.

Charlotte turned back to Alex. "You won't like this, but I'm going to confine you to quarters. At least until my people have figured out what's going on."

"I don't think that's a good idea. You need me to bring in the other Generation Ones."

"Ideally I'd like to keep to that plan, but the risk has just increased."

"It's increased for the other EHBs too. At least I know what's going on."

"No you don't. None of us do right now. We've lost our advantage and we need to get it back. Everyone connected to Station Helix could be in danger. How do you think the CIA spotted Carter?"

"What do you mean?"

"Think about it. You knew where she was last night.

Why didn't they grab her then?"

Alex paused. "They didn't know where she was."

"Your would-be abductors were watching someone else. We've examined the CCTV footage from this morning. We were able to back-track them to Regent's Park."

Alex reached the obvious conclusion. "They were following Joseph Talbot. They have the names of the observers as well."

"I've recalled them and asked MI5 to take over – for now at least."

"Jennings had better come up with some answers soon."

"He will."

"I still think you need me."

"Why?"

"We need to find out who killed Stone. If we're right, they won't stop there."

"What are you suggesting?"

"Forgive the fencing analogy, but sometimes the best tactic against a dominant opponent is a counter-attack. We need to catch these people off guard."

"Something tells me I'm not going to like your idea."

Alex leaned back in his chair. "I don't like it either, but it's our best chance. You need to use me as bait."

EIGHT

1

Jack Caldwell never raised his voice when he was irritated. Undisciplined people who needed to shout to get their point across failed to impress him. There was more weight in silences, prolonged eye contact and softly spoken comments. He shuffled through the ten by eight inch CCTV prints that Clare Quinn had handed him: grainy images that the CIA technical team had extracted covertly from the British Museum's security system. He gathered the photos into a stack, aligned them by tapping the edges and placed them on his desk. He looked up at Clare. "What happened?" He already knew the answer.

"Our guys located Joseph Talbot and followed him all morning. We didn't know if he was planning to watch Carter but we got lucky. He went to the museum and they spotted her. The idea was to track her and pick her up discreetly, but there was an unanticipated intervention. They had to make a decision."

"So they chased her through one of the most public buildings in London?" Caldwell's tone stayed calm but his words told her he considered the operation an utter failure.

She shrugged. "Circumstances changed. They were briefed to bring her in. That's what they tried to do. They had to improvise."

"I understand that, but we've just told the Brits we know about the EHBs and we're after their research."

Clare didn't want to speculate on the consequences of her team's bungled operation. "We spy on each other. What are they going to do?"

"They'll go out of their way to prevent us from getting hold of their assets."

"So we come up with a new plan. Let's disappoint them."

Caldwell leaned forward. "Go on."

"Let's ignore the EHBs for now. Maybe we should focus on the data and learn more about the research. This stuff goes back years and we're only scratching the surface. The MOD will be watching us. Let's back off and waste their time."

"I get your point, but it's not that simple. My source inside Station Helix hasn't been able to gather much data yet. We only have fragments. Now that we've announced our intentions to the British Government, they'll replace all of their security protocols. We'll get nothing more from Helix."

"So we need a new approach anyway," she retorted.

Jack paused. He glanced at the photograph on the top of the pile. Despite its poor quality the faces of a man and a woman were reasonably clear. The woman was Lily Carter. He picked up the print and held it so Clare could see it. "Have you figured out who this guy is yet?"

She smiled. "Oh yes. It's Alex Hannay."

He stared. This revelation was completely unexpected. He took a moment to gather his thoughts. "Are you sure?"

"Absolutely. When we first got the stills we had no idea who he was, but Josie was reviewing our old Helix data and she found a photo that was taken when you profiled the

Hannays three years ago. It's definitely their boy. He must be working for the MOD."

Caldwell put the photograph down and leaned back in his chair. "That's interesting."

Clare perched on the edge of his desk. "No kidding. He obviously knows about Helix."

"I'm more curious about why he contacted Carter. The EHBs aren't supposed to know anything about the programme. It's a secret study managed by observers. Something's changed."

Quinn stared at him as an idea snapped into her thoughts. "Holy shit, Jack. They're bringing them in to *protect* them. David Stone – the diplomat – has just been killed in Cairo. And Jonathan Cline – maybe his suicide wasn't suicide. Someone else is after the EHBs and they want them dead."

He held her gaze. "If you're right, we need to find out who it is. We can't be prevented from acquiring the technology. Our superiors have made that clear to me."

"But we need to know what we're up against."

Jack made a decision. "Clare, you're right about changing direction, but I don't want to throw our people into an unknown risk. Let's use Mason."

She hesitated. "I'm uneasy about that. He could be trouble."

He waved his hand dismissively. "We'll use him for as long as we need to. He'll do what we say. He has no choice."

"Okay, but we're still in the dark at the moment. We don't know who killed Stone."

"Speak to the Cairo office. They might come up with

something. And watch Alex Hannay. He could be the answer to all this."

"Will do." Quinn stood and walked towards the door.

"Clare." She turned round but didn't speak. "One more thing. You're correct about the MOD – they'll be scrutinising everything we do. Distract them with mundane matters."

She grinned. "No worries."

2

Greg McLeod was a big-hearted Scot whose life had felt complete since daughter Megan's arrival three years ago. When Kate and he had moved to Pitlochry in central Scotland, starting a family hadn't been a priority, but he'd been delighted when his wife had revealed the pregnancy. From that moment he devoted himself to becoming a loving and supportive father. For a man whose working life in the aeronautics industry was mentally and physically challenging, the routine of his home life provided a calming counterpoint. He loved coming home for dinner with his two favourite girls. Afterwards he'd give Megan her bath before putting her to bed and reading her a story. He'd put up extra shelves in her bedroom for the dozens of Enid Blyton books he'd bought her. Being a dad was even more rewarding than testing flight suits and aviation safety equipment.

Greg pushed open the living room door. A lightweight waterproof jacket was draped over his arm. Kate glanced up from the magazine she was reading. "Is she asleep?"

He nodded. "Two pages before the end of the story."

"I thought she'd drift off quickly. She used up a lot of energy at the playground this afternoon. I'll go up and see her in a moment. Are you going for your walk?"

"Aye." Greg put on the jacket. "Thought I'd take a coat this evening. The weather looks like it might turn. Our summer evenings might be over for another year. Give it a few more weeks and I'll have to take a torch with me." He zipped up the jacket. "That reminds me – I need to pick up some batteries." He took a couple of steps towards Kate, leaned forward and held her face gently as he kissed her. "Won't be long, beautiful. Enjoy the rest of your magazine."

"Thanks. Enjoy your stroll."

As he closed the front door McLeod reminded himself for the millionth time what a lucky man he was. Kate and he had been together for nearly a decade, although they hadn't seen much of each other during the first two years of their courtship because of distance. They'd met at a conference in London – Kate's home city – when she was still working as a university research assistant. After two years of infrequent weekend visits they'd agreed that their relationship was important enough to make more satisfactory arrangements. Kate had given up her job and moved to Scotland and they'd married within a year. At first glance they didn't seem like an obvious match. He was a burly six-foot-two Scot who loved sport and the outdoors; she was a slender attractive woman whose pursuits were mostly academic. At five-foot-four Kate was much shorter than her husband, and she also had a much quieter temperament. She had typically English reserve and had been brought up in a well-to-do family. She'd walked straight into the research job after graduating. Kate was strikingly attractive with long dark hair and captivating dark eyes: Mediterranean traits she'd inherited from her Tunisian grandfather. Her daughter seemed destined to be equally stunning.

Despite his devotion to his family, Greg still enjoyed some solitary time. Every weekday evening he completed a circular walk around the town. The habit was unbreakable even when the Scottish weather was at its most vindictive. On glorious evenings McLeod found the walk inspiring; on terrible ones he found it invigorating. He stayed out for around forty-five minutes, winding down after a solid day's work. The stroll gave him the opportunity to reflect on his achievements and think up new innovations. He pushed his hands into his jacket and headed down the hill towards Atholl Road, the town's main street.

His walk was interrupted briefly for a chat about work and family when he met Angus Donaldson – a local business owner he knew well – but soon he was on his way again, crossing the railway line and heading towards the River Tummel. South of the tracks the footpath passed through parkland as it neared the river. McLeod spotted a young couple and wished them a good evening. He didn't recognise them and thought they looked like tourists. The town was a popular destination for walkers and cyclists. Some came for Pitlochry itself, but others used the town's numerous hotels and guest houses as bases for treks farther afield. It was said that a map of Scotland would balance on a pin if you placed the point at Pitlochry.

McLeod heard the sound of water tumbling over Pitlochry's famous hydro-electric dam before he caught sight of the landmark itself. He'd never understood why the building was so popular with visitors. To him it was an ugly construction of stone, steel and concrete that did nothing to enhance the surrounding hills and woodland. It had been built shortly after the Second World War as part of a project to generate electricity from Scotland's abundance of water. It had altered the landscape, flooding a section of the town and creating an artificial loch. A concrete walkway – under which the river flowed and plunged onto massive concrete ramps below – extended from the north bank. The dam's huge machine house, with its tall windows and square columns, suggested to Greg that the architect had attempted to make the design look Victorian, but in truth its twentieth century origin couldn't be disguised. He didn't like the structure itself, but he did appreciate the view along the river it provided. He stepped onto the walkway and began to cross.

He stopped ten metres before the power station building and leaned on the rail. Here – halfway across the river – he had the best view eastwards. From his elevated position twenty metres above the lower stretch of the river he could see a slender footbridge a quarter of a mile downstream. He'd cross it later to return to the town. He always gave himself time to enjoy the view while the evenings were long enough to allow it.

He noticed something in his peripheral vision and turned to his left, looking back along the concrete span. He saw two men walking towards him. It wasn't unusual to see people walking here in the evening, but he instinctively felt suspicious. Visitors to the dam who weren't alone were usually caught up in conversation about the scale of the building or the impressive views. These men weren't conversing at all. McLeod sensed they'd been watching him because they'd turned their gazes downwards when he'd spotted them. He turned his attention back to the river for a few seconds, but looked towards them again when they were three metres away. "Evening," he said politely. They didn't reply.

Suddenly the man on his left ran forward and grabbed his arm, pulling him off balance. The second man pulled a knife, its metal blade flashing as it caught the evening light. He lunged at McLeod, thrusting the weapon towards his stomach. The tip penetrated his jacket but snagged on the leather and metal of his belt underneath. For a fraction of a second he glimpsed the surprise in the man's eyes. The delay was long enough for Greg to react. The first man still had hold of his left arm, but he grabbed the second by the hair and jerked his head downwards, slamming his knee into his assailant's face. Blood gushed from the injured man's nose and mouth. He dropped the knife and slumped onto the walkway.

The first man released Greg's arm and tried to swing a punch at his face, but he blocked it awkwardly and stumbled against his attacker. Almost slipping on the spray-soaked concrete, he tried to shove the man backwards against the building. To his surprise he found himself analysing what was going on and realised it wasn't fear that propelled him into action but rage.

You bastards aren't going to make my daughter fatherless.

McLeod slammed the man against the building's concrete wall, grabbed him by the throat and shoved his head backwards. His attacker grabbed his arm with both hands and had the presence of mind to tip his head forward as his back struck the wall, avoiding injury to his skull. The man swung his hands down onto McLeod's arm, forcing him to let go. He aimed a punch at his face but was hit with a counter-attack before he could make contact. Greg grabbed him again and shoved him against some railings. The man groaned with pain but fought back, regaining momentum.

McLeod got too close and the man head-butted him, striking him between the eyes. His vision blurred. The attacker swung his left elbow against the side of his head causing him to spin round and lose balance, but he managed to grab the walkway's railing and steadied himself. A punch aimed at his kidneys made his knees give way. The man grabbed his head. Greg twisted forcefully, found a placement for his foot and strained against his assailant as hard as he could, his leg muscles burning with the effort. He used all of his strength to lift the man and push him back. The man's spine struck the edge of the walkway with a grating crunch.

McLeod sensed victory but it didn't lessen his anger.

You evil fucker.

He grabbed the man by the throat and shoved him over the edge. The man slammed into the concrete ramp twenty metres below with a sickening thud and was immediately dragged under by the torrent of water surging over the dam.

McLeod turned, disoriented, the taste of salty blood filling his mouth. He saw the unconscious knifeman sprawled on the walkway, his face in a pool of dark blood, the blade nearby. Greg slumped against the concrete. He felt sick and had to sit on the wet gangway. With shaking hands he unzipped his jacket and reached for his mobile phone. He couldn't focus on the screen and fumbled with the keypad, forcing himself to concentrate.

One more task, McLeod.

He dialled 999.

3

"How was your evening, sir?"

"Fine, thank you, Nicholas," Arnold Rossington replied. His driver held open the black BMW's rear door and waited as his employer climbed inside. As Rossington settled into the comfortable seat and locked his safety belt in place, he realised that his reply wasn't entirely truthful. While he still enjoyed catching up with old acquaintances at these Oxford dinners, the effort of socialising was becoming increasingly burdensome. He'd survived ill-health and several operations over the years, but the toll of disease was something he could no longer ignore. In his heart he knew that serious ailments were never truly defeated. They could be beaten into submission for a few years by medicine but they never really went away. He felt old and tired. "Straight home, Nicholas," he said to the driver as the BMW's engine purred into life.

"Very good, sir."

The car edged forward slowly, the gravel of the college car park crunching beneath its broad tyres. Rossington glanced back at the eighteenth century building, its elegant architecture illuminated by floodlights. A lot of history had been made here, some of which he had contributed to. He reminded himself that, even today, the friendships and associations formed within the Oxbridge colleges still had considerable power and influence. He couldn't imagine society surviving without those networks being in place. A proportion of the general public may have held the rich and well educated in contempt, but he didn't have time for their ignorance and jealousy. Great Britain needed strong and talented leadership, whether the hoi polloi understood that fact or not.

But it wasn't the state of the country which troubled him the most. The decision to eliminate the Generation One EHBs had been a drastic measure; one that had caused him considerable anxiety and sleepless nights. As a younger man he would have found the choice simpler, recognising that aborting an unsuccessful experiment was nothing more than a scientific process. Many times had Falkner, Barnard, Rhodes and he had to make important decisions objectively and with detachment. It concerned him that, as he'd grown older, he'd seemed to develop a nagging conscience. Terminating the EHBs was, he believed, the right and logical choice. They couldn't risk making knowledge of a failed Government experiment public. Nonetheless, doubt pestered him. He wondered if they'd started to make decisions because of self-preservation rather than the best interests of the nation. Perhaps it was time to stop worrying and simply retire with good grace.

Let someone else make the important decisions, Arnold. You're too old for this.

The headlights of the oncoming traffic made him squint. He closed his eyes and rubbed his temples, but doing so didn't relieve his headache. He felt hot and couldn't understand why. Suddenly the throbbing in his head became a stab of intense pain. He tried to call out to Nicholas but found himself unable to speak. His jaw was slack and his face ached. Rossington couldn't understand why words wouldn't form. He wanted to raise his hand to pull off his bowtie, but his arm was limp. He panicked silently, unable to move or cry out as his sense of self crumbled into disorientation and bewilderment.

4

"My apologies for getting you all up before breakfast, but there's been a development." Charlotte Black leaned against her desk, impeccably dressed, her long hair brushed into a ponytail. She'd had only four hours' sleep but looked alert.

Alex wasn't yet as ready to tackle the challenges of the day. He rubbed his face, trying to concentrate. "It'd better be important," he muttered.

Charlotte glowered at him for a moment, unimpressed by the remark. "This is the MOD, Alex. It's always important."

He flushed with embarrassment. "Sorry, I'm still half-asleep."

She ignored his apology and turned to Abi. "Abigail, I want you to take Lily to the estate for her medical. I have a driver ready for you. When you're there, touch base with Stephen. He's looking into the security breach and he thinks he's found something. Keep me updated."

Abi nodded. "Will do."

Charlotte directed her next comment at Lily Carter. "I know this has been disruptive and totally unexpected, but it is important that we keep you safe."

Lily frowned. "It might be too late for that. Your experiment might have sealed my fate already."

"I sincerely hope that isn't so," replied Charlotte. Her

words were genuine but it was clear she intended to say no more on the matter. She turned to Alex. "Have you read Greg McLeod's file?"

"I have," Alex replied. "Are we bringing him in next?"

"In a manner of speaking. He's in a police cell in Perth. He called the police last night, claiming he was attacked in Pitlochry."

"What happened?"

"That's what I want you and Lucas to find out. The police have already been told we're taking over the investigation and that you're on your way."

"Why's he in a cell if he was attacked?"

"He put one of his assailants in hospital and the other in the mortuary."

Lucas offered an explanation. "It's standard practice for the police to detain someone, even if they've acted in self-defence. They can't just take someone's word."

"You think it was an attempted hit?" Alex asked Charlotte.

"That's exactly what I'm thinking. That's why you and Lucas are driving up there as soon as you've had something to eat." Charlotte grabbed a key fob from her desk and tossed it to Lucas. He glanced at it and saw a Range Rover logo. She continued. "The survivor is under MOD Police armed guard in hospital. You have the authority to interrogate him. Get McLeod out of the police station, find out what he knows, and then question the attacker. McLeod might just have given us the lead we're after."

"No problem," said Ingwe.

"Lucas, there's one more thing. You're used to conducting suspect interviews under the rules of the Police and Criminal Evidence Act. Put that behind you. Get me the information I need."

Lucas held Charlotte's gaze for a second then nodded in acknowledgement.

5

Ten minutes after Andrew Mason's train pulled out of King's Cross Station his mobile phone vibrated noisily in his jacket pocket. He looked at the screen momentarily before answering. The caller's number was withheld. He swiped the screen. "Yes?"

"I see you boarded your train." He recognised the American accent – this man had spoken to him on several occasions recently – but had no idea who he actually was. They'd never had a face to face meeting. It occurred to Mason that the CIA controller might be sitting on the same train, but there was no way of knowing from the slightly distorted sound in the speaker. On a moving train his phone would have to connect to different cell sites as his journey progressed. The signal would suffer minor interruptions regardless of whether the caller was nearby or sitting in an office at Langley over three and a half thousand miles away.

The man had called him at six that morning. Mason, being a habitual early riser, had already been awake. He'd been moved from the Crowne Plaza Hotel to a Travelodge near Liverpool Street the day after his capture and had been there ever since. The CIA obviously thought there was an advantage in keeping him in London accommodation, but weren't prepared to go to great expense. He'd wondered why they hadn't put him in a flat – he was certain the CIA owned numerous properties in the capital – but then realised that they were keeping him at a safe distance, making his association with them deniable. He couldn't be linked to one of their safe houses. A hotel was the best solution. No one would be surprised if he came and went without warning.

The early morning call had been to instruct him to collect the train ticket from the hotel's reception desk and to board the 08.00 East Coast Main Line train at King's Cross. He'd been told to pack a rucksack and wear hiking clothes. He'd be more convincing portraying an outward bound enthusiast than a businessman.

He ignored the caller's remark about boarding the train. "Why am I going to Scotland?"

"You'll find out when you get there. You should arrive at Edinburgh Waverley in just over four hours. There's a bagel shop near the ticket office. Get yourself something to eat there and wait for another call."

"A bagel shop? That's a predictable choice for a Yank."

"My ancestors were Polish Jews. I thought you might like to experience some of our culture. It also happens to be a good location that my colleagues can observe easily."

"I could get off the train before then."

"Come on, Mason, you know that would be stupid. You'd be *stranded*."

However much he loathed this situation, he knew he'd go along with every instruction. The lives of his team members depended on his co-operation. Besides, he couldn't run far. The Americans had ensured that his only access to funds was through them. They'd given him a cash card and a forged driver's licence in the name of Karl

Fletcher. He didn't have any other identification, and he wouldn't dare use his real name in case the police found him.

"What do you expect me to do in Edinburgh?"

"Wait for the call."

The line went dead.

6

Lily Carter watched through the side window as the silver Lexus turned onto a private road. The car progressed slowly through the grounds of the estate, passing groves of trees and open pasture. She noticed a centuries-old manor house farther ahead. "Is this Station Helix? I thought I saw a sign saying this was a wedding venue."

"It is a wedding venue, but that's just a convenient cover arrangement," Abi replied. "All of this is owned by the MOD. This isn't Helix – that's on Orford Ness – but we access it from here. The estate goes all the way to the coast. The staff get taken by boat up to the site. It keeps everything discreet."

"How many places like this does the Government actually own?"

Abi smiled. "There are several others like this."

"Researching genetics?"

Abi shook her head. "Helix and the beta site are the only genetics labs."

"The beta site?" Lily's expression was inquisitive.

"The backup location for Station Helix. It's somewhere in the West Country. I can't be more specific than that because even I don't actually know where it is."

"So what else goes on at these sites?"

Abi grinned. "Are you trying to get me to divulge national secrets? Truthfully, I don't know. The MOD conducts a lot of scientific research. I presume most of it is about communications and weapons. It's fair to say that the Government has access to technology that most people aren't aware even exists."

The car drove past the manor house towards a brick-built stable block. A tall man with an expressionless stare stood waiting for them. "Who's that?" Lily asked.

"Stephen Jennings," Abi replied. "He's Charlotte's assistant."

"The one who's been looking into the security leak?"

Abi nodded.

The car stopped. The driver and his colleague opened the rear doors for them. Jennings approached. "Miss Jones, Miss Carter," he said as they stepped out of the car. Abi wondered if the man would ever learn how to make a greeting sound even marginally welcoming. His next comment did nothing to put Lily at ease. "The medical room is ready."

She glanced at Abi nervously and touched her arm as they followed Jennings towards the stable block. "What are they going to do with me?"

"Don't worry. They'll just take a few DNA swabs and a blood sample."

"We're not going to Orford Ness?"

"Not now. They can do the tests here. But Charlotte has no objection to you seeing Helix, so maybe we can do that later if we have time."

Jennings led them inside the building. Worn brickwork and timber frames gave an indication of the structure's age. It had a slightly musty smell that wasn't unpleasant, and cobwebs hung in corners that hadn't been touched despite the addition of modern office partitions and lighting. He knocked on the door of a converted stall and opened it without waiting for a reply. The interior was set out like a doctor's consultation room. A sheet of white paper, pulled from a roll on the wall, was laid over a metal-framed medical bed. Glass-fronted cabinets were secured to the walls. A woman wearing a white coat sat at a desk.

She spun round on her chair and spoke to Lily. "Hi, I'm Rhiannon. I'll be running the tests today. Don't worry – it's all pretty straightforward stuff."

Jennings spoke. "Doctor, we'll be back later. Abigail and I have another matter to attend."

"No problem. We'll be a little while anyway."

Abi squeezed Lily's hand to reassure her. "I'll see you soon. Don't go anywhere."

Lily grinned. "I don't suppose I have much choice."

Abi smiled. "I guess not." She followed Jennings out of the consulting room and closed the door behind her. "Charlotte said you had a lead about the security breach."

"Yes. I've reviewed the computer records. There's an internal system which analyses the registry logs of every file and folder on the network. It works behind the scenes looking for anomalies. It pings up an alert if it spots something it doesn't like."

"Is that how we found out about the leak?"

"Yes. It noticed several documents about the Generation Ones had been downloaded remotely to a mobile device."

"I see. I didn't think the system allowed that."

He nodded. "That's right... well, partly right as it turns out. There aren't any USB ports on the Station Helix terminals, so there's no way a network adapter can be used in the labs. But someone found a way around that by linking a wireless transmitter directly to the on-site server. To reduce the chance of someone spotting a suspicious Wi-Fi network, it was only active for fractions of a second at a time. Fortunately for us, that makes transferring files a fragmented process. Our suspect didn't get very much before the system noticed the error."

"It sounds sophisticated."

"Definitely not your basic off-the-shelf kit. More like something GCHQ would have."

"Or the CIA?"

He nodded. "The experts said our mole had to be logged on to the internal network to make this happen. They've identified the account that was used."

"Who was it?"

"Zoe Sibon."

Abi stopped and turned to face him. "Really? That's a surprise. She seemed like a nice person. Just a science geek."

"That's your professional judgement?"

"No, that's my intuition."

Jennings frowned. "Forgive me for preferring to make a judgement based on evidence. Nonetheless, you can put your intuition to the test. She's here. You can help me speak to her."

"Lead the way."

7

The room Zoe Sibon was being held in was on the first floor of the Tudor manor house, accessible only via a door into a secure corridor. Jennings used a swipe card to unlock it. They entered the corridor. The door swung shut behind them, an electro-magnetic buzz sounding as the locking mechanism re-secured itself. A plain beige carpet covered the uneven floor. Four doors stood along one side of the corridor; leaded windows overlooked a formal courtyard garden on the other. A suited man stood against the wall opposite the third door, alert but relaxed.

The guard handed Jennings a thin bundle of papers. He nodded at the man but didn't speak. He twisted the door handle and entered the room, holding the door open as Abi followed. It occurred to her that he hadn't allowed her into the room first – with his customary reluctant etiquette – thereby indicating to Zoe that he was in charge. She sat in a chair on the other side of a plain table and glanced up nervously, her eyes darting between them. "Why am I here?" she said, her voice cracking with tension.

They sat down opposite her. Jennings didn't speak but held Zoe's gaze with his glacier-blue eyes. Abi wanted to get started but understood protocol. Jennings would invite her to speak only if he judged it necessary. She suspected the paperwork he had just been given was the computer data he'd mentioned. She hadn't seen it so there wasn't much point in commenting on it. It occurred to her that he didn't actually need her there in order to conduct the interview. Had he waited for her because of Charlotte Black's instruction? She dismissed the thought. She wanted to listen and watch.

Zoe spoke again. "Why was I stopped from going to work?" Jennings ignored her. She turned to Abigail. "Tell me!" she pleaded.

"Information has leaked from Station Helix," Jennings stated coldly.

Zoe's nervous stare snapped back to him. "You think I had something to do with it?"

"Did you?"

"*What*?" She sounded incredulous.

"Did you steal data from the Helix server?" He delivered the words without emotion. Slowly he placed the sheets of paper face down on the table. She glanced at them. Jennings waited.

"I don't know what you're talking about. Really, I don't. What information?"

"You tell me."

"Seriously, I can't tell you anything." Her voice trembled. "I haven't done anything wrong."

"Convince me."

"How? I don't even know what I'm supposed to have done." She clasped her hands together to stop them shaking.

"You seem nervous."

"Of course I'm nervous! I haven't…"

"The computer records indicate you *have*," Jennings interrupted.

"Like I said, I don't know what you mean." She delivered the words slowly, her tone turning from fear to irritation. "I turned up here today, ready to get on the boat, and one of the security guys stopped me. I don't know why – he didn't say – but he was quite happy to do it in front of my colleagues. So thanks for that. Now why don't you tell me what I'm here for?"

Jennings pushed the pile of paper towards her. "Data concerning the Generation One EHBs and their observers was gathered from the Helix server. It was transmitted wirelessly to a nearby device. It was your account that accessed the server. Look for yourself."

"Is that why my phone was taken from me? Well you won't find anything on it. It wasn't me."

"Look at the records." He flipped the paper over. Text was laid out in columns. "These printouts show the times and dates when the data was accessed. I've highlighted the relevant entries. As you can see, you're shown as being logged on and accessing the folders."

She looked up in exasperation. "This doesn't mean anything to me! How am I supposed to understand this?"

Jennings bent forward. "Listen," he instructed. Zoe stared at him. He paused before speaking again, holding her attention. "My colleague doesn't think you're the sort who would leak national secrets to the CIA."

She picked up on the change of tone. Abi wondered why she'd been mentioned. Jennings clearly had an agenda. Zoe glanced at Abi, her look desperate. "Honestly, I had nothing to do with whatever he's going on about." Abi remained silent, studying her closely. The woman's eyes were red. "Please believe me." Abi didn't answer. Zoe slumped back in her chair, her eyes downcast.

"Look at the printouts," Jennings instructed.

"What's the point?" Zoe didn't look up.

"We'll be back in a minute. Look at the printouts." He stood. A subtle nod of his head towards the door told Abi he wanted to speak to her outside. They left the room and shut the door. He led her a short way along the corridor. "What do you think?"

"She didn't do it."

"Are you sure?"

"There are only so many signs of distress you can fake."

"I agree."

Abi stared, wide-eyed. "*What*?"

"That's why I brought you here. You're a good observer. We've already checked her phone. There's nothing on it – not even a fragment of a deleted file."

"You knew that before you started questioning her?"

"It doesn't mean she didn't do it."

"So why did you stop the interrogation?"

"She's an intelligent woman. I've left a metaphorical door open for her."

Abi frowned. "What are you keeping from *me*?"

"Like I said, you're here to observe. When we return, her emotional state will be different. Evaluate her behaviour and what she says. I need to be convinced she's telling the truth before I let her go."

"Before you '*let her go*'?" Abi glared at him. "You bastard. You already know she's innocent."

He ignored her insult. "Let's go back in." He walked back down the corridor and into the room. Abi followed, trying to mask her anger.

Zoe slid a sheet of paper across the desk towards her. "Look," she said, putting her finger on the paper. "Look at that date."

Abi hesitated. *Maybe this woman is a better actress than I thought.* "What about it?" she asked.

"Look at the time. I was at work then, but I wasn't logged on to my computer."

"How can you be so sure?"

"Because that was the day you brought Alex Hannay to Station Helix. I logged off and spent an hour or so talking to him. I didn't log on again until after you left."

Abi examined the paper. "But this shows you logging on for two and a half minutes during the time you were talking to Alex."

"*Exactly*. I didn't touch the computer. Ask *him*. Someone must've hacked my account to make it look like I was responsible."

Jennings gathered the papers. "Thank you, Miss Sibon. We had to make sure. Your property will be returned to you. You may take the rest of the day off."

He stood and left the room, not bothering to wait for Abi. For a few bewildered moments Zoe stared at the open door. Eventually she turned back to Abi with an angry questioning look.

"Are you okay?" Abi asked.

"I don't know. What was that about? No one's *ever* questioned my loyalty before."

Abi didn't know how to respond. Whatever she said wouldn't make up for what Zoe had just been put through. "I'm sorry you had to go through that. The leak is real. We're having to scrutinise every piece of information we can find." She reached for a pen inside her jacket. "Give me your hand." Zoe stared but did as she was told. Abi wrote a number on her palm. "I probably shouldn't do this, but that's my mobile. Give me a call if you want to talk."

"Okay. Thanks."

Abi stood up and strode from the room. She glared at the guard outside. "*Where is he?*" The man didn't have time to respond before she stormed off along the corridor.

She found Jennings a minute later outside the stable block. Gravel crunched loudly beneath her feet as she hurried towards him. He turned to face her, his expression devoid of emotion.

"What the hell was that about?" Abi demanded.

Jennings raised an eyebrow. "Get over it, Abigail. We all have a job to do."

"You *knew* she wasn't involved!"

"*Not* true," Jennings snapped. It was the first time she'd ever seen him drop his guard. "She could have been working with the mole. Bluff and double-bluff, that's how this works, and you know it. Perhaps *she* wasn't accessing the data but assisting someone else."

"By using her own IT account? You really think she'd be that stupid?"

"Or that clever."

"Give me a break."

He regained his composure. "I did just that, Abigail. You're good at reading people. Although I was reasonably confident Zoe had been set up, I wanted your opinion. I trust your professional judgement."

"I thought you called it 'intuition' earlier."

"To be fair, it was Charlotte who pointed it out to me.

You're a lot like her. Your intuition complements your objectivity rather than hinders it. It's a great quality."

"You're trying to flatter me to make me feel better?"

"I wouldn't go that far. I'm just expressing *my* professional judgement."

She scowled. "Next time you want my help, perhaps you should be straight with me."

"And lose that spontaneity? That would be a shame. Anyway, the exercise proved to be very useful. By drawing attention to Zoe we've had a little more freedom to work out what's gone on. We know who stole the data."

"Who was it?"

"A relative newcomer to Helix: Warren Ellis. We've looked into his background. He has a biology degree but knows his way around computers. At university he found a cause – something to do with protecting the Amazon rainforest – and went on a few protests. Academically gifted and ideologically ignorant; the sort who can be befriended easily and manipulated. It's common practice for the intelligence agencies to recruit university students. Our people do it as much as the CIA."

"Have you detained him yet?"

"The security team should be bringing him back from Helix as we speak."

"Do you want me to help with the interview?"

"No, you have to get Carter back to London. I don't need your help with this one. Ellis will tell me everything."

"How can you be so sure?"

"There's a difference between people like Ellis and Sibon. She has principles and sticks to them. He's just a misguided fool who'll blab to protect himself. Particularly if he thinks he's going to prison."

"Okay, I'll head back to London." She paused. "*Next time…*"

Jennings nodded and walked back towards the mansion.

8

The clock on the Range Rover Sport's dashboard showed 15.09 as Lucas backed into a parking space at Perth Police Station. Alex and he had stopped twice to refuel but the delays had been brief. They'd bought some bottled water and tasteless sandwiches at one of the motorway service stations and had eaten once they were back on the road. Lucas hadn't worried about keeping to the speed limit, successfully slicing over an hour off the predicted journey time. He turned off the ignition. "Let's find him," he said.

Alex nodded and climbed out of the car. "I texted our MOD contact as we came into town. He's just sent one back. He's waiting for us in the front office. McLeod's wife and kid are with him."

"That's good."

"Why? The poor woman must be out of her mind with worry."

"That's not what I meant. McLeod's still at risk. It's easier for us to explain what's going on *and* protect his family if they're in the same place."

As they neared the police station's front office, the door opened and a man stepped outside to intercept them. "Hannay? Ingwe?" the man asked with a broad Glaswegian accent. He held up an MOD identity card. "I'm Phil Reid. They sent me over from Faslane to assist you." They shook hands.

"What can you tell us?" asked Alex.

"The superintendent's a tad put out but he's doing as he's told," Reid replied. "I've asked him to vacate his office so you can speak to McLeod privately. I thought you'd prefer not to use an interview room."

Alex glanced at Lucas with a questioning look.

"The interview rooms can be monitored," Lucas explained. He turned back to Reid. "We appreciate your help, Phil. I don't think we can let you go just yet, though."

"Aye, no problem. You know about the guy in the Royal Infirmary?"

Lucas nodded. "I take it he's still under guard?"

"Of course. We've taken over from the local police. His face isn't pretty but he'll live."

"Do we know who he is?"

"No. He's refused to give any details, but we've seized his phone and our techies are looking at it now. It was the only possession he had on him… well, apart from the knife he tried to gut McLeod with. We took his fingerprints and are running them now. I'll let you know as soon as I have something."

"I appreciate that. You told Alex that McLeod's wife and daughter are here?"

"Yes. She knows what's happened – or at least some of it. The custody sergeant let McLeod call her as soon as he was brought in last night. She's been here since 11."

"Okay, let's meet her."

Reid took them inside. The public waiting area was small with a row of uncomfortable metal seats bolted to the floor, a noticeboard with out of date crime prevention leaflets, and a glass window and counter. "Mrs McLeod, these are the men from London I told you about."

Kate McLeod glanced at Alex and Lucas. She looked exhausted. Her arms clutched her daughter who had fallen asleep on her lap. "How long are you going to keep my husband locked up?" she asked. She tried to sound indignant but she was too tired to make her tone forceful.

"We should have him out in the next few minutes. The custody sergeant's been instructed to release Greg to us," said Alex, his voice reassuring. "My name's Alex and this is Lucas. We're with the Ministry of Defence."

"How much trouble is he in?"

"As far as the police are concerned the investigation is over, but there are some things we need to discuss with you and your husband. Phil's going to take you to an office where we can talk. Lucas and I will bring Greg up in a few minutes."

"Okay, thank you."

Lucas held up his MOD identification to a blonde police officer in uniform behind the glass. "Officer, would you take us to the custody suite please?"

"Yes, sir, I'll be right out," she replied. Moments later she unlocked a security-protected door and held it open for them.

"Thank you," said Lucas. "Mr Reid is going to take Mrs McLeod to the superintendent's office."

"That's fine; we've already been briefed," the policewoman replied. "Custody's this way." She led them along a corridor. At the end there was a grey metal door with a tiny window. She held a black tag against an electronic reader in the door frame. The door made a loud clunk as the solenoid in the mechanism released the lock.

She pushed the door open. A sergeant was sitting at a desk in front of a computer, conversing with another uniformed officer. "Sarge?" the female officer called out. "These are the men from the MOD."

The sergeant spun round on his chair. "Cheers, Jules." The officer smiled and left the custody suite. "Come in, gents. I'm sure you're not going to tell me why I'm releasing Mr McLeod to your custody, so I'll just get you to sign for him and give you his property. There isn't much. We took his phone, wallet and belt from him when he was booked in."

"Thank you, sergeant. We appreciate it," said Lucas.

"No problem. It frees up one of my cells – that's the way I look at it." He turned to the male officer behind the desk and tossed a bunch of keys at him. "Ronnie, go get Mr McLeod for these guys, would you? Cell four."

"Will do," the officer replied. He walked through a doorway into the cell block.

9

Greg McLeod entered the superintendent's office, hurried over to his wife and daughter, put his arms around them and hugged them tightly. "I'm so sorry you've had to go through this," he said, his voice filled with emotion.

"We're fine," Kate lied. Her eyes were moist with tears. "What about you? Have they treated you okay?"

Greg nodded. "Very well." He turned towards Alex and Lucas. "But I still don't know what's happened. What does this have to do with the MOD?"

Phil Reid coughed to interrupt. "I'll wait downstairs. Give me a shout when you're ready." He left the office and closed the door quietly.

Lucas indicated towards a chair, inviting McLeod to sit. Alex and he sat down opposite. "Greg, this is complicated. We have a lot to discuss with you, and I'm not just talking about the attack last night. I'm assuming you wish Kate to be present during this discussion?"

"Of course."

"That's fine, but you need to know that this conversation must never be repeated. We're about to divulge information to you that is classified and protected by the Official Secrets Acts. You're both legally bound to remain silent. Is that clear?"

"Are you serious?"

Ingwe held McLeod's gaze. "Totally."

"You have my word."

"Thank you. Tell us what happened last night. It's important we understand every detail."

"I'm not sure I can be as specific as you want," Greg replied. "It's difficult to remember."

"We understand," Alex said. "Let's go through it gradually. You were attacked on the Pitlochry dam. Why were you there?"

"I go there every night. I take a short walk after putting Megan to bed. It's become a ritual. I walk down from the house, cross the Tummel at the dam, walk along to the footbridge, cross over again and head back home. When the evenings are light enough I stop at the dam and watch the river for salmon and bats."

"So you stopped there yesterday?" Lucas asked.

"Yes."

"What happened then?"

"I noticed two men approaching me. They came from the same direction I had. I thought they looked suspicious because they were watching me instead of talking to each other."

Lucas nodded approvingly. "You have an eye for detail."

"It helps in my line of work. Testing high spec kit is all about details."

"Did they say anything?" Alex asked.

"No. I said good evening to them, but they didn't reply. One grabbed my arm and the other tried to stab me. Lucky for me he caught my belt buckle. Otherwise…" he didn't finish the sentence. Kate's eyes were wide with horror.

Lucas leaned forward. "You fought them?"

"What choice did I have?"

"I wasn't making a judgement. I just want to know what took place."

McLeod looked away and closed his eyes as he visualised the attack. He paused for a few moments. "I knew I had to do something right away. I saw a chance and took it. I kept thinking about Megan and Kate. The guy with the knife... I grabbed his hair and kneed him in the face. It was enough to knock him out cold. If I'd missed at that moment I don't think I'd be here."

"But you balanced the odds," Lucas observed.

"I can't remember how I beat the other man. I just knew that if I didn't stop him he would kill me. That's why I pushed him over the edge. I called the police as soon as I realised what I'd done. I knew he wouldn't survive that fall."

Alex spoke again. "You had no choice. You did the right thing."

"It doesn't feel like it. A man's dead and I'm responsible."

"Why did this happen?" Kate questioned. "There's rarely any trouble in Pitlochry."

Alex glanced at Lucas, checking for assurance that it was appropriate to provide an explanation. Lucas nodded.

"We don't believe this was a random robbery attempt." Alex's statement was directed at Kate. "Those men weren't trying to steal Greg's wallet and phone. They were sent to kill your husband." Kate gasped in shock. The colour drained from Greg's face. Alex continued. "We don't know *who* sent them yet – we're going to question the knifeman later to try to find out – but we do know *why*." He turned to

Greg. "You wanted to know why the MOD is involved. I'm about to tell you, but you may find the explanation hard to believe."

"Try me," McLeod replied.

"You're not who you think you are."

In the next thirty minutes Alex told the McLeods everything he knew about the EHB programme and Station Helix.

10

Mason parked the light blue Land Rover Defender in a residential street a short distance from the Royal Infirmary. The vehicle – whose keys he'd been given at Edinburgh Waverley Railway Station – was about fifteen years old and a not uncommon model in the rural parts of Scotland. It was similar to the Land Rovers he'd driven during his military service; not comfortable but robust and a logical choice for a trekker seeking outward bound adventure in the mountains. After being given the keys and the location of the vehicle at the train station – by a contact who'd found him at the bagel shop – he'd found the car, thrown his rucksack onto the passenger seat and waited for a call.

It had come seconds later; the American voice telling him to head for Perth to interrogate the prisoner being held under armed guard by Ministry of Defence policemen at the Royal Infirmary. "There's a connection to Station Helix," the man had said. "The man was sent to kill a person of interest to us named Greg McLeod. Find out who sent him."

Mason recalled the rest of the conversation. "Are you kidding?" he'd questioned. "How am I supposed to get past armed police officers?" The manipulation made him feel sick and vengeful in equal measure. The CIA bastards were prepared to send him into a situation where his face would be caught on dozens of video cameras in the hospital. They wouldn't use their own people for such a public task, but they had no compunction about using *him*. This mission would make him even more dependent on them for protection. He'd barely been able to keep his anger contained.

"You're a resourceful man, Mason," the voice had said. "Find a way."

It occurred to him that, had they wanted to, the CIA could have turned him over to the police at any time. They didn't need to send him into a situation which was unlikely to be successful, nor did they have to set him up like this. He tried to analyse what that meant. Did they have less to connect him to the Hannay murders than they'd implied? Did they believe he might be able to pull off the Perth job? Or did they simply want him caught by the police for a criminal offence, thereby eliminating any hint of involvement with the intelligence agency? The possibilities gnawed at his thoughts.

"I'm not going to let you take me down," he'd said aloud once the phone call had ended. He'd have to find an exit strategy, but right now that was impossible. He resolved to find a way. *Damn right I'm resourceful. It might take time, but I'll get my revenge*. Mason was a patient man.

He turned the key in the Land Rover's ignition and the engine stopped. For a moment he sat in silence, forcing himself to calm down and concentrate. The journey from Edinburgh to Perth had taken an hour. He'd made one brief stop at a petrol station to buy a large scale map of the town. He unfolded it and studied it carefully, committing the street plan to memory. It made sense to park away from the hospital's car park. If the alarm was raised while he was still inside the grounds, the police would probably assume he had a vehicle in a hospital parking space. It was counter-intuitive for a suspect to leave a vehicle a ten minute walk away, which was exactly why he'd picked this quiet residential street. He checked the map a final time then folded it again. He climbed out the vehicle, slammed the door shut and locked it. He started walking an indirect route to the hospital.

The hour's drive had given him time to formulate a plan. He was disciplined enough not to let his other thoughts – those of revenge against the CIA puppeteers – become a distraction. His survival was sufficient motivation to make him concentrate on the task. He'd been told where inside the complex he'd find the room he was looking for, but that knowledge alone wasn't enough. The facility was – in common with many British hospitals – a collection of buildings erected over many decades in a rather haphazard fashion. Old and new stood side by side, the numerous departments laid out in no logical order. As Mason entered the grounds he found his bearings, plotting what he saw against his mental two-dimensional image of the map.

Soon he found the building he was after. A dark-haired lad who appeared to be in his middle twenties was pushing an elderly man in a wheelchair towards the door. Mason noticed a family resemblance. He held the door for them and the younger man thanked him. "No problem," Mason replied. "Hey, I don't suppose you know where the charity shop is?"

"Yeah, just around that corner," the dark-haired man replied, pointing.

"Cheers, buddy." Mason walked in the direction the man had indicated and found the shop moments later. With a cheery hello he greeted the white-haired elderly lady with bifocal glasses who sat by the till. He saw from her name badge that Morag was a volunteer.

The shop was small, occupying little more than an alcove in the corridor. Shelves contained a slim selection of toiletries, packets of biscuits and bottles of soft drinks. Mason picked up a cheap toothbrush, a can of spray deodorant and a motoring magazine. He took them to Morag who studied them closely, looking for the price labels. She peered at the front of the magazine, eventually noticing the small print above a barcode panel.

"My granddad still loves his cars," Mason said, making conversation as she pressed buttons on the till. "He'll be pleased I found this for him."

"I hope he enjoys it, love."

"I'm sure he will." He handed her a ten pound note. "Put the change in the charity tin."

"Och, that's very generous of you," Morag replied.

"My pleasure. Take care."

"You too, love. I hope your grand-dey gets well soon."

He walked from the shop, shoving the deodorant can and toothbrush into his jacket pocket. He folded the magazine lengthways and kept it in his hand as he returned to the building's entrance. He walked outside and nodded at a nurse who was smoking nearby before heading to another part of the complex.

The cleaners' locker room was unoccupied; a small windowless location, sufficiently far enough away from the public areas not to be a distraction, but close enough to be practical for the staff. In an open locker he found a dark blue polo shirt with a contractor's logo embroidered on the front. He removed his jacket and pulled the polo shirt over his t-shirt. He couldn't find an identity badge but doubted that any of the hospital staff would be inclined to look closely and challenge him. He took the spray can from his jacket and tucked it inside his belt underneath the shirt. The toothbrush went into the deep left pocket of his hiking trousers, the folded magazine into the right. He grabbed a mop and a wheeled bucket, rolled up his jacket tightly and pushed it into the plastic container. He placed the head of the mop into the bucket and used the handle to push it along. He left the cleaners' area, entered a corridor and made his way towards a reception desk, guiding the bucket with the mop handle, portraying a bored cleaner who had little enthusiasm for his work.

"Are the police still guarding that guy on the first floor?" he asked the receptionist.

"Don't you mean the second floor?" she said.

"Yeah, probably. My manager must've given me duff information. D'you know if we can still clean up there?"

"I haven't heard otherwise," the woman replied. "I don't see why not. They're only occupying the room at the end. They probably won't let you in there, but I can't see the rest of the corridor being a problem."

"That's cool, just thought I'd check. See you later."

"See ya." The receptionist turned to a nurse who had arrived at the desk.

Mason walked away, the plastic wheels of the bucket droning noisily on the corridor's hard floor, the bearings squeaking. He glanced briefly at a building schematic on the wall that had been put up to assist visitors, needing only a second to orient himself. He continued walking, looking for the stairwell shown on the diagram.

As he entered the second floor, Mason saw one policeman at the far end of the corridor. A strap held a Heckler & Koch MP5 close to the officer's body armour. Mason knew the UK police forces only used single-fire versions of the gun – each bullet fired by an individual press of the trigger – because every shot had to be justified. The police use of firearms was completely different from his military experience. The weapon used 9mm rounds – the same ammunition as the holstered handgun strapped to the officer's leg. Standing approximately twenty metres away from the policeman, he knew that at this range the MP5 – with its red dot targeting system – was very accurate. The handgun wouldn't be anywhere near as precise. Over this distance there was a fair chance the officer would miss him completely, but he had no intention of putting the man's skills to the test.

If one police officer was in the corridor it meant there was certainly another inside the room with the prisoner. Mason couldn't see whether the door was closed. Casually he wheeled the cleaning bucket along the corridor. "All right?" he asked the police officer as he approached.

"Yeah, you?" the officer replied.

"Can't complain. You must be bored hanging around here."

"You get used to it."

Mason walked closer. "I take it it's fine for me to clean along here?"

"Sure, but not in the room."

He took another few steps. "There's a drinks machine down the hall. Can I get you and your mate anything?"

"No thanks, we're fine. We're handing over in twenty minutes or so."

"Oh, right. Well I'll get on then."

"Okay mate, have a good one."

"Cheers." Mason turned away. He reached for the deodorant can under his shirt, spun back to the policeman and sprayed him full in the face.

"Shit, you..." The officer put both hands up to his face, the stinging in his eyes and throat preventing him from finishing his sentence.

Mason grabbed the magazine and rolled it up tightly, converting it into an improvised baton. He rammed it into the policeman's throat. The man fell noisily against the wall, gasping desperately for breath, his MP5 clattering against the plasterboard as he collapsed.

Mason heard a man's voice from inside the room call out a name. He positioned himself to the left of the door frame, clutching his rolled-up magazine in his right hand. Suddenly the door opened and a second policeman stepped out, a handgun in his right hand supported by his left.

You should have looked before you came out.

Mason slammed the rolled magazine into the officer's face. He grabbed his arm and shoved it as hard as he could against the door frame. It wasn't enough to make him let go of the gun but it loosened his grip enough for Mason to twist the weapon from his hand. He hammered the handgun's grip against the officer's temple, knocking him out. The policeman slumped to the floor. His colleague was trying to rise but was seriously disoriented. Mason crouched down and positioned his arms around the officer's head and neck in a chokehold. The policeman faded into unconsciousness in seconds as the blood supply to his brain was interrupted.

Mason glanced into the room and saw the only occupant was on a medical bed, propped up by the raised section. He dragged the policemen inside, returned for the mop and bucket and then closed the door. He knew it was a fallacy that a person disabled by chokehold would be rendered unconscious for hours – a subject could recover in as little as thirty seconds once oxygenated blood returned to the brain. He had to act quickly.

The prisoner looked at him nervously. His left wrist was handcuffed to the bed's metal frame. Mason took off the stolen shirt and tossed it onto the foot of the bed. He pulled his jacket from the cleaning bucket and put it on. He crouched beside one of the policemen and unfastened the clip on his holster, removed the handgun – recognising it instantly as a SIG Pro model – and hid it inside his jacket. He did the same with the second officer's weapon.

"Who are you?" the man on the bed asked. His face was badly bruised and a dressing, taped in place, covered his nose.

Mason ignored him. He shoved the mop handle through the bars of the bed, pinning the man's arms. He glanced around the room and saw boxes of latex medical gloves in holders on the left wall, removed two from the box marked *Large* and stretched them over his hands. Next he took the toothbrush from his pocket, tore off the packaging and snapped the head off. He went to the bed, grabbed the shirt and shoved as much of it as he could into the man's mouth.

Holding the cloth firmly in place with his left hand he stabbed the modified toothbrush into the man's right thigh, the hard and sharp plastic puncturing the man's skin and muscle with ease. The man jerked against his constraints and screamed almost silently through the gag. Mason waited a moment and then pulled the shirt from the man's mouth. The man stared at him through red and watery eyes. "I'm not messing about," he said coldly. "Do you understand?"

The man nodded in response.

"Good. Let's keep this simple. I have the ability to kill you swiftly and silently. Co-operate and it won't come to that. All I want is information. You have the ability to give me what I need. Is that clear enough for you?"

"What do you want?" The man's already injured face was twisted in pain. The plastic shaft was still embedded in his leg.

"You were sent to Pitlochry to kill a man named McLeod. Who sent you?"

"I don't know what you're talking about."

Mason shoved the polo shirt into the man's mouth once more, held it in place and pressed down on the toothbrush handle, enlarging the wound in the man's leg. The man screamed again, his wail of agony muffled by the shirt. Mason removed it again. "Stop fucking around. Who sent you?"

The man groaned. "I don't know."

"Not good enough." Mason went to replace the gag.

"No, wait!"

Mason waited.

"I really don't know," the man said, his voice desperate.

"You know how it works. I don't get instructed directly. I just get a text message. That's it. I don't know where it comes from."

"Still not good enough."

"That's all I can tell you!"

"Bullshit."

"It's the truth."

Mason changed tactic. "What's your background? Special Forces? You learned your tradecraft somewhere."

"French Foreign Legion."

"But not any more?"

"No. I'm a civilian security contractor."

Mason recognised the similarities to his own experiences. "What company?"

"Highland-Global. We specialise in protection – looking after oil company workers in dangerous locations, hostage recovery… you get the idea."

"But you do private work too."

The man didn't answer.

"How do you get paid?"

"Swiss account."

"The man you were with… Is he Highland-Global too?"

The prisoner nodded.

"Why were you sent after McLeod?"

"You know I never get told why."

"So there's nothing more you can tell me?"

The man shook his head. "Nothing."

"In that case…" Mason tugged the improvised weapon from the man's leg, reached up and plunged it into his neck, ripping open his carotid artery. Blood spurted. The man writhed, his movements restricted by the mop handle.

Mason watched him for a moment as he removed the latex gloves. He tossed them into a bin lined with a yellow medical waste bag.

As the man bled to death on the hospital bed, Mason stepped over the bodies of the unconscious policemen and left the room.

11

A siren wailed nearby as Alex and Lucas walked from their Range Rover. Seconds later a police estate car turned into the hospital grounds. The siren went silent but the blue strobe lights on its roof bar continued to flash as it headed along the hospital's service road. Moments later the vehicle was out of sight. Lucas frowned. "That was an ARV."

Alex looked at him inquisitively.

"Armed Response Vehicle," Lucas explained. "Going the same way we're headed."

"What's wrong with that? The prisoner's under armed guard."

"By the MOD Police. That was a local unit on a shout. Something's wrong."

"Let's find out."

Nearing the building Phil Reid had described, they saw the firearms car had stopped beside two Police Scotland response cars and two MOD ARVs. Several officers stood outside the entrance blocking access. Alex and Lucas approached one of the officers and showed him their MOD identification.

"What's going on?" Lucas asked.

"I'm not fully aware of the details, sir. Bear with me and I'll get Bronze to talk to you." The officer reached for the radio attached to his stab-resistant vest, pressed the transmit button and asked for an officer to attend the front of the building. The officer listened to his earpiece for a moment and then transmitted again. "Acknowledged, thank you." He released the button. "He'll be right out."

"Thanks," Lucas said.

Thirty seconds later a short and slightly overweight man exited the building and headed towards them. His black shirt and trousers were standard police uniform, but two embroidered Order of the Bath stars on his epaulettes indicated his rank. "Inspector Cliff Barton," he said as he shook hands. "I'm Bronze Commander. What do you need me to do?"

"Hang on, inspector," Lucas said. "We're just here to speak to the prisoner."

"Oh." The police inspector looked surprised. "You're not Silver? I was told to keep things shut down until the MOD command team arrived. I guess that's not you."

Lucas shook his head. "Can we see the prisoner?"

"You can but there's not much point. He's dead. Stabbed in the neck with a toothbrush."

"*What?*"

"Someone caught your guys by surprise, knocked them both out and went in to kill your man. The scene was discovered by the team who were due to take over. They called us for back up."

"How long ago did this happen?"

"Forty-five minutes, give or take. The local units got here soon after the call came in, but the ARV had to travel from Edinburgh."

"We saw it arrive. I take it you're still looking for the suspect?"

Barton nodded. "Our main concern is that he now has

two loaded handguns. We have pretty clear CCTV from inside the reception and the corridor where your suspect was being guarded, but nothing else. I've sent an officer to review the exterior footage, but there isn't much. We've got the attacker leaving the building but nothing from the car park. It looks like he left on foot."

"He must have had a vehicle nearby." Lucas paused. "Shit."

"What is it?" Alex asked.

"As we came into town we passed a light blue Land Rover. I caught a glimpse of the driver for a fraction of a second and thought he looked vaguely familiar, but I couldn't place him. Damn it! I *did* recognise him – from an old MOD file. Alex, it was Andrew Mason who did this."

Alex suddenly felt sick. He didn't respond.

Lucas turned back to Barton. "I need those CCTV stills urgently. Tell your people that the suspect is a dangerous former soldier. Only firearms officers should approach him. It's highly likely he will retaliate if cornered."

Barton's expression was grim. "Tell me about the vehicle."

"A blue Defender, an old model, white roof panel."

"Did you get the index?"

"No."

"Where did you see it?"

"I think we'd just passed a football stadium."

"Okay, that gives me a starting point, but it'll be difficult. From there he could go in any direction: west to Crieff, southwest to Dunblane, south on the motorway, northeast to Dundee or north to Pitlochry. And that's assuming he doesn't just pull off the road and head up a deserted farm track or spin round and take the B-roads somewhere else completely."

"Can you get an air support unit up?"

"Sure."

"Good. Do that. It's unlikely that he'll head for Edinburgh or Dundee because it would be easy to spot the vehicle. He may know we have MOD staff at Pitlochry, so he'll probably avoid the A9 north. He'll assume we've identified him and the Land Rover. The rural roads are more likely."

"Great. No cameras and no ARVs within easy reach."

"The helicopter's our best chance of spotting him."

"I'll get on it." Barton turned away and hurried back into the hospital building.

12

Lucas didn't start the Range Rover's engine when he and Alex got back into the car. Alex hadn't said anything since hearing Mason's name. "Are you okay?" Lucas asked.

Alex looked at him. "I'm not sure." His face was pale.

"I'm sorry I didn't realise when I spotted the Land Rover."

"You did better than me. I didn't even notice the vehicle."

"I'm normally much better with faces."

"Lucas, stop apologising. You'd only ever seen his old photograph before. I'm amazed you recognised him from that. Thanks to you we know Mason is still active, which means the CIA is using him. This is the first lead we've had since you discovered his blood on the lorry he used to…" Alex didn't finish the sentence.

"We'll get him, Alex. Even if the Americans are protecting him he can't hide from us indefinitely."

"I hope you're right."

Lucas frowned. "I have to admit I'm not entirely sure what to make of this. He killed the man who tried to assassinate McLeod. Did the CIA tell him to do that? What benefit do they gain?"

"I guess they wanted the guy silenced before we spoke to him."

Lucas shook his head. "That can't be right. I think the

opposite is true. Remember the fresh wound on the man's leg? Mason tortured him. He wanted information."

Alex understood. "They sent Mason to find out about the McLeod hit."

Lucas nodded. "Just like us they don't know who's responsible."

Alex leaned back in his seat. "Until now. Mason may have that information. That gives the Americans an advantage."

"Perhaps. It's too soon to know."

"We have to prepare for a worst case scenario." Alex changed the subject. "Reid can look after the McLeods' security. We should find Mason."

Lucas hesitated before replying. "Alex, I know how important this is to you. We *will* find him, but we're not talking about your average criminal here. You and I don't have the skills to capture Mason."

"I understand that, but we aren't on our own. We have all the resources we need." He took his mobile from his jeans and touched the screen. "I think it's time we called Charlotte."

"Agreed."

Alex found Charlotte's number in his contact list and dialled it. The phone was answered seconds later. Alex activated the speaker mode so Lucas could hear. "Charlotte, it's Alex."

He spent the next five minutes updating her about the McLeods and Mason's murder of their suspect. As their call came to an end he mentioned Mason once again, emphasising his desire to pursue him.

"Charlotte, there's one more thing. I need a gun."

NINE

1

The aroma of beans and sausages cooking in Mason's mess tin filled his nostrils. He recalled earlier occasions when he'd spent nights camping in forests. Considerably worse conditions during his military training had given him useful skills and shaped him as a soldier. Now he had a vehicle to sleep in and a small camping stove for his food. Of course in those days he hadn't been a CIA puppet and wanted by the police for murder. The luxury of his camping arrangements was relative. He'd packed a few days' provisions into his rucksack – partly out of habit and partly to fit the profile of his cover – but he doubted he'd need to spend much time in hiding. The police search would begin in earnest, but it wouldn't take long for the effort to be scaled down. They'd keep an operation going – at least in name – but wouldn't continue to task firearms officers when they had no information about his location.

He hadn't spent long on the road after leaving Perth. He'd headed towards Crieff but had soon turned onto a narrow unclassified track in the village of Methven, just ten miles outside Perth. His map had shown him large swathes of forest were situated close by, marking the border between the Lowlands and the Highlands. From here it wouldn't take him long to reach the moorlands and mountains, but he didn't intend to stay in the wilderness. He stirred his beans, listening to the distant call of an owl in the twilight, and wondered if the Americans knew where he was right now.

At that moment his mobile phone rang, the ringtone's normally discreet volume startlingly loud in the stillness of the forest. It didn't surprise Mason that he still had a signal – he wasn't far from the village and had noticed a transmitter mast beside the track – but the interruption to his solitude irritated him. He answered the call.

"We see you've gone to ground," the anonymous American voice said.

How do you know where I am? "Of course."

"Good. The police have tried looking for you. We're monitoring their communications. We'll decide upon an extraction strategy for you in the next few days."

I intend to figure that out for myself. "No problem."

"What did the prisoner in the hospital tell you?"

"What makes you think he told me anything?"

"Don't play games, Mason. You're a pawn moving to our rules. If you do something we don't like, we change the rules. You tortured him. He spoke to you. What did he say?"

You bastards won't be controlling me for much longer. Mason exhaled slowly, forcing himself to mask his anger. "Ex-French Foreign Legion. Recently a security specialist for a company called Highland-Global. That's all I know."

"That's not much."

"We didn't really have the time for a more productive conversation."

The American ignored Mason's sarcasm. "We'll look into it. Stay in the area. We'll contact you again within forty-eight hours." The call was cut off.

Mason put the phone back into his pocket, cursing under his breath. He heard the high-pitched buzz of midges near his face and mentally made the association between the insects and the CIA. They were both persistent unseen irritations that he couldn't ignore. He waved the insects away, knowing they'd pester him for at least the next hour before night fell. But he'd coped with much worse. He turned his attention back to his mess tin, focussed on the pleasant smell of the beans and sausages, stirred the food once more and began to eat.

2

"Has Alex called you?" Charlotte held open her office door for Abi.

"I haven't heard from him. Is everything okay?"

Charlotte pushed the door closed. "There have been some developments we need to discuss." She indicated towards one of the chairs in front of her desk and sat down in the other. "Before that, let's talk about Suffolk. Stephen tells me he's identified the mole."

"A computer genius called Warren Ellis. The kid hacked Zoe Sibon's account to make it look like she was responsible."

"You're sure she had nothing to do with it?"

"Yes."

"Fine. I trust your judgement. Stephen hasn't found any links between Sibon and Ellis. She's in the clear."

"Good." Abi paused. "I'm not happy with the way he treated her."

Charlotte's expression was indifferent. "I learned a long time ago that it's necessary to take a pragmatic approach, Abigail. Do you know why I wanted you to help Stephen with the interrogation?"

"To get a different perspective?"

"Partly. You're a good judge of character. But there was a second reason."

Abi looked at her quizzically. "Go on."

"This business is all about friends and enemies; those you can trust and those you can't. You provided the counterpoint to Stephen's ruthlessness. Zoe feels indebted to you. She thinks of you as her ally. You now have a reliable and trustworthy contact inside Station Helix. That might be useful."

Abi stared. "It's all about manipulation with you, isn't it?"

"That's just the way it is. I need every advantage I can get. The EHB project has been running for decades. I may be in charge of it now, but I'm just one more administrator who'll get moved on to something else eventually. I'm sure I've ruffled a few feathers by bringing in Carter and McLeod. I'm under no illusion that my association with the programme may be nearing its end."

Abi leaned forward. "You think they'll replace you?"

Charlotte nodded. "They'll leave me in charge while the situation remains volatile. The Government always needs a scapegoat."

"But you're trying to protect these people."

"As I said, a pragmatic approach is needed." She smiled. "But we're not here to talk about my career. Have Carter's test results come back?"

Abi shook her head. "They'll need a week or so."

"How's she coping with being confined here?"

"She doesn't like it but she knows it's for her protection. We can't keep her here indefinitely."

"We don't have a choice at present." Charlotte changed the subject. "Ellis rolled over. He told Stephen everything. Of course he didn't know who was directly in charge, but he did know he was working for the Americans. It's reinforced my suspicions."

"You have a name?"

Charlotte nodded. "The operation to snatch Carter was run from a CIA monitoring station in Covent Garden. A former Special Forces instructor named Jack Caldwell is the station chief there. My counterpart at Five has a great deal of respect for him."

"What do we do about Caldwell?"

"Right now – nothing. There might be another avenue to explore: Andrew Mason. He's resurfaced."

"Where?"

"Perth Royal Infirmary."

"He's in hospital?"

"In a manner of speaking. He killed the man who tried to murder Greg McLeod."

"Jesus. The CIA must have sent him."

Charlotte nodded. "For information, not to kill him. They want the technology – their attempt at grabbing Carter proved that. They need to stop the killings as much as we do. We don't know if they found out anything because Mason got to the hitman before Alex and Lucas."

"That puts the Americans ahead of us again."

"That's my concern. We don't know who the assassin was, but he had a grenade emblem tattooed on his arm. One of the MOD men recognised it as French Foreign Legion. We have his fingerprints too, but even if the French agree to help us identify him, they may only have a declared identity on record."

Abi didn't recognise the term. "What's that?"

"A false name. The legion doesn't ask many questions of its recruits. It believes in allowing people a new start in life."

"Great. That was our only lead."

Charlotte paused, glancing at her desk and then back to Abi. "Alex wants to go after Mason."

She responded immediately. "That's too dangerous."

"I agree. He's making this personal. He's becoming distracted."

"Can you blame him?"

"I understand how he feels, but if I have to pull him off this I will. A few days ago he asked me to use him as bait in order to see what the Americans are up to. You know him better than me. How worried should I be?"

Abi considered her response before replying. "He was determined to learn about his parents. You recruited him because of that persistence."

"Sifting through files is different from going after a psychotic former soldier."

"He's not alone."

"Even Lucas is out of his depth."

"They have backup teams."

"Of course, but I think Alex wants to do this on his own. He asked me for a firearm."

Abi frowned. "Maybe I should speak to him."

"Do that. Find out what's going on in his head. Right now I want him concentrating on the McLeods. Lucas and he may need to stay in Scotland for a few days. We can get McLeod's tests done in Pitlochry, but that doesn't solve the protection issue. For now the cover story will hold – McLeod's taken a few days off work to recover from the robbery and to be with his family – but that only gives me a few days to decide what to do next."

"I'll talk to Alex." Abi frowned again and looked away. "What is it?"

Abi turned back to her. "We're still not in control of this, Charlotte." She hesitated. "Perhaps it's time to speak to Caldwell."

Charlotte held Abi's gaze for several seconds. She didn't reply but nodded slightly and stood up. "Let me know when you've spoken to Alex." She walked to the door and held it open.

"I will." Abi left the room and turned into the corridor outside.

3

"I can see why you enjoy this walk," Alex said. He and Greg McLeod leaned against the iron framework of Pitlochry's footbridge, looking westwards at the hydro-electric dam. The first signs of autumn's encroachment were visible in the colours of the early evening light.

"It doesn't feel the same any more," Greg replied, his gaze fixed upon the grey architecture upstream. It was the first time he'd followed his habitual route since the attack. Lucas had been reluctant to allow the Scot to leave his house, but with Alex's persuasion he'd relented. An MOD team – under Phil Reid's supervision – had been tasked with protecting the McLeods. Alex and Greg weren't alone, but their minders kept a discreet distance.

"Early days," said Alex. "Trust me, I know how overwhelming this is."

"Aye, I suppose you do. It's just a lot to take in." Greg hesitated. "Is it really possible that this genetic programming is flawed?"

"I can't answer that."

"What concerns me is whether Megan's inherited a problem from me." McLeod's tone revealed subdued anger. "I guess those scientists didn't think their subjects might actually have children one day."

"Let's get the tests done and see what happens."

McLeod stayed silent, watching the river. The rush of

water – normally a relaxing, therapeutic sound to him – did nothing to quieten his mood. He'd felt a deep and burdening sense of vulnerability since the attack, but the fear that harm might befall Kate and Megan troubled him to a much greater degree. The sudden intrusion into his life by MOD operatives was, he understood, a necessary hindrance, but their presence compounded his irritation.

Reid had tasked a woman from his team named Tanya Smith to stay with the McLeods to provide close supervision, using the cover story that she was an old friend of Kate's from London who'd come to visit for a few days. Smith had done her best to keep out of the way, but their house wasn't big enough to give the McLeods any sense of privacy. They didn't have a spare bedroom, so she slept in the living room on the sofa. Other operatives – Greg didn't know how many – were staying nearby. He hoped the upheaval would be temporary, but he didn't delude himself into thinking that life would return to normal. He stared at the river, momentarily lost in the turbulence of the swirling water.

Minutes passed before he spoke again, his curiosity eventually snapping him out of his sombreness. "So how do they change DNA anyway? Don't they have to infect you with a virus or something?"

"That's one way of doing it – it's called a vector – but it's not the only way," said Alex. "It's also possible to inject genetic material directly into cells. Had I followed my parents' career path I might be able to explain it better, but my interest in cameras took over. I can only give you the basics, I'm afraid."

"That suits me." Greg turned back, watching the River

Tummel tumbling over the dam, the water appearing black in the fading light. "Does it actually work?"

"I guess that's what the EHB programme is trying to prove," Alex replied. "In my case, I know my injuries healed much faster than they were supposed to. And I was quicker and more co-ordinated than most of my fencing opponents."

"I always had more endurance than the lads I grew up with," said McLeod. "If I really have the ability to process oxygen more efficiently than everyone else, I guess that explains why."

Alex nodded. "What about your work?"

Greg laughed, but not because of genuine amusement. "Ah yes. Interesting to know that I was encouraged to go into aeronautic equipment testing as an extension of the Government's experiment. I guess I can thank my adoptive parents for that." He exhaled and briefly clenched his jaw. "I was brought up not to keep secrets," he added bitterly. "Don't you just love the irony?"

"My parents kept this from me too." An image of his parents – one of his photographs at home – appeared briefly in Alex's thoughts. "It's still something I struggle to come to terms with, but it doesn't stop me from respecting their work and the life they provided for me. I'm trying not to dwell on the contradictions."

"I'll try to follow your example. I'm just not ready to speak to them yet." Greg changed the subject. "In answer to your question, my job is perfect for someone like me. Now I know why. In order to test the equipment, my colleagues and I have to undergo difficult conditions: increased g-forces, disorientation… that sort of thing. I'm always the one who can stay focussed and functional the longest. You can put me in a helicopter chassis, drop me upside down in a tank of freezing water in the dark, and I'll know where I am even when the wave machine is doing its best impression of the North Sea. We test a huge range of kit and there's very little that I find difficult to handle. My colleagues tend to specialise in certain areas. I do everything."

"Looks like you've answered your question," said Alex. "Come on, let's walk back. Kate will start worrying if you're not home soon."

"Aye, she's been through enough." They headed to the north bank of the river, detecting the slight sway of the bridge beneath their feet. "So what happens next?" McLeod asked as they walked. "How do you tidy up this mess? When does it end?"

Alex stared ahead and didn't reply. He didn't have the answers, but Greg's questions made him think of one name: Andrew Mason.

4

Standing back from the small crowd, Charlotte Black watched Arnold Rossington's interment with disinterest. Protocol dictated that senior Government staff attended the funerals of notable individuals. She wouldn't have come through choice. She'd never met Rossington and had only a vague understanding of his career. She assumed – quite rightly – that a businessman with influence in the oil industry would have political connections. She wasn't interested in the details, but the high profile attendees standing around the Highgate Cemetery grave site included the Prime Minister and a third of the Cabinet. She raised her coat jacket's collar. The chill in the air and the greyness of the sky should have meant nothing more than marking the end of summer, but, beneath the trees in London's most famous Victorian cemetery, the conditions seemed apt for a funeral. She silently wished for the tedious ceremony to end so she could return to her office.

A tall man wearing a long overcoat detached himself quietly from the main group and walked towards her. His demeanour was confident, his appearance styled. William Dawkins was nearing fifty, the grey flecks in his otherwise dark hair giving him an air of authority rather than making him look older than his years. He spoke softly. "Charlotte."

"Home Secretary." She kept her voice low to avoid being overheard.

"Tiresome aren't they?" Dawkins continued. Charlotte glanced at him, not entirely sure what he was referring to. He saw her confusion. "Funerals you're obliged to attend through a sense of duty," he explained.

"Yes, sir." Charlotte wondered if there was any point to the conversation or whether Dawkins was just as bored as her.

"Of course, they can be useful too," he added.

"Useful, Home Secretary?"

"It's interesting to see who crawls out from the woodwork on these occasions. I'm sure you recognise the usual faces from the Government and the Opposition." He looked directly at three men standing beside the grave. "Do you know who those men are?"

"The bald man is Archimedes Falkner. He was a high level intelligence official during the Cold War. I don't know the other two."

"Benjamin Barnard and Edward Rhodes. Together with Rossington the four of them were some of the most influential men in Great Britain. They're all rather reclusive – particularly Rhodes. But there's nothing like a funeral to bring people together."

"You sound as though you're enjoying the spectacle, Home Secretary."

"What I'm enjoying is witnessing the crumbling of an empire."

"Sir?"

Dawkins looked at her for a moment before speaking again. There was a wry smile on his face. "I look forward to the day when the old guard no longer influences politics. Over the decades these men have pulled the strings on everything from Government appointments to foreign policy."

"I think that's called 'friends in high places', sir."

"Fortunately there are a few of us who got where we are today *without* friends like those. I'm one of the new breed, Charlotte. I didn't have the private education or the family influence. People like me are an irritation to people like *them*." He stared at the old men ten metres away then turned back to Charlotte. "The trouble is the old loyalties still run deep. That's why I need people like you."

"I'm not sure what you mean, Home Secretary."

"You will. Do you know the pergola on Hampstead Heath?"

"Yes."

Dawkins glanced at his Rolex wristwatch. "Good. Meet me there two hours from now. I'm sure you'll be interested to know how our 'friends' are connected to your little project on the Suffolk coast." He turned and walked away, not waiting for a reply.

Charlotte reached for her phone, unlocked it and selected the camera function. Standing on the periphery of the crowd she wasn't drawing attention to herself. Touching icons on the screen, she zoomed in and took several photographs of Falkner, Barnard and Rhodes. She recollected Dawkins' words. *It's interesting to see who crawls out from the woodwork on these occasions*. She took a few more shots of people in the crowd she didn't recognise and several of those she did. Satisfied with her intelligence gathering, she returned the phone to her pocket, turned away and followed a footpath through the trees and tombs away from Arnold Rossington's grave.

5

Hidden in a discreet corner of Hampstead Heath the Edwardian pergola was one of the lesser known areas of the north London park, but one that Charlotte had visited on several occasions when seeking an escape from the demands of her MOD career. Its solitude and scarcity of visitors appealed to her, but she knew that its charm was something of an illusion. The location had fallen into disrepair for many years, and only recent efforts had restored the garden's original grandeur. Built over two levels, the pergola consisted of several elegant walkways, paved with brick and stone and lined with timber posts and beams. Climbing plants entwined the woodwork, their foliage creating a canopy overhead. It wouldn't have surprised her if she'd stumbled across a production of *A Midsummer Night's Dream*, for its backdrop of pseudoclassical columns and balustrades seemed perfect for the play. Charlotte entered the west wing of the structure and climbed the steps to the upper level.

A suited man showed her a police warrant card. "Afternoon, ma'am. The Home Secretary is waiting for you." He pointed along the walkway. "He's at the far end."

She thanked him and headed in the direction he indicated. For once she didn't pay attention to the flowers and vines that lined the promenade. Reaching the end of the pergola's west wing, she saw the Home Secretary leaning upon the balustrade of the next section, looking at the shrubs and trees in the garden below. Another policeman stood beyond him at the far end of the walkway.

Dawkins straightened as she approached. "This conversation is confidential," he stated.

"Of course, Home Secretary."

"And completely deniable."

"Understood."

He paused. "You know you've rocked the boat over your handling of the EHB programme?"

"Are you talking about my decision to bring in the Generation Ones for testing?"

"Don't mistake what I'm saying as a criticism, Charlotte. I think you've made a wise choice. But you've upset some important people. Your actions are being watched."

"After the incident with Cline, I didn't have a choice."

"Agreed. But you don't know the full story. Station Helix has a complicated history."

"You said the 'old guard' are connected to the project."

"They're more than connected to it. They created it. Officially, of course, it's always been an MOD project, but the idea came from them and they've never backed away. Every decision that any government has made about Helix has been influenced by them."

"Why wasn't I told about this?"

"You didn't need to know. Most of the hierarchy of Government is unseen. Your superiors in the Ministry have been supported by Rossington and the others for many years. The same is true of the Cabinet. Think of it as layers upon layers. There are plenty of people on both sides of the

House whose political aspirations have been encouraged and sponsored by those four men. But it's not just politicians. Their influence reaches deep into the whole civil service machine."

"Why are you telling me this now?"

"Because you need to know what you're up against. Times are changing, but incredibly slowly. I hold one of the highest positions in Government, but I'm not naive enough to think that I can overcome Cold War attitudes overnight. I'm just a figurehead – guided and advised by an army of faceless civilians who'll still be shaping policy long after I'm gone. Old allegiances are hard to break down. It's political suicide to bite the hand that feeds you, whether that's a wealthy fundraiser or the unions."

"You told me that you reached your position without their help."

"I did, but I work with people who were guided along the traditional route. The old boys' networks thrive. I'm isolated in that respect, which is why I need people I can trust."

"Why me?"

"Because you can achieve things behind the scenes that I can't do publicly. Your involvement with Helix has shown me that you're prepared to take politically dangerous risks."

Charlotte shook her head. "I wasn't thinking politically. Circumstances forced my hand. I won't come through this unscathed."

"That's something I *can* influence. I can protect you." Dawkins smiled for the first time during their conversation. "Fortunately the Home Secretary does have *some* power."

"I'm not clear with what you expect me to do."

"Start by telling me what you know."

"Very well." She paused. "I'll try to keep this concise. Until a few weeks ago, I wasn't going to do anything with Helix. I was appointed to keep an eye on things for the Ministry, nothing more. Then Jonathan Cline jumped off Tower Bridge."

"His suicide was attributable to a problem with the Generation One experiment?"

"There's no proof of that. But things became complicated. The Americans learned about the EHBs and made an attempt to grab Lily Carter. Our hypothesis is industrial espionage. They wanted a live sample. It's likely they're running their own genetics research, but Helix is way ahead of anything they have so far."

"I get that. But you've had some additional interference."

Charlotte nodded. "David Stone was assassinated in Cairo. Someone tried to take out Greg McLeod in Scotland, but he fought back. We still don't know who tried to kill him, but we think the Americans do. They used Andrew Mason to interrogate our prisoner."

"Mason – he's the one who told them about Station Helix."

"Yes – three years ago. We still want Mason for killing two of our scientists."

"But the Americans have him and you don't know where he is."

She nodded. "I'm thinking about approaching them. Their operation is being run by a station chief here in London called Jack Caldwell."

"Do you think they'll help?"

"Not a chance." She hesitated. "Unless we give them something in return."

"Such as?"

"You're the politician. You know more about the Special Relationship than I do."

"But you have something in mind?"

"They've already demonstrated how badly they want our technology."

Dawkins stared. "You want to give them our EHB data?"

"That decision would have to be made by someone with more power than me."

"I don't know that the Special Relationship goes that far."

Charlotte shrugged. "They're supposed to be our allies. They'll work out the science for themselves before long anyway."

"That doesn't mean it's acceptable to give away years of research."

"It's just an option. But I'm running out of them."

"There's something you haven't considered."

She looked hard at him.

He continued. "You thought Station Helix was controlled by the MOD. Today you've learned the true hierarchy behind the EHB programme."

"Go on."

"You've established the Americans want the technology. They don't want to kill the subjects: they want to study them. But the Americans represent the only leak from Helix. That narrows down the number of people who knew about the Generation One problem."

"Oh my god." She stared at him as she realised the implication. "Are you saying...?"

He interrupted her. "I'm not saying anything. I don't have any proof. But there are men out there with a fervent sense of empire spirit who might take extreme steps to protect a national secret."

"But there isn't any evidence that Cline's condition resulted from his genetic programming!"

"Decisions rarely get made on absolutes. We've gone to war on weaker hypotheses."

"They must be mad."

"Now you understand why I want to bring them down. You have the resources, Charlotte. Just stay under the radar. If you can get to one of them, you'll have your answers and I'll have the evidence to sever their ties with Government. I suggest going after Rhodes: he doesn't have the popularity of Barnard or the ruthlessness of Falkner."

"I take it I'm on my own if this goes wrong?"

"You're very astute."

"We still have to deal with the Americans."

Dawkins paused, considering his options. "Agreed. I don't want them running around trying to kidnap our citizens. We have a terrorist under house arrest they've wanted to extradite for over a year. Tell Caldwell that if he gives you Mason, I'll put the package on a military flight to Quantico immediately."

"He'll want your word on that."

"I'll mention it to the ambassador. I'm having afternoon tea with him tomorrow at Claridge's. The station chief will be expecting your call."

6

After a second night in the forest Mason decided it would be safe to head out for provisions. Unfamiliar faces were common in the small Scottish towns due to tourism, so he wouldn't draw attention. It was late enough in the season to justify the dark blue woollen hat he now wore, and two days of beard growth had changed his appearance since he'd been recorded on the hospital's CCTV system. He avoided paying for anything with the card the Americans had given him – he'd used it at a machine in Edinburgh to draw two hundred and fifty pounds in cash – and deliberately chose shops where the security systems were likely to be non-existent or limited to poor quality cameras that probably weren't recording anyway.

He tore the cellophane from the packet of sandwiches he'd bought at a petrol station and took a bite, ignoring the blandness of the chicken. Food served the functional purpose of keeping him fuelled; taste was irrelevant. Sitting on the flat bonnet of the Land Rover he took in his surroundings. Heather and hardy grasses covered the hilly landscape in all directions. A few sheep grazed on the slopes. Apart from the pylons and the electricity wires that stretched between them, this was a spectacularly wild and beautiful location. In the distance the snow-covered angular peak of Schiehallion impressed the eye. He twisted the lid off a plastic Sprite bottle and gulped down a mouthful of the carbonated drink. He didn't have time to screw the cap back on before his solitude was disturbed by his mobile's ringtone. He took the device from his pocket and looked at the screen, not expecting to see anything other than the withheld number message that appeared on it. He accepted the call but didn't say anything.

The familiar American voice spoke. "The information you extracted has proved useful. It's time to make new arrangements."

"I'm pleased you're so happy."

"You're the one who should be pleased. We feel you should get your old team back together."

Mason frowned. "Why's that?"

"We want you to find some more information. This time you'll need assistance. It makes sense for you to work with people you know and trust."

You mean people you can discard at your convenience. "What's the job?"

"We looked into Highland-Global. Its ownership is something of a labyrinth, but we followed the trail back to a company owned by Edward Rhodes."

"Never heard of him."

"Few people have. He keeps himself under the radar, but he's an influential player. We require you to find out why he ordered the hit against McLeod."

"Why do I need my team?"

"Rhodes lives on a hunting estate in the Highlands. You'll be able to get onto his land easily enough, but access to his mansion will be more difficult. He has security staff to protect him. You'll need to watch for a while, studying their routines."

"That's a high risk operation."

"You've managed considerably more problematic tasks."

"That's not the point. My men don't have anything to do with these games you're playing."

"We disagree. They were all involved in your plot to kill the Hannays in Suffolk. We own every single one of you. Don't forget that."

Mason clenched his jaw. *There's little chance of that.* "And when we get to Rhodes?"

"Intimidate him. Make sure he tells you everything about the assassination plot."

"How do I contact my team?"

"We'll text you all the details you need and arrange an equipment drop for you."

"Understood." The line went silent.

Mason put the phone inside his coat and resumed eating his tasteless lunch.

7

Alex reread the text message Abi had sent last night. *Let me know when you're free for a call.* He hadn't replied yet – not because he didn't want to speak to her, but because he knew what she wanted to talk about. His recent discussion with Charlotte had, in all certainty, caused alarm bells to ring. The message had jolted him into a more objective state of mind. He'd become distracted by the hunt for Mason; a task which had rapidly run out of leads. The police hadn't located him even though his image from the Perth Royal Infirmary's CCTV system had been shown on local television broadcasts. Alex forced himself to look at the circumstances rationally. He didn't have the skills to deal with the man who'd eluded the police and murdered his parents on his own. It needed a team effort.

His frustration hadn't been helped by the delay. By now he should have made contact with the final member of the Generation One experiment, but instead he'd had to remain in Pitlochry with Greg McLeod and his family while the ongoing risk to their safety was assessed. The sense of stalemate was intense, but he didn't know how the impasse could be broken. The MOD team couldn't stay in Pitlochry indefinitely. The McLeods – like Lily Carter in London – needed to get on with their lives. He knew they were even more frustrated by their confinement than he was about failing to track down Mason.

Deciding to have some time on his own, he took himself on an exploratory walk north of Pitlochry. A lane led him down an incline to a small boating station on a secluded bank of the Tummel. From there he followed narrow footpaths along the wooded bank of the river. In places the route almost vanished, but he persevered with the terrain. The physical effort helped settle his mind. In the damp margins at the edge of the river he found broad patches of wild garlic flowers. He paused there briefly to enjoy their heady chive-like scent before turning away from the river and clambering upwards into the pine forest. Here there were more substantial paths between the trees, and he picked a route which he expected to take him back towards the town. Gorse bushes and Scots pine dominated the landscape, but the area was not so vast as to completely block the sound of traffic from the bypass a few hundred metres from his position.

He found a wooden bench – cut from the trunk of a felled tree and decorated with carvings of squirrels at either end – and decided to rest for a while. It didn't take long for him to think about Abi again. He read the text message once more. *Let me know when you're free for a call.* Irritated with himself for not replying sooner, he touched the graphic on the screen to dial her number. She answered a few seconds later.

"Hey, Alex." Her voice sounded as though she was walking.

"Hi, Abi. Sorry for not getting back to you sooner."

"No probs. How are things with the McLeods?"

"They're trying not to let their frustration show."

"They've been through a rough time and they're

probably desperate to get back to normality. Having an MOD team watching their every move must be driving them nuts."

"It would be nice to have something to tell them."

"Sure." Abi paused. "What about you?"

"I'm okay. A little irritated by the lack of progress."

"I'd gathered that. I guess you knew that's why I wanted to speak to you."

"I lost focus when Mason resurfaced." The admission embarrassed him.

"It was understandable, but Charlotte needs to be reassured that you're concentrating on the Generation Ones, not Mason."

"I'm back on track." Alex hesitated. "Well, I would be if I weren't stuck here in Scotland."

"We need you to stay there a little longer. There's been a development."

"Go on."

"I've just come from a meeting with Charlotte. She's been given some information by a source – she wouldn't say who – and we think we know who tried to kill McLeod. This is big, Alex. We're talking about a group of people with decades-old connections to the Government, the military and the intelligence services. It sounds crazy but the men who started the Helix project are trying to kill the Generation Ones."

"Nothing surprises me any more. Who are they?"

"Archimedes Falkner, Benjamin Barnard and Edward Rhodes. There was a fourth – Arnold Rossington – but he died from a stroke in the back of his car last week. It seems they've been influencing very important decisions since the

1960s, including persuading Harold Macmillan to set up Station Helix as a secret research project. It was a touch of genius."

"Setting up Helix?"

"No – persuading him to keep it secret from the Americans. As Prime Minister he strived to strengthen the Special Relationship with the States. He ushered in an era of information sharing and strategic alliance. Helix was one of many projects that both nations would normally contribute to, but Macmillan kept this one hidden from Kennedy."

"The argument must have been powerful."

"No kidding. We're talking about unelected men in their twenties being able to entrench themselves in governmental policy-making. Charlotte believes it had something to do with Kim Philby."

"The double agent? How does he fit into this?"

"When Macmillan was Foreign Secretary he'd publicly supported Philby, dismissing MI5's suspicion about his Soviet connections. Philby was finally exposed just months before the Station Helix project began. Macmillan's error haunted him. He became much more willing to listen to the Firm after that. Falkner was a rising star in the intelligence world at the time. Macmillan was never going to refute him and his well-placed friends." Abi paused. "Now we're going to bring them down."

"How do we do that?"

"Firstly, we're going to try to arrange a meeting with Edward Rhodes for you and Lucas. He's just returned to his Highland mansion after attending Rossington's funeral here in London. We're working out the details now. It's basically a divide and conquer exercise. Rhodes is the easiest target. If we can isolate him…"

"We're more likely to get the information we need," Alex interrupted.

"Exactly. It's tricky though. Charlotte doesn't know who in the MOD is linked to Rhodes and the others. She can only use people she trusts."

"And?" Alex asked.

"And what?"

"You said 'firstly'. What else is going on?"

Abi laughed. "*Secondly*, we're going to speak to the Americans."

Alex paused. "When you say 'the Americans'…"

"I mean Jack Caldwell; the station chief who's been overseeing the CIA's attempts to extract information from Helix."

"That's a development."

"Charlotte's arranging the meeting now. She wants me to attend."

"Good." Alex hesitated, unsure if he should ask his next question. "Abi?"

"Yes?"

"Is this the guy who's been controlling Mason?"

"We think so. Don't worry. It'll be a topic of discussion."

"He won't admit to anything."

"Spies never do, Alex. It's just a matter of listening to what they *don't* say. I must admit I'm rather looking forward to the conversation."

"I bet you are."

"Be patient. This situation may be about to change. I'll

keep you apprised."

"You do that."

"We'll speak again soon." Abi ended the call.

8

A sign several miles back had told Mason that a battle had taken place several hundred years ago in the Highland valley where he now waited, but he hadn't thought any more about it. He wasn't an avid student of history and had other matters on his mind. He lifted the binoculars once again and studied the narrow road he'd taken to reach his stopping point, appreciating the image stabilizing system built into the device. The road followed the contours of the valley; above the river but still far below the glacier-carved peaks that gave the scenery its characteristic Highland shape. A black holdall had been left for him in a discreet location. In it he'd found an assortment of gear including the binoculars plus maps and camouflage clothing. The passing place in which he'd parked the Land Rover had been marked on one of the maps with the letters RVP. The abbreviation stood for *rendezvous point*.

He wasn't troubled that the RVP was visible from much of the glen. Few people other than local farmers and Munro-baggers ventured into this territory. If he were spotted there was nothing surprising about a four wheel drive vehicle being here. He scanned the valley sides with the binoculars and didn't notice anyone trekking on the slopes. He directed his attention towards the ridgeline opposite his position. If a sniper were up there he wouldn't spot him. It occurred to him that, had the Americans wanted to kill him, this was the place to do it and he'd be dead by now. He reckoned he was still of use to them – at least for a while.

They'd supplied him with several items of digital equipment. He'd been instructed to record everything Rhodes said, as well as downloading the entire contents of his hard drive. His lack of computer skills wouldn't be an issue – there was a sophisticated decryption program installed on the portable drive he'd been given. All he had to do was plug it into a USB port and wait for it to steal Rhodes' files. He was less confident about his chances *after* the mission. He was running out of time to devise an escape strategy.

A white Toyota Landcruiser came into view half a mile away where the road entered the valley. He watched it approach, adjusting the focus on the binoculars to keep it sharp. Soon it was close enough for him to recognise the men in the front seats. The driver was Curtis Wheeler, an army buddy of many years and his second-in-command. Beside Wheeler, studying a fold-out map, was Lyndon Fleck, an Irishman and adept mechanic. The Landcruiser drew closer and Mason lowered the binoculars. He turned around to see whether anyone else was heading along the valley from the other direction, but the road was empty. The Toyota pulled in behind his Land Rover a minute later. Wheeler killed the engine and stepped out of the vehicle.

Mason nodded. "Curt."

"Andy." Wheeler came closer and they shook hands. Fleck and two other men approached and Mason greeted them. The two he hadn't seen until they exited the vehicle were Paul South and Danny Rush. He was glad to be reacquainted with them, but these four men didn't account for his entire team.

"Where are the others?" he asked.

Wheeler shook his head. "After that job for the Pakistani blew out and you disappeared off the face of the earth, we weren't sure what to do. Travis and Mooney found work in Jordan through a contact. Rowland said he was going to visit family in France. I haven't heard from any of them since. To say it was a surprise when you made contact would be putting it mildly." Wheeler paused, frowning. "What happened?"

Mason scratched the stubble on his face. "The CIA got hold of me." Wheeler stared. "The Pakistan job was a set up," he continued. "The Americans found evidence linking me to the Hannays and devised a scenario to draw me in. They threatened to give the information to the police if I didn't cooperate. I don't know if it's true, but they say they can link all of you to Suffolk as well."

"Shit."

"That's why I haven't been able to contact you until now."

"So what's changed?"

"They want us to do a job."

"Go on."

Mason held Wheeler's gaze for a moment then glanced at the others. "It's an intelligence operation. They want information about a hit that went wrong. I have the name of the man who gave the order. He's a businessman called Rhodes – a landowner here in the Highlands."

"Hold on, will ya?" Fleck interjected in his strong Belfast accent. "Who did this guy try to kill?"

"Someone called Greg McLeod," Mason replied.

"Who's he?"

"I have no idea."

"This is crazy."

"I'm inclined to agree with Lyndon," Wheeler stated.

Mason shrugged. "McLeod must be important to somebody if the CIA are interested in him. But that's not the point. I'm more concerned about how we get out once the job's done."

"This is fucked up!" Fleck's tone was angry. "We have to run a covert operation for the CIA because they know you killed the scientists? And if we don't, we all get shafted?"

"We all knew what we were getting into, Lyndon," Wheeler said calmly. "Hannay deserved what he got. He screwed things up for all of us."

"Only because Andy sold information to the bloody CIA!"

"You accepted your cut. Drop it."

Fleck didn't respond. He shook his head and looked away.

Mason hesitated before talking again. "I actually don't think they care about you guys. After all, if they let the others leave the country… I just don't know. But I have to get to Rhodes and I can't do that without your help."

Wheeler nodded. "What happens after we get the information?"

"Hold on," Fleck repeated. He directed his remark at Wheeler. "Don't agree to help him on our behalf."

Wheeler frowned. "We're a team. We all know the score."

"Normally I'd be in complete agreement, but this is different. We aren't in control. You heard him."

"We're contractors," Wheeler replied. "We've always worked to someone else's agenda. Let's do the job and get out." Wheeler turned to South and Rush. "Are you in?"

"Like you said, we're a team," Rush replied. South nodded in agreement.

"What about you, Lyndon?" Mason asked.

Fleck stared for a moment. "I don't like it, but I'll do it."

Mason nodded. "Good. In answer to Curt's question, I don't know what happens afterwards. As I said, I think they'll ignore you. But, to be safe, you should get out the country. You can take a boat from the west coast to the Isle of Man and fly out from there to Geneva or Dublin. The Americans have been watching every move I make, so I'll have to find a different route. But that's for me to figure out. Right now we need to focus on Rhodes."

"What's the plan?" asked Wheeler.

"We get onto his estate and conduct surveillance. He has a security team, so we watch for patterns. We work out how long it would take the police to arrive if they were called. We study the terrain and establish our routes in and out. I want to know how many people are likely to be on the premises. We get on site and stay there until we're ready to go in. I collected some kit – night vision headsets, camo gear, radios. Everything we need."

Wheeler opened his jacket slightly to reveal a handgun in a holster. "You know us, Andy. We made sure we brought some kit of our own."

Mason nodded. "Let's get started."

9

The conference room – one of several inside the Ministry of Defence building – was furnished in the same sophisticated but understated style used throughout many of the Government offices in Whitehall. Plain drapes softened the bold lines of the tall rectangular windows. A highly polished mahogany table, surrounded by eight wooden chairs, stood in the centre of the room. Sections of the walls were panelled in dark wood. Discreet lamps were placed in shallow alcoves. The post-war building felt centuries old and unashamedly British; a romantic reminiscence of a time long ago. However fabricated the setting might actually have been, it provided a useful show of power and history. Charlotte had chosen this room for the meeting because it would, subconsciously at least, reinforce her purpose. Caldwell would understand exactly how seriously he should take her.

There was a knock at the door and a brief pause before it was opened. An assistant peered in and looked at her. "Ma'am, your guests have arrived."

"Thank you." Charlotte turned to Abi. "Are you ready?"

Abi nodded. "Let's do it." She pushed her chair back and stood up.

Charlotte addressed the woman at the door. "Show them in please."

The assistant opened the door wider, holding it as a man

and a woman stepped into the room. Charlotte greeted them. "Jack Caldwell? Welcome to the Ministry. I'm Charlotte Black. This is my associate Abigail Jones."

"I was intrigued by your invitation," Caldwell replied as he shook hands. "My colleague Clare Quinn." The dark haired woman smiled pleasantly but didn't speak.

"Intrigued but not surprised, I imagine," replied Charlotte. She showed Caldwell and Quinn to their seats at the conference table. "I understand your ambassador had a conversation with you."

"He did. He emphasised the importance of cooperation between our nations."

"That's good to hear."

"He suggested that we talk about our shared interests."

"Did he have any particular interests in mind?"

"He advised finding out what you wanted before drawing any conclusions." Caldwell leaned forward across the table. "I've been working in London for several years. During that time I've had numerous meetings with MI5, but never the MOD. I'm curious. Why exactly did you call this meeting?"

She held his gaze and smiled. "The CIA doesn't normally show an interest in MOD projects. What's changed?"

"You'll have to be more specific."

"Very well. Warren Ellis."

"That name isn't familiar to me."

"Perhaps not. He was working at one of the sites under my supervision. He's now in a holding facility after attempting to steal classified information. Fortunately the damage was negligible and we've ensured that such a leak can't happen again. My investigators found out that Ellis was working for an American contact. I was hoping you might be able to identify the individual concerned."

"I'd need more information before being able to look into that for you." Caldwell leaned back. "What can you tell me about the stolen data?"

"Very little. Names... that sort of thing."

"Why do you think this has anything to do with the CIA?"

"Ellis was working at a laboratory in Suffolk. You found out about the site three years ago when a former employee went to your embassy." Charlotte smiled. "You've admitted to being a curious man, Jack. It would be understandable if you'd tried to learn more. Of course, it would have taken some time to get a mole in place."

"We don't spy on our closest ally."

"Really? The spooks at Five watch you all the time. You're not trying to persuade me that you don't do the same?"

Caldwell smiled. "I doubt I'd be able to mislead you, Charlotte, so let me clarify my position. I do know about the Suffolk MOD facility called Station Helix. My superiors are both impressed and irritated that you kept it hidden right under our noses for so long. They'd certainly like to know the details about what you're doing there. But the little information we gathered over three years ago was from a security guard who only had access to the periphery of the site. He didn't know what was actually going on there."

"That's true, but things have changed since then. You've had enough time to look into Station Helix more thoroughly."

"That sounds like speculation."

"Call it what you will, but a number of recent events have made me suspicious."

"Such as?"

"Andrew Mason resurfacing. Warren Ellis. The attempted abduction of a British citizen by two of your operatives." Charlotte's expression hardened. "Don't take me for a fool, Jack. I know you're involved, and I know what you're after. This situation has evolved. We either find a way to cooperate or we let this become a political embarrassment for our superiors."

"This isn't about politics. I think you need my help."

"That's right. I want Mason."

"Assuming I have the resources to help you track him down, what do I get in return?"

"My Government is prepared to release a terror suspect into your custody."

Jack shook his head. "That's not enough."

"I thought as much. Very well. What was it your ambassador said about exploring our shared interests?"

"You're going to give me the Helix data?"

"Probably not all of it. But I'm sure you're running research programmes of a similar nature in the States. It might be possible to arrange an exchange of information."

"You don't have the authority to offer that."

"I'm more influential than you might imagine. Like I said, there can be political fallout from this or a strengthening of the Special Relationship. We already collaborate on plenty of projects. I believe this one can be added to the list."

"Why now?" Jack studied her face intently. "This isn't just about tracking down one man. What else is going on? Given time, your people would find Mason. You don't need me for that. You wouldn't be offering me Helix data unless you wanted something else."

Charlotte nodded. "It's not just about bringing Mason to justice for murdering two of my scientists. It's also about protecting the project. I can't allow continued CIA interference. If you don't back off I'll have no choice but to shut down Helix. And that isn't in either of our interests."

"It has to be valuable if you're threatening to pull the plug."

"It's valuable enough that you don't want me to carry out my threat."

Caldwell smiled. "All right. I reckon we can come to a mutually beneficial arrangement. I'll have to make some calls though. My superiors would appreciate a gesture of good will."

"You've had your gesture. I've acknowledged the existence of Station Helix."

"My ambassador pointed out that, in accordance with the Technical Cooperation Program, we should have been told about Helix at its inception."

"I'm not going to pass comment on what should or should not have happened over fifty years ago, but, by mentioning the TCP, you've validated my request for us to work together."

Caldwell grinned. He pushed back his chair and stood. "I'd like to think we're on the verge of a constructive collaboration."

Charlotte rose and stepped around the table.

As they shook hands Jack spoke again. "I'll inquire about Mason. We'll speak again soon."

Charlotte walked to the door and opened it. "Thank you for coming in, Jack."

Abi stood as Quinn and Caldwell went to the door. The Americans were about to leave when Caldwell stopped and turned back to Charlotte. "One more thing," he said. "I accept your comment about the gesture of good will, but why don't you tell me something I already know? What goes on at Station Helix?"

Charlotte smiled. She looked into the hallway and gestured to her assistant. "It's a genetics laboratory, Jack. My colleague will show you out."

Caldwell nodded and walked from the room with Quinn. Charlotte pushed the door shut.

10

"That was interesting," Charlotte said as she turned back to Abi. "I have my own thoughts about how that went, but I'd like to hear your evaluation."

"Caldwell's under instruction to cooperate with you," replied Abi. "But it's a peculiar dynamic. The ambassador wants him to test the water. He's entirely capable of doing that, but he sees diplomacy as secondary to his usual intelligence gathering role. Caldwell would usually be tasked from Langley, but the ambassador is a senior figure appointed by the President, so he won't hesitate to follow his instructions. The station chief has a very strong sense of patriotism and loyalty."

"That's thorough," Charlotte remarked.

"That's what you pay me for."

"Will he work with me?"

"Yes, as long as he sees a benefit for the US. He's intrigued by your information sharing proposal. While he's wary about diplomacy, he relishes the challenge. I think he's keen to be noticed by his superiors, but he's also patient. I wouldn't be surprised if he's already anticipated a promotion, but he's not greedy for it. He's a clever man who considers consequences before making decisions. He'll always know when you're holding back."

Charlotte nodded. "I agree. I'm not going to offer anything I can't actually give. We both need to discuss this with our superiors."

"The details about Helix – yes. But he likes you. I think he'll give you something that he can afford to give away."

"You mean Mason?"

Abi nodded.

Charlotte pressed the topic. "He won't admit to controlling Mason."

"It doesn't matter. If he hands him over, it'll be on the expectation that you disregard any link Mason has to the CIA."

"I can live with that." She paused. "Something concerns me though. Jack's been running this operation for over three years. I don't know if he's ready to give it up."

Abi hesitated before replying, considering Charlotte's words. "He won't jeopardise political negotiations because he understands the bigger picture. But he's still a spy. Even if he scales down the operation, he won't end it."

"The only way to ensure the Americans comply with us is to make them equal partners. I'll have to make my argument persuasive."

"I get the impression you already have high level backing."

Charlotte frowned. "That remains to be seen." She opened the door and stepped into the corridor. "Let's get some lunch. I need time to consider the implications of today's meeting."

Abi nodded and followed her from the conference room. "There's something else," she said as they headed along the elegantly furnished hallway. "Clare Quinn. I don't like her."

"Go on. I didn't have much opportunity to observe her.

What's your assessment?"

"She's not interested in the politics. She's an operative and a pretty ruthless one at that. She's obviously an asset to Caldwell because she's very good at her job." Abi paused. "Most of the time, at least."

Charlotte stopped walking and faced Abi, her expression curious. "What did you see?"

"The only flicker of emotion was when you spoke about Lily's attempted abduction. I think she was in charge of that operation."

"I see. Well, she'll have to live with that failure."

"Just be careful. She's less concerned with consequences than Caldwell – she's the sort to go to any lengths to get the job done. Clare Quinn is dangerous."

Charlotte placed her hand on Abi's shoulder. "That, Abigail, is something she and I have in common."

TEN

1

Formulating a plan without adequate reconnaissance was, in Mason's mind, tantamount to stupidity. Getting to Rhodes would be achieved on his terms and timescale. The Americans hadn't made contact again since informing him where the kit was stashed, but they wouldn't wait indefinitely. The freedom was, he understood, an illusion. He still hadn't been able to work out how they were tracking him. It made devising an evasion plan difficult. Their psychological influence was more intimidating than the physical discomfort he'd felt in the interrogation room.

He peered through the eyepieces of his binoculars, watching a conversation between two men approximately a kilometre away. From his vantage point at the wood line across the valley he had a clear view of Rhodes' mansion. The men on the gravel parking area in front of the building stopped talking and resumed their patrols. So far Mason had identified six security guards and two groundsmen, but he needed more time to be certain of the actual staff numbers. He'd stay here – hidden under the green-brown bracken fronds – for at least another night and day until he was ready to coordinate the assault. The musty scent of the pine woodland floor filled his nostrils. Years of army experience made hiding in wild terrain second nature. His camouflaged clothing made him blend with the dirt and vegetation. Even the birds and animals of the forest seemed unaware of his presence. But he wasn't alone. Wheeler, two hundred metres farther along the ridgeline, observed the mansion from a slightly different perspective. The rest of the team was farther away, watching the building's grey gothic façades which Mason and Wheeler couldn't see.

A light was turned on inside the mansion. He glanced up at the sky, seeing the first splashes of gloaming colour. He reached for a night vision scope inside his bivouac and placed it on the ground in front of him. It wouldn't be long before his binoculars became useless in the fading twilight.

He turned his attention back to the mansion across the valley.

2

Light drizzly rain fell from a featureless grey sky as Clare Quinn walked through London's Green Park towards the RAF Bomber Command Memorial. She tried to wipe the dampness from her face with her sleeve but the fleece material wasn't suited to the task. The weather was just too mildly irritating to ignore. Caldwell stood inside the yellow-grey structure, looking up at the bronze sculpture of seven World War Two aircrew on a plinth in the centre of the memorial. His long raincoat appeared to be dry. She knew Jack was deeply passionate about history – particularly military history – and had probably been standing here for some time, reading the inscriptions carved into the Portland stone walls. She stood beside him.

"Sixty-seven years, Clare." His stare remained fixed on the bronze figures.

She didn't understand the context of his remark. "Jack?"

"Sixty-seven years," he repeated. "That's how long it took the Brits to build a memorial to the bomber crews." He turned to face her. "The Allies lost over fifty thousand airmen during their bombing raids. Even Churchill failed to mention them at the end of the War."

Quinn held his look for a moment before speaking. She shrugged. "I guess they had their reasons. Those bomber crews killed a lot of people. It must have been politically sensitive."

A thin smile appeared on Caldwell's lips. "You're not usually bothered by politics, Clare." He paused. "I love this country and its people, but sometimes I wonder if they've got their priorities right. These memorials aren't about celebration: they're here to acknowledge sacrifice. How can it take so long to honour thousands of men who prevented the spread of Nazism in Europe?"

"I don't know. At least this place is here now." Clare didn't want to get drawn any further into a topic she didn't know well enough to discuss. She hoped her remark would sound suitably empathetic and allow her to change the subject. Jack didn't reply. She noticed his collar was turned up. She adjusted it for him and smoothed down the material. "How was your meeting with the ambassador?"

"Political," he replied. "The diplomats are going to work out the details in accordance with our information sharing protocols."

Clare looked irritated. "So we've basically been told to back off?"

"We're to 'nurture our relationship with the MOD' – whatever that means. We have to assist them in any way we can. No more ops on British soil regarding Helix. Officially, this doesn't belong to us any more."

"And unofficially?"

"We're the CIA. We never stop looking for information."

"That's kinda tough when all the doors have been closed."

"We still have options. Go to Scotland and contact Alex Hannay. Tell him how to find Mason."

She gave him a quizzical look. "Mason's our only ace

in the hole. You want to give him up?"

"He's a burden we can afford to lose, but give him time to get the data from Rhodes' computer before you speak to Alex. I'll tell Charlotte Black that you're going to assist her team with the search. That gives us a legitimate reason for staying involved. I want to know how Alex ended up working for her."

"He found out about Mason killing his parents."

"That's not enough to suddenly get MOD clearance for a top secret project. Befriend him, Clare. Make him think you're his ally. He's brand new to this, so he'll be more trusting than a trained operative. Give him the means to find the man who killed his family."

"But not before Mason's completed one last task." Clare shivered from the dampness in her fleece and glanced at the rain that was now falling steadily. "You want to get a coffee? I think there's a place on Hyde Park Corner."

Jack nodded and offered his arm as they stepped into the rain.

3

Kate McLeod was doing her best to cope with the disruption in her front room with good grace, but her silence revealed how she was truly feeling. Three cases and a rucksack were taking up space in the centre of the room. Kate tried to ignore the clutter by gently bouncing Megan on her knee. Next to her on the sofa was Tanya Smith, the MOD operative. Greg and Alex stood by the door waiting for Lucas to come back inside.

Alex's mobile rang. He glanced at the screen, saw Charlotte Black's name appear, and answered the call. He went to the kitchen and kept his voice quiet in an attempt to lessen the disturbance.

"How are they?" Charlotte asked.

"They understand why we're moving them. The disruption's getting them down though."

"That's understandable, but I can't keep Reid's team tied up. They'll be safer on the base at Leuchars for a few days. Has their accommodation been arranged?"

"Reid's sorted that out. We're just waiting for the car."

"Good." Charlotte paused before changing the subject. "Alex, there's someone from the CIA on her way to meet you. Her name's Clare Quinn."

"Does that mean we're working with the Americans now?"

"There have been some developments. I've had to give

some ground. Station Helix has become the subject of formal negotiations with the Americans, but that won't stop the CIA snooping around. You're not authorised to discuss the programme with Quinn."

"No problem, but why is she coming here?"

"They want to be seen to be on our side. She'll help you find Mason. Use her information and Reid's team to bring him in."

Alex suddenly felt a chill. He didn't know how to react to the prospect of capturing his parents' murderer. He didn't answer.

"Alex?" Charlotte's voice refocussed his attention.

"Sorry. I guess I was unprepared for that. I was beginning to wonder whether we'd ever bring him to justice."

"We'll worry about justice later; for now I just want the bastard caught. But leave the operation to the pros. I don't need to remind you how skilled and dangerous Mason is."

"Of course. Is Quinn authorised to join the team?"

"Yes, but keep an eye on her. Caldwell's taking advantage of the fact that we're cooperating. Sending Quinn to you keeps him involved. It tells us something else too."

"Go on."

"They know exactly where Mason is. Caldwell could give me his location right now. He still has an agenda."

"Sounds right. I'll let you know when she gets here. What about Rhodes? We still have to find out what he knows."

"His pilot has scheduled a flight to Glasgow for tomorrow afternoon. The RAF are on standby to divert his helicopter. I'm afraid I don't have the time to come up with something more delicate."

"Lucas and I will be ready."

"I'll call you soon." Charlotte ended the call. Alex slipped the phone into his jeans pocket and stepped into the hall. He noticed a movement at the door. Lucas turned a key and entered the house.

"The Range Rover's here," he said.

Alex nodded. He looked into the living room. "Kate… Greg… It's time to go."

Kate turned to her husband. "Take Megan, will you? She's made my leg go numb."

"Aye, no problem. Come here, sweetheart." McLeod lifted his daughter and cradled her closely. Megan put her thumb in her mouth and rested her head against her father's chest.

Tanya and Alex carried the McLeods' cases as the group left the house. Parked a short distance away was a black MOD Range Rover. Kate closed and locked the front door. Greg reached out with his spare hand and touched her face. He pulled her in gently and kissed her. "Don't worry, love. It won't be for long. We'll be home again before you know it."

Kate attempted a smile. "I hope so." She kissed him and stroked Megan's hair.

The events of the next split-second unfolded in horrifying slow motion. McLeod's knees buckled. A splintered hole appeared in the door behind him. He fell to the ground dead, his daughter's body landing awkwardly on top of him as he struck the pathway. A dark bloodstain seeped through the material of Megan's coat. Her limp body rolled from her father's chest, revealing more blood. Everyone froze in disbelief as they stared at the bodies.

Tanya's training kicked in. She drew a handgun from a holster under her jacket, raised the weapon in a two-handed grip into her sightline and immediately scanned the view opposite the house, searching for the marksman. "Get her inside!" she yelled, anticipating another shot.

The MOD driver sprinted from the vehicle and hurled himself against the door of the house, causing it to slam open and split the woodwork of the frame. He turned and tried to grab Kate by the shoulders. But Kate McLeod wasn't ready to be guided indoors. She fell to her knees beside her husband and daughter's bodies, her expression wide-eyed, her body convulsing involuntarily with shock. She clutched them frantically in wordless terror, refusing to believe they were both dead.

The driver grabbed her more strongly and tried to pull her inside the house, but Kate resisted, clawing at him. She began to scream. "Oh my god, no!" The driver resorted to brute force, breaking her free and dragging her into the hallway. She kept screaming. "Fucking do something! Help them!" The operative pulled her to her feet, but Kate tried to push away and head outside again. He grabbed her tightly, trapping her arms beneath his, and pulled her into the kitchen, refusing to let go.

Alex and Lucas crouched down by the bodies, horrified at the sight. Lucas's years with the police forced him into action. He picked up Megan, knowing she was dead, but determined to attempt resuscitation. He shouted at Alex, pointing at Greg's body. "Grab him!" Alex's face was pale but he responded to the instruction. He hooked his arms through McLeod's and backed into the hall, dragging the Scot's body awkwardly through the narrow gap. Lucas followed and shouted Tanya's name.

The operative glanced around, saw the pathway was now clear and stepped backwards, her eyes still scanning for the unseen shooter as she reached the house. Only once inside did she lower the weapon. She tried to slam the door shut but the damaged frame caused it to stick partially open.

She hurried into the living room where Alex and Lucas were vainly attempting cardiopulmonary resuscitation. She pulled the curtains shut. "Are you guys okay?" She wasn't surprised when they ignored her. "I'll call the backup team and get some medics here."

She walked to the door and glanced into the kitchen. Her colleague still had his arms around Kate, who was now sobbing helplessly. The man looked up, his glance questioning.

Tanya shook her head.

4

As the undertakers' Mercedes Vito pulled away from the McLeods' house, it occurred to Alex that a characteristic of that solemn profession was to use plain vehicles. He couldn't remember ever seeing the name of a funeral director on the side of a panel van. Perhaps it was a matter of discretion, or possibly unnecessary because it wasn't a particularly competitive field. There must have been enough death to go around without the need for advertising. He stared towards the town for several minutes after the Vito had left his field of view.

He felt sick and numb and his head was throbbing; symptoms that had only begun to afflict him the moment the paramedic had told him to move away from Greg McLeod's body. Until then adrenaline had driven his futile attempts at resuscitation, somehow sustaining him through twenty minutes of unceasing effort. Being moved aside had shocked his system. He'd immediately felt physically cold and mentally vanquished. Lucas had suffered the same effects and hadn't even been able to stand up to move out of the way. Seeing his friend struggling hadn't lessened Alex's sense of failure. The sensation was the same as when he'd learned his parents had died in the car crash. He vaguely remembered someone talking about 'normal psychological responses' and 'survivor guilt', but, despite having gone through it before, his brain wasn't yet able to objectively process seeing a man and child murdered before his eyes.

Tanya came out of the house. "Are you okay, Alex?" Her calm voice found the balance between concern and professionalism.

He looked at her for a moment before speaking. "I'm fine," he lied. "How's Kate?"

"The medic sedated her. She's asleep."

"She must be inconsolable."

"It's going to be difficult for her."

"What happens now?"

"To Kate? I don't know yet. I'll talk to her when she wakes." She changed the subject. "This may sound rather insensitive, but you and Lucas should get back to your hotel. Have a hot shower and put on some fresh clothes. You're covered in blood."

Alex glanced at his shirt. He hadn't noticed the dark stains until now. He looked at his hands. They too had traces of blood residue on them, even though one of the paramedics had removed most of it with a handful of alcohol-impregnated wipes. His nostrils caught the medical smell as he raised his hands to examine them. "You're right." He hesitated. "Kate has family in London. She'll probably want to be with them."

"I'll help her with any arrangements she wants to make," Tanya replied. "You go and get yourself cleaned up." She turned to go back inside the house, then paused, looking back at him. "Alex, there wasn't anything you could have done. They were dead before they hit the ground." She pushed open the bullet-scarred door and went into the hall.

Alex shivered as he waited for Lucas, reflecting on the brutality of the world in which he'd found himself. For a second he regretted trying to find out the truth behind his parents' murder, but just as quickly he dismissed the thought. He'd known from the beginning that pursuing the truth was the right thing to do – the *only* thing to do. He'd never expected it to be an easy journey, and now what he knew affected lives other than his own. He turned his eyes to the spot where Megan and Greg had been gunned down. Blood was still smeared on the footpath from where he'd dragged Greg's body. With cold determination he told himself to continue pursuing the heartless bastards who had destroyed Kate McLeod's family.

The door opened again and Lucas and the MOD driver joined him. "I'll drop you off at your hotel," the driver said, holding up the key fob for the Range Rover. Alex nodded. Tanya had been right. He needed to get away from the McLeods' house and smarten himself up. There was work to do.

As the Range Rover manoeuvred down the steep streets of Pitlochry towards the town centre, Alex's phone rang. Half expecting the call to be from Abi or Charlotte he was surprised when an unfamiliar number appeared on the screen. He touched the graphic to answer the call. "Alex Hannay." His voice was quiet. He had no wish to speak to anyone.

Road noise echoed loudly through the speaker as a female American voice spoke. "Alex, this is Clare Quinn. I understand you're expecting me."

"Yes."

"I'm somewhere near Dunfermline. I guess I'll be at

Pitlochry within ninety minutes. Give me time to find where I'm staying, then I'll meet you in the bar of your hotel." She ended the call before he could reply.

He leaned forward and placed his hand on the back of the passenger's seat. Lucas turned round. "Who was that?"

"Clare Quinn. She'll be here in an hour and a half."

Lucas frowned. "Let's hope she actually has something to contribute."

"Charlotte seems to think she will."

"We'll hear what she has to say then we'll formulate a plan with Reid. We're close to bringing him in, Alex."

Alex nodded. Andrew Mason's name tormented his thoughts.

5

It took twenty minutes under a steaming shower to overcome the chill in Alex's body. He couldn't figure out whether the sensation was physical or psychological. After towelling himself dry and putting on a fresh set of clothes he apprised Abi about the shooting but kept the conversation short, saying he had to meet Clare Quinn. She didn't press him to say how he felt, but simply said they would speak again soon and that she would contact Tanya. After ending the call he went to the bar. He waited another ten minutes before Lucas arrived.

"Drink?" he asked when Lucas sat down on the plain sofa opposite him. The former policeman wore pale grey trousers and a light blue shirt without a tie. Alex thought he looked calm for a man who had tried to resuscitate a child only a few hours ago.

"I guess I'm still on duty," Lucas said. "I'll have a Coke. Has she arrived yet?"

Alex shook his head. "Don't think so." He stood and walked to the bar. A minute later he returned with two glasses and set them down on the low table between the sofas.

"Thanks." Lucas didn't reach for his drink. He held Alex's gaze. "You okay?"

"I'm not sure what to feel. It's like when I woke up in the hospital. I'm actually struggling to remember exactly what happened."

"Don't worry about that. The first few days after a traumatic incident can be unpredictable and unnerving. It takes a while for things to feel normal."

"Have you dealt with this sort of thing before?"

"A few circumstances I wouldn't be in a hurry to experience again." Lucas paused. "I'm lucky though; I have Fran to talk to. She's great. As a paramedic she's been through a lot more than me. It takes a special kind of person to do that job."

"That's high praise coming from a policeman. Have you spoken to her?"

"*Former* policeman," Lucas corrected. "Yes, I called her from the room. I'll speak to her again later."

"I told Abi what happened. She said she'd help Tanya look after Kate."

"That's good. We need to concentrate on Mason." Lucas reached for his Coke, sipped it and placed the glass down again.

Alex spotted a woman wearing a grey trouser suit and white blouse enter the bar. Her black hair was pulled back neatly from her face and tied into a long ponytail. In her hand was a tablet computer case. She caught Alex's glance, smiled and walked over, extending her hand as he and Lucas stood. "Alex Hannay?" Her Texas accent revealed her roots. "I'm Clare Quinn."

"Clare," Alex said as he shook her hand. "This is my colleague Lucas Ingwe."

"It's good to meet you guys. Sorry I'm late; the journey took longer than I anticipated. I'm used to straighter roads back home."

"No problem," replied Alex. "We were delayed ourselves. Can I get you something to drink?"

"Sure. A small white wine would be great. Thanks." Clare sat on the sofa opposite Lucas as Alex went to the bar. "I've been looking forward to meeting you, Lucas." Clare placed her tablet on the table. "I guess we have you to thank for bringing Mason to our attention."

Lucas smiled. "My inquisitive nature cost me my job."

Clare shrugged. "Seems to me you now have a better one."

"Maybe. I'm not sure if the MOD pension is any good."

She grinned at his remark. "At least your new employer appreciates your inquiring mind."

"I hope so."

Alex sat down beside the Texan and handed her a wine glass.

"Thanks, Alex. I guess you guys were as surprised as me to find out we'd be working together."

Alex reached for his drink and gripped the glass a little too tightly. "You could say that, considering you've been protecting the man who killed my parents."

Quinn sipped her wine and took a moment to think about her reply. "I'm glad I've been cleared to talk to you. 'Protecting' isn't the right word, but I'll admit we located Mason a little while ago. We should have passed on what we knew sooner."

Alex held her gaze. Her eyes gave nothing away. "So what *do* you know?"

"He's here in Scotland, up in the Highlands, but he's not alone. He's recently been joined by four members of his team. My hunch is they're planning to flee the country. The west coast is so remote that it would be easy to leave unnoticed. After what happened in Perth it would be too risky for him to stay in the towns or to return to England. He's relying on friends and contacts to help him escape."

Lucas nodded. "That makes sense. Can you give us his exact location?"

"Within a few square miles at least. Right now he's in the Fort Augustus area. I have access to a field ops team, but I expect you want to use your own people to bring him in."

"We appreciate the offer, but this isn't a joint operation. We'll use an MOD team."

"Thought so. But I'm cleared to tag along, right?"

Lucas smiled. "Unless you tell us *how* you know where Mason is, we're going to need you with us."

She lifted her tablet computer. "I'm receiving updates on this. You know I'd love to hand this over, but it's CIA kit. I'd get into all kinds of trouble. How soon can you put a team together? After the drive up here I'd really like a decent night's sleep, but I don't think we should delay any longer than we need to. If his team is armed – which we should assume – a pre-dawn strike seems like the best option."

"Agreed. I'll call our man. He'll need to pull in some more resources. I suggest we get our heads down for a couple of hours before moving out. We'll need you to brief the team."

"Of course." Clare stood. "You have my mobile. Call me when you're ready. I'll see you guys soon."

Alex watched as she left the room. He turned back to Lucas. "Can we trust her?"

Lucas raised his eyebrows in mock surprise at the question. "She's a spy, Alex."

"Do you think she's telling the truth about Mason's men?"

"I believe so. She's here to help us – at least as much as Jack Caldwell wants her to."

Alex swallowed the last of his drink. He didn't speak but his expression seemed uncertain.

Lucas noticed. "What is it?"

"All this time I've been focussing on one person. But Mason didn't kill my parents on his own. If his men are here as well…"

Lucas leaned back against the sofa, holding eye contact. "We'll find them."

6

Mason shielded the display of his MTM Special Ops watch as he checked the time, saw it was 02.50, flipped down his night vision goggles and pressed his radio's transmit button. The tiny microphone in his headset picked up his voice as he gave the order to move out. He crept forward, scanning the mansion intently. He was about forty metres from the hunting lodge. He watched a security guard with a torch cross the broad gravel driveway – the night vision image appearing green and grainy in his eyepieces – knowing that it would take the man roughly forty seconds to move around the corner to where South would kill him using a stranglehold. Mason moved nearer the building, stepping cautiously to avoid making noise underfoot. He paused, lifting the radio's earpiece away from his ear for a moment to listen for unusual sounds, but there were none. He readjusted his equipment and took an indirect route towards the low balustrade wall in front of the mansion.

Seconds later South's voice crackled through the radio. "Target One down."

Mason crouched low beside the wall. He peered through a gap framed by its short columns. One of Rhodes' vehicles – a silver Mercedes-Benz S-Class – was parked almost out of sight near a side entrance. He'd seen it arrive late in the afternoon and had watched the chauffeur polish a dirt spot from the windscreen before going inside the house.

Footsteps on the gravel immediately diverted Mason's attention. His training and years of experience prevented him from adjusting his position and looking for the guard. Instead he waited, listening and calculating the shortening distance between him and the patrol. Light from the man's torch flashed across the driveway between the house and the wall. Sensing the man coming closer, Mason prepared to attack. At five metres the security guard stepped into Mason's field of vision. At three he turned the torch beam directly over Mason's head, scanning the grounds just beyond the wall. The man stepped closer to the masonry and paused, the sudden screech of a tawny owl causing him to shine the torch towards the valley and forest, but the woodland and the bird of prey were too distant to be picked out by the light. The man waited a moment before resuming his patrol.

Mason climbed over the wall, stepped behind the guard and grabbed his head. With a sudden wrench he snapped the man's neck. He grabbed the torch before it fell. Making as little noise as he could, he rested the guard's body on the flat surface of the balustrade then carefully rolled him over it, pushing him out of sight from the driveway. He flipped up his night vision goggles and followed the route the security guard should have taken around the mansion, shining the torch here and there in imitation of the man he'd just killed. He depressed his transmit button. "Target Two down. Approaching black side."

Wheeler's voice spoke in Mason's headset. "I have you in sight. Ten seconds behind you."

South confirmed his position on the perimeter of the building which the team had designated 'green side'.

Colour-coding was a tactic used by police firearms teams to simplify the identification of a building's façades. The words 'left', 'right', 'front' and 'back' could lead to confusion.

Mason walked across the gravel, feeling exposed and wincing at the crunching noise the stones made under his boots. The torch's bright light contrasted against the darkness, hiding his features. The man inside the security office probably wouldn't even turn away from his CCTV monitors when he entered the room.

He froze as a gunshot sounded. Seconds later Lyndon Fleck's panicked voice shouted in the radio's earpiece. "Rush is down! He's been shot!"

Mason flicked off the torch, dropped it and ran directly towards the wall of the building. He hid behind a stone buttress, peered over the top and saw Wheeler sprinting towards him. Wheeler dived to the ground as sudden flashes of light and gunshots punctuated the darkness. They unholstered their handguns. Another shot rang out and a bullet struck stone barely a foot above Mason's head. He pressed his transmit button. "Fleck! What's going on?"

The Irishman shouted a reply. "Sniper, white side! Shooting from inside..." The radio suddenly went dead as more shots rang out.

"Fleck!"

The Irishman didn't answer.

Mason turned to Wheeler. "They knew we were coming."

Wheeler nodded, his night vision headset still in place. He spun around as he heard a noise behind him. A figure carrying an MP5 fitted with a night sight stepped into view.

Wheeler fired four bullets rapidly before the man spotted him; missing with one, striking ballistic body armour with two, but puncturing the man's throat with the fourth shot. The man collapsed. More shots rang out in the blackness.

Mason stared, trying to spot the shooters. "Jesus, Curt, they're firing from the car! They've been watching us since we got here!" He reached for his radio. "South! Status?"

"Pissed off! Where are you?"

"Black side, under fire from the Merc. I think Rush and Fleck are down."

"Yeah, I saw Fleck get hit. They've got at least two shooters inside the building and several outside. I've shot one but I can't see the others."

Mason glanced at Wheeler who'd grabbed the MP5 from the man he'd shot.

"The Merc?" Wheeler asked as he checked the semi-automatic's magazine.

Mason nodded. "Let's go."

They sprinted towards the Mercedes, firing repeatedly at the vehicle. Bullets punctured the bodywork and the shooting from the car stopped. They advanced, scanning for movement. They looked inside, noticing for the first time that the saloon's windows had been open. The bodies of two men – one in the front and one in the back – were slumped inside. Each had an MP5 and a handgun which they removed before retreating into the shadow of the building.

Mason tried to call South on the radio but there was no response. He turned to Wheeler. "If we try to leave now, they'll hit us."

Wheeler nodded. He kept his voice low. "Six down?

South got at least two. We can get inside via the security office, but they'll follow us in and block our egress."

"Clear the outside first?" Mason didn't need to ask the question.

Wheeler nodded.

Raising their MP5s they began to move around the building, stepping slowly and keeping close to the wall. Mason took the lead, keeping the weapon raised in his sightline. Wheeler stayed behind him but faced the other way, scanning the area they had come from.

They encountered no one as they progressed along the building's green side. A sniper would have shot from inside a room – to keep his rifle barrel out of sight – and would never be able to see them below if they kept to the contours of the building, but other men would be watching for movement through the ground floor windows. Mason halted at every opening and tapped Wheeler on the shoulder to indicate when they had to crouch.

Eventually they reached the corner that marked the end of green side and the transition to white side. Shielded by a buttress Mason glanced around the building's edge. Twenty metres away South's motionless body lay awkwardly on the ground. Two armed men, wearing ballistic armour and night sights, approached South, their MP5s aimed at him.

South moved slightly, vainly extending his fingers for a handgun that lay nearby on the ground just out of reach.

Mason indicated to Wheeler that there were two targets. Wheeler shifted his position slightly, moving to the side and behind Mason's left shoulder. Mason looked back at the two men. One placed his boot on South's forearm, preventing him from getting any closer to the handgun. South groaned in pain as the man's weight pushed his limb into the gravel. The man fired two shots at his head, their reports shattering the silence. Mason and Wheeler lurched round the corner and immediately opened fire. South's executioner fell dead a fraction of a second before his companion. They stepped back, expecting more guards to fire in retaliation, but they saw and heard nothing.

They waited a full minute before moving. Wheeler kept his voice low when finally breaking the silence. "Snipers?"

"Yeah. Security door."

"I'll take point."

Mason nodded. "We kill them and locate Rhodes. I want to find out how the fuck he knew we were coming."

7

The retreat round the building was even more cautious than before. They abandoned their radios because they only had each other to communicate with. They needed to be alert for noise outside and inside the mansion. Their pace was tortuously but essentially slow. They heard nothing as they followed the building line and crouched under windows. Even the occasionally loud wildlife had fallen silent, scared away by the gunfire. They were wary of assuming that they had killed the last of Rhodes' security squad, but the quiet after they had shot South's killers suggested that – outside at least – there were no other gunmen.

It took them nearly ten minutes of methodical scanning and incremental steps to reach the security office. The door into the building was open but there was no one in the room. It was logical for anyone inside – listening to the gunfire and being unable to raise his team on the radio – to retreat into the mansion and find a tactically stronger position.

They had conducted house searches during their military service and weren't intimidated by the prospect of entering a dangerous building. They crept into the security office through the open doorway, noting the position of the internal door. Wheeler slid a G60 stun grenade from a pouch on his body armour, held the lever down and pulled out the pin. He kicked the door open – aiming his boot near the handle to ensure the bolt would give way – and hurled the flash-bang into the corridor. The device went off a fraction of a second later, emitting a one hundred and sixty decibel bang and a pyrotechnic magnesium flash of blinding light. Mason burst into the corridor and scanned the space for danger. About six metres along the corridor a man leaned against the wall, his head in his hands, disoriented. With his sense of balance in disarray due to the flash-bang's percussive effect and his eyes' photoreceptors temporarily disabled by the intense light, the man was an easy target. Three shots rang out from Mason's MP5 and the guard fell.

Mason deliberately stayed motionless in the corridor while Wheeler joined him. Had he stepped again he would have crossed Wheeler's sightline, putting himself at risk of being shot and preventing Wheeler from seeing the corridor. They readied themselves to check everywhere for hostile shooters. Room clearance had to be completed swiftly but safely. Any undue delay would give their enemy more time to establish a defensive position.

They came to a foyer and noticed a staircase on the far side. The stairs had a landing halfway up, partially obscured from their view. The upper steps rose perpendicular to the lower ones, preventing them from seeing all the way up. They recognised it as a likely ambush site where a second gunman could be lying in wait. Mason removed the pin from one of his G60s while holding the lever against the casing. He indicated to Wheeler to do the same and used a short sequence of hand gestures to explain his plan. Wheeler nodded and raised his MP5, holding his stun grenade against the grip of the weapon.

Mason flung his flash-bang into the hallway. It rattled noisily as it skidded across the tiled floor, exploded and illuminated the foyer for a fraction of a second before plunging the space into darkness. There was a crash as somebody fell against a door. Wheeler stepped into the hall, spun in an arc and saw a badly disorientated man clutching a doorframe, trying to regain his footing. He fired a burst from his MP5 and the man slumped as bullets tore into his face and skull. Wheeler darted towards the stairwell and hurled his stun grenade upwards, covering the lenses of his night vision scope as he let go to prevent the flash from overwhelming the light magnification apparatus inside the eyepieces. The grenade went off. Mason sprinted past Wheeler and ascended the stairs, shooting a one-second volley of bullets into the gunman he found at the top, killing him instantly. He stepped over the body and crouched, scanning the layout as he waited for Wheeler to join him.

Once again they waited, listening and watching. A door a short way along the upstairs landing was open. They advanced, reached the doorway and burst into the room. They didn't see anyone but a sudden thud from behind an old fashioned desk caught their attention. Mason motioned to Wheeler to hold position near the door. Mason let the MP5 hang on its strap and unholstered a handgun. He edged closer, keeping the pistol raised. He caught sight of two elderly men crouching behind the furniture.

When Mason's voice sounded in the darkness, both men tensed in fright. "Listen carefully," he said with cold authority. "Your men are dead. Stand up slowly." The men did as he ordered, bumping awkwardly into furniture they couldn't see. "Now place your hands behind your head and interlock your fingers." The elderly men obeyed. "Good. Keep doing as you're told and we'll get along fine." Mason turned slightly and directed his next comment at Wheeler. "Curt, close the door and flick on the light."

They removed their night vision equipment as the light came on. Mason looked at the two men standing behind the desk, considering his next move. The unhealthy overweight man with grey untidy hair was recognisable as Rhodes from a photo the CIA had sent to his phone. He wore a white long-sleeved shirt but no tie and he'd been sweating profusely. Mason didn't recognise Rhodes' companion. Physically he couldn't have been more different. He was slim almost to the point of being underweight. His face looked hollow beneath his cheekbones. His hair was white and neatly styled with a parting. He wore a tailored waistcoat and matching trousers.

"Come out from there." Mason didn't need to make his voice sound threatening to command obedience. The two men were terrified. "Stand in front of the desk. If anyone bursts into this room looking for us, they'll probably shoot you first. Then my friend will kill them." Mason glared at Rhodes. "How many gunmen were in the house?"

Rhodes' dry mouth made it hard for him to speak. "I... I don't know."

"That's not good enough." Mason raised the handgun, aiming it between Rhodes' eyes.

"No, really... I don't know." Rhodes' voice was anxious. "Two, maybe three? I don't know. One of the guards came in here and said he couldn't contact his team on the radio. He told us to hide, then he left. That's all I know."

"Other staff members?"

"Just Martin. He's my assistant and housekeeper. The others went home hours ago."

Mason knew this was probably true – his team had watched Rhodes' people leave – but they'd missed the arrival of the extra security personnel. He nodded. "I believe you, Rhodes, but I have many unanswered questions. It's imperative that you tell me exactly what I need to know." He pointed the gun at the slender man's chest and fired three times. Rhodes flinched at the weapon's reports and stared in horror as his assistant died. Mason grabbed Rhodes by the chin and jerked his head up, forcing eye contact. "Do I need to make myself any clearer?"

Rhodes shook his head, his eyes wide with fear.

8

Mason pushed Rhodes towards a fabric covered chair. "Sit down."

"Why don't you just get on with it?"

"Get on with what?" Mason went behind the desk and found a curtain pull. He drew the curtains, not wanting his silhouette to be visible from outside.

Rhodes watched him closely. "You're obviously here to kill me."

Mason stood in front of Rhodes, looking down at him. He ignored the remark. "You knew I was coming. How?"

"I had a call. A friend of mine said he had information that my life was in danger."

Mason frowned. "Who called you? What exactly did he say?"

"A friend from the US Embassy in London. He said you and your team had been hired to kill me. I received the call several days ago so I had time to bring in some extra people."

"And they've been here all this time?"

"All but the last two. My chauffeur picked them up a few hours ago. We knew you'd be watching, so they had to stay inside the car."

"They're still there," replied Mason. There was a hint of anger in his voice as he recalled the ambush. Rhodes didn't reply. Mason turned away for a moment, casually checking the handgun's magazine. Rhodes watched, sweating nervously, unable to keep his eyes off the weapon. Mason spoke again. "It seems we've both been set up by the Americans, Rhodes. I wasn't sent here to kill you. I'm here to steal your computer files for them."

Rhodes stared.

"They want to know why you hired someone to kill Greg McLeod."

The older man turned away, his glance downward. "I don't know what you're talking about."

Mason grabbed his face again, yanking his head upwards. "Don't bullshit me! Two Highland-Global 'security specialists' attempted to kill McLeod in Pitlochry. That's one of your companies. You were behind the hit. But why? McLeod wasn't anyone special. Why him?"

Rhodes remained defiantly silent.

Mason shoved the handgun's barrel against the old man's head. "I told you not to fuck me around."

Rhodes winced. "Don't!" He drew breath, trying to regain his composure. "Oh my god. You really don't know."

"I'm running out of patience. What don't I know?"

Rhodes knew it was futile to conceal anything. "The EHB programme. McLeod was one of the first generation subjects."

Mason took a step back. "What are you talking about?"

"Enhanced Human Beings. Genetic engineering. The MOD has been running a secret experiment for decades."

"At Orford Ness?"

"Yes. We called the site Station Helix. You're obviously familiar with it."

Mason lowered the gun. "My team was hired for site security when we came back from the Middle East, but we had no idea what was going on there. No wonder the Americans were so interested." He holstered the weapon and pulled a portable hard drive with a short USB cable from a pouch. He went to the desk, found an empty port on the front of Rhodes' computer and plugged in the drive.

"It won't do you any good," Rhodes said. "Even if I gave you my password, all of my files are encrypted. You don't look like a hacking expert."

"I don't need to be. This device has a CIA decryption system. All I have to do is plug it in. Now, while we're waiting for it to copy your files, why don't you answer my question? Why did you send men to kill McLeod?"

"I told you, he was one of the first."

"That doesn't answer the question."

"There was a problem with the first batch. One of the subjects suffered cellular breakdown. The decision was made to terminate the first generation experiment."

"So you arranged to have them killed?"

Rhodes didn't answer.

"What does 'first generation' mean? Are there others?"

"Two more generations – half a dozen subjects in each – were designed at Station Helix. They're ten and twenty years younger than the first subjects. That way we could learn by observation and develop the science. It's a long-term project."

"You're not MOD. How are you involved?"

"Indirectly. The MOD has administrative control over Station Helix, but ultimately the true power and influence lies elsewhere." Rhodes seemed to have overcome his fear and his tone seemed boastful. "Don't you see what's happening here? You've been drawn into something far bigger than you could possibly understand. You've been used. The Americans don't want you to steal my files; they want you dead. That device probably doesn't even work. And now you've betrayed your country. You'll have nowhere to hide."

"I don't owe my country anything," Mason snapped. He removed the USB device from the computer. "You and I have different perspectives on loyalty. Mine is to my friends – friends you've just killed." He lifted up the hard drive. "Trust me, I have no intention of giving this to the Americans. You're a businessman, Rhodes. You understand about breach of contract. They tried to have me killed today, and I don't take kindly to that." He slid the device back into its pouch. "What else can you tell me about this EHB experiment?"

Rhodes scowled. "Nothing."

"Very well." Mason unholstered the handgun and shot Rhodes twice, the first bullet tearing into his forehead, the second into his heart. He turned to Wheeler. "Let's get out of here."

Wheeler reached forward and turned off the light switch. Both men adjusted their night vision equipment. Mason pulled open the door while Wheeler aimed through the gap. There was no one outside so they began their egress. They moved hastily, determined to get outside with as little delay as possible. It took them less than a minute to reach the security office. They kept their weapons raised as they exited the building, scanning for activity, but all was quiet. Mason gestured in the direction of the hidden

Landcruiser. They unclipped their MP5s and set them on the ground, not wanting to be hindered by the bulky weapons as they fled.

As they sprinted from the house a gunshot shattered the silence. Wheeler exclaimed in pain as a bullet struck his boot, causing him to stumble and fall. Mason stopped running and spun around, searching for the shooter. About fifteen metres away an injured man was lying prone on the ground with one hand outstretched, clutching a pistol. Mason aimed his weapon but the man fired first. Mason felt a sting in his shoulder as a bullet grazed him. Mason fired and the man's arm slumped, his grip loosening on the handgun. Mason stepped closer and fired again, making sure the man was dead.

He went over to Wheeler and helped him stand. "You okay?"

"I think so," he said. "I can feel blood in my boot but it's not too bad." Supported by Mason he put his weight on his injured foot but recoiled from the stab of pain caused by the pressure. "Maybe not. How about you?"

Mason put Wheeler's arm around his shoulder. "Just a scratch. We'll get to the Toyota and clean up. There's a med kit inside. For now, just keep your gun handy. I can't carry you and shoot straight at the same time."

"You never could shoot straight anyway," Wheeler joked.

9

Alex looked at Lucas Ingwe's face, faintly illuminated by the Range Rover's dashboard lights, and noticed his friend's look of concentration. Police driver training had given him the skills to safely tackle the winding roads at speed. Lucas stared at the road revealed by the Sport's bright headlamps. Occasionally he glanced up at the rear-view mirror to check the other vehicles in the convoy were keeping up. The BMW behind them was being driven by Reid, accompanied by Quinn. Two vans – containing firearms teams – followed Reid's car.

Lucas spoke, keeping his eyes focussed on the road. "It's more than coincidence."

"Quinn suddenly finding Mason on the periphery of Rhodes' estate? I'm inclined to agree with you."

"We're missing something."

"Let's concentrate on finding him. We'll figure out the rest later."

Lucas nodded. "How close are we now?"

Alex checked the sat-nav display in the Range Rover's console. "I think we're already in the grounds, but still about four miles from his house. The lane to the RVP should be coming up any moment now."

"Keep watching the screen for me. We're relying on the sat-nav."

"Nearly there. Two hundred metres."

As Lucas steered the Range Rover around the next bend, the headlights caught a white Landcruiser veering sharply from a side turning. The vehicle accelerated, racing towards them, blinding them with its headlamps and roof-mounted spotlights. Ingwe slammed on the brakes to avoid a collision, the anti-lock system kicking in as he was forced to steer into the dirt at the side of the road. The Range Rover came to a halt. The Landcruiser rounded the corner, forcing Reid in the BMW to take evasive action. The Toyota ploughed on, side-swiping the first firearms van, forcing it into the gorse bushes at the roadside. The driver of the second tugged on the wheel to avoid a head-on crash but in doing so drove off the road. The Toyota's bull-bar crunched into the van's rear panel, tearing the metal.

Inside the Range Rover Alex grabbed the radio as Lucas used the dirt track to turn the vehicle round. "Reid! That was Mason! We're going after him." The Sport's engine roared as Lucas pursued the Toyota, skilfully navigating the gaps between the three stationary MOD vehicles.

Reid's voice crackled over the radio. "Not without backup!"

Another voice followed. "This is Alpha Team. We're still mobile."

"Do it, Alpha Team," Reid ordered. "Don't lose them. Bravo Team – status?"

"The vehicle's dead," a voice replied.

Reid spoke again. "Okay, debus. We'll hold position here in case the other target vehicle shows up."

The radio went silent. Lucas drove as fast as he could on the narrow Highland roads. Occasionally he caught glimpses of the Landcruiser, but the geography of the terrain meant, for most of the time, the Toyota was out of sight.

Lucas gradually succeeded in lessening the gap, bringing the distance between the four wheel drives down to about one hundred metres. The narrow road – wide enough for only a single vehicle in most places – wound its way through the depressions and summits of a Highland pine forest. The Range Rover gripped the road doggedly, responding precisely to Ingwe's control. The gap continued to narrow.

"How close is our backup?" asked Lucas.

Alex glanced round, looking for the van's headlights. "Twenty seconds, maybe thirty. They're doing well to keep up."

"Let's hope they can stay with us for a while longer. Get ready on the radio. I'm going to try to get Mason to crash. The team will have to be ready to react. I'll tell you when."

Suddenly the Toyota's brake-lights illuminated and the vehicle slid to almost a standstill. Lucas stomped on the Range Rover's brakes in response. The Toyota turned off the road sharply, its wheels spinning on the dirt and pine needles of the forest floor as they fought for traction. The vehicle roared up a hill between the trees, its wheels bouncing over rocks and fallen branches.

Lucas stopped the Range Rover and cursed under his breath. "Clever bastard."

Alex transmitted over the radio. "Alpha Team, they've gone off road. Two of you get in the Range Rover with us. The rest of you see if you can work out where to cut them off."

The firearms van pulled up behind them. Two men

climbed into the rear of the Sport. Lucas floored the throttle as soon as the doors were closed, turned the steering wheel and drove up the hill in pursuit. There was no finesse to his driving now and the vehicle bounced and lurched as the rugged tyres traversed the hostile terrain. Despite the frantic momentum, the speed of both the Landcruiser and the Sport was considerably slower now as both drivers had to negotiate the outcrops and hollows with caution, relying on the vehicles' traction to carry them over and around the obstacles of the forest.

Lucas realised that Mason's military training had given him an advantage in this landscape. While he could keep the Landcruiser in view – the Toyota's bouncing headlights cut through the darkness like a beacon – his lack of off-road training hindered him considerably. The Toyota moved neatly through the trees, increasing the distance that Lucas had managed to shorten on the road. Suddenly the Landcruiser's lights went out. Lucas stopped and stared through the windscreen. "Where are they?" he murmured.

"Open the window and cut the engine," said the firearms officer behind the driver's seat. Lucas followed the instruction. In the distance the roar of the Toyota's powerful engine could be heard. "They've switched to night vision," the officer said. "We have to keep going or we'll lose them."

Lucas restarted the Range Rover and continued. There were signs of disturbance on the woodland floor – patches of dirt where the Landcruiser's wheels had carved hollows and disturbed the blanket of pine needles – but the marks were unclear and infrequent. Progress slowed as uncertainty increased.

A steep hill rose in front of them at an angle that appeared impossible to climb, but the Range Rover's four wheel drive system maintained its grip, edging slowly up the incline. The vehicle reached the summit and returned to a more level orientation, but from here Lucas wasn't able to see how steep the next descent was. He throttled too hard, causing the Sport to accelerate. The front end dipped, the headlights illuminating the other side of the hill. Trees crowded the hillside, making the route to the bottom indirect. Realising his mistake too late Lucas stomped hard on the brake pedal instead of relying on engine-braking. The Range Rover began to slide.

Loud reports of gunshots cracked through the air. A headlight shattered a second before the windscreen fragmented. Lucas flinched and raised his hands to protect his face, unavoidably losing control of the vehicle. The Range Rover spun slowly on the mud, turning sideways on to the descent. The vehicle was now under the control of gravity and building up momentum. Its wheels struck an unseen object and the car flipped onto its side, scraping its way down the incline.

The roof crunched inwards as the Sport struck a tree trunk and was brought to a shuddering halt.

10

The grey light of an autumnal Scottish dawn was creeping over the hills when Mason steered the dirt covered Landcruiser into the entrance of the Fort William Golf Club. The clubhouse was a drab single storey building that didn't draw attention. Without the benefit of the sign outside, passing motorists might have mistaken the golf club for a transport café; a blot on an otherwise charming forested landscape. But aesthetics were far from Mason and Wheeler's minds as they drove slowly along the driveway and turned left into a secluded parking area. Here they could tend to their injuries knowing they were out of sight. They were almost three miles from the town of Fort William and far away from security cameras.

Mason parked a short distance from two cars and a campervan. He switched off the lights and killed the engine. After three minutes of watching and listening through their open windows, they glanced at each other and nodded in silent agreement. Mason grabbed the medical kit and two small backpacks which contained spare clothing and footwear. They made their way towards the clubhouse – Wheeler hobbling on his injured foot and supported by Mason – where they found a discreet spot behind the building and sat down against the wall.

Mason glanced at Wheeler. "You okay?"

Wheeler nodded. "I will be when I get this boot off. It

feels like my foot has swollen up."

Mason opened the kit bag and found a pair of medical scissors. They had angled serrated blades capable of cutting through sturdy fabric. "There's plenty of sterile bandaging in here." He handed Wheeler a torch. "Hold this. I'll need to cut through your boot laces."

"No, you first," said Wheeler. "My foot will be okay for a while longer, but your arm needs cleaning up. You've driven through a forest with an injured shoulder and probably damaged it some more. Besides, I don't want you working on me one-handed."

"Fair enough. You'll have to help me get out of this kit."

"No problem, just turn around a bit." Wheeler unfastened Mason's body armour and tossed it to one side. Shining the torch, Wheeler saw Mason's injury wasn't deep, but it wasn't clean and had bled considerably. Half-dried blood caused his shirt to stick to his back. Wheeler used the scissors to slice through the ruined garment. Once it was removed he opened a packet of alcohol-impregnated cleaning wipes and began to clear some of the congealed blood from Mason's shoulder. After a minute he stopped suddenly.

"What is it?" Mason asked.

"I was about to ask you the same question," Wheeler replied. He shone the torch onto Mason's back, studying a small mark near his upper spine. "Hold still a minute." He touched the mark and realised it was slightly raised. A fine red line, about half an inch in length, ran vertically down the centre of the bump. He pressed a little harder and felt something solid beneath his fingertip. "Andy, I think there's something in your back. Have you had any surgery recently?"

"No, none," replied Mason. "What is it?"

"Hard to say. It's only tiny, but there's something solid in there."

Mason suddenly felt a chill. "Get it out."

"Hang on, mate, I don't know what it is yet."

"I have an idea. There's a scalpel and forceps in the bag. I need you to get it out."

"Okay, you're the boss. I just hope I can keep the site clean."

"You're doing fine already."

Wheeler rummaged through the kit bag, opened packets containing swabs and dressings, and found the tools. "There's no anaesthetic."

"Get on with it." Mason leaned forward and braced himself.

Wheeler used the scalpel to cut into Mason's back, keeping the incision as precise as he could while holding the torch. Blood flowed and he quickly pressed swabs against the cut. He picked up the forceps and used them to try to grasp the object. He slipped a couple of times and had to readjust the tool, but finally he succeeded in pulling out a small plastic capsule from Mason's back. He cleaned the area as thoroughly as he could and applied a dressing. Blood oozed through the fabric, so he attached another and taped it in place.

"Let's have a closer look at this thing," Wheeler said softly as he shone the torch beam onto the object.

Mason picked up the scalpel and carefully sliced into it. Inside the capsule there was some miniature electronic circuitry. "CIA bastards. This is how they've been tracking me. They must have cut me open when they abducted me in London."

"It's so tiny that they wouldn't have had to stitch you up," said Wheeler. "They inserted it under your skin – next to your spine where you wouldn't have reached it – and probably used medical superglue to repair the incision. No wonder you didn't notice it."

Mason put the capsule on a paving stone, placed a flat pebble on top and then stood on it, grinding with his boot. He dislodged the stone and saw the remains of the device were now sufficiently damaged to prevent it from working again. "We have to go. They know where we are."

Wheeler nodded. "We'll have to hotwire one of those cars in case the Landcruiser has a tracker on it too."

Mason helped him to his feet and picked up the bags. They started walking back to the car park.

"So what exactly are we going to do?" asked Wheeler. "We're pretty fucked if the CIA come after us."

"You should get out of the country. It's not you they want."

"We're a team," Wheeler protested.

"We'd draw attention travelling together. We'll use the e-mail account to communicate when we can." The account had been set up a year ago for his team's use, but no e-mail had ever been sent from it. Messages were only ever saved as drafts. Doing so allowed each team member to log in, read the messages and respond without risking an e-mail intercept. Later they would abandon the account and create a new one with a different service provider.

Mason dropped the bags at the entrance to the car park. "Wait here. I'll see if I can get that old Montego started."

He approached the grey vehicle, glanced inside to check it was empty, smashed a quarter light then reached inside and released the rear door catch. He entered the vehicle, clambered into the front and tore off the steering column's casing. Moments later the engine coughed into life. Mason selected first gear and slowly drove to Wheeler's location. Wheeler threw their bags onto the rear seat before getting inside.

"Fort William is too obvious," he said. "We need somewhere we can dump this car but still have access to transport. Any ideas?"

"South to Glasgow. That'll give us some options. It'll take about two and a half hours, but I need some thinking time." Mason reached into his pocket and pulled out the USB device he'd used in Rhodes' mansion. "I need to figure out what to do with this."

ELEVEN

1

A succession of shots rang out from the SIG Pro pistol as Alex fired towards the paper target. The weapon's slide clicked back. The firearms instructor stepped forward and took hold of the weapon, checked it was empty and placed it on the floor of the indoor range. Both men removed their ear defenders.

"You're getting quicker," the instructor said. "Let's see how accurate you are."

A dozen round holes were clustered a few inches apart and slightly to the left of the target's centre. Alex had realised that, even standing seven metres from the target, being accurate with a handgun took a lot of practice. During his first session the instructor had allowed him to try an MP5 as well as the SIG. The simplicity of aiming and firing the MP5 had been a revelation. He'd been close to the centre of the target with each shot. The pistol, however, was proving more difficult to use.

The instructor faced him. "You're pulling to the side slightly as you're firing. You need to relax your stance a little. Your finger is still too tense on the trigger, but you're improving. We'll practise some more at seven metres before trying the ten metre line." He glanced at the far end of the range and saw Charlotte Black watching through the glass of the viewing area. "Looks like your boss is here. Let's take a break for lunch."

"Sure. Thanks, Rick." Alex put down his ear and eye protectors and headed for the exit.

"Going well?" asked Charlotte as Alex stepped through the doorway.

"Improving," he replied. "I still need a lot of practice." He rolled his head, stretching his neck muscles. He'd had suffered some pain since the crash in the forest.

"How's your neck?" Charlotte asked.

"Better, thanks. I'm glad none of us were badly hurt." He frowned. "We were close, Charlotte."

She nodded. "Caldwell claims not to have any more information about Mason, but we won't stop looking." She changed the subject. "I want to get you out to Greenland. It's imperative you make contact with Robert Grier."

They walked into a small empty canteen with round plastic tables and hard moulded chairs. The hum of a vending machine's refrigeration unit was the only noise. Alex pushed some coins into the slot and pressed the button for a Pepsi. "Can I get you a drink?" Charlotte shook her head. Alex popped the can open and sat down. "Wouldn't it be simpler just to recall him to the UK? He's British Army."

"That's not strictly true. He runs Arctic survival courses for the Army as a contractor, but he's a glaciologist by profession. That's why he spends most of the year conducting surveys on the ice sheet. It's fortunate for us that the expedition works out of our Greenland base camp. We've been lucky with Grier. So far no one has targeted him, but that probably has a lot to do with being on an army base in one of the remotest parts of the globe."

"Or because Rhodes and the others haven't arranged the

hit yet."

Charlotte shrugged. "We don't know. Stephen's team has been looking at the computer we seized from his mansion. They've found plenty of data concerning operations at Orford Ness and the names of the EHB subjects, but nothing else."

"Rhodes wouldn't keep anything on file about the assassinations."

"Of course. Unfortunately there's nothing connecting Falkner and Barnard to the killings either, which presents me with a problem."

"Go on."

"I have no evidence to link them to illegal activity. They're old school patriots with a Cold War mentality, but they still have considerable influence over many people in Government. Others want Falkner and Barnard exposed as corrupt ideologists of a bygone era. The reformers want the old ties severed, but it's not easy. I'll have to rethink my plan."

Alex sipped his drink. "What do you want me to do when I find Grier?"

"The same as with Carter and McLeod. Tell him about the programme. Ask him to fly back with you so the scientists can conduct their tests."

"And if he refuses?"

"Hopefully his scientific background will make him curious."

Alex smiled. "When do I leave?"

"Soon, but there are still some details to work out. My staff are liaising with the RAF to fly you out to Iceland and then on to Kangerlussuaq on Greenland's west coast. I'm sending Tanya Smith with you. She's familiar with military protocols."

"Not Abi?"

"No, I need Abigail here in London. She's assisting with the diplomatic negotiations. Besides, I want you to work with Tanya again. She's a competent operative, plus she's looked after Kate McLeod very well since the shooting. I'm thinking of bringing her into the team."

"Phil Reid will be sorry to lose her."

"He'll get over it." Charlotte pushed her chair back and stood. "We'll discuss this more when you return." She hesitated. "I realise you haven't had the training you need for these missions."

"There hasn't been time."

"I know that, but I'm not comfortable with putting you at risk."

"I told you I wanted to be involved. I wouldn't have it any other way."

Charlotte nodded. "When this is over, we'll discuss things properly. The EHB project might be shut down."

"I can still be on your team."

"Assuming I'm not moved onto something else."

"Would they do that to you?"

"I'm anticipating exactly that. That's why I need everyone to pull together right now."

"I'll do my part."

"I know you will." She put on her coat. "I'll let you know when your transport is ready. For now, keep practising on the range. It'll be helpful knowing how to handle weapons."

Alex stood. "There's one thing I've learned already. I

wanted revenge for my parents' murder. But now? Firing at a target on the range is one thing, but I don't think I could take someone's life. Not even Mason's."

Charlotte placed her hand on his shoulder. "That's why I trust you with a gun, Alex. You understand the consequences of pulling the trigger. I've had firearms instructors tell me the same thing over and over – if you want to carry a gun, you're the last person who should have one." She headed for the door. "I'll see you back at the office later."

"Will do. Thanks for the talk."

Charlotte smiled and turned to the door.

2

"I discovered this place by accident," said Jack Caldwell as Clare Quinn sat down beside him. The Broad Court walkway ran between London's Drury Lane and Bow Street. Their seat was a flat stone circle with a bronze Enzo Plazzotta statue of a seated ballerina at its centre. Caldwell pointed towards the row of five red telephone boxes nearby. "You know there are hardly any of those left?"

"How quaint." Quinn wasn't in the mood for a conversation about vanishing cultural icons. She stared at the bollards at the end of the street.

"You haven't said much since coming back from Scotland."

"What is there to say?"

"Come on, Clare. You speaking your mind is as certain as death and taxes. You're pissed because I didn't tell you everything."

"That's your prerogative as station chief."

"True."

"You could have put me in the middle of a firefight."

"Unlikely."

"But possible." She turned to face him. "I'm sure you had a plan, Jack, but this turned into one prize screw-up."

"I don't share that perspective."

"Well it was hardly a success!"

"You downloaded the Station Helix data Rhodes had on

his computer."

"Only because Mason and his boys turned the place into a war zone!"

Jack held her gaze. "Sometimes you have to take an engineered gamble, or, as I like to call it, plant a serendipity seed."

"Sounds like sociology nonsense."

He smiled at her bluntness. "Scotland was going to play out in one of several ways. I made several beneficial outcomes possible. Relying on Mason to get hold of Rhodes' data was a long shot, so I needed a backup plan. Telling Rhodes his life was in danger created two possible opportunities. Either his men would kill Mason – thereby eliminating a threat and saving us a job – or Mason would succeed and create enough of a mess for us to take advantage of. As you were already working with the MOD, you were able to go to the scene. Liaising with Alex was secondary to getting onto the estate. Knowing my plan would have negatively influenced your interaction with him."

Clare shook her head. "You're a devious bastard, Jack. It would've been nice if you'd mentioned this beforehand. And you forget that Rhodes ended up dead and Mason got away. How does that help us?"

"Rhodes being dead benefits us and the Brits. He had a long-standing association with Helix and used his resources to target people connected to the project. I don't know why yet."

"I'm sure Charlotte Black will thank you for arranging his death."

He grinned. "It probably won't come up in

conversation. Rhodes was killed by a hit squad of renegade ex-British Army soldiers. We have no connection to the incident."

"Convenient. And Mason?"

"An unfortunate loose end, but not a particularly troublesome one. His team is dead and he doesn't have any resources. I wouldn't be surprised if the police pick him up soon."

Clare stroked her hair and tightened her ponytail. "Thanks for explaining the bigger picture to me – *eventually*. Are you going to tell me what happens next?"

"The diplomats will continue their discussions, but behind the scenes we're looking at the data you collected. It's proved rather intriguing already."

Quinn's curiosity displaced her annoyance. "Really?"

Jack nodded. "Remember I asked you to find out how Alex came to be working for Charlotte?"

"I didn't get the chance to speak to him properly."

"It doesn't matter; he wouldn't have told you anyway. He's a Helix subject."

She stared. "I thought we had all their names? Besides, he's ten years younger than Carter and the others."

"Warren Ellis extracted just a handful of files from the Helix server before he was caught, so we only had a tiny amount of information. It turns out that the five people on our list were just the first batch. They repeated the experiment ten and twenty years later. Alex is part of the Generation Two group. This is a lot bigger than we thought."

"Should make finding a live subject easier."

Caldwell shook his head. "We're not doing that."

Quinn glared. "Because Black asked you not to?"

"Because the ambassador made his position very clear to me. The CIA will not jeopardise the diplomatic talks."

"Great."

"It's of no consequence. Right now I'm curious about something else – the hits that Rhodes arranged. He was going after the Generation Ones. Why not the others?"

"Maybe that was the next step."

Caldwell shook his head. "I don't think so." He stood and brushed his coat out of habit. "Let's get back to the office. I want to have another look at the Jonathan Cline file."

3

The clock on Edinburgh Zoo's gatehouse showed the time as twenty past three when Mason's bus drove by the entrance. A small crowd of tourists was outside but he ignored them and turned his attention back to the sheet of paper in his hands that he'd torn from an Edinburgh *A to Z*. Murrayfield Stadium was close to his destination but he had no interest in the rugby venue. He folded the paper again and placed it in a pocket. He turned back to the window, reading the street name signs as the bus made progress along Corstorphine Road.

Wheeler and he had made it to Glasgow without incident and had abandoned the stolen Montego as soon as it was practical to do so. Their concern about having to wait so long to tend their injuries had proved to be misplaced because their wounds were relatively minor. They had the field experience to clean and patch themselves up without needing to seek professional medical attention. They'd found a rundown B&B, rested overnight and left after an early breakfast. Wheeler's plan was to catch a train south to Liverpool from where he would take a ferry to the Isle of Man. Mason had boarded a coach for Edinburgh.

The bus continued eastwards for another three minutes. On the right the metalwork of the rugby stadium became visible through a gap in the buildings. On the left a glass-fronted bus stop was attached to a stone wall. Foliage from a row of tall trees behind the masonry hung over the pavement. The bus came to a halt. Mason made his way to the front, mumbled an acknowledgement to the driver as the doors opened with a hiss, disembarked and waited for the traffic to clear before crossing the road towards a modern five-storey office building. Wall-mounted CCTV cameras covered each aspect. A large red flag hung from a pole protruding from the roofline.

He saw a small sign with an arrow and the words *Reception and Deliveries*, went a short distance in the direction it indicated, and saw a satellite receiver dish mounted on a metal platform against the rear of the building. He walked a little farther before finding the entrance. He hesitated for a moment, feeling uneasy about the decision he'd made, but quickly dismissed the thought. He removed the USB data device from his jacket pocket and walked into the reception of the Chinese Consulate.

4

The last time Alex had attended a funeral he'd sat at the front of the room and found it difficult to pay attention to proceedings. Now he sat at the back, sharing a pew with Abi, Lucas and Tanya. It occurred to him that, having seen the interior of one crematorium's chapel, he'd seen them all. The same pastel drapes interrupted the blandness of the same painted walls. The same carefully-vacuumed carpet fitted neatly against the same wooden pews. But it was seeing two coffins at the front of the chapel that made him experience the same emotional bewilderment he'd struggled with during his parents' service. This time one casket was much smaller than the other. An image of little Megan McLeod being zipped up in a black body bag filled his thoughts and guilt knotted his stomach. He wondered if Lucas and Tanya were still finding it difficult to come to terms with what had happened. He turned slightly and glanced at their faces. They were looking straight ahead. He couldn't read their expressions.

A click sounded and the coffins were transported slowly out of sight by the rollers in the plinth. After an appropriate pause the minister opened a side door and waited beside it as the McLeods' family and friends filtered slowly from the building. The man shook hands with everyone, offering much-repeated and meaningless words of comfort. When everyone else had gone outside, Lucas stood. Alex, Tanya and Abi did the same, shuffled out from the pew and walked to the exit. Alex shook hands with the minister and instantly forgot whatever he said. They took a moment to glance at the neatly placed flower bouquets, but none of them wanted to stay for long. Abi had summed up their sentiments when she'd said that being an official representative at a funeral felt like intruding on someone's grief.

They walked a short distance away, endeavouring to give Kate McLeod and her family space. Kate spent several minutes thanking the attendees for supporting her. She finally separated herself from them and walked over to Alex and the others. Her dark hair had been tied back apart from loose bangs which framed her olive face. Her smudged mascara betrayed earlier tears, but now her expression was calm and reflective. "Are you guys okay?" she asked.

The question caught Alex by surprise. It bemused him that a grieving woman would have time to concern herself with the wellbeing of others. He didn't answer but nodded and attempted a half-smile.

Kate placed her hand on his arm. "I know this must be difficult for you. It's so soon after your parents' funeral."

"I hadn't thought of it like that. I just wanted to attend. I'm sorry things…"

"It wasn't your fault," she interrupted. She glanced back at her family who were reading the message cards attached to the bouquets. She looked back round. "I had to get away from all that." Her voice made the comment sound confessional. "All that sobbing and well-wishing was making me feel sick." Kate directed her next words at Abi and Tanya. "Thank you for helping me get this arranged. I couldn't have coped on my own." She hugged them in turn. "I'd better go. I…" She hesitated.

"What is it?" Abi asked.

"I need you to keep your promise," Kate replied. "You told me you'd find out who killed my daughter and husband. I even agreed to keep the truth from my family. They still believe the cover story about the hit and run accident. I hate lying to them but I know why I have to keep this secret. Just don't break your word."

"I won't," Abi assured her. "You have my number. Call me whenever you want and we'll talk some more."

Kate nodded. "I will, but right now I need to spend some time with my parents and sister. I'll call you soon."

"Do that."

"Thank you all for coming today." She turned and walked away.

Alex faced Abi. "Are you really going to discuss everything with her?"

Abi returned his look. "We can't make her sign an official secrets agreement about her child's death and not give something in return. She deserves more."

Tanya pulled a car key from her suit pocket. "Right now she knows more than I do. I've been told to see Charlotte Black for a briefing later. I thought I'd be heading back up to Scotland after today."

"We're going a little farther north," said Alex.

5

"Your team's found nothing?" Charlotte Black watched through the rear side window as the Ministry Lexus passed Hampstead Underground Station.

"They found plenty," answered Stephen Jennings. "Unfortunately there's nothing of use. Rhodes had plenty of data about the EHB programme including Cline's autopsy report, but we knew he'd have that. We can't prove any connection to the McLeod and Stone hits."

Charlotte turned to face him. "What about his associates?"

He shook his head. "Again, nothing helpful. We've found documents where Falkner and the others are mentioned, but they're legitimate records."

"It was always a long shot." She turned back to the window.

Thirty seconds later her mobile began to ring. She glanced at the touchscreen as she took the phone from her pocket. The name *Mark Booker* appeared on the screen. She answered the call. "Mark? What can I do for you?" Seconds into the conversation she glanced at Jennings, her expression uncharacteristically revealing. "Thanks, Mark. I appreciate it. Yes, don't hesitate. Keep me informed. I owe you lunch. Will do." Black lowered the phone, smiled slightly, and touched the graphic to end the call. Jennings waited for her to speak. "That was Mark Booker."

"Your counterpart at the Security Service?"

She nodded. "They've had a facial recognition match on Andrew Mason getting out of a car with diplomatic plates outside the Chinese embassy here in London." She put her phone away. "I thought he would show up, but I'd never have predicted that."

"I don't recall seeing anything about the Chinese in his file. I'll look again."

"Don't bother; you won't find anything. I know his file inside out. No, this is new. He's got hold of something and found a buyer."

Jennings nodded. "The Chinese are no strangers to industrial espionage. We can only speculate what he's given them."

Black shook her head. "We have a pretty good idea. He got into Rhodes' computer."

"There were security protocols on the data."

"That means nothing. Besides, Rhodes had a gun to his head. He probably told Mason everything."

"If the Chinese have that information – and we should assume from the CCTV footage that they do – the whole programme is at risk."

"Let me worry about that." Charlotte paused as the driver pulled off the road into a small lay-by. She reached for the door handle. "I might be able to take advantage of this. Wait here with the driver. I'll be about twenty minutes." She stepped out from the car, shut the door and set out along a footpath leading away from the road.

She passed trees and shrubs displaying their early autumnal foliage and headed down an incline as the path took her past buildings on Hampstead's Inverforth House estate. One hundred metres farther on she reached the mansion's pergola and garden. A plain clothes police sergeant met her at the entrance and directed her to William Dawkins' location.

"I'm not sure whether Rhodes being shot helps or hinders our mission, Charlotte," said Dawkins as they shook hands. They were on a ground floor walkway with a solid brick wall on one side and views over the garden and footpath on the other.

"I'd be inclined to go with the former, Home Secretary," she replied.

"Really? I thought you were going to interrogate him."

"Things change. This outcome is better."

"Explain."

"The risk was substantial. If he'd held his nerve, we'd have lost. We had nothing else to go on. I couldn't have held him at one of our facilities without his friends noticing very quickly. Attempts to link him and the others to the assassinations would have failed."

Dawkins nodded. "You're probably right. I take it we still have nothing on Falkner and Barnard?"

"Nothing at all."

Dawkins rubbed his brow, uncharacteristically anxious. "How did you clear up the mess in Scotland?"

"The McLeod deaths have been attributed to a hit and run accident. The paramedics and undertakers who attended have signed non-disclosure agreements for national security."

"And Rhodes?"

"A murder-suicide. We've implied that Rhodes had an intimate relationship with his assistant that went tragically wrong. The other bodies were dumped in the North Atlantic."

Dawkins stared at her. "Remind me never to upset you."

"I'm paid to be a problem solver."

"For the most part you're damn good at your job, but Falkner and Barnard remain untouchable. Recent events will make them even harder to reach."

"Forgive the political analogy, sir, but I think it's time for a U-turn."

He looked at her quizzically. "I don't follow you."

"A change of perspective. Until now we've been doing this under the radar. Perhaps it's time to invite them in for discussions."

"I don't see how that would work to our advantage."

"I have some news that they'll definitely want to hear. The Chinese know about Station Helix."

"Jesus!" Dawkins glared. "I didn't think this could get any worse. Are you sure?"

"Mark Booker at Five called me a few minutes ago. Andrew Mason was seen in one of their diplomatic vehicles outside the embassy. It's safe to assume he's given them information in return for protection from us and the Americans."

"Do you realise what this means? This has all happened on your watch. Everyone – and I'm not just talking about Falkner and Barnard – *everyone* is going to want your head on a platter."

She smiled. "That's what I'm counting on, Home Secretary."

6

Alex reached the top of the Ministry building's accommodation floor staircase, pushed open the fire door and stepped into the hallway. As he dug around in his pocket for his key he noticed that the door to Lily Carter's room was open. He heard chords being strummed on an acoustic guitar. He walked along the corridor but didn't show himself. Lily's melodic voice sang the opening lines of *I'm So Lonesome I Could Cry*.

Alex knocked on the open door and looked into the room. "That was beautiful, Lily. Hank Williams?"

She looked up from her chair, rested her arms over her blue Takamine and smiled. "I definitely thought you were too young to know about him, Alex."

"My dad was a fan."

"Your dad had good taste. It's hard to beat Hank Williams for pure poetry and insight into the human condition."

Alex smiled as he sat down. "So our rock chick knows her musical roots."

Lily laughed. "Hey, it's not all *Train, Train* and *Sweet Home Alabama* with me, sunshine. I like including some of the old stuff in my sets. Besides, it's good for a performer to tackle songs like *Lonesome*. You have nowhere to hide with tunes like that."

"I'd like to see you perform that one on stage."

Lily held his gaze for a moment. "When artists take breaks from performing they usually do it because they're knackered or in need of rehab, but I'm out of public view because my life is in danger." She gave an ironic half-smile. "At least it's given me time to write some new stuff."

"I hope your enforced exile doesn't last much longer."

"Can you be sure of that after what happened in Scotland? Those poor people."

He shook his head. "There are still matters which need resolving."

She leaned back in her chair. "I'm glad you found me when you did. I regret I was rude to you the first time we met."

Alex grinned. "And the second. It was understandable though."

"I thought you were a fruitcake stalker."

"Well, you're forgiven."

"Thank you. So when are you off to Greenland?"

"Hopefully soon, but there's a huge storm in the North Atlantic that's disrupting flights. I'm waiting for an update from the RAF. Then we have to travel across the ice sheet to reach the base camp. They won't let us attempt that until the storm has passed."

"Sounds like fun. You might even get to see a polar bear."

"Hopefully from a safe distance."

"You're a photographer. You should take your camera."

"I'd like to but this isn't exactly a sightseeing trip."

"You'll have time to take a few pictures. Hey, maybe when this is all over you could get some shots of me on stage. I could do with a few portfolio shots."

"I'd love to." Alex stood. "I'll let you get back to your practising. You sound great."

"Thanks. Drop by before you get on your plane."

"I will." Alex smiled and made his way out of the apartment. He thought about Lily's words and wondered how soon it would be before their situation really would be over. He couldn't help feeling that hoping for normality was wishful thinking.

7

A clear autumnal sky greeted Charlotte Black, Abi Jones and Stephen Jennings as they left the Old Admiralty Building and strode purposefully across the open ground of Horse Guards Parade. They didn't have far to go – their destination was the Cabinet Office on Whitehall – and they walked briskly to avoid being chilled by the low temperature of the season. Beneath their overcoats all three wore smart and formal attire. Both Charlotte and Abi had chosen elegant but empowering trouser suits. Jennings, whose demeanour always made him look both sophisticated and aloof, wore a tailored suit and a finely made regimental tie.

As they headed south across the parade ground Charlotte's phone rang. "Morning, Jack," she said as she answered the call.

"Morning, Charlotte." Jack Caldwell's voice sounded clearly through the speaker, undistracted by background noise. "In the interests of being a good neighbour, I thought I should let you know your man Mason has appeared on the radar again."

"Yes, I'm aware. I wanted to thank you for everything you did to help us capture him in Scotland." She didn't attempt to hide her irritation.

Jack ignored her tone. "Mason is of no interest to us but his new friends are. We probably keep a closer eye on the

Chinese here in London than MI5 do. I'm sure you've already got GCHQ eavesdropping, but I'm in contact with Langley over this as well. If we get wind of what the Chinese are up to, I'll let you know. I'm concerned they know as much as we do."

"Why the generosity, Jack?"

"As I said, I'm just being neighbourly. Have a good day." Jack ended the call.

Charlotte didn't break her stride as she placed her phone in her pocket. "Interesting. Caldwell's being unusually forthright. He's just informed me – indirectly – that he has everything from Rhodes' computer."

"Why would he do that?" Abi asked.

"To remind me about information-sharing protocols. The diplomats are negotiating the release of information that the CIA already has. Secrecy is blown. Clever bastard. I like him more and more."

8

The conference room on the first floor of the Cabinet Office – used to host the Government's Cobra crisis meetings – lacked the grandeur that might be expected of a Whitehall venue. It was a plain room dominated by a table which left little space for the twenty dark grey office chairs around it. Bottles of still and sparkling water had been placed on the table besides upturned glasses on cloth napkins. A monitor occupied almost the entire wall at one end of the room. Today it was switched off, but when in use it could be used in a split-screen format to receive several video feeds at once. A strip light, fitted into an alcove in the ceiling, emitting a tired yellow-tinted fluorescent glow. Fortunately the drab beige blinds were open, allowing some much-needed daylight into the characterless space.

William Dawkins sat at the head of the table sipping water from a glass as he waited for the remaining attendees to arrive. Charlotte Black sat to his left with Abi beside her. Both looked immaculate in their tailored suit jackets. Stephen Jennings stood by the door. Abi and he had been instructed to refrain from contributing to the discussion. Charlotte had wanted them there for several reasons; the simplest of which was to balance the numbers, but also to observe and assess Barnard and Falkner's reactions during the discussion.

A smartly-dressed man stepped into the room,

unwinding a dark blue woollen scarf as he did so. Dawkins rose from his chair and extended his hand. "Good morning, Jon. Thanks for coming."

"Not sure what this is all about, William," Jon Vestal commented as he sat down in the chair opposite Charlotte. "Charlotte."

She smiled. "Defence Secretary."

Vestal leaned back in his chair and turned to Dawkins. "Your other guests are on their way up. This all seems pretty irregular. They have no idea why you've asked them here."

"I'll be sure to make everything clear," the Home Secretary replied.

Two minutes later Archimedes Falkner and Benjamin Barnard entered the room. Falkner shook hands with Dawkins and smiled warmly. "Good morning, Home Secretary. I trust you're keeping well?" His affable manner revealed his calm confidence.

"Very well, thank you." Dawkins turned his attention to Barnard, greeting him as they shook hands. Barnard didn't share Falkner's aquiline features but looked no less self-assured. The Home Secretary motioned towards the chairs beside Vestal.

Jennings stepped forward and addressed Barnard who was the only one wearing an overcoat. "May I take your coat, sir?"

Barnard removed the garment and handed it to Jennings, thanking him. Jennings left the room. He returned moments later, closed the door and sat beside Abi.

"Right, let's get started now that we're all here," said Dawkins as he sat and pulled his chair closer to the desk.

"For those of you who haven't met, I'll do the introductions. Benjamin Barnard and Archimedes Falkner; respected former senior civil servants. Jon Vestal; Secretary of State for Defence. Charlotte Black; one of Jon's senior staff and adviser to the Cabinet. Abigail Jones and Stephen Jennings; Miss Black's assistants." He caught Falkner and Barnard's eyes and directed his next comment to them. "You are undoubtedly aware that discussions have begun with Washington about sharing the data from the Enhanced Human Being research programme. I initiated this dialogue because of necessity and practicality. In doing so, I've pulled rank on Defence Secretary Vestal." Dawkins turned to Vestal. "Jon, I'm grateful that you've taken an important part in the talks, despite your misgivings. I hope you haven't felt like I've pushed you aside."

"Not at all, Home Secretary," Vestal replied, his tone betraying his words.

Dawkins pretended not to notice. "While I'm confident that the dialogue with the Americans is going well, I'm also mindful that recent events have become troublesome to say the least. For this reason I've decided to shut down the Orford Ness site and transfer the research to the beta facility in Dorset. The project will continue, but it will be in collaboration with the Americans and on a much smaller scale. The Government can't continue to fund the research at its current level."

Falkner leaned forward. "Home Secretary, forgive me for asking, but why are Ben and I here? These are decisions for Government. As you said, we're retired."

"I felt it was important to apprise you and seek your opinions. You conceived the project and persuaded Prime

Minister Macmillan to back it. Many of the protocols you established are still in place. For no reason other than professional courtesy, I'd like you to be involved in the next stages."

"That's gracious but unnecessary," Falkner replied.

"Maybe so, but I feel it is appropriate. Your wealth of experience can only be beneficial to the transition. I'd like you to be available to Charlotte's staff at all times."

Barnard lifted his hand to interject. "I'm afraid I have my concerns about Miss Black's suitability for the task. Her management of the EHB project has led to the circumstances in which we now find ourselves."

Vestal nodded. "I have to agree with Benjamin. I wasn't informed by her regarding certain decisions, which, had I known about, I would never have endorsed." Vestal faced Black. "I'm sorry, Charlotte. I think it's time to replace you."

She held his gaze. "Would you care to elaborate, Defence Secretary?"

Falkner spoke again. "Perhaps I can answer that, Miss Black. The EHB programme was meant to be *Eyes Only*. The EHB subjects were never supposed to have known about the experiments. As for allowing the Americans to become involved..."

"With respect, sir, bringing in the Generation Ones was forced upon me when David Stone was murdered in Cairo. It was obvious that these people were in danger. The project was compromised. My efforts have been directed into finding a resolution."

"Your idea of a resolution is misplaced," Falkner retorted. "You're out of your depth. Your appointment was simply to oversee the project, not to make independent decisions behind the Defence Secretary's back."

Barnard glared at Charlotte. "The project worked perfectly for decades. In a matter of weeks you've jeopardised the whole thing and forced us into unwanted negotiations with the Americans."

"Unwanted by whom?" she snapped. "In accordance with the Technical Cooperation Program the Americans should have been involved at the outset."

"That's a matter of opinion and one with which I disagree," said Falkner. "Helix was set up as a research facility based on new science. There was never any certainty that anything useful would come of it. We had no obligation to speak to them."

"We're not here to debate interpretations of Special Relationship protocols," Dawkins interrupted. "I won't accept the accusation that Miss Black was responsible for the Americans finding out about Helix. There was a leak before she was put in charge. It was only a matter of time before they realised what was going on at the facility."

Vestal raised his hands submissively. "All right, that's a fair point. But I stand by my decision that Charlotte has to be taken off the project. She hasn't managed it effectively. It's bloody chaos."

"I'm over-ruling you, Jon," Dawkins said. "Charlotte stays in charge of Helix."

Vestal glared. "Home Secretary, I must object."

"Your objection is noted. She stays. In fact, it's thanks to Charlotte alone that we know of other risks to the project."

Barnard looked quizzical. "What are you talking

about?"

Dawkins looked at Charlotte. "Perhaps it's time to apprise our colleagues about what happened to Mr Rhodes."

"Yes, sir." Charlotte leaned forward, making eye contact with the three men opposite her in turn. "Edward Rhodes wasn't shot by his personal assistant following a lovers' tiff. He was murdered by a hit squad. I arranged a suitable cover-up to hide the truth."

Barnard stared, his expression disbelieving. "This had better not be a sick joke."

"Quite the opposite," she replied. "This is deadly serious. Someone knew about your friend's connection to the EHB programme. Not only did the team kill Rhodes but they stole the data stored on his computer. That information is now in the hands of the Chinese. So you see the Home Secretary's decision to shut down Orford Ness is not just about budget cuts. It's about protecting your project from industrial espionage."

Falkner stared at Dawkins. "Is this true?"

"Unquestionably."

"There is one puzzle I haven't yet been able to solve," Black lied. "I don't know whether those responsible for Rhodes' death also killed Stone and McLeod."

"That's the other reason why I want you to be accessible." Dawkins directed his remark at Barnard and Falkner. "We have to assume that you are both in danger."

"Thank you for your concern but we can take care of our own security," Falkner stated.

"Rhodes believed that too," said Dawkins. "You're not entitled to diplomatic protection, but I'm sure Jon will be able to arrange something through his department if you wish it." He pushed his chair back and stood. "Gentlemen, do you see now why I invited you here today? It was imperative you were told about the risk to not only the EHB programme but yourselves as well. Charlotte is now working under my direct authority and I expect you to give her your full support. My apologies for cutting this short, but I have a meeting at Downing Street with the PM. Good day."

9

Benjamin Barnard had never been fond of London despite having spent a considerable proportion of his working life in the city. He found England's capital drab and overcrowded. He could taste the traffic pollution in the air and saw its sooty fingerprint upon buildings which would be grander if only someone were to take responsibility for cleaning their stonework occasionally. In his mind the royal palaces in which he had worked were jewels surrounded by coal. Civic pride was a contentious issue to him; knowing how magnificent British culture *could* be, it irked him that much of the population seemed indifferent towards it. Living outside London had always provided him with the balance he needed; at heart he was a lover of rural life. The restfulness of remote villages and broad painterly landscapes appealed to him considerably more than the city's urban greyness.

Leaving London for the countryside normally settled his thoughts, but this time the journey northwest from the city towards the Chiltern Hills was anything but calming. Discovering the truth about his friend's murder had unnerved him, and Dawkins' obvious move to usurp him and Falkner had caused him frustration. He wasn't used to being manipulated. Sitting in the rear seat of his Bentley Continental he uncharacteristically said barely a word to his driver for almost the entire journey.

The car turned off the carriageway and headed down a long private road bordered by white fences, passing chalk meadowland and trees resplendent in their autumnal colours. Several buildings of various ages – utilitarian as well as residential – were located on Barnard's estate, but his home was a Tudor brick structure of three storeys with tall windows and angular gables. An oval driveway, with a neatly mown lawn at its centre, was situated in front of the mansion. Braking gently the chauffeur stopped the car outside the house. Barnard thanked him and let himself out of the car.

He watched the car pull away, took out his mobile and, instead of going inside, headed across the lawn towards a walled garden. He found Falkner's name in his contact list and dialled the number as he walked through the archway of a ruined mediaeval tower.

Falkner answered the call. "I wondered when you were going to ring." His voice sounded unperturbed.

"Are you not bothered by what was said in that meeting, Archie?"

"I'm not going to concern myself with matters beyond my control."

"That's my point. We're being pushed out."

"Dawkins is an intelligent man. He's played this astutely."

"You sound like you admire the fellow."

"I respect him. There aren't many men in Government who would have the nerve to take us on. It's a clever move to involve us in the dismantling of our own creation."

"Are you willing to let that happen?"

"I – *we* – don't have a choice. If we attempt to jeopardise his plan we'll be portrayed as having a negative influence. You and I will go along with his request. We'll assist Black's staff, make a few suggestions and then retire with good grace."

"That doesn't sound like the Archimedes Falkner I know." Barnard sounded irritated.

Falkner's tone became more direct. "You're failing to see my point."

"Explain it to me."

"Dawkins wants us to react. He knows we have considerable influence and he's expecting us to use it. We'll do the opposite. He's trying to call our bluff."

"I don't like it. We should talk to Vestal."

"It's safe to say he'll be taken off Defence and given a minor portfolio in the next Cabinet reshuffle. We can't use him any more."

Barnard hesitated. "I'm worried Dawkins knows more than he's letting on."

"Of course he does," replied Falkner. "I made a call to an old acquaintance at Five. The Chinese found out about Helix from Andrew Mason. Mason was in Scotland working for the CIA. It's possible that *he* killed Edward."

Barnard's face went grey. "Jesus, Archie! What if Edward told Mason about the Generation Ones?"

"I can't speculate on that."

Barnard raised his voice almost to a shout. "Don't you at least have a bloody opinion?"

"In my opinion you're allowing yourself to become unduly anxious. The reasons for Edward's demise are not connected to us. Anything he did, he did independently."

Barnard wasn't swayed by the inference. "We were all

there. It was a collective decision to terminate the Generation One subjects. And it wasn't only Edward who made *arrangements*."

"You remember incorrectly, Ben. The agreement was to terminate the *experiment*. It is unfortunate that our late friend apparently misinterpreted that conversation. You and I know nothing about what he did subsequently."

"But *they* know! Dawkins and that Charlotte Black."

"I doubt that. We wouldn't be having this conversation now if that were the case."

"No, because we'd be in police cells under arrest for conspiracy to murder!"

"You're getting carried away. We did nothing untoward. Is that clear?"

"I don't know how you can remain so bloody calm about this."

"Edward is dead. His actions died with him. Let's focus on the matters at hand."

"You're a cold bastard, Archie."

"I don't have time for sentimentality. We will assist Charlotte Black in accordance with the Home Secretary's request."

Barnard clenched his jaw. "Even you must admit we misjudged that woman."

"I'll concede that," Falkner agreed. "Dawkins has found himself a perceptive and ruthless ally in Black. It may prove beneficial to give her our unwavering support."

"Ever the tactician," said Barnard. He turned around and followed the path back towards the mansion, passing through the mediaeval tower's archway once again. "All right, Archie, we'll do it your way."

"Enjoy your evening, old friend," Falkner replied.

The line went dead.

Barnard shook his head and dropped his phone into his coat pocket.

10

Thick grey bands of stratocumulus clouds hung low over the shingle expanse of Orford Ness as Abi Jones and Lily Carter disembarked from the MOD launch and made their way towards the seemingly derelict Station Helix buildings. The low diffused afternoon light seemed to partially desaturate the colours from the isolated landscape; the effect adding to the character of the remote site rather than detracting from it. At times like this, when the sun had all but abandoned this stretch of Suffolk's coastline, the place had an endearing near-monochrome quality that was as enigmatic as the colour-rich light usually associated with the region.

Lily took a moment to study her surroundings, intrigued by the buildings' dilapidation and nature's understated elegance. A flock of seabirds flew overhead, the din of their raucous calls disturbing the quietness as they headed for the nearby salt flats. Lily turned to Abi. "This place is amazing."

Abi nodded. "I promised I'd bring you here." She turned her head, looking at the vista. "At least all this will still be here after Station Helix is shut down. Left for the wildlife and the tourists. Come on, I'll show you the lab." She led Lily towards the brick-built building whose weather-worn doorway accessed Station Helix's reception area, pushed the door open and took her inside.

Waiting for them were Michael Hearn and Zoe Sibon.

"Zoe, Michael," said Abi. "This is Lily Carter. I promised her she'd get to see the laboratory before we closed it down."

Hearn offered his hand. "Welcome to Helix, Miss Carter."

Zoe looked anxious. "Is Jennings with you?" she asked.

Abi shook her head. "No, he's doing something for Charlotte this evening."

"Good," Zoe replied. "I don't want to see that man ever again."

"I can understand that. Don't worry, I've been given the responsibility for ensuring the transfer to the beta site goes smoothly." She grinned. "Of course what that actually means is I'm relying on you two to make it work."

"We've already started packing up," said Hearn. "Moving the equipment is the easy part – it's the archived paperwork and the tissue samples that need care. We have a great quantity of material. Zoe is packing up the documents. There's a lot that isn't on computer. I'm taking care of the rest."

"That's fine. Zoe, call me if you need anything."

Zoe nodded. "I will. I've been given access to the Dorset site's archive room so I can find the space for our material. If you're happy for me to begin I'll start sealing up the crates and get the MOD to transport them down there."

"Absolutely. We need to act promptly." Abi turned to Hearn. "Do you anticipate any difficulties with the organic material?"

"None. We have some organ transplant ambulances at our disposal. Getting the samples to the beta site will be straightforward."

Abi pulled her mobile from her jacket. "Charlotte wanted me to call her as soon as I'd spoken to you. Zoe, would you take Lily to the lab and show her around?"

"Sure." Zoe smiled and pointed at the door behind the reception desk. "It's this way. If you have any questions, please ask."

"There's one thing I'm anxious to know," said Lily. "Is there any news on my test results? I haven't heard anything yet."

Zoe took her by the arm. "Your tests came back negative. I'm delighted to say there's absolutely nothing wrong with you."

11

It was 8.45pm when Jennings arrived at Barnard's mansion. The grey Ford he'd driven from London was owned by the MOD but not registered to it – one of several ordinary and unmemorable models that Ministry staff could use without drawing attention. He twisted the key in the ignition and the engine stopped. Only a few lights were on inside the house.

He headed towards the oak door at the front of the building, aiming the Ford's remote behind him to lock the car as he walked. He knocked twice with the door's large black knocker and waited almost a minute before Barnard greeted him.

"Thank you for agreeing to meet me, Mr Barnard," said Jennings. "I hope the late hour isn't inconvenient."

"Not at all." Barnard stood to one side, allowing Jennings into the mansion's elegant hallway. He pushed the door shut. "I was surprised to hear from you so soon, though."

"My superior is keen to make progress."

"Of course." Barnard paused for a moment, studying Jennings' expressionless face. "Shall we go to the drawing room?" Jennings nodded and followed him.

It was apparent from the light-coloured soft furnishings in the room that Barnard had chosen to decorate parts of the house in an informal style. Simply-patterned fabrics gave the drawing room an atmosphere that was modern but notionally rustic. "Very pleasant," Jennings remarked, although his tone betrayed his indifference.

Barnard didn't notice. "Thank you. A few airy rooms are good in a place like this. So much of the house seems rather formal." He pointed towards a cushioned chair, inviting Jennings to sit. "Can I get you something to drink?"

"No thank you. I shan't keep you for long."

Barnard sat down opposite. "So what brings you here?"

Jennings held his gaze. "New information has come to light. It's rather fortunate, actually. We were beginning to wonder how we'd resolve a nagging issue."

"The Chinese?"

Jennings shook his head. "The Chinese situation is something we'll address in due course. This matter is closer to home."

"I'm intrigued. Please explain."

Jennings reached inside his coat and pulled out a small digital voice recorder and placed it on the table between them. "We've known for some time that you and your friends arranged the murders of David Stone and Greg McLeod. Finding the evidence has been difficult. You're remarkably good at covering your tracks."

Barnard stared, endeavouring to look shocked at the accusation, but his sudden discomfort was evident in the redness of his face. Perspiration made his collar itch. "That's a ridiculous assertion. I have no idea what you're talking about."

"Your phone call to Archimedes Falkner suggests otherwise," said Jennings.

He reached forward and pressed a button on the recording device. Barnard's voice sounded tinny through the speaker. *"We were all there. It was a collective decision to terminate the Generation One subjects. And it wasn't only Edward who made arrangements. But they know! Dawkins and that Charlotte Black... No, because we'd be in police cells under arrest for conspiracy to murder!"* Jennings stopped the playback. Barnard stared at him, his expression fearful.

Jennings placed the recorder back inside his coat. "An interesting excerpt," he remarked quietly.

Barnard remained silent, his eyes wide.

Jennings spoke again. "You're wondering how I managed to record you when your phone is encrypted. Let me explain. Moments after you handed me your coat in the Cobra room, one of my technical experts inserted a tiny device into the lapel. An old-fashioned spying technique, but an effective one. I didn't have the opportunity to set up Falkner in the same way, but fortunately I got enough from you."

"It proves nothing." Barnard didn't believe his own words.

Jennings shrugged. "A good defence barrister might agree with you, but we don't intend to take you to court. We want to present you with a choice."

"What are you talking about?"

Jennings stared at him for a while before changing the subject. "What risk is there to the remaining EHB subjects?"

"I have no idea what you mean. You're deluded. I had nothing to do with those deaths."

Jennings bent forward, staring at Barnard through narrow eyes. "You're not answering my question. Are there any more active contracts?"

"You're insane."

"It's imperative you tell me what I want to know."

"I didn't allow you into my house for you to insult me with fictitious allegations. I thought you wanted my help with relocating Station Helix."

Jennings leaned back. A thin smile appeared on his lips. "Do you really think we need you for that? You're clinging onto the belief that you still have some influence."

"I'm more influential than you could possibly imagine."

Jennings shook his head. "Past tense, Mr Barnard. You *were* influential. Now you're *nothing*. This brings me back to the choice I mentioned." He stood. "Let me get you a drink."

"I don't want a fucking drink."

"I don't care." Jennings took a pair of white cotton gloves from his suit pocket and pulled them over his hands. He went to a drinks stand and picked up a glass and a nearly full whiskey decanter, placed the glass on the table in front of Barnard, removed the lid from the decanter and filled the glass. Reaching inside his jacket he found a large plastic pill bottle. He twisted off the lid and set the container beside the whiskey glass.

Barnard stared at the objects for a moment before glancing back at Jennings. "What is this?"

"One of your choices," Jennings replied coldly.

"You're mad." Barnard choked on the words.

"You do have an alternative."

"Which is?"

"You could try fighting us. Put those connections of yours to the test. However, we're fairly confident that the tabloids will tear you to pieces once this recording is given to them. Demolishing public figures has become something of a sport to editors these days. Of course, you might still know enough people to silence the story in the press. The Internet is a different matter."

"You wouldn't go public with this. It would ruin the EHB programme."

"We could handle the speculation of a few conspiracy theorists. Your admission that you were involved in murder is far more newsworthy."

"I haven't admitted anything."

"Not directly, but the recording will be enough to destroy you."

"You think I'd rather kill myself than take my chances with the press?"

"The press would only be the start of it. You'd live out the rest of your days being hounded by every angry blogger and activist who's ever held a grudge against injustice. You'd have nowhere to hide."

"You bastard." Barnard stared at the bottle of tablets in silence. A minute passed before he spoke again. "What sort of tablets are they?" His voice was quiet.

"It doesn't matter. The inquest will be a formality. The pathologist's report has already been written."

"Damn it, I asked you what was in them!" Barnard shouted.

Jennings raised his eyebrows. "Have it your way. For all intents and purposes, they're high dosage Paracetamol. Combined with the liquor they'll ensure you die from liver failure. Some additional elements have been added to help speed up the process. We don't want you taking three days to die."

"How considerate."

"Not really. It's a matter of practicality. Ideally we want you dead by the time your housekeeper arrives in the morning."

"And if I'm not?"

"It'll be too late anyway. You won't even know who you are. The damage will be irreversible."

"You're barbaric."

"Make your decision."

Barnard glared; anger and fear knotting his stomach. The cold sweat stains on his shirt caused him to shiver. He loosened his tie and undid the top button of his shirt. "You evil spook bastard."

He reached for the pill bottle.

TWELVE

1

Mist hung over RAF Northolt's mile-long runway as Alex and Tanya pulled their rucksacks from the boot of the MOD car. Beneath the grey dawn sky the hangars and terminal buildings seemed plain and functional. Much of the site was obscured from view by the damp mist. A No. 32 Squadron British Aerospace 125 aircraft stood nearby on the tarmac, white in colour and adorned with a narrow red and blue stripe from nose to tail. The loud drone of its engines made it impossible to talk without raised voices.

A man wearing an impeccably smart RAF uniform walked over to them. He shook hands and introduced himself. "Flight lieutenant Cliff Bradbury. Welcome to Northolt." His endearing personality and military bearing seemed unaffected by the cold or the early hour.

"Thank you, flight lieutenant," said Tanya, her voice raised. "Is everything in order?"

"Yes, ma'am. Are you aware that you're sharing the flight?"

Tanya nodded. "Embassy staff?"

"They're returning to Reykjavík. You'll drop them off, refuel and then proceed to Greenland."

"We heard the conditions are pretty rough at the moment," said Alex.

Bradbury nodded. "There's a storm stuck right over the ice sheet, but that won't stop you from reaching

Kangerlussuaq – the aircraft will fly above it. When you're on the ground it may be another matter, but I'm sure my Army colleagues will get you safely from the airport to the basecamp." He motioned towards the jet. "If you're ready, may I suggest we get you on board?"

They hefted their rucksacks over their shoulders and followed Bradbury to the aircraft. The cabin door – hinged downwards to provide stepped access – was attended by one of the aircrew. They shook hands with Bradbury again as he wished them luck for their mission.

The interior of the aircraft was small but luxurious. Cream leather seats were located either side of the carpeted aisle. The two nearest the cockpit were rear-facing and separated from the chairs opposite by wooden tables. Farther back a fifth seat was located on the port side of the aircraft. Bulbs in round recesses in the cabin's roof provided illumination. Windows – larger than those found on bigger passenger aircraft – lined the cabin and would have given a good view of the airbase had the mist been absent.

Two members of diplomatic staff sat opposite each other in the starboard seats and acknowledged them briefly as they sat down.

Minutes later the 125 began taxiing onto the runway. There was a pause and then a roar from the jet engines as the pilot applied power. The aircraft accelerated rapidly, reaching take-off speed in seconds, and lifted into the air. Alex pinched his nose and gently equalised the pressure in his ears as the aircraft gained height, watching as they broke through the mist and gained altitude.

2

An uneventful flight took them over central and northwest England, the Dumfries and Galloway region of Scotland, and several west coast Scottish islands before venturing over the open ocean shipping areas of Hebrides and Bailey. Cloud blocked sight of the North Atlantic for most of the flight, but, when glimpsed through patches in the sky's greyness, the near-black water appeared featureless and uninviting.

It took the jet less than three and a half hours to complete the eleven hundred mile trip from London to Reykjavík. The occupants of the 125's cabin said little to each other, choosing instead to occupy themselves with books or MP3s. Diplomatic staff were uninclined to discuss their business. Tanya and Alex were equally guarded.

The sky over Iceland's capital had cleared by the time the aircraft descended towards Reykjavík's coastal airport, revealing an ordered city of inelegant but functional and colourful architecture. There were signs of industry but the tallest building in the city – at two hundred and forty feet – was the twentieth century church called Hallgrímskirkja, standing less than a mile away from the airport.

Once the 125 had taxied to the terminal building, the pilot invited the embassy staff to disembark. They exchanged pleasantries with Alex and Tanya as they exited the cabin. The cool breeze which entered through the open door was welcome after several hours of breathing recycled air, tasting clean as they inhaled. The temperate climate – influenced by the Gulf Stream – was milder than might have been expected for a country so isolated and northerly. The reprieve was short-lived as the door was resealed. They decided to use the two hour wait for take-off to eat some lunch and to discuss their plan to meet Robert Grier.

Grier had set out alone from the British Army basecamp eight days earlier; one of many study trips he made during the course of the year. He had use of a mobile laboratory – an elderly Bandvagn 206 all-terrain carrier – which had been adapted for scientific research from its original military design. Contacting him wouldn't be difficult – the vehicle had modern radio and satellite communication systems – but the length of his journey back to the camp depended upon how far he had travelled in pursuit of his scientific studies. On Charlotte Black's instruction, the aircraft and flight crew had been allocated to Tanya and Alex for a week, but they didn't anticipate having to wait that long for Grier to return.

After the lunchtime delay – during which the jet was refuelled – they took off once more and headed west from Reykjavík over the Denmark Strait towards the largest island on the globe. The arctic storm had barely lessened in intensity, lingering above Greenland and extending over the sea. Flying above the clouds the occupants of the aircraft saw little of the ice sheet which covered four-fifths of Greenland's landmass, but the storm's slow eastward progression meant the west coast and their destination of Kangerlussuaq Airport were under a calmer sky. Two hours after leaving Iceland the jet began its descent.

The ice sheet was visible now, although from the aircraft it seemed almost featureless. Only as they closed in on Kangerlussuaq did the landscape begin to change. Countless fjords and rivers dominated the western fringe of the country. The aerial view of the ice-carved hills and valleys was breathtaking. Hundreds of lakes – from tiny pools to miles-long snaking waterways – occupied every depression in the fragmented land. Even among the grass-covered mountains the ice was never truly absent. Signs of human occupation were all but imperceptible until the jet began its approach into Kangerlussuaq. Alex saw that the airport had been built on the edge of a fjord still dominated by migrating ice flows.

Less than half an hour after landing, Alex, Tanya and the RAF pilots cleared immigration and made their way to the hotel situated inside the terminal building. Luxury wasn't in evidence at Hotel Kangerlussuaq, but it was comfortable enough for a single night's stop over before heading out to the army basecamp.

When they checked in at the hotel's reception Tanya was handed a note with her room key. She unfolded it and took a couple of seconds to read it. "Good." She turned to Alex. "The base captain will meet us here at eight tomorrow morning. I suggest we clean up, get something to eat and have an early night. Their helicopter has been grounded for repairs. We'll be driving to basecamp."

Alex grinned. "Over the ice? Sounds like fun."

Tanya chuckled. "We'll see if you're still as keen after four hours of Greenland terrain."

3

Survival specialist Dr Robert Grier steadied himself against the force of the arctic blizzard as he traversed an expanse of snow and ice on the way back to his research vehicle. Visibility in the swirling snow was extremely poor, but not as bad as some whiteouts he had experienced. Today he could still see between fifty and a hundred metres, depending on the gusting wind. Had the visibility been much less he would have stayed inside the carrier and waited for the storm to ease up, but in these conditions he was confident and – relatively speaking – comfortable.

He wiped the snow from his ski goggles and continued down a slight incline towards the Bandvagn 206. The vehicle, designed in Sweden for carrying troops in the Arctic, consisted of two box-like cabins connected by an articulated mechanism. A reliable diesel engine spread power evenly between four caterpillar tracks. Part of the front section was now sleeping accommodation and the rear compartment was fitted with workstations and computer equipment. It was the sole 206 in use by the British Greenland Survey Team; a small group of scientists of whom Grier was the expedition leader.

Grier reached the vehicle, pulled open the cabin door and tossed his walking poles inside. He was about to climb inside the compartment when he thought he heard something. The high-pitched whine grew louder, but it wasn't possible to tell which direction it came from against the noise of the wind. He grabbed a pair of binoculars, lifted up his ski goggles and held the optics to his eyes. At first he couldn't see anything other than swirling snow against the endless grey vista, but the sound grew louder. Grier recognised it as not one but two snowmobile engines. Soon the noise was loud enough for him to estimate its source and close enough not to need the binoculars. He saw two riders heading towards him from the east. Seconds later they rode up to him, stopped the skis in the lee of the wind beside the 206 and switched off their engines. They dismounted and approached.

"Dr Robert Grier?" one asked, his voice muffled by the neoprene shield he wore over his nose and mouth.

"Yeah, that's me," Grier replied. "What can I do for you guys?" He indicated upwards at the sky. "You've picked an odd time to visit."

"Tell me about it," the man replied. "We're here to collect you. Unfortunately our helicopter could only bring us so far. We had to complete the rest of the journey on the ground. You'll have to accommodate us until the chopper can land here."

"Hang on – what's this about a helicopter? I'm not leaving my work." Grier looked at the men's snowmobiles and realised he didn't recognise the models. He turned back to the man who had spoken, frowning. "You're not with the British Army. Who are you?"

"Very astute, Dr Grier." Andrew Mason lifted his ski mask. "My colleague and I are in the employment of some people who want to meet you. Apparently you're something of a scientific curiosity. They're very keen to study you."

"Let me guess. Your employer is a wealthy global warming denier who wants to discredit me?"

"Not at all," Mason replied. "You misunderstand me. It's not your *work* they're interested in – it's *you*."

Grier shook his head. "I have no idea what you're talking about. I suggest you get back on your skis and turn around. I don't need this sort of hindrance."

"What you need is irrelevant."

Grier stared. "I don't know who you are but you have no right to be here."

Mason glared. "I'm getting tired of this, Dr Grier. Let's get inside the vehicle before we freeze to death."

"Sorry, friend, I don't like your tone."

Curtis Wheeler pulled a handgun from his jacket pocket and aimed it at Grier's head. "My acquaintance tried to speak to you nicely. I'm not so tolerant. Get inside the vehicle."

Seeing the weapon, Grier raised his hands submissively. "All right." He opened the cabin door and stepped up. Wheeler went up next, followed by Mason. Mason tugged the door shut, sealing out the blizzard that had already begun to deposit snow on the two snowmobiles outside.

4

The red-hulled Chinese research vessel Xuĕ Gōngzhŭ, or Snow Princess in translation, held position fifteen nautical miles from Greenland's east coast; three nautical miles beyond the territorial waters defined by the United Nations' *Convention on the Law of the Sea*. The one hundred and sixty-five metre icebreaker was ostensibly a research ship, fitted with sophisticated equipment for the study of numerous scientific fields. She had a forward mounted superstructure of seven storeys, accommodating thirty crew and over one hundred additional personnel. Behind the superstructure two giant cranes and a loading platform were situated in the ship's central section. A helipad for a Russian-built Kamov helicopter was located at the stern. While genuine study did take place on the vessel – from the mapping of ocean trenches to weather monitoring – not all of the passengers were involved in such activity. One fifth of the passenger manifest were operatives from the Chinese Ministry of State Security, their purpose intelligence gathering about persons of interest and to conduct industrial espionage for foreign technology.

In a secure room below the bridge Zhang Hu glanced at the sea and sky through the salt spray covered window, but he couldn't see far. Persistent low cloud meant visibility was less than a hundred metres. Zhang didn't like being on the ocean and had been dismayed when the ministry posted him aboard the Xuě Gōngzhǔ for six months, but he knew the work he achieved on board would assist his promotion prospects. Fortunately the vessel had proved to be more comfortable than he'd anticipated and seasickness hadn't troubled him much. Now, four months into his assignment, he had found his sea legs and the Greenland storm caused him little discomfort.

Zhang had used his technical expertise to launch cyber-attacks against several American companies, even managing to steal the design of a prototype submarine propulsion system. A number of similar successes gave him confidence about being rewarded with a higher status upon his return to Beijing. He hadn't anticipated being given a new task just before the end of his posting on the Xuě Gōngzhǔ. Being put in charge of the two Britons and supervising their mission had caught him off-guard. He'd taken an instant dislike to Mason and Wheeler and had been glad that their presence on the ship was subject to constant scrutiny by armed guards.

Zhang's superiors hadn't told him much about Dr Grier and he knew not to ask. Pinpointing the British scientist's location on the Greenland ice sheet had been a simple task − Zhang had satellite access − but getting Mason and Wheeler directly there had been impossible. The storm had prevented the Kamov from completing the whole journey, forcing the former soldiers to travel twenty-five miles on the ground, assisted by Chinese tracking technology.

Zhang's Iridium satellite phone began ringing. The screen displayed the number of the phone he'd given Mason. He picked up the handset and answered the call, speaking clearly in English. "Yes?"

Mason's voice came through the speaker. "Mr Zhang?"

"This is Zhang."

"We've acquired the package." Mason's voice was clear. Zhang assumed he was speaking from inside the scientist's vehicle. "When can we expect extraction?"

He glanced at his watch. "We are monitoring the weather. The storm should pass from your location within twelve to eighteen hours. Stay by your phone, Mr Mason. When the helicopter is ready to fly, I shall call you to confirm."

"Understood." Mason terminated the call.

Zhang tossed the handset onto the desk beside a bank of computer screens. "Damn mercenary," he said softly.

5

Alex and Tanya saw their Army contact waiting for them as they walked into the hotel reception area at 7.50am. Captain Tim Drake was short but broad and had a self-assured but understated demeanour. His bright blues eyes were his most striking feature. His dark hair was neatly styled beneath his Army beret. He greeted them warmly, glancing at their attire as he did so in order to assess its suitability for the arctic conditions. His lack of comment indicated he approved of their equipment. The brightly-coloured synthetic materials of their kit contrasted with the Army issue smock and trousers Drake wore, but the quality was comparable.

"If you're ready we'll get going," he said. "It's quite a trek to basecamp. I'd hoped to fly you up there but the mechanics have grounded the helicopter for maintenance. We're using our polar-adapted Hilux instead."

He led the way from the hotel. Outside the sky was a vivid blue. The lack of moisture in the air made the temperature feel less cold than the minus ten Celsius it really was. "I suggest you put on those hats and gloves," said Drake. "Frostbite can occur pretty quickly out here. While it's a myth that you lose most of your heat through your head, you do need to protect it as much as the rest of your body."

"Does Dr Grier know we need to speak to him?" asked

Tanya as she secured a Velcro fastener on her jacket's sleeve around her glove.

"That's something I wanted to talk to you about," replied Drake. "He was informed as soon as we received the message about you coming here from London, but he was already out on the sheet. He said he'd wait for you to call on the satellite phone before returning to basecamp. But there might be a problem."

"What sort of problem?"

"He hasn't checked in since yesterday afternoon."

"That's out of character for Dr Grier?"

Drake shook his head. "Not exactly. He frequently forgets to call in at the arranged times. It's become something of a running joke with the survey team. They call him up, he says he's fine and apologises for missing the slot. But this time no one's been able to get hold of him."

"Could the storm have affected the communication equipment?" asked Alex.

"It's a possibility, but the equipment in the module is shielded against magnetic interference. Besides, there are three separate systems: an analogue radio, a digital radio and a satellite phone. He hasn't responded on any of them."

"What about moving out of range?"

"The 206 hasn't moved in three days. Grier was collecting data in a specific area and comms have been fine with him up till now. There's a GPS locator on the vehicle, so we know it's exactly where it's supposed to be. Hopefully our guys will have heard from him by the time we get to the camp, but if not, we'll have to organise a search. He knows what he's doing out there, but even the best survival experts can fall ill or have an accident. It's fortunate that the weather is clearing."

"How long will it take to reach Grier from basecamp without the helicopter?" asked Tanya.

"Two or three hours depending on conditions."

"What did you tell him about our visit?"

"Only that you were from the MOD and that you needed to speak to him concerning a personal matter. That's all the information we were given by London."

"He was fine with that?"

"Absolutely, although he implied that whatever it was could wait until he'd finished his work. He was due back in a day or two anyway."

Tanya glanced at Alex and frowned. "What do you think?"

"I don't know. Hopefully it's nothing."

"Is there something I should know?" asked Drake, stopping in his tracks. He turned to face them.

Alex held his stare. "I can give you the edited version, captain. Grier's life may be in danger. I can't tell you why. That's one of the reasons we need to speak to him. The fact that you haven't heard from him gives us cause for concern."

Drake frowned. "With respect, if I'd known this I could have brought him in already. This is a game changer." His voice revealed his irritation. "Sending a rescue team after Grier is one thing, but if he's in danger it makes it a military operation. My response as base captain has to be an informed one. What exactly is the risk level?"

"We can't be certain," replied Tanya. "We thought the risk to Grier had been eliminated. We weren't expecting this either."

"I need more than that."

"Let's not jump to conclusions. Do you have a satellite phone in the truck?"

Drake nodded.

"Good. I'll call London to arrange for an imaging pass of the area. We'll take a look at the pictures and decide what level of response is needed after that."

"Very well. Just don't withhold information that could put my men in danger."

They reached the modified Toyota and saw a soldier in grey and white arctic camouflage gear standing beside it. Tanya and Alex hefted their rucksacks into the cabin. For a large vehicle the interior was compact. The small side windows gave only a limited view of Kangerlussuaq airport and its neighbouring buildings. Drake and his subordinate entered the front part of the cabin. The private started the Toyota's ignition and its powerful engine roared into life.

The roads leading east from the airport were little more than rough tracks which followed the contours of the hills into difficult terrain, but the vehicle progressed effortlessly along routes which, for a few miles at least, were traversable by ordinary four wheel drives. Even with his restricted view through the side window, Alex was able to appreciate the wilderness. Only a few minutes away from the airport he spotted herds of musk oxen grazing on the valley slopes.

The roads ended as the landscape became more remote and the terrain more inhospitable. The view was spectacular as they crossed wildflower meadows and rocky outcrops before finally reaching the edge of the ice sheet.

The ice was not uniformly smooth in texture or colour; it was fractured and pitted with peaks and troughs reflecting white and blue and grey in the autumnal morning air, as though painted upon a vast canvas whose appearance changed depending upon the angle of view and direction of light. For the next two hours Alex allowed himself to be distracted from the Toyota's noisy growl by gazing upon Greenland's intriguing natural landscape.

6

The Metropolitan Police warrant card in Abigail Jones' possession identified her as Detective Inspector Sue Davey. Police identification drew less attention than the Ministry equivalent. The card had been issued under special protocol between the Met and the MOD. Had she still been alive, the real Sue Davey would have been Abi's age, but the girl had died from a heart condition a few days before her seventh birthday. The use of dead children's identities by police undercover teams and the security services was commonplace.

Abi snapped shut the warrant card holder, preventing the inquisitive staff member from reading it properly. Access to the exclusive Morrell Club in Soho was normally limited to members and it was clear that the smartly-dressed attendant in the lobby did not approve of her interruption. The tall man peered through round wire-rimmed glasses. "I don't believe Mr Falkner is expecting you, detective inspector. Guests are not normally allowed."

Abi resolved to bring the conversation to a swift conclusion. "Your house rules don't interest me. Where is he?"

"I must object. We do not disturb our members."

"Do you know what is meant by the term 'obstructing the police'?"

The man understood the threat and took a short step

backwards. "I believe Mr Falkner is at his usual spot in the corner of the lounge."

"Thank you." Abi walked past the man to the lounge door and twisted the brass handle. She pulled the door shut behind her and glanced around the room. The lounge was more opulent than she had expected. At street level the Morrell Club didn't catch the eye; its Georgian architecture seemingly duller and less interesting than the glass-fronted galleries and cafés which surrounded it, but the façade concealed an interior of sophisticated old-fashioned elegance. A portrait of a Dutch noblewoman by Rembrandt occupied a central space above a wide hearth at the far end of the room. Wooden panels reached from floor to ceiling, framing the fireplace. The softly crackling fire and the ticking of a mantel clock were the only discernable sounds. Unoccupied leather chairs were clustered around low wooden tables. The light from outside wasn't bright enough to illuminate the room comfortably, despite the height of the windows. Lampstands and wall-mounted fittings compensated; their light throwing a soft glow on the intricately plastered ceiling. Fleur-de-lis wallpaper, matching the soft red of the carpet, provided the backdrop for more lavish artwork including a Turner and a Gainsborough.

Falkner sat alone near the fireplace concentrating on a book through reading glasses. A glass of orange juice, barely touched, stood on the circular table in front of his chair. Abi walked the length of the room and sat down in the chair opposite, not waiting for an invitation. Falkner looked at her for a moment without speaking. He closed the book, removed his glasses, and placed them both on the table. "I had hoped for a quiet afternoon," he remarked. "I trust you're here on a matter of importance, Miss Jones?"

Abi looked around the room briefly then turned her attention to Falkner. "This seems like a lonely place."

"I enjoy the solitude," he replied. "Why are you here?"

She noticed Falkner's book was a collection of poems by Shelley. "Keen on poetry, Mr Falkner?"

"I find it disciplines the mind."

"That must be useful."

"Extremely. I'll ask you again – why are you here?"

"Because we need to talk about recent events."

"To what are you referring? The sudden and unexpected suicide of Ben Barnard? The Home Secretary's imposition on my retirement?"

She shook her head. "The murders of David Stone and Greg McLeod."

"Tragic events."

"Police superintendents trying to sound caring at press conferences say 'tragic', Mr Falkner. Your disciplined mind is much more objective. Men like you don't have time for sentimentality. You're an illusionist; a master of misdirection and deception. You influence events but keep your involvement hidden. But even the greatest tricksters get found out in the end. We've seen through the smokescreen. You've lost your touch. We know you killed those men."

Falkner smiled and leaned back in his chair. "All right, Abigail, let's pursue this hypothesis of yours. What if I admitted to you right now that I killed them? Where would you take that confession? The statement would be useless as evidence. You've been involved in Charlotte Black's little conspiracy to sever my connections with the Government for weeks. If you could actually prove something you would have done it by now. I suggest you stop wasting your time and find something useful to do."

"You know you were wrong about them? The EHBs?"

"What do you mean?"

"There were no genetic abnormalities attributable to the Generation One experiment. We conducted thorough tests on Carter and McLeod. We also took samples from Stone's body when he was repatriated. There was nothing wrong with any of them. We anticipate the same from Grier. Your desire to protect your national secret was based on an incorrect assumption." Abi frowned. "And you have the audacity to talk to me about evidence."

"And *you're* not qualified to talk to me about secrecy," Falkner retorted. "The protection of this country depends on people like me. While you were playing with your dolls during the Cold War, I was managing assets on the wrong side of the Iron Curtain and thwarting IRA attacks at home. I don't care whether you approve of my actions or not."

"You should have retired."

"To be replaced by unpatriotic fools like you? You haven't the first idea how to keep Britain safe."

"Murdering British subjects achieves that?"

"An absurd and baseless accusation." Falkner sipped his orange juice and placed the glass down. "What do you want? Are you trying to intimidate me? You're playing a game without knowing the rules and it makes you look incompetent."

"You crossed a line," Abi said quietly. "You and your friends stopped looking after the country's interests because you became paranoid about your own. Now you're the only one left and you've ceased to be relevant. Great Britain doesn't need you any more." She stood, holding his gaze. "You're right about one thing, of course. I don't have the evidence to lock you up. But what I *know* is much more powerful. As a former spy, you should appreciate that. You asked me what I want from you. The answer is simple. I want you to fade into obscurity. Don't delude yourself into thinking you still have influence." Abi glanced down at the book on the table momentarily. "It's ironic that you enjoy Shelley."

"Why is that?"

"'*Round the decay of that colossal wreck, boundless and bare the lone and level sands stretch far away.*' Good evening, Mr Falkner. Enjoy your retirement."

7

Rain was falling heavily as Abi left the Morrell Club. Shallow puddles were forming in the uneven London pavements, reflecting the lights from the numerous business premises lining the street. She hurried to the illegally parked silver car outside, let herself into the passenger side and quickly tugged the door shut. Lucas Ingwe turned the wheel and pulled out into the narrow street. "You spoke to him?"

"I think he got the message. He knows we'll be watching his every move."

"That's good, but as a former policeman I wish we could bring the bastard to justice."

"The conventional method doesn't apply to people like Falkner. We're talking about a former high-ranking MI5 agent who's been building dossiers on every politician and judge since the 1960s. We'd never get the chance to prosecute him in court even if we had a case."

"I understand that. I'm still getting used to looking at things from a different perspective."

Lucas drove steadily and slowly along the narrow back streets, compensating for the downpour that now lashed against the windscreen. The route back to the Ministry took them through London's busy Theatreland where hundreds of pedestrians – caught out by the rain – hurried in the miserable conditions to find their chosen entertainment venues, ignoring the vagrants huddled in doorways near the theatres under blankets and sheets of cardboard.

Abi's mobile phone rang and she answered it. "Hey, Zoe."

"Hi, Abi." It sounded as though Zoe was outdoors, competing with the wind to be heard. "I thought I'd call you with an update. Everything from Orford Ness has been moved down here. Helix is empty."

"Great. Where are you? I can't hear you very well."

"I had this crazy idea of having a takeaway on the sea wall. I'm on Chesil Beach. It's pretty wild down here tonight."

"It sounds it. Thanks for the call."

"No probs. I'll be heading to London at the end of the week."

"The meeting with Charlotte?"

"Yeah." Zoe hesitated. "Abi, there's one more thing. I was going through the archive room down here and found a couple of references to something called the Elzevir Collective. I think it's the name of a project the beta site ran a while back, but I can't find any more information. Do you know what it is?"

"I haven't heard of it. Mention it to Charlotte when you come to London."

"I will. See you soon."

"Bye, Zoe." Abi swiped the end call graphic on her phone and tucked it inside her jacket. She turned to Lucas. "Zoe's ahead of schedule. We can shut down Station Helix."

Lucas nodded then turned his attention back to the road as the car passed under the crescent-shaped architecture of

Admiralty Arch.

8

The basecamp shared by the British Greenland Survey Team and the British Army comprised of ten semi-permanent buildings; each one constructed from enamel-coated steel panels. The prefabricated sections had been transported to the camp's location and assembled on site, connected to generators and water processing units, and fitted out for numerous functions from accommodation to vehicle maintenance. The Army engineers had enhanced the protection afforded by the insulated walls by allowing snow banks to accumulate against the structures, thus forming natural barriers against the prevailing winds. A geodesic dome containing electronic hardware was mounted on the flat roof of the communication hut and was the highest structure on the half-hectare base. The smell of hot food, emanating from the aluminium chimney of the canteen building, was welcoming and homely in an otherwise intimidating landscape. Even under a clear sky the beauty of the ice sheet was tempered by a sense of absolute isolation.

Although the base had a well-equipped vehicle workshop, the limitation on space meant vehicles were parked outside unless being repaired. Half a dozen Polaris Indy snowmobiles and their trailers were located in the lee of the quartermaster's building. A second adapted Toyota Hilux four wheel drive stood near the medical centre, its bright red paintwork in contrast to the subdued camouflage of its neighbour: a tracked personnel carrier known as a Warthog. The base's currently grounded Westland Puma transport helicopter was situated forty metres from the buildings.

Inside the communication hut a grainy photograph was displayed on a flat screen computer monitor. Grier's survey vehicle could be made out in the top left corner of the aerial picture but the detail was poor. The computer operator leaned back in his chair to allow Tanya to take a closer look at the screen. "I'm sorry, ma'am, but this was the best of the batch."

"No problem. Given the timescale, I'm impressed that we've received anything. Can you zoom in on the 206 for me?"

"Sure. I can compensate for the grain with a filter, but I'll lose even more detail." The soldier altered some settings in the image viewer.

She turned to Drake. "The vehicle's where it should be?"

He nodded.

Tanya looked back at the screen. "Where are you, Dr Grier?" she muttered.

Alex rested his hands on the back of the operator's chair and leaned over his shoulder. "Is there any way of adjusting the tone curve of the image? When I edit my photos I sometimes boost the contrast to make details stand out."

"Let's try it," the soldier replied. "Snow's pretty featureless though." He opened a panel on the screen containing a histogram. The graphic had a diagonal line running through it from bottom left to top right. "I'll keep the adjustments small. You want to try an S-curve?"

"Yes, but keep it shallow."

The operator manipulated the line with the mouse. The picture's dark tones became slightly darker.

Alex spoke again. "Hold it there. Now drag the top of the line. Yeah, stop there." He scrutinised the image for a moment before looking at Tanya. "I think I've spotted something. Look there." He pointed at the screen just below where Grier's vehicle was located.

Tanya looked at the adjusted picture. "Tell me I'm looking at something other than snow."

"You're half right," replied Alex. "Snow-covered shapes. Two of them. They're the same size."

The computer operator nodded and turned to Drake. "He's right. I think they're snowmobiles." He pointed at the screen. "They're hard to see, but I think these are what's left of track marks."

"Good work." Drake turned to Alex and Tanya. "I have to assume those sled riders are still there and are the reason Dr Grier hasn't responded. How does this fit in with your risk assessment?"

Tanya glanced at the screen briefly. "It's consistent. It looks like a small team. But we're almost certainly too late. Dr Grier is probably dead and the killers gone."

"I'm not prepared to conclude that yet," replied the captain. "I intend to find Grier and I'm not waiting for the helicopter to be flight-ready. I'll take a team in the Warthog. This is now an Army operation in hostile territory. You're welcome to stay here and monitor communications. I'll call in with a sitrep as soon as I reach Grier's study site."

"Actually, this is an MOD operation and that involves all of us," said Alex. "We're coming with you."

Drake stared at him. "It's not protocol to take civilian staff on this sort of mission."

"Our designation isn't as clear-cut as that, captain. We have Whitehall authority to get involved in pretty much anything we like."

Drake nodded. "I don't have time to argue the point, but if you do come, you're to adhere to my instructions. Is that clear?"

"Understood."

"Good. Let's get moving."

Tanya raised her hand to interrupt. "We need to visit your armoury."

"Excuse me?"

"What handguns do you have on site?"

"Glock 17s."

"We'll need your quartermaster to issue us with those. You're welcome to call London to check our firearms authorisations. This may be your mission but Grier is our responsibility."

The captain held eye contact with her for a few seconds. A wry smile appeared on his lips. "I don't need to check with London. Whitehall made it clear that I was to comply with your requests before you arrived." He opened the door and they instantly felt the coldness of the air on their faces. "I just didn't expect to be handing out guns. The armoury is next door."

9

For two hours the fifteen tonne armoured carrier powered across the ice sheet, its heavy-duty caterpillar tracks coping easily with the rugged terrain. With its broad footprint and all-wheel drive system the Warthog traversed stony escarpments and valleys with little effort. On flat ice it came close to reaching its top road speed of almost forty miles per hour. Drake's instruction to the driver had been brief but clear. The lance corporal had driven flat out all the way from the basecamp, navigating with the aid of a military specification GPS system that pinpointed the location of Dr Grier's vehicle on a digital display in the cabin.

Travelling on the ice – whether by vehicle or on foot – was always inherently dangerous. The Greenland sheet was a sea of compressed ice and snow under constant physical pressure from its own weight. The entire mass was permanently on the move; usually imperceptibly but sometimes in abrupt and unexpected tremors that tore gaping crevasses in the ice. The clearing sky meant visibility was greatly increased, but spotting danger in the largely uniform colour of the landscape required constant alertness. The driver didn't allow complacency to interrupt his concentration and refrained from engaging in dialogue with the vehicle's other occupants.

The Warthog climbed another incline, slowing

gradually as it neared the summit. The driver brought the vehicle to a near crawl as they crossed the ridgeline and started their descent. Grier's 206 was approximately two hundred metres ahead of their position. Drake leaned forward, peering through the arch of relatively clean glass cleared by the Warthog's wiper blade through the muck of dirty ice particles that had accumulated during their journey.

He addressed the occupants in the rear seat. "Load up. The snowmobiles have been dusted off. Whoever has Dr Grier is still there." Drake focussed on Tanya and Alex. "I want you to stay out the way. My boys will conduct a tactical entry into the 206." He turned to the lance corporal. "Take us in close – round to the rear section. If anyone opens those doors I don't want them used as cover."

The soldier acknowledged the instruction and drove the Warthog down the gradient towards the survey vehicle. The two Army privates who had joined the group prepared to disembark, readying their L85A2 assault rifles. Drake drew his handgun and glanced around again. "Vigilance, boys. We'll provide cover. Try to detain these guys but remember Dr Grier's safety is the priority."

The lance corporal stopped the Warthog twenty metres short of the Bandvagn and killed the engine. On Drake's command the soldiers exited the vehicle, raised their weapons and scanned ahead, studying the survey vehicle intently through their rifles' sights. They advanced slowly, watching for any sign of movement.

The lance corporal stepped down from the front compartment and crouched beside the vehicle's caterpillar track, aiming his rifle. Drake adopted a standing stance behind the Warthog's door, his Glock held out in a two-handed grip, his eyes scrutinising the scene as his men continued their cautious approach. Tanya and Alex positioned themselves behind the lance corporal, their newly-issued pistols with rounds in the chambers and ready to fire.

The report from a firearm at close range shattered the silence. Blood spurted from the throat of one soldier, the force of the bullet tearing through his neck and felling him instantly. A second shot cracked loudly in the frozen air. A bullet embedded itself in the shoulder of the other private causing him to spin and fall involuntarily. He dropped his rifle as he hit the icy ground. Drake held his nerve, drawing upon years of combat experience to identify the location of the shooter. He noticed a minute movement. "Contact on the roof! Get inside!"

From the roof of the 206, wearing white camouflage and partially hidden by snow, Curtis Wheeler aimed at the captain and fired three shots a fraction of a second apart. Two shots ricocheted off the Warthog's armoured door but the third struck Drake in the ankle. Fighting to ignore the pain Drake tossed his pistol inside the cabin, grabbed hold of the door and screamed a command at the lance corporal. "Knock that fucker off!"

The soldier clambered back into the carrier, fired up the engine and slammed the vehicle into gear. The Warthog lurched forward, building just enough speed over the short distance to ram the 206's rear section hard. Wheeler slid awkwardly from the flat roof. Drake lost his grip on the Warthog's door frame and fell, landing painfully on his damaged foot. The driver slammed the carrier into reverse and backed away. Wheeler scrambled to his feet, looking for the rifle that had fallen from his grasp, but it was too far away to reach. He drew his pistol, cocking it as he aimed it at Drake. Tanya almost slipped on the ice as she sprinted around the retreating Warthog, clutching at the front of the vehicle to steady herself with one hand as she aimed her pistol with the other. She fired one-handed and hit Wheeler in the chest. He fell backwards, an expression of disbelief etched on his face as he died.

A sudden impact against the bullet-resistant windscreen caused the glass to fracture directly in front of the lance corporal's face. He ducked down and crawled across the floor of the cabin, pulled himself out of the open door and slid out, half falling onto the snow. He ran to Drake, grabbed him and tugged him awkwardly towards the Warthog's passenger section. Tanya helped him lift the wounded captain into the compartment.

The soldier glanced at her. "There's a second shooter."

"I know." She hesitated. "Damn, where's Alex?" She screamed his name.

"I'm okay," he shouted. "It's Mason! He's got Grier!"

"Stay where you are. I'll come to you!" She glanced at the soldier. "Drake's losing blood. You're going to have to keep pressure on the wound."

"I've got it ma'am. I'm a field medic."

"That's the best news I've heard all day. You're going to have to multitask though. Get on the radio and tell basecamp we need backup and a medevac. They need to get that Puma in the air even if it's held together with cable ties. I'm going to help Alex."

"Yes, ma'am."

Tanya hurried around the rear of the carrier and spotted Alex at the vehicle's front corner, his Glock raised and aimed at two figures now standing beside the Bandvagn. Mason stood behind Grier with a pistol pressed hard against the scientist's temple. "I'm here, Alex." She adopted a stance behind him, weapon raised.

"I can't be certain of hitting Mason without injuring Grier," said Alex. His voice sounded choked.

"I know. It's a twenty metre shot."

"I can't let this go on any longer. We've finally got him."

"And we'll bring him in." Tanya attempted to sound reassuring. "Just hold your nerve. We have a wounded man out there and we have to figure out how to get him and Grier back safely."

"Drake?"

"He's down. The lance corporal is treating him. We're on our own. It's time to improvise. Mason's cornered but he'll be trying to figure out an exit strategy. Let's see what he wants."

"We aren't going to let him go." The anger was clear in Alex's voice.

"I have no intention of letting him go. Ease up on that pistol grip will you? I need you to focus."

"Oh I'm focussed."

She placed a hand on his shoulder. "You're too tense. Just relax your stance a little while I talk to Mason."

Alex inhaled and bent his elbows slightly, easing the tension in his arms and shoulders while still keeping the Glock aimed at the mercenary.

Tanya shouted to draw Mason's attention. "Mason!

You're not going anywhere. Let Grier go."

"That's where you're wrong," he shouted back, instinctively shrinking behind his human shield, further reducing his target size. He pushed the gun harder against Grier's head. "Grier is my way out of this. Back off now and no one else gets hurt."

"We're not going anywhere. Your friend is dead. You're on your own."

"Actually my backup is on its way right now. You won't survive a firefight. Get back in your carrier and turn around."

Tanya shook her head. "We won't do that."

"Then you'll die. My employers' determination is something to behold."

"The Chinese? You think they'll protect you?"

"As long as I have Grier. I guess you know how valuable he is." A faint sound became detectable in the distance, its source unseen. The noise grew louder, increasing in intensity until it became recognisable as the distinctive mechanical throbbing of a helicopter. Mason smirked. "That'll be my evac!" he shouted. He suddenly noticed the wounded British soldier in the open ground trying to aim his rifle one-handed. Mason pointed his handgun and fired four times. The private slumped, killed by a headshot. "I warned you! No one else has to die! Get aboard the carrier and stay there till I'm gone."

Tanya glanced up at the approaching helicopter, now visible over Mason's head. "I suggest you re-evaluate!" she shouted, but the roar of the aircraft was too loud for Mason to hear her.

The US Air National Guard Pave Hawk helicopter

roared overhead, banked tightly and circled back. Mason stared in disbelief as an airman aimed a machine gun and fired a volley into the ground five metres in front of him, churning up the ice into flying dust and razor-sharp fragments. Mason instinctively shielded his face, loosening his grip on Grier. The scientist rammed his elbow into his chest, taking advantage of his captor's disorientation. The strike wasn't forceful enough to cause injury but Mason let go. Grier ran but slipped on the ice and fell. Mason glared at the Pave Hawk as it descended and hovered five metres above the ground, its machine gun aimed directly at him. He clenched his jaw, angrily accepting defeat. He tossed the pistol aside, raised his hands in surrender and linked his fingers behind his head.

Tanya and Alex stepped out from the cover of the Warthog, keeping their weapons aimed at Mason's chest. Thirty metres behind the vehicle the American helicopter landed on flat ground. Moments later the pilot cut the engines and the giant rotors slowed to a halt. A single figure, wearing civilian clothing, disembarked from the aircraft and jogged towards Tanya and Alex.

Tanya shouted at the scientist but kept her eyes on Mason. "Dr Grier? Are you all right?"

Grier pushed himself up. "Somewhat alarmed but otherwise unhurt."

"Please step over here."

He obeyed and began walking towards her, but, after just a few steps, he stopped suddenly, sensing movement beneath his feet. With a deafening, grating roar the ice began to split around him. He began to sprint but slipped again, losing his balance. A rift opened in front of him and the ice buckled. He vanished from sight, plummeting into a thirty metre abyss. Collapsing masses of ice and snow were sucked into the void with him as he fell.

The rift expanded beneath the Bandvagn. The survey vehicle lurched suddenly and toppled into the gap. Mason threw himself forward, narrowly avoiding the same fate. He sprawled on the ground just metres in front of Alex and Tanya. As quickly as it began the earth tremor abated and silence fell.

Mason pushed himself onto his hands and knees and looked up to see the barrel of Alex Hannay's Glock inches from his face.

Alex pulled back the hood of his coat. "I've been waiting for this moment, Mason. Do you have any idea who I am?"

10

Mason studied the barely contained fury on Alex's face, momentarily uncertain of his captor's identity. But then he leaned back and laughed, his expression mocking. Still on his knees, he locked his fingers together behind his head once again. "Well isn't this ironic? Captured by the Hannay kid. What are you going to do, Alex? Go on – pull that trigger. That's what you want."

Alex could barely speak. "It's what you deserve."

"Do it then!" Mason snapped. "I have nowhere to go. Put an end to it." He grinned. "Make your parents proud."

"Don't speak about my parents!"

"Why not? They're the reason you're here. I didn't understand everything to begin with, but I discovered something about you. You're a freak. Your 'parents' experimented on you. You're a stain in a fucking Petri dish."

"You're a murderer!"

Mason shrugged. "I hold grudges. It looks like I'm not alone in that respect. Come on, Alex! Man up! Pull the damn trigger. Or is your genetic disposition too sensitive? Have those MOD bastards programmed the guts out of you?"

Alex tensed, pushing forward with the gun, aiming at Mason's forehead. The taste of bile filled his mouth. His focus was so tight on Mason that he became oblivious to what was happening around him.

Tanya noticed his locked jaw and shaking hands. "Alex," she said, endeavouring to draw his attention. He didn't hear her. She shouted his name. He glanced at her quickly then turned back to Mason. "He's goading you. Don't let him push you. We've won."

"My parents didn't win." He didn't look at her as he spoke. "He deserves to die for what he did."

"Your parents wouldn't want this."

"How do you know what they would want?" He clenched the gun tightly, unable to control the shaking in his hands. Despite the cold, sweat beaded on his face.

"Because I know *you*. I don't believe they were vengeful people."

"Well maybe that's where I differ from them, Tanya. Besides, I'm not completely their son, am I? Mason got that part right. Maybe there's a gene inside me that wants to punish scum like this."

"You're not a killer, Alex." The voice wasn't Tanya's. Recognising Clare Quinn's Texan accent, Alex glanced round and saw the CIA woman standing near Tanya. She pulled her hood back and removed her sunglasses. "You won't do this."

Distracted by Quinn's arrival, Alex took his attention off Mason for a second before realising his mistake. Hurriedly he turned back and repositioned the gun. He kept his eyes on Mason. "Clare? What are you doing here? How did you…?"

She stepped closer. "We knew Charlotte would want you to find Grier." She looked at the crevasse for a moment then refocussed on him. "I guess *that* didn't turn out as expected." She paused. "We've been monitoring a Chinese ship in the North Atlantic: the Xuě Gōngzhǔ. She's owned by the Chinese Ministry of State Security. When she repositioned off the Greenland coast, we suspected they'd decided to find Grier for themselves. They're into stealing other countries' technology."

Alex sneered. "They're not the only ones."

"Point taken, but we're allies now." Clare looked at the man on his knees in the snow. "Of course, we didn't actually expect the Chinese would send Mason here." She directed her next remark at the mercenary. "Boy, you must be fed up with intelligence agencies treating you like a whore."

Mason ignored her.

Quinn spoke again. "We keep an Air National Guard presence at Kangerlussuaq. When we realised you had plans to come here, I arranged to be flown out from Lakenheath. I thought you'd be glad of the help."

"How gracious of you, Clare. The thing is, I know what kind of help you have to offer. You could have given us Mason weeks ago."

"Sure, but we'd never have got to know each other. It's more fun this way."

"I didn't get into this for *fun*." He pressed the gun against Mason's head. "*He* murdered my parents – *that's* how I got into this."

Mason shouted at him. "So what are you going to do about it? Your parents had it coming. They betrayed me."

Alex glared. "So how did you do it? How did you plan their murder?"

Mason smiled. "I'm methodical. I watched you and

your family for over two years. I knew your routines. I knew the places you liked to visit. I knew you'd be at the fencing tournament. I even knew there was a good chance you'd win it. Congratulations, by the way. Picking the time and place was easy. Of course, I had several contingency plans lined up."

"So what's your contingency now, Mason?"

"You've got me there."

"You're a psychopath."

"You're the one who's ready to kill an unarmed man."

"You deserve to die."

"So kill me or let me get up off this damn ice." Mason slowly got to his feet.

"Stay where you are!"

"Make a fucking decision. The more you deliberate, the colder we all get."

"Don't move!"

Mason stood still, his eyes fixed on Alex.

Clare spoke again. "Is your helicopter still grounded?"

Tanya shook her head. "Not any more. It should be here within twenty minutes."

"So you'll be able to get your people out?"

"Yes."

"Good. Well I guess that more or less concludes the matter." The CIA operative turned to Alex. "Put the gun down. You're not going to shoot."

"Listen to her, Alex," Mason goaded. "You don't have what it takes."

Alex lowered the gun and stepped back. "You know what, Mason? You're going to spend the rest of your life in prison."

Quinn suddenly drew a handgun from inside her coat, cocked it and fired it three times at Mason, the weapon's explosive reports unbelievably loud in the still air. Every bullet found its mark and tore into his chest. He died where he stood and his body slumped onto the ice. The smell of propellant filled their nostrils. Blood emanated from the wounds in Mason's body, spreading and making random patterns in the ice's tiny fissures. Alex stared at the body, still clutching his handgun. Quinn stepped closer and put her hand on the Glock, encouraging him to release it. He did so and she gave the weapon to Tanya.

Clare placed her hand on Alex's shoulder. "Like I said, you're not a killer. I, on the other hand, became part of this a long time ago. Mason was unfinished business for us too." She hesitated. "Don't forget who you are. Don't dishonour your parents' memory. Take care, Alex. I'll see you around."

She signalled towards the pilot of the Pave Hawk and a few seconds later the machine's engines powered up, the great rotors slowly turning, building momentum.

Quinn turned back to Alex. For a brief moment they looked at each other; an expression of understanding on his face and a thin remorseful smile on hers.

Author's Note

Thank you for reading STATION HELIX. I hope you enjoyed the book. If you'd like to learn more about me and my writing, please visit my website: *www.ashgreenslade.com*. There you'll find behind the scenes details about the story and the 'real' Station Helix, as well as information about forthcoming books.

Ash Greenslade

Made in the USA
Charleston, SC
16 August 2016